Mary Wesley was born near Windsor in 1912.
Her education took her to the London School
of Economics and during the War she worked
in the War Office. She has also worked part-time
in the antique trade. Mary Wesley has lived in
London, France, Italy, Germany and several
places in the West Country. She now lives 'rather
a hermit's existence' in Devon. She has previously
written for children and comments that her 'chief
claim to fame is arrested development, getting
my first novel published at the age of seventy'.
That first novel was *Jumping the Queue*. Her
later novels, *The Camomile Lawn*, *Harnessing
Peacocks*, *The Vacillations of Poppy Carew*,
Not That Sort of Girl and *Second Fiddle* are
also published by Black Swan.

Author photograph by Kate Ganz Dorment.

Also by Mary Wesley

JUMPING THE QUEUE
THE CAMOMILE LAWN
HARNESSING PEACOCKS
THE VACILLATIONS OF POPPY CAREW
NOT THAT SORT OF GIRL
SECOND FIDDLE

and published by Black Swan

A Sensible Life

Mary Wesley

BLACK SWAN

All of the characters in this book are fictitious and
any resemblance to actual persons, living or dead,
is purely coincidental.

A SENSIBLE LIFE
A BLACK SWAN BOOK 0 552 99393 X

Originally published in Great Britain
by Bantam Press, a division of
Transworld Publishers Ltd.

PRINTING HISTORY
Bantam Press edition published 1990
Black Swan edition published 1990
Black Swan edition reprinted 1990
Black Swan edition reprinted 1991

This book is set in 11/11½ Melior

Black Swan Books are published by
Transworld Publishers Ltd., 61–63
Uxbridge Road, Ealing, London W5 5SA, in
Australia by Transworld Publishers
(Australia) Pty. Ltd., 15–23 Helles Avenue,
Moorebank, NSW 2170, and in
New Zealand by Transworld Publishers
(N.Z.) Ltd., Cnr. Moselle and Waipareira
Avenues, Henderson, Auckland.

Printed and bound in Great Britain by
Cox & Wyman Ltd., Reading, Berkshire

for James Hale

PART ONE

One

There was no wind; sea flat as a plate met sky the same colour as the water. Only an occasional glint betrayed their meeting. The beach sloped so slowly to meet the sea it might have been an illusion that it inclined at all. Sand, dry as a biscuit near the shore, changed colour gradually, growing wetter, more sea-coloured as it smoothed close to the distant water.

On an unexpectedly warm February day birds inland were rehearsing their spring song, but the beach was silent; it stretched wide and empty. A heron flapping its way with lazy sweeps emphasized the emptiness as it left the estuary to travel inland. The boy, imagining he could hear its wings, lowered his binoculars in disappointment; he had come to watch sea birds and there were none. He blinked into the sun, already low in the sky, and decided to go home.

A movement half a mile out at the water's edge attracted his attention: a tiny figure moved. The boy screwed up his eyes against the shimmering light. The figure split in two. A child and a dog? It must have climbed down the cliff to the west and walked along the water's edge; there was no line of footprints from the beach, no mark on sand still damp from the last tide and the fresh water sweep of the stream from the estuary seeping its clandestine way to the sea.

The boy moved higher up the beach to see further, limping, placing his right foot with care, using a stick for support. He trudged up through dry sand heaped with detritus, crisp dead seaweed, bits of bleached wood, broken razor shells, glass smoothed by pounding

9

seas, mussel shells. At the top of the track he sat on the short stiff grass which led inwards to the estuary and rested. His knee was recovering from an injured cartilage. He eased the bandage, wishing it was less tight, and swept his hand across a clump of thrift which retained a few seed heads. He was sweating, unfit since his injury.

He wondered just how far the sea went out at low tide. Distances were deceptive; he did not know this coast. He adjusted his binoculars and focused them on the distant figure.

He saw a child dawdling at the water's edge, kicking up small spurts of sand to amuse a dog almost as large as itself, which scrambled madly, tail tucked joking between its legs, ears flopped back, jaws gaping in hysterical amusement. He fancied he could hear it bark, but just then his ears were filled by the cry of gulls swinging round the headland and the peep of oyster-catchers crossing the bay from one embracing headland to the next. Simultaneously the sun, shut off abruptly by a cloud, reminded him that February was a tricky month.

He followed the oyster-catchers with his glass until regretfully he lost them rounding the headland. Their passing roused a cormorant he had not noticed on a rock above the sea; he watched it fly towards the sun, fighting a losing battle with the clouds. He buttoned his jacket against a chill breeze signalling the evening.

The child was now running, loping ahead of the sea which to his amazement rippled across the sand faster than a man could walk. The child chirruped to the dog in tones similar to the oyster-catchers' but the dog, obsessed with enjoyment, had begun to dig in the sand. It worked in a frenzy, scooping showers of wet sand towards the sea, biting the sand, shaking its woolly head, excavating a pit into which it dipped head and shoulders, barking.

The child, a girl, trotted along, crossing the beach at an angle. She had thick black hair in pigtails and wore a light brown sweater with a matching skirt which she had stuffed into elastic-bottomed knickers; it gave her the grotesque silhouette of a toffee apple. Her long legs were thin. She paused at intervals to whistle to the heedless dog.

The boy, who had been watching idly, became interested. The tide was coming in so fast the child would have to change course. She would not be able to reach the side of the bay, she must run towards him. And the dog was being pretty stupid; it lifted its head from its pit and whimpered with indecision, unwilling to leave its game.

The boy now noticed that the beach, which had looked so flat, had deceived him. The incoming tide swirled round islands in the sand and the dog, standing on one of these elevations, was cut off. It lifted its head and howled. There were seventy yards of frothing water between the dog and the child. She raised her voice and shouted to the dog to be brave. It was not encouraged; it stood shivering, tail between legs. She turned towards it.

The boy stood up. 'Leave it,' he shouted, 'let it swim.' From his viewpoint he could see the depth of the water, the smallness of the child. 'Let it swim.' Could she at this distance hear him?

The child, unheeding, was stripping off her clothes, bunching them in a bundle, wading half-naked back to the dog, balancing the bundle on her head with one hand. Reaching the dog she yanked it, plunging into the rushing tide which swirled round her chest.

The boy yelled: 'You fool, you bloody fool!' and began to hop and hobble down the dune to the beach while the dog, swimming strongly now, desperate head above the water, splashing paws, paddled ahead of the child who, encumbered by the bundle of clothes, waded slowly.

The boy reached the water's edge as the dog bounded ashore and, shaking itself, soaked him liberally with spray. Still yards from the shore, the child tripped on an underwater hazard and partially submerged, but still she managed to keep her bundle clear.

Remembering that he was in France, the boy now

yelled: '*J'arrive! Idiote! Espèce de con! Attendez. J'arrive. Au secours!*' Wading into the sea, he caught her hand. '*Tenez fort*,' he cried, '*ma main*. I'll pull you out. *Venez vite. Quel horreur!*' He dropped his stick and grabbed the bundle of clothes. '*C'est dangereux*.'

The child snatched up his stick as the sea reached for it and handed it to him as she came out of the water. She had brown eyes and was blue with cold. 'Can I have my clothes?' She snatched the bundle from him. 'Look the other way,' she said, dragging on her skirt, hauling her sweater over her head, insinuating knickers up under the skirt and wringing out the edge of a vest she had not taken off. She was shaking. 'You need not have bothered,' she said ungratefully, her teeth chattering. 'I was quite all right.'

'So you're English?' said the boy, wringing water from his trouser bottoms, feeling a fool.

'Yes.'

'My name is Cosmo,' said the boy.

'Is it?'

'That's a pretty stupid dog,' said Cosmo, watching the dog roll on the short dune grass, grinding its spine against a tussock.

'Just doesn't like water.' She re-tied a ribbon which hung loose from a plait. 'Must find my shoes.' She moved away, picking her way barefoot towards the rocks. The dog stopped rolling, jumped up and followed her.

'What's your name?' Cosmo called after her as she reached the rocks which circled the foot of the cliff. The child did not answer, but the cliff threw back ''ame – 'ame – 'ame.' He stood by the tide which, having reached its peak, sighed gently to and fro, smoothing the sand trustfully. 'You might have drowned,' Cosmo yelled in case she didn't know.

She had found her shoes and stockings; he watched her put them on. Then she went leaping up the cliff like a young goat, followed by the dog. At the top she stood for a moment looking back at him, raised her arm, waved and was gone.

'Con,' shouted Cosmo. He had learned the word the day before. 'Con!'

His trousers were wet, his knee was painful and it was a long way back to the road where he must catch the conveyance, half-train, half-tram, which would carry him through St Briac and St Enogat to Dinard.

In the tram, attempting to ignore fellow passengers' interested observance of his wet legs, Cosmo consoled himself. She was only a child, not really a girl. At fifteen he was anxious and eager to meet girls, find out about them.

Two

In the spring of 1926 middle-class English families took their young to Brittany for the Easter holidays. It was thought good for them to catch a glimpse of foreign soil, see some sights, learn a few words of French.

It was easy to get to St Malo by steamer from Southampton; as cheap or cheaper than travel by rail to Cornwall, a similar country, in many ways equally foreign. Dinard, across the river Rance from St Malo, had a beach, a casino, a tennis club and many excellent hotels and *pensions*. By early April the dining-rooms of the Hôtels Angleterre, Britannique, Bristol and Marjolaine rang to the sound of British vowels discussing the weather (so similar to that of South West England), the delights of shopping at the favourable exchange rate (a really splendid number of francs to the pound), and the nice rest for mothers of families from a servant problem grown acute since the War.

Some fathers of the English families had taken part in the War. Several families were fatherless, having lost them at the French or Italian front, in the Dardanelles, in Mesopotamia or at sea. But the War was scarcely mentioned; people hoped to forget it; there was a new generation to consider. What was discussed with vehemence and alarm was the attitude of the coal miners. Would there be, could there be another strike? Was it true that there was the possibility of a General Strike? All the British parents could remember the railway strike in 1919. One father with a bristling moustache, who had not taken part in the 'let's forget

14

the War' War but was, in spite of a gammy leg, a Master of Foxhounds, had driven a railway engine and drawn the train between Taunton and Minehead for the duration of the strike. He was prepared to repeat his exploit; he had found confounding the strikers enjoyable. Some people thought him boastful, for it was difficult, if you knew the peaceful people of Somerset, to visualize them in the Bolshie role he described. Surely the railwaymen on the branch line which ran past the Quantock Hills were not in the same league as the miners of Wales, the Midlands, the North and Scotland – Bolshies to a man, it said in *The Times*.

The word 'Bolshevik' bounced from table to table in accents of contempt tinged with fear; everyone knew what had happened in Russia in 1917, the poor Tsar murdered with wife and family.

'They could learn a lot more if they took the trouble to get to know the inhabitants of some of the lesser *pensions* and lodgings, where Russian refugees live with considerably less money to spend. Their trip abroad is of necessity permanent,' murmured Blanco Wyndeatt-Whyte to the friend with whom he was spending the holidays, Cosmo Leigh, as they sat at lunch in the restaurant of the Hôtel Marjolaine.

'Do you know any?' asked Cosmo, sotto voce. 'I have heard that they moan and groan about their lost estates and are living on the vast hoards of jewelry they brought out with them.'

'The person I have found to give me piano lessons is one of them,' murmured Blanco. 'She's Armenian, really, originates from Baku. She's an absolute knock-out at bridge. I started lessons with her when I was here with my aunt last year.'

'Bridge and piano?'

'Yes. We scamper through a few scales for form's sake, then get down to bridge. We need a fourth. Why don't you come along this afternoon?'

'I'm no good at cards, not interested.'

'Backgammon, then?'

'Does she play?'

15

'Does – she – play!'

'Right, I'll come.' Cosmo was delighted.

'You'll have to endure a rubber or two first. I'm not giving up my bridge.' Blanco kept his voice low.

'All right. You're on,' said Cosmo.

'What are you boys doing this afternoon?' asked Mrs Leigh. 'It's a bit wet for tennis and doesn't look promising for bird-watching, Cosmo. How is your poor knee?'

'Lots better, thank you, Ma. Cured.'

'What shall you do, then? You should get some fresh air.'

'We thought we'd go for a walk,' said Cosmo.

'Don't let your walk end up in the casino,' said Mrs Leigh.

'Oh, Ma, we are too young.'

'But I know you, and you both look older than fifteen.'

'What shall you do, Ma?' asked Cosmo.

'I'm having a fitting at that splendid little dressmaker. I want to get finished with her before your father arrives.'

'Is he not to know?'

'Know what?'

'How much you are spending on clothes.'

'Clothes here are an economy. Don't be silly, darling.' Blanco thought his hostess looked ruffled.

'I hope you are having a wonderful dress made with a tremendous *décolletage*. Father would like that, he could tell his joke.'

'He can manage that without a new dress,' said Mrs Leigh wistfully.

'Father tells this terrible old chestnut—' began Cosmo.

'Cosmo!' warned Mrs Leigh. 'Stop it.'

Cosmo laughed and bent to kiss his mother's cheek.

'Actually, I have my piano lesson, Mrs Leigh,' said Blanco tactfully. 'If Cosmo would like to keep me company, we could walk there.'

'Mrs Whatshername – such a difficult one – seems

16

to have inspired you. Your mother told me your report said you had "neglected your ivories". These schoolmasters are getting frivolous.'

'It's relief at having survived the War. My teacher is frivolous, cowardly too. He screams with pain and outrage when I play wrong notes. I was hoping to give up the piano but Madame Tarasova is no screamer, so I'll carry on through the holidays to please my mother.'

'Your mother wrote particularly to stress the importance of music—'

'My mother merely wishes to placate my cousin Chose. She is not interested in the arts.'

'Don't call him Chose, Blanco; it's terrible manners and it makes me laugh.'

'Thing, then.'

'Not that either. He deserves respect, remember, even though you haven't met. He has a name.'

'Nor am I likely to. His choice, not mine. We have the same name, that's all,' said Blanco. 'I would like to drop either Wyndeatt or Whyte but my mother won't hear of it. Never mind, music is an extra at school, and she won't mind much if I drop it once I have grasped the rudiments.'

'And Mrs Whatsit can help you?'

'One hopes so.'

'Was – er – was your father musical?' Mrs Leigh hesitated to mention Blanco's father, who was buried, she supposed, in Flanders.

'Neither the Wyndeatt part nor the Whyte part, Mrs Leigh. He was tone deaf even before he was blown up, so I've heard. Bang, bang.'

'Honestly, Blanco, I – er – you—' Mrs Leigh felt she must say something. 'Wyndeatt-Whyte is a very fine name, you shouldn't mock—'

'Sorry, Mrs Leigh, I didn't mean to upset you. It just seems monstrously unfair that my father, an only son, should get killed when Cousin Thing had six to spare,' said Blanco tersely.

'I thought all six were killed in one way or another. Come now, you be fair,' said Cosmo, hoping to stem

Blanco's anger and save his mother embarrassment. His own father had been a staff officer and survived without mishap, which put Mrs Leigh in a delicate position with the widows and orphans of those who had disappeared in the front lines.

'How terrible. Six. Six sons, oh,' she murmured.

'There's one long bathroom in my cousin Chose's house with six baths in a row, or so I hear,' said Blanco. 'Of course, I haven't seen it myself.'

Mrs Leigh gathered up her bag and a book she hoped to read. 'Odtaa,' she said, looking at the title. 'I have not started this yet. I wonder what it means? It's supposed to be good.'

'What Cousin Chose said about my cousins as they got killed: one damn thing after another?' suggested Blanco.

There was something aggressive about her son's friend. Mrs Leigh wondered whether she had been right to invite him to stay for the whole holidays. 'Well,' she said, 'try to be good. I shall see you both at dinner.' Blanco stood up and pulled back her chair while Cosmo went ahead and opened the dining-room door. Other families still at lunch watched her go.

'I suspect your mother sees through us,' said Blanco, as he and Cosmo made their way down the street towards Madame Tarasova's a little later.

'She sees what she wishes to. My father will be here tomorrow; she will stop being interested in our movements then. She's been rather bored all these weeks on her own with me since I hurt my knee—'

'Could it not have recovered at home?'

'Of course it could. Father thought I should take the chance while hors de combat to learn French, and Mother took to the idea because of the shops. She adores shopping. She has been to Paris three times since we've been here.'

'To see your sister?'

'Officially, yes, but in truth the shops.'

'When is your sister arriving?'

'Next week. She is getting a bit old for family holidays. She's seventeen.'

'Does she play bridge?' asked Blanco.

'Perhaps she does by now. I don't know. Why do you want to learn?'

'Money,' said Blanco. 'I'm a poor relation.'

'I am not interested in money,' said Cosmo. 'I am obsessed with girls.'

'How do you get the one without the other?'

'Charm?' suggested Cosmo, grinning.

'Huh!' said Blanco. 'Charm won't hold them, but money will. What's this story your father tells? His chestnut.'

'It's about some woman at a grand reception who curtsys to the King of Egypt; she has this low-cut dress and her bosoms pop out and the King of Egypt says, "*Mais, Madame, il ne faut pas perdre ces belles choses comme ci comme ça etcetera,*" and he flicks them with his finger.'

'Eugh.'

'Mother and I feel eugh, too.'

They walked on in silence.

'I heard the manager tell the head waiter that a Dutch baroness is arriving with her five daughters, and to put them at their usual table,' said Blanco.

'Five girls?' exclaimed Cosmo. 'Five?'

'That's what he said. It may be a case of Odtaa.'

'Oh, I hope not. Five beautiful girls, ah!'

'What about your sister, Mabs?'

'She's my sister.'

'Beautiful?'

'Passable, I'd say. She's bringing a friend.'

'That's one girl for you.'

'Mabs will have put her off me. I am too young to be interesting,' said Cosmo gloomily.

'Better set your sights on the Dutch five, then.'

'An embarrassment of daughters. Let's pray they are pretty and speak English.'

'The quantity makes the quality doubtful,' said Blanco.

'Why?'

'If they are of marriageable age there would not be five arriving; some, at least, would have been snapped up. On the other hand—'

'Yes?'

'They may have no dowries, poor things.'

'Your mind runs on money; first it's bridge and backgammon, now it's dowries.'

'Only because I'm strapped. I plan to remedy my plight,' said Blanco cheerfully.

'There goes my mother,' said Cosmo. 'Look! She really is letting rip, two hatboxes!' Further down the street Mrs Leigh crossed with springing step and disappeared into a boutique. 'Father says there has been no holding her since she had her hair shingled, but I believe it's to do with Mabs leaving school.'

'Short skirts suit her,' said Blanco judiciously. 'Seen from behind, your mother might be you in drag.'

'Have a heart,' protested Cosmo. 'She has not got knobbly knees.'

'Same hair, same features—'

'My mother is beautiful,' protested Cosmo.

'You are a coarser version, that's all, and you have those terrible spots.'

'Only two now. French food has done wonders; you have more.'

'Handicapped in the Dutch daughters stakes. When we are old and rich, shall we look back on our spots with nostalgia?'

'I am not planning to grow old. I just want to grow up and get at the girls,' said Cosmo boldly.

'You are terrified of girls.' Blanco was aware of his friend's shyness. 'Perhaps the five Dutch are tiny little girls. You could not be frightened then.'

'Oh, don't! What is the Dutch baroness's name?'

'It sounded like shove halfpenny. Here, turn right down this alley. We are nearly there.'

'It's a bit smelly along here.' Cosmo looked about him.

'Madame Tarasova is poor; she brought no jewels

20

from Baku. She teaches the piano to dolts like me to make ends meet. Here we are. She lives there, above where the horse's head protrudes.'

'*Boucherie chevaline*,' Cosmo read. 'I say,' he said, 'how awful.' Then, seeing his friend's expression of amusement, he flushed and said, 'Sorry, I am extremely insular. Lead on.'

'For insular, read ignorant,' said Blanco angrily. 'Don't come in if you don't want to, not if you find Madame Tarasova's lodgings distasteful. I told you she is poor, she teaches the piano and tells fortunes, she dressmakes and alters people's clothes to keep the wolf at bay. If you must know, I could have given up the piano ages ago, but she needs the money. She teaches, eats, works and sleeps in one small room. Why don't you go back to the hotel?'

'I don't want to go back to the hotel,' said Cosmo.

They stood facing each other in the mean street, Blanco white-faced and angry, Cosmo confused and pink. After an uncomfortable pause Cosmo said: 'Perhaps I should have piano lessons too?' Both he and his friend doubled up with laughter.

'Here comes my pupil,' said Madame Tarasova, looking out from the window on the first floor of the house in the Rue de Rance.

The room where she prepared to meet her pupil held an upright piano, a square table covered with a red baize cloth, four upright chairs, a *chaise longue*, a pedal sewing machine and a bookcase stuffed with Tauchnitz paperbacks. Balanced on top of the books were piles of sheet music and a crystal ball wrapped in a black velveteen cloth. Under the table there was a dog basket and reposing in it a small Pomeranian dog, asleep.

'Time you took Prince Igor for his walk. Do not bring him back tired and wet, as last time his beautiful fur was full of sand,' she said in heavily accented French.

'Who is the pupil?' Flora peered out, following

21

Madame Tarasova's gaze. 'Oh golly,' she said. 'Is it one of those boys?'

'The one with the dark hair is Blanco. The other, the fair one, I do not know.'

'I'll get out of the way.' Flora pulled a jersey over her head. 'Come, Prince Igor, buck up.' She snapped a lead onto the little dog's collar. 'How long will the lesson last?' she asked, making her way through impeding furniture to the door.

'An hour. I wonder why Blanco brings a friend? Does he too require lessons? What do you think, child?' Madame Tarasova's voice rose hopefully, but Flora was already catapulting out of the room and down the stairs, dragging the dog behind her. She brushed past Blanco and Cosmo on the doorstep and disappeared running.

'That's Madame Tarasova's only luxury,' said Blanco, prodding the bell button with his thumb.

'The little girl? I've seen her somewhere – I know, she was with another—'

'The nauseating Pom. Just touch the piano and it starts howling. Madame T. has to send it out whenever she gives a lesson.'

Cosmo was not listening: 'She was with another animal, a great big—'

'Come on, it's up this way.' Blanco led the way. 'Bonjour, Madame, this is my friend Cosmo Leigh,' he said, as they reached the landing. 'I am staying with him for the holidays.'

'In the hotel? C'est chic. And how is your maman?'

'She's well. Cosmo would like lessons too. No, not the piano, backgammon. What's the matter, Cosmo?' For Cosmo had crossed the room through the jungle of furniture and was peering out of the window. 'He seems to be interested in dear little Igor. I apologize for his uncouth manners, Madame.'

'He is perfectly couth, he is welcome.' Madame Tarasova shook hands with Cosmo as he turned back into the room. 'So you too are a player of backgammon, my national game.'

'No, but I'd like to learn,' said Cosmo, looking

down at Madame Tarasova who, less than five feet tall, looked up at him. She was tiny, with miniature hands and feet, greying hair pulled severely back in a bun, a paper-pale skin, large black eyes and an enormous arrogantly hooked nose above a sweet-tempered mouth. She looked considerably older than her twenty-nine years. 'Blanco tells me you play a demon game, are a great gambler,' he said, smiling.

'The wicked fellow seduces me from his scales, and the bridge too! I play as reward for his piano if he tries hard. *Alors*, Blanco, we make a *début*?'

'If we must.' Blanco sat astride the piano stool.

'And your friend? Will he be happy waiting? After some Chopin, some bridge. Shall you be patient, Monsieur Cosmo?'

'I shall be quite happy.' Cosmo edged himself onto a chair by the window.

Blanco, sitting side by side with Madame Tarasova, embarked on his scales.

I could do better than that, thought Cosmo, watching for the reappearance of the child with the dog, wincing at Blanco's false notes. Those heavy lidded brown eyes last seen when the child had come out of the sea, half-naked and shivering, had made him jump. Half-listening to the excruciating sounds his friend was creating, he wondered whether the child's eyes, briefly glimpsed, were as mysterious and mischievous as they seemed. Was it perhaps the effect of enormously long lashes? Could the term voluptuous be applied to the eyes of such a small and skinny child?

Three

Flora Trevelyan ran fast, twisting and turning through alleyways and short cuts, down the hill to the *plage*. No longer in his prime, over-indulged on succulent scraps from the horse butcher, Prince Igor had trouble keeping up. He trotted protestingly, his neck twisted sideways by the taut lead. When they reached the beach Flora let him free. He snapped at her hand before running across the sand to prance, yapping, as the sea rippled in and out. He advanced and retreated with the water, afraid of getting his paws wet. Flora kept watch in case the German Shepherd who had pounced on the Pom and rolled it into the water the week before should reappear and terrorize it afresh. When Igor tired of his futile pastime, she re-attached the lead and proceeded at a sedate pace across the town to the quay where the *vedettes* came in from St Malo, laden with returning day-trippers and passengers from the Southampton ferry. She had friends among the crews of the *vedettes* and would chat with porters sent from the various hotels to meet arriving guests.

'When does your mama return? Will she be accompanied by your papa?' Gaston, the porter from the Hôtel Marjolaine, threw the butt of his cigarette into the water.

'I do not know. She has not written.'

'Does she know that your Mademoiselle lets you run free about the town and adventure into the countryside without protection?'

'I have a dog with me.'

'You call that a dog? That specimen? Is a Bolshevik toy sufficient chaperone for a child, one asks?'

'Madame Tarasova is not a Bolshevik; I often have a larger dog; Igor has teeth.'

'Igor has teeth.' Gaston snapped his fingers derisively at the Pomeranian, who leapt up snarling shrilly. Gaston stepped back. 'Bolshevik,' he hissed at the little animal.

'Don't tease him.' Flora loosened the lead so that the dog could close up on the man. 'If you go on, I will let him loose.'

'Does this courageous animal bite your Mademoiselle? Does Mademoiselle know the animal?' Flora did not answer. 'Your maman was expected back weeks ago. I was told so by Mademoiselle, who sits in the hotel reading love stories and eating chocolates while you run wild,' teased Gaston.

'She changed her mind and stayed with papa. He has business in London. He goes back to India soon; she wants to be with him as long as possible,' said Flora defensively.

'One understands. But you, do you not wish to be with your papa?' The porter from the Hôtel Britannique, lounging beside Gaston, joined in the quiz.

'Sometimes,' said Flora cautiously, 'not always.' She sensed that Gaston and the other porter might be surprised if she told them that she hardly knew her father and was not all that keen on knowing him better. These family men were unlikely to understand or approve the mores of an Indian civil servant and his casual acceptance of constant separation.

'I am all right,' she said.

'And your lessons? You do your lessons with Mademoiselle?' queried Gaston, whose eldest son was working for his *baccalauréat*.

'Of course I do,' lied Flora, conscious that with Mademoiselle's connivance lessons had dwindled to a bare minimum. The porter from the Hôtel d'Angleterre, younger than his colleagues and unmarried, now remarked: 'She amuses herself, this English child, she runs wild with old women's dogs. It is laughable.' He laughed. '*C'est fou.*'

'Madame Tarasova is teaching me Russian. In exchange, I exercise Igor.'

'Of what use is Russian, a filthy Bolshevik language? Your situation is not *comme il faut.*'

'Not *convenable*,' agreed the porter from the Hôtel Britannique, who had so far not contributed his opinion.

'I wish you would all mind your own business,' said Flora unhappily. 'What visitors are you expecting?'

'English families,' said the porter from the Hôtel Britannique.

'For me the same,' said the porter from the Hôtel d'Angleterre. 'There are too many; I spit on them and their money.'

'And I,' said Gaston, 'am here to meet General Leigh, husband of the beautiful Madame Leigh.' Unconsciously Gaston drew himself up.

'Lots of spit for him?' suggested Flora. 'Oh,' she exclaimed, 'look! Here comes the *vedette*! Quick, Igor, run, I must get you home.'

The group of porters watched her disappear, dragging Igor behind her. 'Has she seen the devil?' asked one.

'Her parents,' said Gaston. 'I recognize the mother; the man with her must be papa, that one in the black hat who feels the cold. The tall robust one beside them will be my client, the General, husband of the lady who spends so much of the money you despise patronizing our modistes. Does not your sister work for the hat shop in the Rue de Tours?'

The porters stopped lounging against the wall, straightened their caps and adopted obsequious expressions.

While Flora raced through the town to deliver Igor to Madame Tarasova's and on, panting, to rouse Mademoiselle from the sofa where she lolled with her novel, in the annexe of the Hôtel Marjolaine, Denys

Trevelyan only marginally looked forward to meeting his daughter. He had disliked the crossing from Southampton and felt cold crossing the bay. He took his wife's hand and tucked it against his side. She had introduced herself to Angus Leigh and was questioning him about the likelihood of a General Strike as though he were a politician or a trade unionist, in spite of his modestly explaining that he was a retired Army man, no better informed than anyone who read *The Times* or listened to the news on the wireless. If there were a General Strike, he said, he proposed leaving his wife in Dinard and motoring back by himself.

'Just in case of trouble I'd like my wife to be out of things. One never knows these days whether things may not get rough.'

'Oh, Denys. Did you hear that?' Vita looked up at her husband. 'What shall we do if there is a strike? Will there be a revolution?'

Denys Trevelyan repeated for the benefit of the General what his wife perfectly well knew. Come what may, his leave was up at the end of June and he must sail for India. Anyway, he said, more for the benefit of the General than his wife, he thought talk of revolution was alarmist. He did not add that he wished to God that Vita was coming with him, that he loved her jealously and passionately, that the prospect of leaving her made him feel ill, that he thought it unnecessary for her to stay with Flora until the autumn. In India she could go to the hills for the hot weather, as she usually did, where he would know what she was up to. He thought the child could have been deposited in the school they had picked at once, instead of at the start of the school year. Pressing his wife's arm against his ribs and his lips into a tight line, he wished that when Vita nearly miscarried, five months pregnant, she had lost the child. Children and the Indian Civil Service did not mix. It was not, he thought bitterly, as though Vita liked children. Flora was the result of a passing and regrettable fancy. The child was an expense, an inconvenience, a wedge between himself, his wife and his career. He was an uxorious man; he flinched from sharing any part of her. Spending the summer with Flora, Vita was bowing to the convention that this was what parents did. She had been happy to leave her with the governess all the weeks they had spent in London, he thought grimly. He knew Vita, alone with Flora, would get bored. And what then? At least when she was in a hill station, and he not too far away, there was some control. Most wives could be counted on not to do more than flirt with bachelor subalterns. Vita was welcome to that, but alone in France—

Beside him, Vita was telling the General that they had a daughter and the idea was that she should learn to speak French before she went to school; that she already spoke good Italian after a year in Siena with an Italian governess. 'Denys is keen on languages,' she said. 'She is also learning Russian.'

'Ah, hum, yes, a good thing, I suppose. Are you yourself a linguist?' Angus included Denys in the conversation.

'Native languages.' Denys did not specify how many. 'In my job, you have to.' He despised Vita for her falsity, and perversely loved her for it. Flora's year in Italy and her present sojourn in France were nothing to do with the acquisition of languages, everything to do with the rate of the lira and franc to the pound. He had no independent means (the sight of General Leigh's rather splendid luggage annoyed him). Standing up in the *vedette*, looking towards the quay, he decided Vita could manage without Mademoiselle until Flora went to school. While despising his wife's manipulation of the truth, Denys felt a sharp lust for her. She may be silly, he thought, but I desire her.

'Is your daughter meeting us?' he asked, disassociating himself from parenthood. Then, noticing Angus Leigh's quick glance, he laughed. 'Our daughter is so unlike either of us, I make a joke of it, but since discovering a portrait of my great-grandmother I have put aside doubts of her provenance.'

Angus Leigh said, 'Oh,' on a polite note.

28

Vita said, 'Oh, Denys, you are the limit,' and to Angus, 'We are both fair, you see, and Flora is dark.' Then to Denys she said, 'No, darling, I don't think she will meet us. It seemed better not to tell her we were coming today; the sailings might have been delayed by the strike.'

'The strike has not happened yet,' said Denys, aware that they would have stayed on in London if they had been able to get tickets for a particular show. 'I want to get you into bed,' he muttered in his wife's ear.

'And I you,' she said. 'Here we are, we have arrived.' The boat bumped against the quay. 'See you at the hotel later on,' she said to Angus.

'Yes, yes, of course,' said Angus, not sure that he wanted to. He handed his bags to Gaston and set off at a brisk clip towards the Marjolaine, leaving the Trevelyans to find their own way. As he walked he thought Vita Trevelyan pretty but tiresome, foreseeing that she might make friends with his wife. Nor was he drawn to her husband.

Four

Since the hotel was filling up, the management had asked Cosmo and Blanco if they minded moving into the annexe. They would share a room with a balcony larger than the one they occupied in the main building. Perhaps they would not mind the inconvenience of crossing the garden to the hotel dining-room for their meals? The servants would, of course, move their things. Cosmo and Blanco did not mind.

'We can sneak out at night and go to a brothel,' Cosmo suggested. 'If there is a brothel. I wonder what goes on?' he said wistfully. They surveyed their new room.

'We would be turned away as under age. You know what goes on, idiot,' muttered Blanco.

'In theory. What's the use of theory?'

'We could try the casino, wear false moustaches.'

'Same applies to the casino; they guess your age to a week, I've heard,' said Cosmo. 'Ah me, you know why they moved us, don't you? It's all those Dutch girls. I bet they will be strictly chaperoned, kept well clear of sex-starved us.'

'And your sister and her friend? What's the friend like?' asked Blanco.

'No idea. She's called Tashie Quayle. Are you going to have a bath?'

'I might do. Oh God! They've mixed up our clothes. Look at this.' Blanco jerked open a drawer with one hand as he unbuttoned his flies with the other. 'Let's get them sorted; it's not good for my best shirt to consort with your pants. I like this room. I wonder

30

whether there is anyone interesting in this annexe. I say, that's my pullover you are putting in your drawer.' He stepped out of his trousers and snatched at the pullover. 'But you can have it if you like, it's the sort of thing the Prince of Wales wears – puts me off.'

'No thanks, I don't want it, Blanco.'

'I wish you'd call me Hubert, that's my proper name,' protested Blanco.

'With a name like Wyndeatt-Whyte you must resign yourself to Blanco, Blanco.' Cosmo ducked as his friend aimed a blow.

'I thought your cousin Thing was called Hubert, and since you don't care for him—'

'My father was Hubert, too. My family are repetitive with names. I say, these walls are paper thin. Listen.'

Footsteps tapped along the corridor and someone knocked at the door of the room next to theirs. The door opened. A woman's voice said, 'Mademoiselle? Are you in here?' The door closed.

'Oui, Madame, I am here. The child ran in and said – I was not expecting you just yet – if I had known that you were arriving today, I would have—'

'Sent Flora to meet us? Where is she?' The voice was sharp.

'I let her run out to buy flowers for your room. She planned to please and surprise you and her father. I gave her some money, her next week's pocket money to be exact.'

'A nice thought, I suppose.'

'It was the child's idea.'

'Well, yes – I see— Well, actually, while she is out, perhaps I'd better speak to you.'

'Of course, Madame. Won't you sit down?'

'I'd rather stand.'

Cosmo and Blanco listened. Cosmo unbuttoned his shirt and slowly pulled it off and, as Blanco watched, slipped off his shoes and tiptoed to the French window which opened onto the balcony. Blanco, already in socks, joined him.

31

In the next room Vita Trevelyan dismissed the governess, giving her her salary and a month's money in lieu of notice. For the rest of the holiday, she explained, and the summer months until Flora went to school, she would look after her daughter herself.

'It would be nice for the child to see something of her papa.' Mademoiselle's interjection was hoarse. Vita Trevelyan did not seem to hear. It would be convenient, she said, if Mademoiselle packed up and left the following day; she had arranged with the manager for Flora to move into a single room. 'The single rooms are all at the back looking out on the street, not the garden,' said Mademoiselle.

'The arrangement is suitable,' said Vita Trevelyan.

'And more economical,' said Mademoiselle. Cosmo and Blanco drew in their breath.

'That is a consideration,' said Vita coldly.

'Madame will give me a reference?' asked the governess.

'Of course,' said Vita flatly.

'Thank you,' said Mademoiselle.

There was a pause. Cosmo and Blanco waited; Cosmo's mouth was open, Blanco's hands held his vest pushed half-way up his chest.

Vita Trevelyan spoke again: 'Well – that's about it, I think – we are sorry, of course – we shall see you at dinner? I must go and unpack.'

'If Madame will excuse me, I have a headache.'

'Very well.' The door opened, closed, footsteps died away down the passage; Blanco pulled his vest over his head.

In the next room Mademoiselle said, '*Salope*,' very loudly.

Cosmo reached for a pencil and wrote '*salope*' in his notebook.

'One can guess what it means,' whispered Blanco. 'Oh, look.'

Flora was running across the garden, her feet crunching on the gravel. She looked very small, dwarfed by a vast bunch of narcissus.

'That's the child who takes Madame Tarasova's beastly Pom out when I have my piano lesson,' whispered Blanco.

'I've seen her before, weeks ago on a beach up the coast with another dog, a great big thing. She nearly drowned,' whispered Cosmo. 'Listen.'

They heard the garden door snap open, feet race up the stairs and along the passage. The door of the next room was pushed open. 'I got these, aren't they wonderful?' said a joyous voice. 'I bought the whole bucketful.' Then, 'What's the matter?'

'Your mother has dismissed me. I am to leave tomorrow. I am an unnecessary expense,' said Mademoiselle.

'Oh,' said the child. 'Oh—'

Cosmo and Blanco shrank back into their room as the windows next door were pushed wide. They saw Flora come out onto the balcony, open her arms and let a cascade of narcissi fall into the garden.

There was an air of anticipation in the hotel dining-room. The centre table, usually heaped with hors d'œuvres, cheese and fruits, was laid for seven people. English families coming into the room took covert note. The table was laid with an abundance of knives and forks, scintillating glass, superlatively white napery. The adolescent English who were beginning to know each other raised their eyebrows, exchanging questioning looks.

'That will be for the Dutch family,' said a widowed mother of three. 'There are five daughters, I hear. What a—'

'She's a baroness, the mother, sounds like—'

'Then all the girls will be baronesses, too. That's how it goes with continental families.'

'Rather diminishes the éclat,' said the widow.

'But there are seven places—' counted her friend.

'Perhaps six daughters, not five?' suggested the widow.

'Don't speak so loud, mother,' whispered the widow's daughter, catching Cosmo's eye.

Cosmo looked away; the girl had white eyelashes, buck teeth and was only fourteen.

'Don't be ridiculous, the seventh place will be for her husband, the father of—'

'The baron.'

'What? Oh, I see. Yes, of course, the baron.'

Cosmo and Blanco ate their dinner with circumspection while keeping an eye on the door. They listened with a polite ear to Angus Leigh explaining the state of the British nation to his wife. Cosmo was used to his father's opinions and knew exactly what he thought of Mr Baldwin; he secretly hoped his father would irritate Blanco sufficiently for Blanco to contradict him and say something daring. Champion Ramsay MacDonald, for instance. But Blanco kept mum, mollified by Mrs Leigh's efforts to call him Hubert every now and again, or Bluebird or Blinko; her mind, he knew, was wandering towards the shops where she would presently take his sister Mabs if, that was, Mabs would condescend to provincial shops after the delights of Paris.

Both boys wore suits for dinner and had slicked back their hair. From time to time they caught the eye of some junior member of another English family, winked and looked away. Later in the evening they would congregate in the lounge or in the shadows of the hotel garden where in the dusk they would fix up fours for tennis, or suggest expeditions to Dinan or Mont St Michel, where there was a restaurant famous for its omelettes, and the tide came in faster than a galloping horse. Cosmo was not particularly interested in all this, having been in Dinard for two months with his mother while recuperating from his knee injury. Half-listening to his father, letting his eye stray surreptitiously round the room, he dreamed of five exquisite Dutch girls: they would have long legs and wear flimsy dresses so that he could see through to their mysterious breasts. His mother was saying: 'No, Angus darling, I can't bear it. If you go home, I want to go with you, I don't want to be left here on my own.' Her voice bordered on the tremulous. 'What should I do?'

34

'Do a bit more shopping. Trip up to Paris. Take Mabs out from her school.' Angus munched his steak. He liked women to fuss; he knew his wife was doing it to please him. He swallowed some wine. 'Stock up with shoes while you are about it. If I go, I go alone. The situation hasn't arisen yet.'

'Then you shall pay for your desertion with dresses and hats. I will betray you with enormous bills for fripperies.'

'That's about it.' Angus beamed, pouting out his fine moustache. 'How are you off for gloves?'

At the table in the alcove behind them Denys and Vita Trevelyan ate in silence. Between them, staring at her plate, sat Flora.

Still the centre table remained unoccupied.

Denys Trevelyan was peeling an apple. Angus Leigh helped himself to wine. Cosmo dreamed.

Then the dining-room door swung open and the manager bowed in Baroness Habening, followed by Elizabeth, Anne, Marie, Dottie and Dolly. All round the dining-room people noted their entrance.

'What a swiz,' muttered Cosmo. 'Not one of them is nubile.'

'The three youngest are wearing wedding rings,' said Blanco, who had observant eyes.

'They are not even remotely pretty,' whispered Cosmo.

'Homely,' said Blanco. 'Home sweet homely.'

'They'll never leave home looking like that.'

'What are you two whispering about, Cosmo?' said his mother. 'Manners, darling.'

'Nothing, Ma. Sorry, Ma.'

'The Welsh miners are the worst of the lot,' said Angus Leigh, whose mind was on the troubles in England, 'but the northern lot may get stroppy. It's that lot I expect to—'

'There's a great deal to be said for the miners. I think their case is—' Had Blanco gone too far? Cosmo wondered. What would the rest of the holidays be like?

But his father had not heard Blanco. He too had

seen the newcomers, who were setting their ample bottoms on the spindly restaurant chairs. 'I *say*,' he exclaimed, 'if that isn't my old friend Rosa. Darling, come over and meet Rosa. You must remember how often I've told you about Rosa and Jef Habening. Used to shoot wild boar with him, remember? And duck. Friends of my youth—' Angus put his napkin down and stood up.

'All those girls,' said Mrs Leigh.

'She didn't have them in those days; I'm talking about the Dark Ages. There may have been one or two, but well out of the way, in their cradles. Come along, you must—' Angus led his wife across the room to the centre table. 'Rosa? Remember me?'

'Angus!' The baroness threw up her hands. 'Angus, of course—' There were exclamations, introductions, hand-shakings, standings-up, sittings-down.

'Look at the shape of them,' whispered Cosmo. 'Huge. What a crashing disappointment. I had pinned my—'

But Blanco was listening to what was being said at the table in the alcove. They heard, '—so greasy it can't have been washed since I left you with her. Filthy nails and chipped. When did you last have a bath? She hasn't even seen that you wear clean clothes. Your vest is grey, it's disgusting and you've got blackheads. Look, Denys, she's got blackheads.'

'Send her to the hairdresser.' Denys Trevelyan spoke remotely. 'Have some of it off. I don't care for pigtails.'

'She's too young to go to the hairdresser, Denys.'

'Do whatever you think best. Why don't you answer your mother, Flora?'

'I think I will go to bed.' Flora stood up. 'Goodnight,' she said steadily. 'Goodnight.' She began to edge away.

'Flora,' Vita snapped, 'sit down. Come back.'

'Oh, let her go,' said Denys as the child moved past the Leighs' table. 'It's not your fault, darling.' He put his hand over his wife's. 'I wonder if we can find a couple to make up a four for bridge. I daresay

36

the governess was pretty slack.' He squeezed his wife's hand.

Watching Flora cross the room, Blanco and Cosmo saw her run smack into a man hurrying into the restaurant. He steadied the child, putting both hands on her shoulders, then stood aside to open the door for her.

'She didn't see him, she was crying,' said Cosmo. 'I shall ask Father to get our table moved,' he said without lowering his voice.

'I think I shall give up bridge,' said Blanco. 'Look, your pa's waving at us to join them.'

'That will be the baron. Her son, of course.' The widow with the buck-toothed daughter leaned towards a neighbouring table. 'Isn't he good-looking? And so young.'

'Angus, introduce me,' said the baroness.

'My son Cosmo, his friend Hubert Wyndeatt-Whyte who is with us for the holidays, a bit of a bolshie. And let me get this right: Elizabeth, Anne, Marie, Dottie and Dolly.'

'And my son Felix,' said Rosa, holding the young man who had bumped into Flora by the sleeve. 'What kept you, Felix? We had given you up.'

'A puncture, Mama.' Felix sat beside his mother. 'Hello, hello, all my sisters.'

'What an astonishingly handsome young man,' said Milly Leigh as they moved away, 'and what disastrously lumpy girls. It simply isn't fair.'

Five

Denys changed his mind about finding a four for bridge; catching Cosmo's eye had given him a chill.

He walked with Vita's hand tucked in his arm. From time to time he squeezed it. 'What will you do with your time? Shall you be happy in this hotel? You will be bored, alone with the child.'

'Play bridge, tennis; write you long, long letters; swim.'

'In this climate? You'll die of cold.'

'Overhaul my wardrobe so that when I join you in September you will think you have a new wife.'

'I want the one I have – preferably without clothes.'

'Not in this climate!' she teased, then, 'Let's turn in soon, shall we?'

'What about the child?' He was petulant.

'She's probably helping Mademoiselle pack. I shall be all right, Denys. I'll find someone to teach her maths; she's learning the piano with Madame Tarasova. Maths aren't that important, though, she will catch up when she gets to school. When I first brought her here, before you got home on leave, I heard of an Italian family who will be glad to chatter to her so that she doesn't forget her Italian.'

'Darling.' Denys stared at the sea; they were walking along the road above the beach. 'If she's so occupied, what's the point of you being here at all?'

'She's only ten. She needs me.'

Denys snorted. 'I need you.'

'Darling, we've been into all this. Everybody in India goes through it. They come home, spend time with their families and see to the children. We would be thought odd if I didn't do this. What would people say at the Club?'

'But we have no families. I don't care if I am thought odd. Is it odd to love one's wife?'

'I know, I know. We can't blame my mother for dying, and I love you too, darling, you know I do.'

'It's the disappointment. She was prepared to take charge of the child. We could have spent my summer leave in Kashmir—' Denys was resentful.

Vita shivered in the April wind. 'I am just as sad about it as you.'

'We should have had the child adopted.'

'Denys!'

'It's not as though she were a son. I know you feel the same. Every time we have a chance to have fun together, she gets in the way. We could have stayed on in London but oh no, to save money, because of the child, we come to this tedious place. I hate France. I can't stand the French.'

'Denys!'

'And I do not like this hotel. I could hear someone cleaning their teeth in the next room when I was changing for dinner, farting.'

'Denys!'

'I don't like that family we were next to in the restaurant; one of those hulking boys stared at me most insolently.'

'You liked his father on the boat.'

'You liked his father on the boat.'

'Denys—'

'I shall ask tomorrow. There may be a flat we could rent. We'd have privacy.'

'A nice double bed in it, perhaps?'

'Good idea, you think?'

'Yes, I do. It might even be an economy. We could go to Kashmir for longer next summer, or up there to ski in the winter.'

'Next summer is a long way off.'

'Tonight isn't. Let's go back and go to bed.'

39

They turned about and walked up the hill. 'I cannot believe any man loves his wife as I love you,' he said.

'Oh, Denys.'

'I do not mind being honest about it. Do you mind?'

'I love it.'

'Or saying what I think about the child.' He paced doggedly.

'It's a bit unconventional.'

'She was shockingly impertinent at dinner.'

'But she never uttered a word.'

'That was it.'

They walked on, leaning into the slope. Vita said, 'I know. Listen. If I can get someone to say they'll keep an eye on her, we could spend the last weeks of your leave in London. I see now it was a rotten idea to come here.'

'But we have sacked the governess.'

'We don't need a governess for such a short time, just someone who is in the hotel. And I can ask Madame Tarasova to do it too. We could pay her a little something. Leave our address, of course.'

'Could you arrange it? It would put my mind at rest with this tricky situation of the strike interfering with my voyage. It may well, if it spreads.'

'And we could see that show.' They had reached the hotel. 'The one we couldn't get tickets for.'

'That's an idea. But if we move into a flat, what about the child?'

He never called her Flora.

'Leave her in the annexe until I come back? See. I think of everything. She's perfectly all right there and we can have the flat to ourselves at night.'

They mounted the stairs to their room. Denys put his hand on his wife's neck as she unlocked the door. Such white skin. In a flat, he thought, nobody would hear her cry out when they made love, there would be no inhibiting hotel walls.

Vita brushed her teeth with salt; Denys did not like the taste of toothpaste.

'Hurry up,' he called from his bed, and when she joined him, 'Take that thing off,' jerking at her nightdress. She would be at a disadvantage; he would not, she knew, take off his pyjamas.

'Look out,' she said, 'you'll tear it.'

'Those bloody boys,' he said, tearing the nightdress. She feared this mood, made herself pliant.

'Just boys,' she said, 'young.'

'The fair one was bloody arrogant. I know his kind, but the dark one reminded me of someone, the eyebrows meeting above the nose. Didn't you notice him?'

She had preferred not to, had deliberately looked elsewhere. 'Not particularly.' She unbuttoned his pyjama. (It was only the eyebrows, all else was different.) 'Don't do that,' Denys snapped.

'What about this, then?' she murmured.

Presently Denys whispered, sweating, 'Where did you learn to do that?'

'I just did it. It came naturally.'

'You've never done it before.'

'I have wanted to.'

'You would have made a wonderful tart,' he said. She knew the mood was over.

Asleep, Denys relaxed his hold. Cautiously, so as not to disturb him, she retrieved the torn nightdress and, a little shaken, got into her own bed to lie wakeful in the cool sheets. The man had played that trick on her; it had been dangerous to use it on Denys. She forced herself to push the memory back where it belonged, buried deep. Usually she managed. Only occasionally, when there were spats as there had been tonight, did the memory surface. Once she had made up her mind that whatever happened Denys came first, she had stopped having nightmares. She swore to herself to get through the next months with the child unscathed. If we had had her adopted, Vita thought, I might have had nightmares about meeting her, wondered what she looked like; as it is, I know what she looks like and mercifully I am not maternal.

Six

Milly Leigh was seldom pleased to meet people, women especially, whom her husband had known in his youth. Angus was a large, confident, handsome man who talked in a large, confident way. He had travelled much, served far afield, made friends wherever he went. When she married him in 1908 at eighteen, she came straight from the schoolroom. Fifteen years older than Milly, Angus had a host of friends, male and female, intelligent, gifted and amusing. Milly felt herself at a disadvantage. She resented Angus' bachelor years, was inclined to fear his friends, was jealous. Angus paid not the slightest attention. Rather, if he thought about it, he was flattered; Milly's jealousy boosted his ego. He knew, too, that sooner rather than later she made friends with his friends, forgot she had bristled with fear when introduced and would soon be ganging up with them against him, so that they became as much her friends as his. He adored his wife, thought her by far the prettiest woman he had ever loved and would, if asked to stop and think, have concluded that Milly was the only woman he had loved. There had been lots of other women, of course, but nothing serious; he had never lost sleep.

Cosmo and Mabs watched for their mother's reaction on meeting what they referred to as Father's misspent friends. They bristled with her, closed ranks with their mother, glared when strangers were bonhomously introduced.

Cosmo tried to explain this to Blanco as they sauntered through the town after dinner. 'We know she has nothing to fear, of course. Father dotes on her but he's a fool; he expects her to know there was nothing between him and the women. It's the women who terrify her. Some of them act as though—'

'What?'

'As though they and Father had had an affair. It's ludicrous.'

'And did they?'

'How would I know? With the men she's afraid she'll appear stupid. Father has friends who are much brainier than he is and think women should be good listeners.' (Blanco laughed.) 'And Ma isn't a good listener. She chatters from nerves,' said Cosmo.

'Wish my nerves made me chatter. I go dumb.'

'But tonight,' Cosmo exclaimed, 'did you notice? When introduced to the baroness and her five Amazons Ma was ever so jolly, joyfully accepted the invitation to join their table, all of us with all of them. That will be seven of them and six of us, gosh!'

'We shall be thirteen.'

'Are you superstitious?'

'Just simple arithmetic.'

'It's amazing,' Cosmo marvelled. 'She was so spontaneous. It's not like my mother; it usually takes weeks to reach that stage.'

'The old girl said, Let's catch up on lost years, let our children get to know each other. D'you think – well, she's as old as your father or looks it.'

'Even so—'

'She's fat.'

'That wouldn't faze my mother. She'd be seeing a slender little Rosa peeking out from the fat.'

'Your father was speaking as though her husband had been the great friend—'

'Wouldn't fox Ma. No, I think it's something else, all those daughters and only one son.'

'Plain daughters at that,' Blanco agreed.

'And Mabs is a smasher.'

'Why didn't you tell me?' asked Blanco, surprised.

'Because you haven't a hope. Mabs is seventeen.'

43

'And her friend?'

'Same goes for her.'

'Do you think the baron and baroness went on trying: pop, pop, pop, pop, pop, five little girls, then great big pop, she's done it at last, Felix, a son, hurrah, we can call a halt?' suggested Blanco.

Cosmo and Blanco clung to each other, screaming with laughter.

Recovering, Blanco said, 'I think your mother realized that if we join up with the Dutch, it gets us away from that horrible couple at the next table who were bullying their child.'

'Ah yes, I caught some of it. They said she had blackheads. Poor kid. I say, Elizabeth, the eldest Dutch daughter, plays backgammon and they all play tennis. They seem friendly. One of them asked why don't we dance at the casino. It seems age doesn't matter, we can all go and dance.'

'Dance?' said Blanco, interested.

'Can you dance?'

'A bit,' said Blanco modestly.

'If you want to get off with Mabs you must dance.'

'Actually, I can dance. See me dance the Charleston.' Blanco began to dance, bobbing and kicking on the pavement, 'Come on, Cosmo, dance!'

'Stop it, you'll attract a crowd. Shut up,' hissed Cosmo, alarmed by his friend's high spirits.

'Don't be so English,' sang Blanco, dancing.

Cosmo took to his heels.

Blanco joggled and kicked down onto the beach, where he danced patterns in the sand. As he danced he hummed the tune he had seen Jack Buchanan dance to with Elsie Randolf. Exultantly he danced towards the waves, crunching up the sand. The breeze from the sea stung his eyes and ruffled his hair. He flung out his arms and whirled about in ecstasy.

He stopped at last; he had the beach to himself. He stood watching the lights from the town reflected on the water and considered the colour of the waves in the moonlight. Were they silver or emerald? Was the sea black or bottle green? A cloud passed across the moon. He felt cold and turned to walk back. It was then that he saw Flora.

Flora was wading into the sea with her eyes shut. She was fully dressed. When Blanco caught her, she bit him.

Blanco pinned her arms to her sides and carried her up the beach. She kicked his shins; her heels, drumming on his shinbones, hurt abominably. Blanco held her tightly with his left arm and smacked her. 'Keep still.' She bit him again. 'Bitch.' He shook her. 'Stop it.' He was horrified by her silence. She dodged his raised hand and tried to bite him again. 'I know who you are,' he said. 'I shall take you to Madame Tarasova.' Still Flora said nothing. 'Come on,' Blanco said, putting her down, 'walk.' He kept a tight hold. 'If you can walk into the sea, you can walk up the hill.'

'I've ruined my best trousers,' he said presently to Cosmo.

'Send them to the cleaners. Then what happened?' Cosmo was already undressed and in bed.

'I just said to Madame Tarasova that I had caught her walking into the sea. With her eyes tight shut!'

'God!'

'And not a word said! Look where she bit me. Look at my shins; she's broken the skin. They are going blue.'

'What did Madame Ta—'

'Said something in Russian, something about hot milk in French. She sort of folded the child up.'

'Enfolded.'

'All right. Enfolded. She said quite a lot more in Russian, then she thanked me in French. She was kissing and cuddling her all the time, sopping wet. She said leave it to her – just look at these trousers!' Blanco wailed.

'Go on.'

'Then her bloody little dog came hurtling down the stairs – we were half in, half out of the house – and

45

tried to bite me. That seemed to wake the child; she started to laugh. The Tarasova waved me away, shut the door in my face and I came on home. D'you think the cleaners will get this water mark out? Look, here, where the salt is drying.'

'Was she sleep-walking, d'you suppose?' Cosmo hugged his knees.

'You don't bite people in your sleep.' Blanco put his trousers across a chair.

'I think we should tell my mother.'

'Let's wait and see. See what la Tarasova does. She looked so private, somehow. One wouldn't want to barge in more than—'

'Perhaps my mother would be more help if we didn't tell her.'

'Why?' asked Blanco.

But Cosmo did not know why he thought this to be so. He said, 'Surely children don't actually—' Neither he nor Blanco uttered the word suicide. Blanco said he thought he would have a hot bath.

Seven

'I think I will stretch my legs before turning in.'
Angus stood with Milly in the vestibule. They had
said goodnight to Rosa and her daughters. 'I'd like a
breath of fresh air before bed. Would you care to keep
me company?' he asked Felix.

'Thank you, sir, I would.'

'Goodnight then, darling, don't be too late.' Milly
climbed away from them up the stairs. 'Don't forget
the girls are arriving tomorrow. You will need all your
strength.'

Angus and Felix stepped out into the street. 'I find
coming to terms with an adult daughter rather daunt-
ing,' said Angus, 'though your mother is a fine example
of survival in that context.'

Felix laughed. 'My parents stopped counting after
a while and now three of my sisters are married. My
mother only has two at home.'

'What I really want,' said Angus as they walked,
'is to get to the casino without my wife knowing.'

Felix said, 'Oh,' and wondered how much money
he had on him.

'Not what you think,' said Angus. 'I have a hunch
there may be one of those ticker machines. Waiting
for a day-old newspaper is no good; I need to keep
in touch with news from home.'

'There is one in the foyer of the casino,' said Felix.
'I take it you are concerned about the possibility of a
strike?'

'A strike which may lead to a revolution.'

'Surely, sir—' Felix was amused.

'Plenty of young men in Moscow and St Petersburg said, "Surely, sir," in identical accents to yours,' said Angus grimly. 'I am not saying there will be, but if boys like Cosmo's friend Wyndeatt-Whyte know enough to sympathize with the miners, think what a lot of sympathy there must be in the country generally.'

'I thought it was a Conservative delusion that your trade unions are influenced by the Communists.'

'It's a pretty general opinion. Hotheads like Winston Churchill are spoiling for a fight. A man like Simon, who is too clever by half, half believes it. It's a spreading fungus. It makes good headlines for the press barons. Then there is Birkenhead, one wonders about him, and of course Joynson-Hicks sees Bolsheviks everywhere.'

'Your Home Secretary?'

'Yes. Don't know any of them personally, I am just a retired soldier. I hate politicians. Don't trust them an inch. If you ask me the King has more sense than the whole Cabinet. Shut him in a room with A. J. Cook and he'd settle the whole thing in a trice, and fairly at that,' grumbled Angus.

'He represents the miners, this Cook?' Felix's English was good but hesitant.

'Yes, he does. And the King loves the miners. I love the miners, perfectly splendid fellows.'

'I understand from the newspapers that they want a living wage. What is a living wage?'

'What they are not going to get,' said Angus shortly. 'Hence the deadlock in negotiations.'

'So?'

'So there is anti-Bolshevik panic which I find myself joining, with every possibility of a National Strike and ugly scenes. If there is one, I have to be at home to give my services to the Civil Commissioner of my area. Bloody fool he is, too. I served under him at one moment in the war. I don't want to get embroiled with the minister, but if I'm there I may be able to stop him doing something idiotic. He's afraid of me. He's a distant cousin of my wife's.'

'Oh,' said Felix. 'Ah.'

'I don't want to alarm my wife, but in the event of trouble I shall leave her here and go home on my own. I shall rest easy if she and Mabs are in France.'

'What about your son?' asked Felix. They were reaching the casino.

'Cosmo? He has to go back to school; he's missed quite enough with that bad knee. Oh! I say, I know those fellows. Hi, Freddy, and is that Ian with you?' Angus hailed two men coming out of the casino. He introduced Felix. Freddy and Ian, it seemed, had come on the same errand as Angus. They stood exchanging news and views, men much of an age, voice and opinion as Angus. Felix watched the group with a mixture of fascination and amusement. It would be impossible to mistake them, he thought, for anything other than English. He tried to pinpoint what was so English. The voice? The way they stood? The clothes? The way they placed their feet? What was it? The group was joined by several more fathers of families Easter-holidaying; they all bore the same invisible stamp.

There was consultation, accord, an agreement reached. The group broke up – 'Goodnight,' 'Goodnight,' – and went their various ways.

'Sorry about that,' said Angus. 'Boring for you. You should have gone in and had a bet or two, there's still time. Would you like to? Or is it a bit late?'

'A bit late, sir, and not boring at all. I enjoyed watching you. You all looked so English.'

'One of them was a Scot,' said Angus, pouting his moustache.

'Perhaps I should have said British?'

'English will do. What else would you expect us to look?' They were walking back towards the Marjolaine.

'What I was trying to say, sir, was that seeing you standing there with your friends – er – that if I had not met you or heard you speak, I would still have known from something about you that you were English. I was trying to guess what it was.'

Angus was only half-listening. 'Talking to those

49

chaps has put my mind at rest. I can enjoy the holidays now.' Then, 'My dear fellow, what you say is absurd. Look at any group from any nation and you know what they are. Everybody knows that the Dutch are stodgy, just as the French are flash. You have but to look at them—'

The two men walked on a few paces without speaking, then Angus, glancing at his companion, began to laugh. 'My dear fellow, what an awful fool you must take me for. Perhaps that is intrinsically English?'

'My father used to describe you to us as slightly larger than life,' said Felix, smiling. 'We used to watch you from our nursery window.'

'Come to think of it, he wasn't stodgy either. Goodnight, my dear fellow, thanks for your company.' They parted laughing.

On his way up to his wife's room Angus remembered Jef, Felix's father, tall as himself, blue-eyed and fair, and Rosa when young, a little fair girl with blue eyes. How on earth had these two managed to produce dark-haired, dark-eyed Felix who remotely resembled neither parent? As he walked along the corridor to his wife's room Angus frowned, remembering the couple on the boat; had not the man made a remark in dubious taste about his dark child? There was an intensity about the man, something alien; would Felix class him on sight as English? Would he immediately recognize Felix as Dutch? What a horrible pattern this carpet had. Angus looked despisingly at the red and black lozenges stretching ahead; they reminded him of something. What was it? Got it. Rosa, in a similar patterned dress, showing him photographs of herself with her brothers as children, her hair cropped short and her expression serious. He could hear her voice: 'Don't laugh, we really looked like that.' Until tonight he had not thought of Rosa for years; friend Jef was long dead. One had coveted Rosa in a jolly sort of way, but now she had grown too stout. Angus knocked on his wife's door and went in. 'Ah, there you are,' he said, sounding pleased.

'Who did you expect to find?' Milly, already in

bed, laid down her book. 'I can't get on with this,' she said, 'it's rubbish.'

'Could you get on with me?' Angus made his voice gruff.

'Of course I could.' Milly held out her arms.

Flora, in pyjamas and dressing-gown, watched Mademoiselle pack. Having laid shoes in the bottom of the suitcase, missal and bundles of letters along the sides, she now levelled a platform to receive her best clothes by padding over lumps with underclothes, stockings, handkerchiefs and scarves. Her one good dress was neatly folded on the bed with tissue paper, as were her two blouses, waiting to be packed last after the tweed skirt and cardigan of daily wear.

'Labels, I need labels,' muttered Mademoiselle. 'Run, child, and ask at the desk for two labels.'

'Like this?' Flora spread her arms, exposing skimpy pyjamas and bare feet.

Mademoiselle sighed gustily. She was a fat young woman. 'You are no help; I must do everything myself.'

'The desk will be closed in five minutes.' Flora eyed the open suitcase. 'Won't tomorrow do?'

'Tomorrow is too late.' Mademoiselle left the room, taking with her a musty smell of perspiration overlaid with cologne. Flora wondered whether she would miss Mademoiselle more or less than she had missed the Signorina with whom she had spent a year in Italy. The Signorina's smell had been of lesser strength, but had the same base. Flora raised her arms and sniffed at each armpit. She tightened the belt of her dressing-gown. As she leaned down to peer into Mademoiselle's suitcase she remembered quite jolly times singing the Fascists' song *Giovanezza* with the Signorina, who had a brother who wore the olive-green uniform and black top-boots of the Fascisti and thought Mussolini wonderful. Among Mademoiselle's letters were postcards; one of particular interest. Flora knew the message: 'We visited this museum yesterday – we return Paris tomorrow – Danish food does not suit Maman – Copenhagen

51

disappoints – Hans Andersen lacks panache – Babette.'
The card was from the Thorwaldsen Museum; the picture on the card was of a sculpture of a naked man
reclining on his side. With her back to him, also naked,
a girl lay, her back and legs fitting into the curve of
the man's body, her head supported by his arm. On
receiving it Mademoiselle had remarked that Danish
sculptures were peculiar; to her mind the pair would
look better upright. On receiving an identical postcard
from her mother she had observed that the Danes were
a repetitive people and refused to explain what she
meant. Flora thought the recumbent figures wonderful;
how delicious, she thought, to lie like that against the
marble man. She asked Mademoiselle to give her one of
the postcards since she had two. Mademoiselle refused;
she collected stamps, she said.

Flora leaned down and with finger and thumb
extracted one of the postcards from the bundle. About
to look at it just once more, she heard Mademoiselle
returning, talking as she came to Gaston.

'If you give me the suitcase now,' said Gaston, 'I
will send it to the station with a visitor who is taking
the train to Paris. That way you will save a taxi and a
porter's tip. What else have you got?'

'My overnight bag,' said Mademoiselle as she opened
the door. 'I can carry that.'

Flora pocketed the postcard. Mademoiselle finished
packing. Gaston helped her shut the case and tied on
labels, picked it up and departed, saying goodnight and
bon voyage.

'Go to bed, child. I shall be gone before you wake.'
Mademoiselle pecked drily at Flora's forehead. 'Bonne
chance, petite.'

Too late to return the postcard. Flora mumbled
a token kiss onto Mademoiselle's plump cheek and
went to her room, where she put the postcard in a
drawer and covered it with a vest; she would gloat
over it tomorrow. But now she pulled the spare pillow round so that she could lie with her back pressed
against it and imagine smooth, cool, comforting marble.

Eight

The friendliness and good humour of the Shovehalfpennies, as they inevitably became known after Angus'
mention of the late Baron's first name, acted as a cata-
lyst among the visitors of Dinard. It did not matter to
Elizabeth, Anne, Marie, Dottie and Dolly to what age
group anybody belonged. They played tennis with
young children, bridge with their parents and roulette
with Angus, Milly and their mother. They danced with
Cosmo, Blanco and their brother and went through the
shops like a dose of salts. Sophisticated Mabs and
Tashie, arriving from Paris, were not to have it all
their own way. If, at seventeen, they outshone the other
girls, had shingled hair, wore lipstick when Milly was
not looking, had shed their puppy fat and could dance
not only the Charleston but the foxtrot, they had yet to
acquire the ease of manner of the Dutch sisters. Under
their benign influence the young people from the various hotels coalesced into a homogeneous group which
ebbed and flowed about town, forming and reforming
like a flock of birds. Three girls from the Britannique
knew a boy and his sister in the Marjolaine and they
had a cousin in the Angleterre whose school played
Cosmo and Blanco's at cricket. Fours were made up
for tennis, riotous rounders were played on the beach.
There were expeditions along the coast and from five
o'clock onwards dancing in the Casino, le Thé Dansant.
All the girls were in love with Felix.

Flora Trevelyan, too young and too shy to join
in, watched from a distance, awed by the exuberance.
She was painfully jealous of Mabs and Tashie; she had

seen them arrive from Paris and noted their smart navy blue suits, dazzling white blouses, knee-length skirts, their cloche hats pulled low over pert noses. She too was in love with Felix.

Felix might have belonged to some other breed than his sisters. They were dumpy, he was tall; they were fair, he was dark; they were high-spirited, he was quiet, soft-spoken, gentle. From time to time he disappeared in his car with his sister Elizabeth.

'He takes her with him because she is so old he is sorry for her. She is twenty-six, poor thing, not a sign of a husband.' Tashie sat with Mabs and Cosmo on the hotel terrace trying to decide what to do next.

'Actually, she's an archaeologist. They go to look at the menhirs,' said the sandy-haired girl with buck teeth who was listening to the group, though not exactly of it.

'What's a menhir?' asked Tashie.

'A standing stone,' said the buck-toothed girl, whose name was Joyce.

'What's a standing stone?' asked Mabs.

Cosmo, foreseeing his sister about to be caught displaying ignorance, got up and sauntered down the street to where he could see Blanco staring through the window of the patisserie. 'What's a standing stone, Hubert?'

Surprised at being called by his proper name, Blanco said, 'What's a what?'

Cosmo repeated his question.

'Lots of them in Cornwall and Wales, all the way from Asia Minor to the Orkneys. Something to do with Druids, Stonehenge, that sort of thing.'

'What a lot you know.'

'Been talking to Elizabeth Shovvers. Shall we go in and eat some of those?' Blanco pointed at the alluring display of cream cakes. 'My mother sent me some money. I'll treat you.'

'Terrible for our spots,' Cosmo demurred.

'What do spots matter with Felix around? We might as well not exist.'

'True.' Cosmo led the way into the patisserie. They

54

sat at a table, ordered cakes, leaned back and surveyed the street through the plate-glass window.

'The married Shovvers are leaving tomorrow to return to connubial bliss.' Blanco bit into an éclair. 'Delicious.' He licked his fingers.

'Elizabeth told you? I wonder what their connubial bliss is like.'

'Your parents?' suggested Blanco.

'Oh, come on!' Cosmo laughed. Then, 'Elizabeth and Anne are coming to meet the Tarasova; they want to get some pointers for backgammon, crafty Armenian dodges. Oh look, there goes that peculiar child.' Through the window of the patisserie the friends viewed Vita and Denys Trevelyan window-shopping on the opposite side of the street. Flora trailed several yards behind them.

'My shins are still bruised,' said Blanco. 'She looks rather miserable.'

'One would with those parents.' Cosmo watched the Trevelyans move out of sight.

'They'll be back in India soon, with hordes of native servants and all that jazz. Anne says the Dutch are the same.'

'As what?'

'Downtreading and squashing the inferior race, that sort of thing – grinding their noses into the shit in the East Indies.'

'Father says—'

'Your father is an imperialist warmonger. Have another cake?'

'Thanks. I'm missing lunch.' Cosmo was laughing. 'The imperialist warmonger is worried to death about the strike,' he said. 'He's no nose-grinder, though.'

'I hope for a revolution. *Encore de gâteaux, s'il vous plaît, Mademoiselle.* What is your father going to do about it? Can he take on the strikers single-handed?' Blanco enquired, teasing.

'He's—' Cosmo stopped what he was about to say, then said, 'He isn't a warmonger. Yes, he votes Conservative and yes, he is a magistrate, but he thinks war

55

is an abomination, and revolution leads to war. That's why he is so twitchy at the moment. All our fathers are Conservative.'

'Speak for yourself, I have not got one.'

'Don't use your war orphanhood as a damper.' Cosmo was good-humoured. 'My point is that were he alive, your father would vote Conservative.'

'I like to think he wouldn't,' said Blanco. 'Anyway, your father has got it back to front: revolutions are nourished by war, they start in wars. Look at Russia—'

'No thanks. Look, Blanco, thanks for the cakes. I have to go and do something for my father.'

'What?'

'Just a chore.'

'Shall I come too?'

'No.'

'Shall you be long?' asked Blanco.

'I might be.'

'Right, I can see I'm not wanted. I have a chore of my own for Madame Tarasova. She is going to write a letter in Russian to my cousin Thing; Anne can post it in Holland.'

'What for? What about?'

'Just a little tease. He was beastly by post to my mother. It's just a silliness.'

'Sometimes I can't make you out, you and your cousin Thing. It's an obsession.' Cosmo ran a surreptitious finger across his plate to catch the last of the cream and, licking it, rose to go.

As he walked towards the quay he patted his pocket to make sure the money his father had given him was safe. Reaching the quay, he saw the vedette had disgorged its passengers and was casting off, ready to leave.

Perched on a bollard with her back to him, her legs wound about it, sat Flora, watching the *vedette*. On impulse, as he ran past, Cosmo caught her by the hand and said: 'Come with me to St Malo.'

Flora was surprised, but allowed him to run her down the steps and jump on board. 'Let's sit up forward.' He pushed her ahead of him. They sat in the bows. 'D'you know St Malo well?' he asked. Flora nodded. 'You've had some of your hair cut off,' he said, watching her hair swished across her face by the wind.

'And washed. The hairdresser tried to charge extra for the shampoo.' Her tone was flat.

'Because it's so thick.' Cosmo remembered Vita's voice saying blackheads. He wanted to say her hair was lovely, which it was, but did not; he said, 'All women's heads are shingled, the man must save a packet on shampoo.' He caught a quick glance from Flora's enormous eyes. 'I wonder what they charge to shampoo eyelashes,' he said. Flora looked puzzled. Perhaps she did not know that she had extraordinarily long lashes? He would have liked to touch them. 'I see you about sometimes,' he said, remembering now that he had noticed her during the last weeks, glimpsed alone or with Igor, disappearing round corners. 'I saw you this morning with your parents,' he said and wondered belatedly whether he was getting her into trouble taking her off without permission. 'I was in the patisserie.'

'They've gone to Dinan,' she said. 'They've taken a flat; they are buying things for it.'

'So you've left the hotel. I thought—'

'They have, I haven't.'

Cosmo couldn't take this in. 'When will they be back?' he asked, remembering his dislike, fearing a confrontation, explanation. What explanation?

'Tomorrow, perhaps.'

'Do they leave you on your own often?'

'They like to be together.' Her lips closed with almost adult discretion.

Cosmo said, 'Oh.' Then again, 'Oh.' After a while he said, 'I am on an errand for my father. Secret from my mother. Nobody is to know. He doesn't want to alarm her so you mustn't tell a soul. I am to buy a revolver.'

'A pistolet?'

'Yes. He is going to travel up north in his car

when I go back to school. Afraid of trouble, he feels he should be armed.'

'I shan't tell anyone.'

'I only told you because I asked you to come with me and you might be surprised to see me buy a revolver.' Cosmo felt he should regret his impulsive action, but did not. 'Father said, "Find a gunsmith, there must be one," but I haven't the foggiest. I don't even know what a gunsmith is in French or how to ask; my French is still pretty basic. I can ask for patisseries and that sort of thing, but I don't know the word for gunsmith.'

'I do.'

'You do? What is it?'

'Armurier.'

'Oh, thanks. I must write it in my notebook. D'you think you could ask someone?'

'There's one in a side street round the corner from where your sister and her friend bought hats. Your sister bought a green one, her friend a blue.'

'What an observant little thing you are.' Flora shot Cosmo a glance of amusement. The hats had not noticeably impressed Felix, which had been the object of their purchase; she had observed that also. 'You'd better pretend you are eighteen,' she said.

'I'm not half-witted,' said Cosmo crossly.

Nine

Cosmo felt relief stepping out of the gunsmiths; he had felt rather ridiculous making his purchase. He could hardly believe that the parcel he carried concealed under its wrapping a lethal weapon. The man had asked no questions but casually laid out a choice of revolvers, naming the price of each as he placed it on the counter, turning the price label towards Cosmo.

Cosmo picked the make his father had asked for; there was no need to display his ignorance. All the same, while perfectly polite, the man had angered him. A heavy man, no taller than five and a half feet, large-stomached, heavily jowled, with black eyes which slid over his customer. Coming from behind the counter when there was no apparent need, he twitched at a display of knives in the window, straightening a row that was already straight. Returning, he let his hand rest on Flora. It did not rest long; she moved so that the hand fell to his side. Wrinkling her nose, she removed herself into the street. A word passed. The shopkeeper looked sharply from the closing door to Cosmo, pursed his lips, finished wrapping the parcel, took the money, gave change and wrote a receipt. 'Merci, Monsieur.'

Flora waited across the street.

'Let's find somewhere that sells ice-cream. What did you say to that man?' asked Cosmo, intrigued.

'Maquereau.'

'He didn't look too pleased. What does it mean?'

Flora grinned. 'They have lovely ices in Jules' café by the harbour,' she said.

59

Cosmo memorized 'maquereau'; he had come out without his notebook and was disinclined to use his pocket dictionary in front of Flora. As they walked, he thought Blanco would have called the gunsmith 'priapic'. He was not sure what that meant, either. He said, 'How old are you? And I still don't know your name.'

'Flora Trevelyan. I am ten.'

They threaded their way through the narrow streets to the harbour. Flora indicated a café facing the quay. 'Will this do?' They sat.

The patron came out in a rush and gave Flora a smacking kiss on each cheek: 'Alors, petite, ça va? Tu veux une crème glacée? Fraise? Vanille? Chocolat? Et monsieur? Bonjour, monsieur.' He shook Cosmo's hand. 'Alors, votre choix?'

Cosmo chose chocolate, Flora strawberry.

'Do you come here often?' She was obviously a favoured customer.

'With Madame Tarasova.'

'Oh.'

'Once or twice with Mademoiselle.'

'Oh.'

'Madame Tarasova alters dresses for Jules' wife; she is getting rather fat.' Flora spread hands outwards from her stomach. 'Madame Tarasova lets them out.'

'I see.'

'Jules likes fat ladies.'

'Does Madame Tarasova teach you the piano?'

'Russian, and they are asking her to coach me at maths before I go to school.'

'Where are you at school?'

'Nowhere. I start in the autumn.'

'So you haven't been yet?'

'No.'

'What school are you going to?'

'Some place they have chosen.'

'How peculiar.'

'Why?' She seemed indifferent.

'It seems peculiar not to know where you are going.'

'They decide. It's in England. I can't live with them in India because of the climate.'

Cosmo thought it odd the way she referred to her parents as 'they'; he was reminded of Blanco's name for his cousin, 'Thing' or 'Chose'. 'Mabs and I were taken to see our schools,' he said, 'to see whether we thought we'd like them.'

'You are different.'

Feeling different, Cosmo said, 'Has Madame T. taught you backgammon?'

'Yes, we play. On wet days when Igor doesn't want to go out.'

They watched the boats bobbing beside the quay until Jules brought two large ice-creams, placing them down with care.

Flora sat straight on her chair, pointing her toes down so that they reached the ground. She ate her ice with calculated enjoyment.

'I take Jules' dog out for the day sometimes,' she said.

'The animal I saw you with the first time we met?' Cosmo remembered the idiotic dog, Flora wading, the vast expanse of beach beyond St Enogat.

'He belongs to the curé of St Briac.' She acknowledged their first encounter. 'Jules' dog is a mastiff.'

'Really?'

'Very busy people do not have time to exercise their dogs.' She sipped primly at her ice, making it last.

'That's a wonderful beach,' said Cosmo. 'I was birdwatching. I imagine it's the sort of beach which would be great for sand eels.'

'It is.'

'What does "maquereau" mean?' Cosmo succumbed to curiosity.

'Pimp,' said Flora.

'Do you know what a pimp is?'

'It's not polite.'

'No.'

'He smelled.' She laid her spoon regretfully in the saucer and sniffed the harbour air. Rope, tar, fish,

61

salt, seaweed, drying nets. She filled her lungs. The shopkeeper had smelled stale. She caught her breath, remembering the foetid smell in her parents' bedroom when she had evaded her ayah and run in to say good-morning. They had yelled at her to go away and scolded the servants. 'I didn't like it in India,' she said.

Cosmo said, 'Would you like another ice?'

'No, thank you. It was delicious.'

'Then I suppose we should be getting back,' he said.

'It's been absolutely lovely,' she said. 'Thank you very much.'

He wondered whether she listened much to people talking. Some of the turns of phrase were reminiscent of his mother.

On the *vedette* crossing back to Dinard, Cosmo said: 'Why don't we make up a party, ask everybody, have a great bang-up beach party on that beach? An end-of-holidays party? Dig for sand eels, have a bonfire and a fry-up on the dunes. They are delicious with bread and butter. My parents, your parents, the Shovelhalfpennies, and all the children. It would be fun, wouldn't it?'

She said, 'Yes,' without enthusiasm.

As they reached the quay he said, 'Perhaps Blanco and I could take you on some day at backgammon?'

'Oh, yes!' she said. 'Yes.' And her face lit up.

Ten

The holiday, as holidays do, had begun by stretching pleasurably ahead. But now, like elastic, it snapped short; there were only ten days left.

Cosmo's idea of a grand picnic party received short shrift when he mooted it. The weather had changed; the wind blew unkindly from the east. It rained, a persistent driving rain which sliced at people's legs and gargled down the gutters. Queasy children were sick crossing from St Malo. Families stayed indoors and played snap and racing demon, draughts or chess. They ventured out only to make a dash to the cinema or the casino. The intermingling of the young from the various hotels dwindled.

The three younger Dutch girls, Marie, Dottie and Dolly, left the Marjolaine to return to their husbands in The Hague and Amsterdam; the party at the centre table shrank to ten, and sometimes eight since Felix and Elizabeth, regardless of the elements, were often out quartering the countryside for menhirs. Sometimes they ventured so far that they stayed the night. Elizabeth, it transpired, was writing a thesis. On these evenings Mabs and Tashie did not go to the casino; it was not worth running through the rain if Felix was not there to invite them to dance the foxtrot and the Charleston. Schoolboy partners who offered were rebuffed; they were unpractised, trod on the girls' feet, ruined their shoes, smelt of perspiration. Yet, persistent little shoppers, they skipped through the puddles by day, darting from hatshop to boutique, hoping in their young optimism to attract the

63

object of their desire by the brilliance of their plumage.

Rosa and Milly settled on a sofa in the lounge with their novels, knitting and growing friendship, and watched, the one with amused tolerance – she was used to the effect her son had on girls – the other with pity. It was painful to see the girls making fools of themselves; it reminded her of her social agonies before Angus, godlike, had snatched her from youthful insecurity, married her and made her happy ever after. Well, almost. It did not make her happy to see Cosmo dragged off to play golf in the wind and the rain by his father. Cosmo detested golf; being forced to play would not make him like it any better. She said as much to Rosa.

'Playing with a pretty girl in any weather, he would like it.' Rosa counted stitches. 'One can see he is ready and eager for girls.' She caught Milly's eye. 'Not my lumpen girls, of course. He and his friend watch for girls. It is natural, but their hopes are dashed with each new family's arrival, poor boys.'

'A pity Tashie is just that much too old for him, and Mabs too old for Hubert. They consider themselves grown-up. I had hoped that these holidays Cosmo might – with some other girl perhaps—' Milly looked round the hotel lounge, sadly lacking in suitable girls. 'Cosmo was off on his own into the country bird-watching before the holidays. I had hoped he would practise and improve his French. He carries a notebook with him and looks up the odd word in his dictionary, but that's about it. I hardly think what he learns is useful; he only bothers when he overhears an argument or people shouting at each other.'

'The first English word I overheard and looked up in the dictionary was obscene,' said Rosa, knitting steadily.

'And not useful?'

'It was useful,' said Rosa, suppressing a smile. 'I must concentrate on my knitting or I shall make a mess and have to unpick.'

64

'I wonder what it was.' Milly let her knitting, golf stockings for Angus, rest in her lap.

'I don't suppose you know it,' said Rosa, remembering what Jef had said apropos Angus: 'After all that he will pick someone innocent.' Thinking of her dead husband, she murmured, 'I miss him.'

Milly, not as innocent as Rosa supposed, thought, What she misses is the carnal side and the use in bed of those words one has to look up. She imagined Rosa's Jef to have been a Dutch version of Angus. She knitted a row of purl thoughtfully.

'There is the redhead called Joyce,' said Rosa. 'She is of an appropriate age for your Cosmo and his friend Hubert; she is fourteen.'

'Have you seen her teeth?' exclaimed Milly.

'She is intelligent. Do her teeth rule her out?'

'Definitely,' said Milly.

'Her mother tells me she is to go to one of those American dentists who do marvels. She has beautiful eyes, and a good figure.'

'Cosmo and Hubert do not see beyond the teeth; they say she looks like a horse.'

'Most English girls of the better class resemble horses, as do the German "hoch". It is a racial characteristic.'

'You generalize,' said Milly, laughing. 'I do not look like a horse and nor do Mabs and Tashie.'

'When you and those girls are excited, you look like fine Arabs. Flaring nostrils, the toss of the head, the shaken mane.' Rosa smiled down at her knitting; she enjoyed watching Mabs and Tashie tossing their heads at Felix. Elizabeth had remarked that she expected them to whinny. Elizabeth, of cart-horse build, was fortunate that she had a future in the world of intellectuals. 'I mean it as a compliment,' she said. 'Have you not heard men refer to girls as fillies?'

'God, yes,' said Milly, 'it sets my teeth on edge. But Cosmo does not seem to have had luck with any girls, be they like horses or frogs. Soon he will be back at school and be kept too busy to think of girls.'

Rosa sniffed. She did not believe any amount of being kept busy suppressed adolescent lust. Her husband had told her about British public schools; he had first-hand knowledge of what young males got up to when herded together. Was Milly as uninformed as she sounded? What did she imagine those boys did? 'Jef was sent to an English school by his father,' she said. 'It was hoped he would learn an upper-class accent, but he ran away.'

'I wonder why,' said Milly.

'The only friend he made at that school was Angus,' said Rosa. 'Jef was a very pretty boy.' If Angus had not enlightened his wife about the mores of public schools, it was not for her to shatter her complacency.

'Angus says a bit of healthy buggery never hurt anyone,' said Milly, knitting, 'and he drags poor Cosmo out in all weathers to the golf course to toughen him up. Cosmo says he swings his driver and thwacks the ball and shouts, "And that's for Baldwin" and "That's for Joynson-Hicks" and "That's for the Bolsheviks, curse their guts". He really is worried about the miners.'

Rosa knitted for several minutes before rallying. 'There is the child of that couple who are so wrapped up in each other,' she said. 'She has potential.'

'Do you mean the Trevelyans, who were staying here when you arrived? Angus met them on the boat from Southampton; he thought the wife pretty. I remember they had a child, but much too young to interest the boys. They moved on somewhere. Cosmo took a dislike to them for some reason.'

'They are still in Dinard,' said Rosa. 'They moved to a flat near the quay, leaving the child in the annexe where she has spent the winter with her governess. The mother was here for part of the time, they got special rates for a long stay – out of season – the mother has been in England with her husband for the first months of his leave. He goes back to India at the end of June.'

'What a lot you know,' said Milly.

'I talk to the hotel servants, they are fond of the child.'

66

'Oh,' said Milly, who hoped she disapproved of gossip.

'The Mademoiselle has been sacked; no great loss, I gather. The child is left to her own devices.'

'But her parents—'

'I suspect that in this weather they spend their time in bed doing the things you look up in the dictionary,' said Rosa. 'One sees the child, but she is rarely with her parents.'

Milly thought Rosa's suggestion coarse. She was of course Dutch, but even so . . . She kept her eyes on her knitting. She and Angus had never done anything like that in the daytime.

Rosa gave her an amused glance. 'That child is having a slap-dash education,' she said. 'A couple of years with a governess in Italy on the cheap, small pensions, that sort of thing, and then the same in France. I hear she is learning Russian from one of the émigrés and now the parents plan to put her in a school in England when the mother rejoins the father in India.'

'That's what happens to the children, long separations. It's sad, they hardly know their parents in some cases,' said Milly.

'Perhaps this child does not wish to,' said Rosa.

Milly thought Rosa was being rather harsh; she had probably got a garbled version from the hotel servants. 'I expect she has a grandmother or kind aunts who will take care of her in the holidays.' She felt it necessary to present a happier picture; the child's parents were, after all, English.

'There are no aunts or uncles. The only grandmother died recently, I hear.'

From the hotel servants, thought Milly. 'Many parents have quite a struggle these days,' she said. 'Look, for instance, at Hubert's mother, Mrs Wyndeatt-Whyte—'

'Such a ridiculous name,' said Rosa.

No more ridiculous than yours, thought Milly.

'She has only her widow's pension,' she said. 'She

67

tries to manage on that, and his rich relation will not help with one single penny.'

'Hum,' said Rosa, feeling she had teased Milly enough. 'He is a good-looking and nice-mannered boy. How does he spend his time while Cosmo plays enforced golf?'

'He learns the piano,' said Milly, 'goes for walks.'

Eleven

Blanco's walks took him no further than Madame Tarasova's lodging above the horse butcher. On his way he called at the patisserie to buy cakes to share with his tiny Armenian teacher. After a certain amount of heart-searching she had been persuaded to drop the piano lessons in favour of French conversation. This arrangement suited Madame Tarasova; she could stitch at whatever garment she happened to be making while they talked. When she had placed the cakes on a plate, she would resume her sewing while Blanco, sitting astride the piano stool, asked questions. He was consumed with curiosity about the Revolution, thrilled to meet someone who had been in Russia in 1917. Maybe she had played no actual part, but she would have met people who had, people who would have given her first-hand accounts. He questioned her in schoolboy French. 'Tell me what you saw. Your experiences, were they exciting?' He was avid for history at first-hand.

Madame Tarasova, sitting opposite the plate of cakes, savoured them with her eyes.

'Have one, go on, they are for you,' urged Blanco.

'Presently,' said Madame Tarasova. 'I like to look at them. Look,' she said, 'this is for the child, isn't it a pretty blue?'

'The one I—'

'Her maman has commissioned three – this blue, a green and a pink. Quite cheap material, but it is pretty. I would myself have chosen silk.' Madame Tarasova sighed. Blanco pushed the plate of cakes towards her. 'Oh, Hubert, you spoil me.'

'Tell me about the Revolution, the Bolsheviks; what were they like?'

'Bolsheviks, Bolsheviks.' She helped herself to a cake.

'Tell me what you saw,' urged Blanco.

Madame Tarasova threaded a needle. 'She will look her prettiest in the pink, but the material is rather ordinary.'

'The Revolution, Madame?'

'It was terrible. I was twenty years old in 1917, the year of disaster. So many young officers were killed in the war. They were so elegant, such fine uniforms, sable linings to their greatcoats. There is no sound to equal the musical clink of spurs. You could see your face reflected in their boots – such polish.' On either side of her large nose Madame Tarasova's eyes gazed into the past. 'All their underclothes were silk, of course.'

Had she been engaged to one of these creatures? Had she lost a lover? How to ask? Blanco helped himself to a cake. 'Were some of these officers relations of yours?' He screwed the stool round to watch her face.

'I watched them riding or driving in their carriages, such fine horses. They went to the great balls and to parties. This was before the Revolution. My heart went with them.'

'Ah.'

'The nobles, the princes, the Tsar and Tsarina, their beautiful children. Murdered by the Bolsheviks, oh, the shame and desecration.'

'Tell me about the Bolsheviks—'

'You should have seen the clothes the court ladies wore. The magnificent jewels, oh, the pity. Where are those jewels now?'

'I don't know, Madame Tarasova. In hock?'

'The silks and velvets, the lace, those incredible furs. Imagine the sable and mink, Hubert.'

'Tell me about Lenin.'

Madame Tarasova pursed her mouth. 'I cannot speak

that name without wishing to spit. *Je crache!*'

'Trotsky, then, tell me about Trotsky.'

'I would spit on him too.'

'Stalin? More goo?' suggested Blanco.

'I will tell you of the wonders of Holy Russia. Of Petrograd, that exquisite city, of the grandeur of Moscow. I know nothing of the monsters who destroyed my country. Where are the beautiful people who drove to the opera, the ballet, the court balls in their sumptuous carriages and sleighs? I can tell you about the beautiful people—'

Blanco tried again. 'Did you ever see Lenin?'

'Certainly not. Such badly cut suits, he had no idea of dress.'

'Did you see Trotsky?'

'He dressed a little better. No, I did not see him.'

Blanco pushed the cake plate towards her. She was stitching hard, hemming the bottom of the pink cotton dress with swift jerking movements. He would try another tack.

'The poor, Madame Tarasova. The serfs. What about the poor?'

'They were there. They served the beautiful people, cared for their jewels, their clothes. But let me tell you about the clothes, not the serfs; their clothes were dull, of no importance.'

'Tell me about the common people, the soldiers who died in the snow at the front.'

Madame Tarasova threaded her needle, holding it to the light, squinting. 'They died. There were plenty of them. They had uniforms of rather coarse material.'

'They were poor,' said Blanco. 'Poor.'

'Jesus Christ made it clear that the poor are always with us, did he not?'

'And not the officers?'

'Come to think of it, he never mentioned the officers.' Was she teasing him? 'It was the officers who were beautiful. The soldiers were drab.'

'I don't believe Jesus Christ was a particularly snappy dresser,' said Blanco. Madame Tarasova did not seem

71

to hear. 'So you were not, are not, interested in what Lenin did for the common people?'

'Only,' Madame Tarasova was stitching fiercely, vindictively, 'in that his interference in the natural order of things has made me a poor and common person without even the security of a passport. My Imperial Russia is no more.'

'If you had stayed in Russia, would you have had jewels and silks and furs?' Madame Tarasova did not answer. 'Forgive me for asking,' said Blanco, embarrassed, 'but was your family very rich?'

'What does it matter now?' said Madame Tarasova, sitting in her cramped lodging above the horse butcher. 'Look, the dress is nearly finished. It is all the fault of Rasputin and his influence on the Tsarina. He wore filthy clothes, he was a disgusting, drunken, devilish man; the nobles who killed him had great difficulty. He had inhuman strength.'

'What were they wearing? Were they hampered by their fancy clothes?'

'Hubert,' she reproached him, 'do not mock.'

'Another cake, Madame Tarasova?'

'I shall keep one for the child.'

'And Igor. Igor would make a nice waistcoat lining. Where is Igor, the princely Pom?'

'With the child. Please do not make such jokes, Hubert.' She was quite cross.

'Sorry, Madame. Tell me about Rasputin. Wasn't he a monk?'

'The Tsarina should have spoken to the Orthodox priests, not to Rasputin.'

'Properly dressed, were they?'

'Oh, Hubert, their vestments! Their wonderful vestments of blue and crimson, embroidered with gold. The Metropolitan's robes resembled those of the holy angels. The Tsarina should have been advised by him.'

Blanco reassembled his ideas; angels in his book had always dressed in outsize nightdresses. 'Russian angels sound rather dressier than ours,' he said, laughing. 'Why didn't Rasputin—'

But Madame Tarasova, losing patience, was angry. 'You are making fun of my lost country, my lost life. All you want to talk about is the ugliness, the violence, the horror, while I want to remember the beauty.'

Blanco felt ashamed of the one cake left on the plate. He wished he had bought more; he could find nothing to say as he watched the little woman. She was whispering now in Russian, then, as he leaned forward to hear, in French, 'et vous êtes sacrilèges—'

'I apologise, Madame. Jesus Christ would never need to bother about his tailor. He would dress in clouds of glory, would he not?'

'Tailor?' Madame Tarasova choked. Blanco wondered how he had put his great foot in it now.

Flora came into the room. 'I say,' she said, 'what's going on? I couldn't keep Igor out in the rain any longer; he has done his jobs twice and has no squirt left for pipi. Am I interrupting?' ('Am I interrupting?' She talked like an adult.) 'Oh, Madame Tarasova, is that my dress finished? How lovely! May I try it on?'

'Turn your back, Hubert, while she tries the dress. Look out of the window.'

Hubert looked out into the grey street. In the glass he saw a faint reflection of the woman and child, saw the child pull her ugly brown jersey over her head, let her baggy tweed skirt drop, saw her standing white-skinned in vest and knickers, heard Madame Tarasova say, 'Don't your underclothes scratch you, child?' Her voice low. 'In Russia you would wear silk.' The dress was dropped over the child's head, straightened and buttoned. 'There,' said Madame Tarasova, 'how is that?'

'Lovely.' Flora climbed onto the table so that she could see herself in a glass on the wall. 'Thank you so very much.' She looked down at Blanco.

'Hello,' said Blanco, looking up. 'Hello.'

Flora flushed. 'Hello,' she said.

'I don't know why you had to go out in this weather,' said Blanco. 'We've given up the piano. French conversation shouldn't make Igor howl. Are you living here?'

She was taller than him standing on the table. He had the illusion that she was adult.

'I spend most of the day here. I'm learning Russian and maths and keeping Madame Tarasova company.' She got down from the table carefully, so as not to spoil the frock. 'I am still sleeping in the annexe,' she said.

'We never see you,' said Blanco, realizing as he said it that she did not mean to be seen. 'There is one cake left,' he said. 'We kept it for you.'

'Is it really for me?' Her pale face grew pink. 'You kept it for me?'

'Madame Tarasova, actually.'

'Oh.'

'I have some parcels for ladies at the Marjolaine,' said Madame Tarasova. 'Will you help Flora carry them there?'

'Of course I will,' said Blanco.

'Take the dress off, Flora, I have one more button to sew on.'

He could see she did not wish to take the dress off. The dressmaker had cut it with a square neck which showed the hollows above her collar bone. 'It's too cold to wear the dress today,' he said. 'If the weather changes before we go back to school, you could wear it at the picnic.'

'What picnic? Oh, I—' She bit her tongue, remembering discretion. 'Could you look the other way,' she asked, 'while I dress?'

'All right.' When he turned round she was back in her drab jersey and the tweed skirt which, much sat in, made her look as though she had a large bottom. But she had a neat bottom, he had seen it reflected in the window. 'You haven't eaten your cake,' he said. 'Eat it.'

Flora ate the cake as they stood by the work table, watching Madame Tarasova pack the parcels of dresses for the ladies at the Marjolaine and writing bills which she pinned to the tissue wrapping-paper. The cake tasted of coconut, which she detested. She gave a piece to Igor, who sat on his haunches and begged, his black eyes glistening like pins. Igor spat it out onto the worn carpet.

They walked up the street carrying Madame Tarasova's parcels.

'How can I persuade Madame Tarasova to tell me about the Revolution?' Blanco looked down at his companion.

'Playing backgammon reminds her of nice things; she sometimes talks of them.'

'We've rather missed out on backgammon. D'you suppose, if I can rescue him from the golf course, I could bring Cosmo tomorrow?'

'Cosmo?' Her voice lifted. 'Would you?'

'Why not? He's keen. Would she talk freely to him?'

'Not about the Revolution, but she likes telling her escape story. She hates the baboonery of Bolshevism.'

'Where did you learn that expression?'

'My father read it in *The Times*; someone called Churchill said it. I told Madame T. She likes it.'

'If I keep off the Bolsheviks, will she talk?'

'Oh yes. The Tsar, the Tsarina, the beautiful people.' Flora mimicked Madame Tarasova. 'You are going to have a very funny accent if you learn French from Madame T,' she said, laughing.

'I don't mind,' said Blanco. 'How did she escape?'

'She and her husband—'

'She's married? Where is he?'

'In Paris. They escaped from Petrograd to Moscow, to Kiev, to Baku, then back to Odessa, to Constantinople where they got stuck for months, then Egypt, to Italy, to France. It took two years. I looked it up on the map. They were half-starved. She'll tell you all that. I know it by heart.'

'What does her husband do?'

'He's a taxi-driver. Lots of Russians, princes, generals and nobles drive taxis in Paris.' Flora threw the parcel she was carrying up in the air and caught it.

'Really?'

'All the best people drive taxis. *C'est plutôt* snob.'

Flora mimicked Madame Tarasova again. 'And get her to tell you the "insult" of the underclothes.'

'No, you tell me about the underclothes.' Blanco felt a sudden urge to bully her, as he sometimes bullied small boys at school. He pushed Flora up against a wall between two shops. 'Go on,' he said, towering over her. With his arms full of parcels it was quite difficult to keep her trapped; he thrust a knee between her legs, pinning her. 'Go on,' he said. 'Tell me.'

'It was winter and bitterly cold,' said Flora hurriedly. 'In Constantinople the British ambassador's wife organized a collection for the Russian refugees. She bought masses and masses of Jaeger underclothes and sent them to the refugees.' Flora tried to wriggle free, but Blanco had her pinned. 'Madame Tarasova sent them all back with a message to say thank you very much but none of them ever wore anything except silk next to the skin.'

'Bloody cheek,' said Blanco, pushing.

'Do you like scratchy pants? Here, take this.' Flora thrust the parcel she was carrying into his arms, ducked and was gone, racing up the street.

Blanco, his arms full of parcels, watched her go. He was not thinking of the Russian refugees and the woollen underclothes; he would remember them later and tell his hosts, the Shovelhalfpennies and Cosmo at dinner to make them laugh. With Flora pressed against the wall he had wished he was not burdened with parcels. He would have liked to hold her throat and put his thumbs in the salt cellars above her collar bone. He felt a prickle of sweat on his upper lip and was startled to feel he had an erection.

Twelve

Finding the door beside the horse butcher ajar, Cosmo was surprised, when he pushed it open, to see Flora squatting half-way up the stair leading to Madame Tarasova's lodgings. 'What are you doing?' he asked.

Equally surprised, Flora countered, 'Why aren't you playing golf?'

'My father is in confabulation with other *pater-familiases* plotting how to get us back to school. If there is a General Strike there will be no trains.' Cosmo stood on the bottom stair looking up.

'So you could stay on in Dinard?'

'They'll get us back somehow, even if they make us walk. How do you know I play golf?' Flora did not answer but pulled her skirt over her knees.

'What are you doing?' Cosmo climbed the stair. 'I'm rather sick of golf,' he confided, 'but don't tell Pa.'

'I am playing myself,' said Flora primly.

'Backgammon?' Cosmo noticed the board balanced on the step. 'Playing left hand against right? Which is winning? Do you play fair?'

'There would be no point in cheating.'

'Let me watch you.'

'No.' Flora clenched the dice in her fist and began stacking the pieces into their box. 'Elizabeth and Anne are having a fitting,' she said. 'There's no room in there to move. They are rather large.' She gestured with both hands, indicating the size of the Dutch bosoms. Cosmo was reminded of the trip to St Malo, when they had bought the revolver for his father. She had made a

77

similar gesture but lower down to indicate the café proprietor's wife's obesity. 'How is your friend Jules' wife?' he asked, settling himself below her on the stair.

'She's grown thin. Jules says he will give her new dresses and she's got a little baby.'

'Ah,' said Cosmo, 'that's interesting. Are they pleased, Jules and his wife?'

'Very. Jules says they've wanted a baby for ages. They had prayed for one, gone on a pilgrimage to Lourdes. It didn't come from Lourdes, though. He said, "*Voyez ma petite on s'est beaucoup appliqué.*" They managed to find one somehow.' Flora looked puzzled. 'It's a girl. They want to find a boy next.'

Cosmo said, 'I see, yes, that's nice.' In the room above he heard Elizabeth laugh and a burst of talk. He said, 'Would you give me a game?'

'If you like.' Flora began setting out the board.

'I know the rudiments,' Cosmo said, watching her, 'but not the finer points. Madame Tarasova hasn't taught me how or when to double. Let's see how we get on.'

'It's Alexis who is the gambler. D'you want black or white?'

'Black. Who is Alexis?'

'Her husband. You start.'

Cosmo shook the dice and threw. 'A three and a one. What shall I do? No, don't tell me.' He moved a piece four paces.

Flora's nose twitched. She shook the dice, threw a double six and rapidly – chunk, chunk – blocked Cosmo's six-point as well as her own. Cosmo threw a three and a two and moved his men, leaving himself grievously exposed. Flora took him off and consolidated her board. Cosmo, who had been feeling kindly and patronizing, now realized that Flora might not know where babies came from, but knew this game. As she took her last man off, he said, 'Either I am a complete fool or you are extremely lucky.'

'It's a knack.' Flora began stacking the pieces. 'Were you meeting the Shovels here?' she asked, nodding upwards towards Madame Tarasova's door.

'I'm making myself scarce, actually; when Pa's finished, his mind may turn golfwards. I was hoping to find Blanco; my mother, Mabs and Tashie are at the hairdresser's and going to St Malo for lunch. It's amazing what a lot of time they spend beautifying themselves. Who for, one asks? Who would they find in St Malo?'

Felix, thought Flora, who had seen him board an early *vedette*. 'I saw them,' she said, 'go into the *coiffeur*.'

'You funny little thing, d'you spy on us?'

Flora flushed. 'No! I just notice people.' And Felix does not notice anybody, she thought. 'I'd better go now.' She shut the board.

'Don't run away.' Cosmo caught her by the ankle. 'Stay here, sit down. I have an idea. When Blanco comes for his bridge and conversation, you can teach me how to play this game properly. Will you?'

Flora said, 'Oh – I—'

'Got something better to do? Does your mother want you, or your father?' He gripped her ankle, squeezing it hard.

'No, I—' She tried to move. Cosmo was hurting her.

'Hello,' said Blanco, entering from the street. 'There's a skinned horse's head next door; spooky. What are you two doing? Its teeth are rather like young Joyce's, except that it never needed a brace.' He kicked the door closed. 'Eugh, horse blood. Are Anne and Elizabeth still here? What an age they take. I've been out to buy cakes and blown the last of my francs as it's the last but one of the hols. I bought enough for everybody except Igor. Cakes make him throw up. Has the little horror had his run?' he asked Flora.

'Yes.' Flora jerked her ankle free and stood up.

Above them the volume of talk grew louder. Elizabeth opened the door. 'Look at you all,' she said. 'Why don't you come up? We are quite decent, we've finished our fittings. Anne and I thought we would stay and

79

make a four for your bridge, Hubert, but since you have Cosmo we shall be *de trop.*'

Cosmo said, 'Please stay. Flora is going to teach me to win this bloody game, aren't you, Flora?'

Flora did not answer, but sprang ahead into Madame Tarasova's room.

'You've been teasing her,' said Blanco.

'I don't tease little girls.' Cosmo went ahead of Blanco into the crowded room. 'Hello, Madame, bonjour, bonjour.' He shook her hand with the hand which had held Flora's ankle vice-like.

Madame Tarasova chirruped with pleasure over the patisseries, moved her sewing onto the *chaise longue*, bundled Prince Igor's basket underneath it, brought out the cards, placed chairs for the card players and arranged the cakes on a plate.

Elizabeth, Anne and Blanco squeezed round the table, while Cosmo and Flora, using the music stool for the backgammon, sat on the floor. 'Now, start at the beginning,' said Cosmo. 'Explain everything. Tell me all the hows and wherefores and how to win.'

Gaining confidence, Flora was soon demonstrating the game, showing Cosmo when to double, when to draw back, when to give in. When presently Madame Tarasova made tea, serving it in glasses with a slice of lemon, Elizabeth and Anne conducted a bridge post-mortem, accusing each other of crass mistakes with the utmost good humour, leaning back in their chairs, sipping tea, nibbling their cakes. They aired their excellent English in accents which charmed the ear. Cosmo, from his position on the floor, was impressed by the size of their breasts, which jutted like the prows of galleons under their jerseys; so unlike his sister Mabs and her friend Tashie's fashionable flatness or his mother's discreet curves. Holding his steaming glass in one hand he unconsciously cupped the other, until, aware of Flora eying him across the piano stool, he made a fist and feinted a punch at her nose. Flora did not flinch but, leaning across the stool, whispered,

'Jules' wife's tummy has moved up high like Elizabeth and Anne's fronts.'

'Has it really?' Cosmo calculated the length of her eyelashes. 'Keep still,' he said, 'I won't hurt you,' and tweaked an eyelash out. 'Nearly half an inch, I'd say.' He laid the eyelash on his palm.

'Is that dangerous?' Flora's eye watered.

'Another rubber?' Blanco called the bridge players to order. 'And cut the frivolity. I shall never survive in the gaming houses of Europe at this rate or support myself in the world of Cousin Thing; I need all the help you girls can give me.'

Elizabeth said, 'Very well, Hubert, but tell us about this cousin and his world. We do not know the secret.'

'It's no secret,' said Cosmo from the floor, 'he tells anyone who will listen about the merde his cousin has landed him in.'

'Do not use that word, Cosmo. Tell us, Hubert, the history of your cousin,' said Madame Tarasova.

'Be brief,' said Cosmo. 'I know it by heart.'

'Hush,' said Elizabeth. 'We want to hear.'

'My cousin, this old man, had six sons. My father was the distant residual heir. My father was killed, then all my six cousins, sons of the old man, were killed too. Voilà!'

'The war exaggerated,' said Anne.

'All wars exaggerate,' murmured Elizabeth. 'Go on, Hubert.'

'Get to the primogenital point,' said Cosmo.

'All right,' said Blanco. 'The point is that this cousin's house is entailed on the nearest male heir, that's me, but none of the money. The old bastard is spending it while he lives so that when I eventually inherit, I shall have nothing to keep the house going. I shall not be able to sell the beastly place because it is entailed. So now perhaps you grasp why I have to make money?'

Everybody said, 'Ah!' in a variety of sympathetic tones. 'Poor Blanco, poor Hubert.'

'To add to the injury,' said Hubert, 'I have been

made to take his name, add Whyte to my father's Wyndeatt. Double-barrelled names are ridiculous.'

'Only if you are a socialist,' said Cosmo, hoping to irritate his friend.

'What is he like, this old monster?' enquired Anne. 'If he knew you better he would be charmed and alter his will.'

'He categorically refuses to meet me,' said Blanco.

'Like Little Lord Fauntleroy,' said Flora. Cosmo gave a whoop of laughter, throwing back his head and cracking it on the piano. 'Ouch!'

'So you are a milord?' Madame Tarasova's eyes sparkled with interest.

'Oh witty, very witty,' cried Cosmo and everybody laughed except Madame Tarasova. Cosmo leaned across the piano stool, caught Flora's head in both hands and kissed her. Flora jerked away as Blanco aimed a kick at his friend. Between the friends there was a sudden surge of anger such as happens when a small child makes free with a little friend's toy.

It was then that Felix rapped on the door and came in. 'I knocked at the street door,' he said, 'but you were making such a noise you did not hear. Forgive me, Madame, my mother sent me to find my sisters. What is going on?' he asked. 'Oh, I see, the rejects from the casino have created their own establishment. Why, you have everything – cards, backgammon—' His eyes darted round the room. 'And even fortune-telling. Isn't that a crystal ball I see? Will you tell us our fortunes, Madame?' He wove his way past his sisters and picked the crystal off the mantelshelf.

Madame Tarasova took the ball from him and replaced it on the shelf. 'I do not tell fortunes,' she said stiffly. 'This is an ornament, a sphere.'

Flora caught Blanco's eye and looked away. Felix said easily: 'Apologies, Madame. If you had been able to tell the future you could have told us the outcome of the General Strike in England, which starts at any minute. This is official.'

'Welcome the revolution,' exclaimed Blanco.

'Perhaps your cousin Chose will end up in a tumbril,' said Anne optimistically.

'The miners will lose,' said Elizabeth. 'One hardly needs a crystal ball to tell that.'

'Oh God,' said Blanco, 'there is no justice.'

'And my father will get us back to school whatever happens,' said Cosmo gloomily.

'Well, cheer up,' said Felix. 'While you have been cooped up here gambling, the rain has stopped and the sun has come out. It's a beautiful day.'

Cosmo said, 'Then we can have the picnic after all. I know the perfect place, a marvellous beach. Let us invite everyone, all the families.'

Cosmo and Blanco followed Felix and his sisters up the street. 'Seen from floor level,' said Cosmo, 'those two women's bosoms are quite something. It would be fascinating to see them naked.'

'Rather much for my taste,' Blanco demurred.

'If it keeps fine we could take our swimming things and bathe at the picnic,' said Cosmo. 'Brave the chill.'

'D'you think your sister and Tashie could be lured into the ocean?' asked Blanco, his mind following the line of his friend's thought. '*C'est une idée.*'

'Only if Felix swims too,' said Flora, who had been walking unnoticed a step behind them.

The two friends spun round, collided, and Flora made off running fast. 'Oh, let her go,' said Cosmo, 'the skinny little beast,' and to entertain his friend he repeated Flora's account of Jules' baby. 'She's as ignorant and innocent as they come,' he said.

'I wouldn't say that,' said Blanco. 'She caught my eye when Madame T. said she doesn't tell fortunes, and would someone that innocent walk into the sea?'

'I thought we decided she was sleep-walking,' said Cosmo, conscious as he spoke that they had decided no such thing, merely failed to discuss it, put the incident aside, almost forgotten it. 'Come to think of it,' he said, 'the first time I saw her was on that beach, the one I want for the picnic,' and he remembered then Flora's chilled white face and enormous eyes. 'She came in with the tide,' he said.

Thirteen

'Where have you been, darling? I've missed you.' Vita Trevelyan held out her arms.

Denys bent to kiss her. 'M-m-m, you smell good.' He sat beside her on the bed, slid a hand under the bedclothes. 'I have not been gone long.'

'It seemed ages.' She held his hand.

'Shall I join you? Did you have lunch?'

'I nibbled a little snack. Hurry up and undress.'

Denys took off his shoes and socks, stood up to remove his jacket, unbuttoned his shirt and looked down at his wife. 'You are lovely.'

'Yes, I know.'

'I was delayed by General Leigh—'

'Oh, him.'

'– and his friends Ward and MacNeice at the casino.'

'Freddy and Ian, go on—'

'They have a plan to get all the children back to school in spite of the strike. They asked if we wanted to join in.'

'Is the strike official, then? What's the plan?'

'As good as. They are hiring a bus at Southampton, packing in all the children and driving around the country dropping them off at their schools until they are delivered at their various academies. MacNeice called them that. His son is at Fettes, he will be the last.'

'Take off your trousers, darling.'

'I explained that much as I would like her dropped, preferably out of sight and forever, Flora is staying in France. Have you asked anyone to keep an eye on her, by the way?'

85

'I hope you didn't really say that.'

'They thought I was joking.'

'Take them off, darling. Yes, yes, I've asked the Russian dressmaker, and I thought I'd ask Milly Leigh. She's staying on in France. And perhaps the baroness.'

'Left it a bit late, haven't you?' Denys unbuttoned his flies. 'We leave the day after tomorrow.'

'I know we do. I'll say I wasn't absolutely sure I was coming with you until now. By the way, I wrote for seats for Charlot's Review, we can't miss that. If you throw them down like that, they'll lose their crease, darling.' Denys retrieved his trousers, shook them, folded them and hung them over a chair. 'I shall ask them this evening,' she said. 'We could have dinner at the Marjolaine.'

'With the child?'

'Why not? Do get in, darling, I am waiting. Cuddle up.' She held the bedclothes aside. Denys got into the bed. 'I simply adore being in bed in the afternoon,' she said.

'Me too. Leigh is going to drive up to his home – his car is at Southampton – and as he goes report on pockets of revolution when he comes across them. He has Bolsheviks on the brain.' Denys laughed. 'This is nice.' He stroked his wife and kissed her gently. 'I don't believe in Bolsheviks myself, even in the North of England.'

'Go on doing that.'

'These little marks on your tum, darling?'

'Stretch marks, you know they are.'

'Left her bloody mark on you.'

'Can't be helped now. If I'd known I could have oiled myself, they say it helps. Yes, yes, go on doing that, yes.'

'Did you do anything about the Italian family?'

'How you fuss. Yes, I did. I telephoned them; she can go there any time and chatter in Italian. Why are you so concerned all of a sudden?'

'I just want it fixed so that after tomorrow we needn't bother and can enjoy the rest of my leave. If she grows up as plain as she is now, she may not marry, but if she speaks Italian, Russian and French she can get a job when she leaves school and be off our hands.'

'That would be nice. Clever you are.'

'Another seven or eight bloody years.'

'We shall be in India—'

'Have you told her she has to spend the holidays at school?'

'I did, but she may get invited to stay by friends. I was invited all the time at her age.'

'But you were lovely.'

'She'll improve.'

'Let's hope so. Is that nice? And this?'

'What?'

'What I am doing, of course.'

'Yes, yes, it is. Do it again just a little higher, and again, go on doing that, aiah! Gosh! Oh gosh, Denys, how marvellous. Oh phew, that was colossal. Was it for you?'

'Yum.' Denys lay back. 'I have a suggestion.'

'What is it?'

'If you come as far as Marseilles with me on the boat, we could have an extra week. What d'you think?'

'And come back here alone?'

'You were going to do that anyway. You'll have the child.' His tone implied that the child was her fault, her penance.

'It would mean a week's less separation—'

'A whole week. It's nice going to Marseilles by sea at this time of year.'

'We could pretend I was coming all the way to Bombay. Let's do it, Denys, and let's do what we've just done again, shall we?'

'If you are up to it.'

'Let me show you. Then a little sleep before a large bath and a walk by the sea before dinner—'

'With the British families at the Marjolaine. I bet they can't wait to get their awful children back to school. All this family love is hypocrisy. When we've done our parental stuff we can hurry back to bed.'

'You are so good at this, Denys!'

'And so are you.'

Vita watched her husband fall asleep. He always fell asleep when she, exhilarated, would have enjoyed a longer period of chat. His profile, she thought, resembled the bow of a yacht, with its prominent nose and a chin which did not match in strength. The term runaway crossed her mind. He had once remarked that it was fortunate Flora had not inherited his nose. Vita smiled. Turning on her side she considered what to wear that evening. Nothing too frivolous; Milly Leigh and Rosa always managed to look caring and parental. The evening would be dull but they could get back to bed early or pop into the casino for a bit. It was marvellous, she thought dreamily, how cosy they had made this funny little flat, with a few bright cushions, the yellow rug, the Breton lace bedspread. They would look nice later on in India in the bungalow. She would find something to keep her mind occupied, hurry the weeks along to the end of September and back to Denys. Another yellow rug? Why not? A trip by herself to Dinan to buy it.

Fourteen

Arriving at the Marjolaine for dinner, Denys and Vita found themselves caught up in the plan for the picnic. The change in the weather and Cosmo's suggestion had galvanized the British families into action. For parents steeling their hearts against imminent partings from children who, toward the end of the holidays, indulged in sulks, impertinence and tears brought on by premature homesickness, the picnic plan was a heaven-sent distraction. Others, genuinely worried about the strike and its possible consequences, were equally pleased. Some who had been guiltily looking forward to the blessed peace of termtime were particularly enthusiastic, coming forward with generous and imaginative suggestions. Freddy Ward and Ian MacNeice, whose minds were already engaged on hiring the bus in Southampton, proved game to find a charabanc or even two to transport the picnickers to and from the beach. Children with swift legs were despatched by their mothers to alert the families in other hotels, urging them to bring food and drink, bathing suits and warm jerseys, and to rendezvous at the Marjolaine at eleven the next morning. (No, no, darling, we cannot start earlier; nobody will be there, there is too much to do.)

A convulsion of energy swept from family to family. Spirits which had flagged in wet weather rose sky high. Boredom was banished.

In this bonhomous atmosphere it was easy for Denys and Vita to join in and casually, while discussing picnic food, rugs, thermoses, and would a first aid

89

box be a good idea, we always take one to picnics in India, mention to Milly and Rosa that, wishing to be together for Denys' last days of leave, could they possibly ask Milly and Rosa to keep a friendly eye on Flora who would be staying on in the hotel until Vita got back, when of course she would move into the flat? She would not, Vita felt, be a nuisance; she had her lessons with Madame Tarasova to keep her occupied and Italian conversation with an Italian family, quite a full routine. It would be a relief to Vita and Denys to know that there was someone other than Madame Tarasova for Flora to turn to if in need. Milly and Rosa agreed to keep an eye; it would not have been possible to refuse.

There had been awkwardness when, arriving at the hotel and looking around for Flora, they had found her eating her dinner off a tray in her room. Neither Denys nor Vita had known Flora did this; it had not occurred to either that the child might be averse to eating alone in the restaurant. The arrangement had been dreamed up by Gaston in connivance with the head waiter, Flora told them. 'We should have been consulted,' said Vita angrily.

'It frees a table for someone else in the restaurant,' said Flora, careless.

'Come along and have dinner with us as you normally do,' snapped Denys.

'What's normal?' muttered Flora, following her parents into the restaurant. 'I don't want a second dinner,' she said, taking her place at the table.

'Then watch us eat and make yourself agreeable,' said Vita, sitting on the chair the waiter held for her. 'Mademoiselle isn't hungry,' she said. Flora and the waiter exchanged looks.

If her parents were tempted to hit her they gave no sign, chatting amiably through the meal to parties at neighbouring tables. Several people remarked on what a good-looking couple they were and one old lady said to her husband that it was a pity the child looked so disagreeable. 'I expect she is spoilt,' she said. 'It's all

90

those servants in India. School will knock the knobs off. The parents look so much in love.'

'What's this Italian conversation?' asked Flora in a low voice.

'There is an Italian family who live a few kilometres out on the Dinan road. They are willing for you to spend afternoons with them and talk to you in Italian.'

'Have you met them?'

'Actually, no, but I will give you a note. I have arranged it by letter. You can reach them by bus.'

'Oh.' Flora was dubious.

'The man is a stud groom,' said Denys.

'Horses?'

'Presumably, if he is a stud groom.'

'Then I can talk to the horses.'

Vita did not care for Flora's tone but felt it best to say nothing in front of the people in the dining-room. 'You had better go to bed early,' she said, 'so that you are fresh for this picnic tomorrow.'

'May I go now?'

'Wait until we have finished dinner. You really must learn some manners and consideration.'

'Is there anything more we can do about this picnic?' asked Denys. 'Or can we nip into the casino for an hour before bed?'

'Lovely idea, darling. Let's do that,' said Vita.

Having watched her parents leave, Flora hovered inconspicuously around the hotel listening to the various plans being made for the picnic. Mabs, sitting near the entrance with her friend Tashie, did not notice her as they discussed what they would wear the next day, whether to wash their hair or change the varnish on their nails. 'I have to take this varnish off; my mother objects.'

'It is a bit purply.'

'But will he notice?'

'Does he ever notice?'

'Of course he notices, he must.'

'Where is he now?'

'Gone out with boring Elizabeth.'

'No, she's with her mother and Anne and my mother.' The girls' eyes roved around the hotel lounge seeking the object of their desire.

'When he danced with me, he—'

'He has danced eight times with me, only seven with you.'

'Oh, Tashie.'

'I don't care.'

'Nor do I.'

'Why should we care?'

'Wherever he is, we shall see him when he comes back if we stay here.'

Cosmo and Blanco came by. 'Lying in wait for Felix?' enquired Cosmo.

'Of course not,' said Tashie.

Mabs put out a foot to trip him.

'Felix is in the casino dancing with a beautiful blonde,' said Joyce, hopping up the hotel steps from the garden on long springy legs.

'Oh,' said Tashie.

'Shall we?' suggested Mabs, rising to her feet.

The two friends pulled their skirts straight, adjusted the seams of their stockings and strolled negligently out into the dark. Joyce doubled up with laughter; she had an infectious laugh.

'What's the joke?' asked Cosmo.

'Felix isn't in the casino.'

'Where is he, then?' Cosmo resented others than himself making a fool of his sister.

'No idea.' Joyce wandered off.

'A bitchy trick.'

'They do rather invite—' murmured Blanco.

Flora shrank back out of sight and presently made her way by a back alley to Madame Tarasova, who spent lonely evenings with Igor wishing she was in Paris with Alexis. Pushing open the street door and skipping up the steep stair, Flora knocked and went in to find Felix sitting in Madame Tarasova's usual chair, drinking a glass of wine. He had taken off his coat and for some reason his shoes and sat in his shirt sleeves. Opposite him Madame Tarasova reclined on the *chaise longue*, wearing a sleeveless dress with a very short skirt. Her tiny hands were folded in her lap and her slender legs crossed at the ankles. Her high-heeled shoes were on the floor beside Felix's.

'Oh,' said Flora, 'am I interrupting?' Prince Igor yapped sharply from his basket.

'Come. Join us.' Felix held out a hand. 'I came to persuade Irena to tell my fortune. She refuses, so we sit here discussing the state of the world with our shoes off. Take yours off too and sit here.' He patted the seat beside him. 'Kick them off, kick them off.' Flora sat, pushed the heel of her right shoe with her left foot, eased off one shoe, eased off the other.

'Good.' Felix and Madame Tarasova watched her indulgently. Felix sipped his wine. Madame Tarasova smiled. Igor snuffled in his basket, then scratched his neck, his nails clicking sharply against the name-tab on his collar.

'I did not know your name was Irena.' Flora broke the silence.

'You never asked me.'

'It's a lovely name.'

'Isn't it.' Felix smiled at Irena. 'Flora is lovely, too.'

'Why won't you tell his fortune?'

Irena laughed. 'Because I do not know how. Sometimes I pretend to amuse young girls or middle-aged ladies. The girls want to know whether they will fall in love and marry, the older ladies want to know whether their husbands will grow rich or richer. It is easy to make them happy.'

Flora digested this piece of misinformation, sure that at some time Irena had told her that she saw the future in her crystal. But meeting Irena's smiling eyes she decided that perhaps she had only imagined this. 'Are you coming to the picnic?' she asked.

'No.' Madame Tarasova looked down at her hands.

'I have tried to persuade her.' Felix bent to retrieve his shoes and began putting them on. 'But she refuses.'

'Why?'

Madame Tarasova shrugged. 'It would not amuse me. I am too busy. I have work to finish before the English families leave the day after tomorrow.'

'That's not true. I helped deliver all your parcels,' protested Flora.

'Put on your shoes,' said Felix. 'Come, Flora, we will walk back to the hotel together.' He put on his jacket. 'Your shoes look sad alone,' he said. 'Thank you for an enjoyable conversation.' He took the hand Irena Tarasova held out to him.

'They will survive,' said Irena crisply.

In the street Felix took Flora by the hand. 'Look at the moon,' he said. 'It will be full for the picnic.'

Flora had been about to allude to Irena's shifty misuse of the truth but now she dared not speak. Never in her life had she been so happy. Felix was holding her hand.

'I tried to persuade her to come to the picnic,' he said, 'but she won't; too many of the women are clients. I hate this émigré mentality, half-servile, half-snob. Presumably in her Holy Russia she would have come to the picnic? She seems to have had some connection with the Tsar's court; my sisters tell me she is forever talking about it.'

'Of course she has.' Flora was glad to tell Felix about her friend. 'Her father was the court tailor who made all the lovely uniforms.'

'Who told you?' Felix paced slowly, holding Flora's hand in his.

'I think she did. No, it was Alexis, her husband.'

'I don't think she would like you to tell everybody that her father was a tailor.'

'I'm sorry. I have only told you.'

'Good.'

'I suppose it's something to do with wearing silk underclothes—'

'Um, yes.' Felix had heard the tale of the charitable underclothes and their reception from Anne, who had heard it from Cosmo. 'Yes,' he said gravely, 'I see the

94

connection. I confess I wear warm pants in winter.'

'And silk in summer?' Flora absorbed this information.

'Cotton, actually.' Felix laughed and squeezed Flora's hand. 'Can you keep a secret?'

'Yes, I can.'

'I am going to bring my gramophone to the picnic. I thought it would be fun to dance. Will you keep a dance for me?'

Flora had difficulty breathing; she felt she might suffocate. She managed to gulp, 'Yes.'

'And a concertina.'

'What's a concertina?'

'A squeeze box.' Felix squeezed Flora's hand again. 'You squeeze and stretch and twiddle with your fingers and it makes music. It's rather like making love but you wouldn't know about that.'

Flora felt she did know and that she might die of it.

Fifteen

The charabancs arrived at the Marjolaine as ordered. Actually a rendezvous at the Britannique would have been more convenient, its driveway being wider. Also, from the Marjolaine the bus must double back past the Bristol, which possessed more parking space, to reach the coast road to the beach of Cosmo's choice. But since the inspiration for the picnic, which in the memories of the Dinardois became known as 'le pique-nique des Anglais', had come from the Marjolaine, so from the Marjolaine they would set forth.

From ten o'clock onwards families arrived bearing food. One family called Stubbs, whom nobody had hitherto spoken to much, brought armfuls of rugs and several groundsheets and, as if this were not enough, went back to their hotel to collect a cooking pot and a portable stove which burned methylated bricklets under its matching kettle.

Mrs MacNeice brought a basket of potatoes to roast in their jackets and a fine supply of tomatoes. Her husband Ian brought a case of wine and a box of glasses.

Mrs Ward brought a hamper filled with oranges, apples, bananas and lettuce; her husband Freddy staggered under the weight of a crate of lemonade.

Anne and Elizabeth arrived with an armful of baguettes hot from the baker, a basketful of ham, garlic sausage, pâté and several pounds of unsalted butter.

All the mothers carried thermoses of tea and one father brought a couple of ripe camemberts. Felix caused surprise by contributing a pair of dressed chicken. 'We can make a spit and roast them.'

'Has anybody brought matches?'

'Corkscrews?'

'Napkins?'

'Who on earth is going to eat all this food?'

'Plates?'

The Stubbs family had tin plates; there would not be enough to go round, but it would be friendly to share.

'Oh.'

'Knives and forks? Spoons? We shall need spoons.' The Stubbs family had these too and a competent-looking first-aid box. They had not thought it necessary to bring food. Just as Joyce's mother, Mrs Willoughby, was showing her contribution, bars of plain chocolate, Denys and Vita arrived bearing, each, a large flat box. When they lifted the lids they displayed a pair of open fruit tarts from the patisserie decorated with sticks of angelica and whipped cream.

'So suitable for a sandy beach,' said Tashie to Mabs without lowering her voice. They stopped giggling when Mrs Leigh hissed, 'Shut up, girls, manners.'

Rosa strolled out of the hotel at ten to eleven with an armful of giant thermoses full of black coffee and a packet of sugar. At five to eleven Cosmo and Blanco raced up from the quay carrying a large cardboard box tied up with strong string.

'What have you got there? What were you doing in St Malo? What is it? Tell us, do.'

'A secret.' They kept the box shut. 'No peeping.'

At half a minute to eleven Angus Leigh, to the fury of his wife, who knew he did it to annoy her and never in their long years of marriage got used to it, strolled up. He carried The Times newspaper of the previous day, field glasses, and in his coat pocket a flask of whisky.

At precisely eleven Mrs Stubbs, owner of knives, forks, spoons, groundsheets and rugs, started a roll call. Was everybody there? Had they got warm jerseys,

97

bathing dresses, buckets and spades, spare socks? 'In that case, start getting into the buses. Don't push, dears, don't jostle, but look sharp.'

'Whose picnic is it? Isn't she bossy!'

Later, when discussing the picnic, Mrs Stubbs was dubbed a natural leader by the more charitable; indeed, long after memories of the picnic had blurred, she was referred to as the Natural Leader. 'Oh look, there's the Natural Leader,' people would say at point-to-points, concerts, Wimbledon or the winter sales, giving their companion a reminiscent nudge. 'Do you remember Dinard in the twenties?'

All the youngest children got into the first charabanc with Mrs Stubbs and their mothers. Most of the fathers chickened out, piling into the charabanc which held adults and adolescents. They sat in a group looking guilty, but openly congratulated one another when in the nursery bus, as it was immediately dubbed, Mrs Stubbs organized a singsong (to keep the little ones quiet) so that the charabanc carrying adults and adolescents trundled in the wake of shrill voices singing 'Knick Knack Paddy Wack', 'John Brown's Body', and 'It's a Long Way to Tipperary'.

Mabs and Tashie, who had pushed their way to the back of the bus, sweeping Flora along with them, looked down their noses and pretended not to hear. Flora, perching between them, kept quiet, considering herself fortunate to be distanced from her parents who sat immediately behind the driver. She did not question whatever instinct it might be which had caused Mabs and Tashie to befriend her, but was glad that from where they sat she had a view of Cosmo and Blanco two seats ahead and, across the aisle from them, Felix with his sister Anne. Nobody asked her what was in the wicker basket she had put under the seat. Since she was so small and insignificant, it was naturally supposed that anything she carried had no significance either. In any case, she was so overawed by the proximity of Mabs and Tashie that she kept even quieter than usual.

98

As they drove out of Dinard, along the road which led through St Enogat and St Briac to the beach, Cosmo and Blanco joked with Anne and Felix about Blanco's Cousin Thing (or Chose).

'Why can't you get to know him? Why don't you visit him? Surely, Fauntleroy, it would be correct to try.'

'I did write to him once. It was when I understood about being his heir. I asked him whether I could meet him. He never answered. My mother invited him to stay; he never came. I wanted to get to know him all right, but nothing doing. So now I plan a tease.'

'What sort of tease?'

'I thought I would send him the occasional postcard just to remind him of my existence.'

'Wish you were here?' asked Mabs.

'Something more subtle. I thought something on the lines of: I shall be passing your way soon, or I contemplate calling on you 'ere long.'

'Signed or anonymous?'

'Initialled.'

'Unsigned would be more cryptic, more sinister,' said Felix.

'True.' Blanco considered this. 'I thought, posted from different countries—'

'What about in lots of different languages?' suggested Tashie.

'I don't know any.'

'We do, though. Look what we have in this bus: English and Dutch, and Flora speaks French, I've heard her, and Italian, don't you?' Tashie leaned down to look at Flora, who nodded mutely. Everybody turned in their seats to look at her.

Seeing Flora flush Elizabeth volunteered: 'We all speak German and I have Spanish.'

'You are learning Russian, too, aren't you?' Mabs also looked down at Flora. 'Quite the infant phenomenon, aren't you. Anyone got a pencil and paper? We can write the messages for you, Hubert, as we go along.'

'Thanks,' said Hubert, used to being called Blanco.

99

Felix produced an envelope and Anne a fountain pen.

'What about Russian?' Mabs persisted.

'Can't spell in Russian,' Flora muttered.

'I can ask Madame Tarasova,' said Blanco, enjoying himself.

They wrote the messages in the different languages on the envelope. 'He will think he is being pursued by plotting Bolsheviks,' said Cosmo. 'Oh look, everybody, we are nearly there. The beach is over that hill. I hope the tide is out.'

'What's the name of Cousin Thing's house,' asked Tashie, 'and where is it, anyway?'

'It's called Pengappah, it's somewhere in the West of England.' Blanco pocketed the envelope. 'There are six baths in the bathroom, that's all I know.'

'Lord Fauntleroy of Pengappah sounds like a row of teeth.' Mabs laughed.

'Shall you really send postcards?' Anne questioned.

'It's the sort of thing one does in the middle of a long winter term when Christmas is far away and you feel it will never happen,' said Blanco.

'He might think it some sort of code,' said Tashie.

'Or a preview of death,' said Mabs.

'You mean premonition.'

'Here we are,' shouted Cosmo. 'Look. There's the beach and, oh gosh, the tide is just right, going out.'

'And Mrs Stubbs is already organizing the little ones to collect driftwood,' said Felix drily.

'I'll race you,' Tashie shouted in Mabs' ear and they raced across the sand along the edge of the water, followed by a throng of small children.

'Really, those girls!' said Milly Leigh, exasperated. 'You are supposed to watch them,' she said to Felix, who with his sisters was helping to unload the picnic baskets.

Sixteen

From where she sat on the top of the cliff Flora
had a panoramic view. Scarred across the beach the
children's fathers had dug a system of moated castles. These were intricately interconnected by fresh-
water canals fed from a system of dams leading from
the stream which, flowing down the valley, normally
fanned out in glittering streaks across the sand.

Having taken off their jackets and rolled up their
trouser bottoms, the fathers worked barefoot in shirt
sleeves. They laboured with enthusiasm and imagination and showed tolerance towards interfering children
who hopped and skipped around, getting in the way.

There had been tears when a child who had ventured
off to the rock pools at the foot of the cliff brought back a
bucketful of crabs and snails. He could not understand
why he should not put them in the moats. Mrs Stubbs,
hearing screams, hurried down from the dune where
she was organizing the building of the bonfire, took
the child by the hand and led it, carrying its bucket,
back to the rock pool. 'It is unkind to move the poor
little crabs from their homes. Look, they will hide in
the lovely seaweed. They would not be happy in the
Daddies' moat. They need salt water, dear.'

Six or eight of the smaller adolescents played a
frenetic game of rounders. Their feet scoured a rough
circle in the pale khaki sand. Far out, following the
tide as it receded, Cosmo and Blanco dug for sand
eels.

The high tide line had been cleared of driftwood
by Mrs Stubbs and her children. They heaped it into

a pyramidal pyre. Everybody looked forward to its lighting.

The picnic lunch which had been eaten immediately on arrival had rendered some of the elders somnolent. Angus Leigh slept with his hat over his eyes; Freddy Ward slept, too; Ian MacNeice was reading a book. Rosa and Milly, without waiting for a Stubbs suggestion, had collected the picnic debris and buried it in the fire where, later, it would make aromatic smells of burnt orange peel and not so nice banana. Now, with their backs to a rock protecting them from the wind, they sat chatting.

Joyce, having seen Mabs and Tashie run, was now teaching them how to do handstands and cartwheels. All three girls hoped to persuade Felix to join in, but Felix had walked up the valley with Elizabeth and Anne to look for a farm which would sell fresh milk, milk for the little children having been inexplicably forgotten by the commissariat.

From her elevated position Flora watched all this; she could, too, view the progress of her parents as they clambered round the base of the cliff. They would shortly reach a gulley which, as the tide receded, formed a small cove sheltered from the wind, well away from the crowded and desecrated beach.

Hot breath on her neck apprised Flora of the arrival of the curé's dog. She greeted him with affection but, sighting the movement on the beach, the dog galloped off to join in.

'Tonton deserts you. He has a passion for company, a veritable beach dog. Everybody's friend, as his master should be but is not.' Louis, the garde champêtre, crept up on Flora. 'The curé heard that there were two charabancs full of people. What is going on?'

'English families picnicking,' Flora answered guardedly.

'English? I hate the English.'

'One English papa is a general.'

'I hate generals.' Louis lowered himself to sit on a stone near Flora.

'There is a Dutch baron and some Dutch baronesses.'

'I hate the Dutch; they have given sanctuary to the Kaiser.' Louis brought a pipe out of his pocket and filled it.

Wrinkling her nose, Flora edged away.

'Why are you not playing with the other children?'

Flora did not answer. Below her she saw her parents reach the cove. Louis struck a match and lit his pipe. Tonton, having reached the beach, was bounding in friendly fashion among the picknickers, wagging his tail and jumping up. A small child shrieked in terror; the child's father threatened Tonton with a spade. Tonton, moving away in a jolly, forgiving way, lifted his leg against a sandy battlement. Louis chuckled: 'Un chien patriote.'

Down below Denys and Vita kissed in the privacy of the cove. Denys held Vita close, Vita put her arms round Denys. Denys nuzzled Vita's neck and began bunching her skirt up over her bottom.

'Some of the English are going to swim when they have digested their lunch,' Flora informed Louis.

'That I must see.' Louis got up and began moving diagonally down the cliff. 'Monsieur le curé is anxious about the proprieties. It is my job to see that the law is adhered to, no indecencies committed.'

'I thought you were anticlerical.' Louis had explained this term one day the previous winter, when meeting her with Tonton. He had told her he hated all clerics and the curé in particular. Below her, Vita drew her dress over her head and stepped out of her knickers. Flora was quite glad that her mother was out of Louis' sight. What funny things people did: she remembered Felix and Madame Tarasova shoeless. Not being fond of her parents she was not interested in what they took off, she was up here to keep others in sight. Down on the beach Tonton now ran in a crazy circle, his tail tucked between his legs. Louis paused in his descent to watch. As Tonton's circle included one of the larger castles there was the risk that he might misjudge his leaps, but he leapt clear each time.

'He is a clown,' Louis called back to her.

Denys and Vita were lying down now; Flora thought they might find the sand wet and cold but see, Tonton had stopped in midrush to squat, strain and do his jobs against a sand battlement. Almost out of earshot Louis cried, '*Bravo!*'

Sandcastling fathers shouted indignantly and children began pelting the dog with wet sand, which thumped against his woolly flanks. Flora gave a shrill whistle and started trotting down the cliff. Louis was out of sight, but she could see Felix, Elizabeth and Anne returning along the path by the stream carrying jugs of milk. Tonton came up from the beach and ran on past her, following Louis. Flora walked to meet Felix and his sisters. They put the jugs of milk to stand in the shallow water near the picnic site to keep cool.

'There seems to be a move to go in and swim,' said Anne. 'The tide is coming in. Shall you swim, Felix?'

'The sea will be icy.'

'It would be a good thing if some of us were at least prepared in case the small children get into trouble,' said Elizabeth.

'I can't,' said Anne, *sotto voce*.

'You are fortunate to have a valid excuse,' said Elizabeth slyly.

Flora was puzzled by this exchange.

Around the picnic site children were clamouring to be allowed to bathe, tearing off their clothes and hitching themselves into bathing costumes. Their mothers said, 'You must not stay in long,' and 'You must come out the moment I call you,' in doubting tones.

Seeing Felix resignedly pick up his towel and bathing suit, Mabs and Tashie rushed behind a rock to change; Joyce was already in her swimsuit, prancing on long legs, showing her teeth. 'Show-off,' said Tashie enviously, as Joyce hurdled a sandcastle.

Cosmo and Blanco had little luck. 'There were so few eels, we put them back,' they said. 'No thanks, no bathing for us, it's far too cold.'

'It would be tactful if you did swim, darling,' said Milly Leigh. 'If you don't, the children's fathers will feel they must; somebody should go in with the tinies.'

'Oh God!' said Cosmo. 'Must I?'

'The cold water might give one of them a heart attack,' persisted his mother.

'Oh, all right.' Cosmo gave in ungraciously. He took the towel his mother handed him and retreated behind a rock to join Felix. 'Now you know why the English are considered mad,' he said. 'Come on, Blanco, don't leave it all to me.'

'I hope the mothers don't allow them to stay in long,' said Blanco, beginning to undress.

'I went in, or partially went in, in February,' said Cosmo. 'I'd been bird-watching; the beach was empty that day.' He then remembered Flora had been there and the idiot dog, who was here today. It had all looked different: the sand had been wet, flat, shimmering and Flora had seemed very small at the water's edge. He ran down the beach with Blanco, catching up with Felix and Freddy Ward who had decided to go in. Ahead of them the small children trotted, followed by their mothers carrying towels. When they reached the water they tested the temperature, gasped and retreated, skipping back up the sand emitting shrieks. 'If you are going in, go,' said the mothers. 'Don't stand there shivering, dip.'

Freddy Ward and Felix waded in, dived and swam out. 'Gosh, they are brave,' said Blanco. As Felix turned to swim back Mabs, Tashie and Joyce, who had found a rock on the side of the bay dived, hoping that Felix would see and admire.

'Aren't you going to swim?' Anne asked Flora, who sat now above the high tidemark.

Flora said: 'No, thank you.' She was not going to admit that she could not swim in case somebody, Mrs Stubbs for instance, volunteered to teach her.

The bathers, risking their deaths from cold, raced and played by the water's edge until somebody noticed that the tide was advancing and it was time to retreat.

The small children, enjoying themselves now, were reluctant to come out, but their mothers cried: 'That's enough,' and, 'Come out, now let me give you a rub.' Felix picked up a child and piggybacked him up the beach. All the others followed.

On the dunes Angus had put a match to the bonfire which crackled, spat, and flared up. While people were dressing, Milly and Rosa helped by Elizabeth and Anne set out the picnic tea. Only Freddy Ward, far out, kept on swimming.

'I call that really lunatic,' said Cosmo.

'Didn't you know? He swims all the year round,' said Blanco. 'One of his children told me.'

Everybody was getting dressed now, dragging off sticky bathing dresses, standing blue-faced, teeth chattering near the fire, while mothers tried to rub wet heads dry. Angus thought everyone looked so chilly that he shivered in sympathy and took a swallow from his flask.

Flora watched the water swirling up across the sand and Mabs and Tashie, who had lingered, break into a run, their figures silhouetted black against the sun. As she watched Vita and Denys came into view, clambering round the rocks, having lingered longer in the cove than was safe. If they had been cut off by the tide they might have been drowned, thought Flora dispassionately. Watching her parents scramble round the slippery rocks, she savoured the thought.

'Wait a moment, darling, these beastly rocks are cutting my feet. I must put on my shoes,' Vita complained.

'I love your feet.' Denys handed his wife the shoes he had been carrying for her. 'I love every part of you.'

'But you don't love our child.'

'She is not part of you.'

'There was a time when she was.' Vita massaged the sand off her soles. 'How this beastly sand sticks.'

'I cannot bear to think of it.' Denys remembered his wife's distorted stomach. 'The idea of her being part of you is to my mind purely academic and rather disgusting.' He flinched from the memory.

Vita laced her shoe. 'Disgusting? You never said that before.'

'Not you, sweetheart. I do not mean you.'

'I should hope not.' Vita tied the shoelace tight and reached for the second shoe, snatching it from his hand. 'I've had enough of this picnic,' she said, standing up, 'and these happy families. We'd better look sharp or we'll get wet.'

'Somebody might have told us about the tide,' said Denys. 'It's jolly dangerous, we might have been trapped.'

'As we are trapped by Flora,' said Vita crossly.

'When she is seventeen we'll get her out to India and be shot of her.' Denys laughed and his wife joined in. 'I do love your honesty and lack of hypocrisy,' he said. 'I think I have had enough of all these people.'

'They will keep an eye on Flora, that was the object of our coming—'

'We could surely have achieved that without taking all day.' Denys jumped down onto the sand and, turning, held out a hand to his wife.

'Well! We found our little cove and achieved something there.' Vita sprang down to join him.

'So we did.' Denys was pleased by her return to good humour. 'A great feeling of well-being. I feel I can endure that managing matron for a few more minutes; there she is, waving.'

'Everybody come up close to the fire and have a drink of hot tea,' shouted Mrs Stubbs. 'That way you won't catch your deaths.'

Freddy Ward was swimming back with long steady strokes, coming in with the tide. Mothers made their children sit down and distributed sandwiches. 'I can't think who suggested bathing, it's only the last day of April,' said one of the mothers. 'We would never let them do this at home.'

'We're in France now,' said Mrs Stubbs.

Flora moved to one side, putting the fire between herself and her parents.

'I know we are in France,' said the mother who had raised the objection to bathing.

Cosmo, Felix and Blanco came back from behind the rock where they had been dressing. Mabs, Tashie and Joyce joined them; they had all put on warm sweaters, but still had bare feet.

Tonton, coming up behind Flora, nudged her; she put an arm round his woolly neck. She was watching Freddy Ward coming out of the sea. He had a hairy chest, hair on his shoulders, and tufts sprouting from under his arms. He wrapped a rug round his waist and wriggled out of his swimsuit. Coming up to Angus Leigh, he said: 'I could do with a swig from your flask, old boy. The water here is colder than at home.' Angus handed him his flask. Holding the rug with his left hand, Freddy Ward raised the flask with his right.

It was at this moment that Louis pounced. Nobody had observed his approach. He snatched at the rug and Freddy Ward was exposed, standing naked, head thrown back, drinking from the flask.

'He did look extremely indecent,' said someone who had been present at the picnic, recalling the incident long afterwards.

'The Natural Leader was quick off the mark restoring the rug, though.'

'All the same, snatching it from the garde champêtre and calling him her good man didn't help.'

'There might have been real trouble if the Shove-halfpennies hadn't known about French byelaws and explained our ignorance.'

'Curious that they used that child – what was she called? – as interpreter. Her father was in the Indian Civil Service, wasn't he?'

'Anyway, what might have turned into a nasty incident was smoothed over quite amicably. Nobody laughed until the man had gone on his way.'

'It didn't seem terribly funny at the time.'

108

'Catholic country, of course, France.'

'I don't suppose the children had ever seen a naked man. One didn't in those days—'

'I remember it had the most extraordinary cohesive effect; we all gathered round the bonfire and enjoyed our tea—'

'I seem to remember we were all leaving for home next day. Wasn't it the General Strike?'

'Yes, and the end of the holidays.'

Flora, who was one of the people who had never seen a naked man, was filled with an immense pity for Freddy Ward. It was terrible for him having that dreadful growth between his legs. No wonder he kept it hidden. She thought him extremely brave to carry on as though he was normal and to be so uncomplaining.

Seventeen

When the Natural Leader announced that it was time
for the little ones to go home, everyone was secretly
pleased. The little ones, charming and tractable earlier
in the day, were fretful; parents were glad to collect
picnic baskets, bathing dresses, towels, buckets, spades
and passionately collected seaweed and shells, and
head for the charabanc. They looked forward to the
relief of their children in bed, a long drink before
dinner, and quiet packing before tomorrow's journey.

'Come with us,' said Cosmo to Flora. 'Help us fetch
our surprise from the bus. You are not going back, are
you?'

'Of course she isn't,' said Blanco. 'I need her for my
message in Russian to Cousin Thing. She can dictate
it phonetically, can't you, Flora?'

'I don't think it's a very kind idea,' said Flora surprisingly.

'I am not a very kind person, nor is my cousin,
but you will do it because I ask you to.' Blanco held
Flora's arm. He was about to pinch or twist it when,
catching the eye of Felix who was walking abreast, he
desisted, saying, 'What about it, Flora?'

Flora muttered, 'All right, Hubert,' thinking that
if she told him the words for 'I hope you are happy
and blessed', which she happened to know in Russian,
Blanco was unlikely to discover the difference.

'Your parents are going back with the smallest children,' said Felix. 'Do not forget that you promised me
a dance.'

'Dance?' said Cosmo.

110

'I have my gramophone, I left it with the driver, and a box of records. I thought dancing would be good.'

'A great idea,' said Blanco. 'Have you got the Charleston?'

'Of course.'

Flora watched her parents strolling ahead.

'We could visit the casino after dinner for the last time,' suggested Vita. 'Our next chance of a casino will be in Calcutta next winter.'

'And the child?' Denys glanced over his shoulder.

'Looks as though she is staying. She'll be all right, with Mrs Leigh to keep an eye on her. Mind you behave yourself,' Vita said to Flora. Flora did not reply but disengaged her arm from Blanco. They stood watching the Natural Leader shepherd the little children and their exhausted parents into the charabanc. Vita and Denys, without waiting to be shepherded, had claimed the seat behind the driver, apart from the *mêlée*. The driver started the engine and engaged the gears with a crash and the charabanc lurched away. As it gathered speed the watchers heard a ragged rendition of

'Show me the way to go home,
I'm tired and I want to go to bed,'

led by the Natural Leader's strong contralto.

'Your parents will really enjoy that,' said Cosmo. 'Now let's find our box of surprises.' He went with Blanco to claim the cardboard box they had brought from St Malo, while Felix collected the gramophone and records. Flora dived under the charabanc to pull out her wicker basket from where it had been reposing in the shade. 'What have you got in there?' Felix asked curiously.

'*Langoustes*.'

'What?'

'Crawfish.'

'Gosh! Where d'you get them?'

'Jules heard about the picnic and sent them to me.'

111

'Who is Jules?' asked Blanco.

'He keeps a café in St Malo and is her—'

'Her what?'

'My friend,' said Flora, opening the basket to make sure that all was well.

Felix, Cosmo and Blanco stared in admiration at scarlet *langoustes* reclining on a bed of seaweed, packed round a jar of mayonnaise. 'What a brilliant contribution,' said Cosmo. 'Clever little Flora!'

Flora blushed.

'Let me help you carry it.' Felix took one of the handles. 'Did your parents know?'

'Oh no,' said Flora. 'No.'

'They might have stayed on if they had,' said Blanco. Flora shot him a look.

Back at the beach Mabs, Tashie and Joyce had rebuilt the fire, and parties were returning from exploratory trips up the valley with fresh fuel, branches of furze and dry sticks. Mrs MacNeice had put potatoes to roast in the hot ash; her husband was busy with the wine and a corkscrew. Elizabeth and Anne contrived a spit for Felix's chickens and set them to roast.

Everybody exclaimed in approbation when they saw the *langoustes*, and Rosa held out a hand to Flora, saying: 'Sit near me, Flora, have a glass of wine. You deserve it.'

With the departure of the very young, Flora's parents and the Stubbs family, the picnic entered a fresh phase; people achieved a second wind, grew more relaxed, more intimate. As it grew dark they gathered round the fire to feast and, presently, when they had eaten the delicious *langoustes*, the not very successfully roasted chickens, the sausages, the pâté and salad, and filled in corners with cheese and fruit, they started asking riddles and telling jokes. The fire flared up with salty blue flames and the driftwood crackled and spat. There were bursts of laughter and ripples of merriment as Cosmo told limericks which were capped by Joyce, and with her tongue loosened by wine Flora dictated a message in Russian to Blanco, who wrote it on the back

112

of an envelope borrowed from Felix. Then, 'I say!' cried
Tashie or Mabs (the two girls were indistinguishable in
people's memories of that period), 'what happened to
those frightful open tarts?'

'Open tarts? Open tarts?' the boys asked, laughing as
at some brilliant witticism. 'Tarts? What tarts?' Some
of the adolescent boys were a little tipsy by now and
repeated the word, finding it both humorous and ris-
qué. 'You know. What the sahib and memsahib brought
from the patisserie, those tarts. What we thought would
get full of sand, those tarts. What happened to them?'

Nobody knew and after eating so much nobody
cared. 'Perhaps they ate them themselves? They went
off on their own,' a boy persisted, 'for a little quelque
chose behind the rocks.'

'Enough of that,' growled Freddy Ward. 'Their child
is here.'

Hurling himself into the breach, Angus Leigh cried,
'And so she is! Now I must tell you the story of the
lady at the King of Egypt's ball. She had an extremely
décolleté dress and very large you-know-whats. Have
you heard this one, Rosa? Stop me if you have—'

'Here we go,' Mabs and Cosmo groaned. 'Go, go,
go.'

'Well, when she was presented to His Majesty she
dropped a deep curtsy—'

'Dropped a deep curtsy,' sang Mabs and Cosmo.

'—and out popped from her bodice her beautiful
breasts, and the King said—'

'*Mais, Madame, il ne faut pas perdre ces belles
choses comme ci comme ça etcetera,*' chorused Mabs
and Cosmo.

'Oh, you are rotten,' said their father, laughing, and
Rosa, leaning towards him, said, 'I seem to remember
you first heard that story from Jef years and years ago,
and he learned it from his father.'

'Ah, Rosa, once we were young. How Jef would
have enjoyed this picnic,' and as Rosa and Angus
remembered her husband, Flora's possible embarrassment was saved and Jef's children Felix, Elizabeth and

113

Anne looked at one another and said, 'Father never told that sort of story.'

They had all eaten so much and joked so much that there came a lull; people fell silent, sitting and sprawling round the fire which was sinking low, glowing red with only the occasional spit of blue. A few yards away the tide turned, sighing as each small wave whispered up the sand a little less optimistically than the last. Out at sea an orange moon came surging up, and all the people gathered round the dying fire on the last day of April 1926 sat gaping as miraculously it changed from orange to gold to silver, swinging up into a cobalt sky.

Then Mabs and Tashie, breaking the silence, sang:

> 'Au clair de la lune
> Mon ami Pierrot,
> Prête-moi ta plume
> Pour l'amour de Dieu,
> Ma chandelle est morte,
> Je n'ai plus de feu;
> Prête-moi ta plume
> Pour l'amour de Dieu.'

Years later, at the moment of his death, Felix would remember those young voices and the recollection of their purity would purge him of his fear, but at the time he cried out: 'What about a dance?'

Felix wound his gramophone and put a record on the turntable. Soon they were dancing on the flattened grass round the fire, and some with more temerity barefoot by the edge of the sea.

Blanco danced the Charleston with Joyce, who danced freely, kicking and twisting; there was no time to notice her teeth. Angus danced with Rosa and his wife. Felix danced with Mabs, Tashie, Joyce, Elizabeth and Anne. Cosmo danced with anyone who would risk their toes.

Felix had the Charleston, foxtrots quick and foxtrots slow. Everybody danced. Then, winding up the gramophone, he put on a record of a Viennese waltz and only the older people could remember how to waltz, which they did while their children watched, applauding. Felix, snatching Flora by the hand, said: 'You promised to keep me a dance,' and half-carrying her, for she was small and light, said, 'Put your arms round my neck,' and whirled away with her along the edge of the sea until the record stopped when he put her down and said, 'That was good, wasn't it?' and Flora said nothing, how could she? She had thought he had forgotten her, but he had remembered.

Then, as they thought the dancing was over, Felix picked up his concertina and began playing a tango.

Sitting or crouching round the fire everybody listened as they gently revived it, poking small twigs into the embers, little scraps of furze, and they tried, for many of them were out of breath, to breathe in time to the music.

Then it was that Freddy Ward caught Ian MacNeice's eye and they rose to their feet and walked without speaking down onto the flat beach and began to tango. They danced holding themselves erect, wearing their hats as men do in the streets in Argentina, intimate, masculine, absorbed, weaving the threatening graceful steps. And as they danced they shed the years of war and work and love which intervened between now and their youth, when they had worked and become friends in South America, recapturing for a few minutes the fluidity of movement they had then possessed. When the music stopped their wives and children who had watched, amazed, sat silent, afraid to applaud. It was Louis the *garde champêtre*, lurking suspiciously in the shadows half-way up the cliff, who shouted: '*Bravo! Bravo! Encore, les messieurs, encore!*'

'After that,' said Cosmo respectfully, handing a glass of wine to each performer, 'one hardly dares, it seems an anticlimax to have fireworks.' Freddy Ward and Ian MacNeice, smiling rather sheepishly, said, 'Fireworks? Are we to have fireworks? So that's what you have in your mystery box. How wonderful, what fun, what a surprise!'

People recollecting the picnic in later years remembered the surprises and how each surprise had surprised. The food, the wine, Flora's *langoustes*, the jokes, Mabs and Tashie singing, Felix's gramophone, Freddy and Ian dancing, the moonrise, and finally the rockets and Catherine wheels. We forgot we had to go back to school, they said. We forgot the General Strike, and of course next day it rained. My God, how it rained: we piled into the *vedettes* in pouring rain and that curious child, what was her name, can you remember, stood on the quay without a mackintosh, weeping. She can't have been weeping for her parents; they had no time for her, they were so obsessed with one another it could almost be said they neglected her; some people actually said so. It was quite odd to see a child cry like that.

Flora, watching the *vedette* chug out in the driving rain towards St Malo, wept for Cosmo and Blanco leaving on the boat, for Felix who had already gone in his car, for the terrible discovery that she was in love with three people at the same time.

When in old age she constantly forgot people's names, things which had happened a week before, titles of books, the ephemera of living, Flora would brilliantly remember standing on the quay at Dinard in the driving rain, watching the launches pull away.

There were so many travellers, such a rush to get back before the strike, that there was a supplementary boat, and both boats were overloaded and low in the water. Passengers unable to crowd into the shelter of the cabins stood shoulder to shoulder, collars turned up, hats crammed low over noses. Cosmo and Blanco had tried ridiculously to open an umbrella, but it instantly blew inside out. The umbrella's owner had bellowed in protest while the wind whipped away their laughter.

Her parents, who had found room in a cabin in

116

the first boat, were out of sight as she watched the launches bounce into the choppy cross-current. Had they waved goodbye? Her view had been partially blocked by the group of porters who had brought the travellers' luggage from their various hotels; they stood gossiping and counting their tips while Mabs and Tashie, forgetting that they were grown up, reverted to excited childhood, waving umbrellas as they shrieked into the wind: 'Goodbye, goodbye, see you next holidays.'

They had waved the same umbrellas half an hour earlier when Felix had driven away with Elizabeth. 'Come and see us in England,' they had yelled. 'Come and *stay*. Why not come and *stay*? Do, do come and stay!' Somehow, somewhere they had found coloured umbrellas, a rarity at that time, Mabs a green, Tashie a blue. Then, when Felix was lost to sight, they had asked Joyce Willoughby, all packed up and wearing her school uniform, for her address, as though they had been great friends, equals even, throughout the holidays.

Flora had followed the travellers to the quay and watched them board the *vedettes*. Joyce had become separated from her parent and attached herself to the Leighs; Cosmo had given her a hand down to the boat. Perhaps her parents had said a perfunctory goodbye? Flora could not remember. There had once been a terrible accident with an overloaded launch, a lot of people drowned; she did not wish this to happen today. Neither Cosmo nor Blanco had waved to her; why should they? She had kept out of sight, not wishing them to see the tears coursing down her face. In age she recollected the sensation of hot tears mixing with cold rain. She remembered that perfectly.

And she remembered the grief; it had been tempered by a despairing rage, a passion which shook her whole body as she stood in the rain.

When the *vedettes* were lost to sight, disappearing in the sheeting rain, she had turned and run through the wet streets to the beach, across the sands, up the hill past the casino, past the turning to the Rue de Tours and Madame Tarasova, to the tram/train which, raising steam for its journey across the coast to St Enogat and St Briac, was letting off loud shrieks and whistles as it began to move. She had scrambled on board breathless, crippled by a stitch, gasping as she sought to elude her unbearable loss, her shocked realization that she loved, was in love with Felix, Cosmo and Blanco all at once, equally.

In old age Flora would smile, remembering the child who believed that love was for one person, for ever, for Happy Ever After.

The conductor, working his way along the tram, swinging in and out of the compartments – 'Alors, messieurs, mesdames, vos billets, s'il vous plaît' – had nearly caught her; she had no money. She moved ahead of him along the train. Since the carriages had no sides it was possible to swing out, clinging to a rail as the conductor did, and back into the next carriage; then, when you reached the carriage behind the engine, to drop off, let the train go by (it never went faster than five or six miles an hour) and rejoin it behind the conductor. Flora had watched bold boys do this but, afraid of getting crushed, had never attempted the prank herself. That day, emboldened by grief and despair, she had carried out the risky manoeuvre to the amusement of fellow passengers and the irritation of the conductor. I wish I still had that agility, she would think in age. Arrived at St Briac she had loped across the headland, tiring a bit from the feeling that her heart had dropped in her chest and, turning to lead, lodged across her solar plexus. Her tweed skirt was soaking and its friction rubbed sore patches behind her knees.

The tide had erased yesterday's footprints, smoothed flat the battlemented castles, filled in the moats. The stream from the valley reached across the sand with watery fingers to where the waves cracked onto the beach with a smack and a hiss as the tide turned to come in.

She walked the long distance towards the water

and, as she walked, tried to bring back the feel of Felix's warm hand when they had walked up the street, the taste of Blanco's blood when she bit him, and Cosmo's smile when he bought her an ice in St Malo; but memory was evasive and cold.

She crouched by the water's edge and wrote in the sand, spelling out the names with her forefinger: Felix, Cosmo, Blanco. When I am seventeen, she had thought, I could marry Felix. He will be twenty-seven when I am seventeen. I could marry Blanco or Cosmo; they will be twenty-two. But the sea rushed in, smoothing away the names, filling her shoes with frothy, sandy water. She had stood up and screamed into the wind, 'I shall, I shall, I shall.' Then the sea, egged on by the wind and the rising tide, began chivvying her along so that she took off her waterlogged shoes and stockings and ran ahead of it until she reached the high watermark. Clambering up the dune she found the remnants of the picnic bonfire, a circle of black bits, made cold by the rain. She had crouched by the charred embers for a long time so absorbed in her grief that she did not notice the dog Tonton come and join her, nudge her with his nose before departing, puzzled, back over the cliff. In age she would not remember him that day, nor how she found her way back to the Marjolaine; there was a gap in memory; she would suppose she got back in the tram.

PART TWO

Eighteen

'I found it impossible to like Mrs Trevelyan,' exclaimed Milly.

'Who was Mrs Trevelyan?'

Milly and Rosa, meeting for tea at Gunters, had their memories of the Easter holiday of 1926 sparked by the recent discovery by Mabs or Tashie – it did not matter which, since the two friends were as close as sisters – that the little dressmaker Madame Tarasova, patronized by the ladies from the Hôtel Marjolaine in her cramped room above the boucherie chevaline, had set up in business in rooms above an antique shop in Beauchamp Place SW3.

'Of course she charges a great deal more than she did in those days,' said Milly, apropos Madame Tarasova, 'but the girls say she is extremely good value.'

'I had heard she had moved to London. One of my girls, Dolly I think it was, heard it from Felix. Or it might have been Anne heard it from Felix, but more likely Dolly; she is the most interested in clothes. Felix would have told her.'

'Why should Felix—?' Milly raised her eyebrows.

Rosa said: 'Felix took an interest in refugees about that time. The little Russian was one of those who only had a Nansen passport; he would have given her an introduction to my brother-in-law, who was concerned in such matters, when she wanted to come to England. It must have been something like that. I wasn't suggesting that he was having dresses made.' Rosa laughed cheerfully.

Milly joined in Rosa's laughter. 'Of course! It was

Mrs Trevelyan who had the dresses made. There is the connection of thought, why I said I found it impossible to like her. I have not thought of her for years. She spent the whole summer having clothes made to take back to India; she monopolized the woman. None of us liked her at the time, did we? I wonder why. I remember her as pretty, almost beautiful.'

'Too preoccupied with her husband? There was something abnormal there. Neglectful of her child? You must remember the child. She left her in the hotel when she went back to England with her husband; you and I were supposed to keep an eye on her. I should like some more cakes, if I may. I don't torment myself about my figure as you do, Milly.' Rosa signalled to a waitress. 'Have an éclair, they are delicious. We should get you on a visit to Holland and plump you up.'

'No, thank you. I don't remember doing much for the child. How awful, Rosa. It just strikes me. Should we have done more? I can't remember doing anything.'

'As far as I remember,' said Rosa, as she studied the display of cakes offered by the waitress, 'the child had lessons with the Tarasova woman. I suppose she got paid for it. And wasn't she learning Italian? Something of that sort. There had been a French governess, I believe. I'll have one of those' – Rosa pointed at the cakes – 'and one of those. Thank you. I remember the child was no bother; she kept herself occupied, took people's dogs for walks.'

'I remember now, I asked her whether she wouldn't like to eat at my table,' said Milly. 'But she refused. I don't know where or when she ate; it is awful to be so vague.'

'She would have had some plot with the hotel servants. Children are good at that sort of thing.'

'Oh, Rosa! I should have done more. I do feel guilty.'

'Retrospective guilt is a pretty useless emotion.' Rosa bit into a cream cake.

Milly thought, She is greedy. I am paying for all these cakes. I invited her.

She wondered why she liked Rosa, whether the

only reason she kept up with her was because she suspected Angus had once flirted with her, or even been in love? She felt reassured when she met Rosa on the rare occasions she visited England and saw her for what she was: fat, unglamorous, grey-haired, in her fifties. Come to think of it, she had been pretty unglamorous in 1926 and so had her five daughters, in spite of their tremendous niceness.

She said: 'Of course I was worried sick about Cosmo going back to school and Angus driving up through England on his own. He really thought there might be a revolution or riots. I only found out recently that he had armed himself with a revolver. He was convinced the situation was serious. He insisted that I stay safe in France. Mabs, of course, was at her finishing school in Paris; it was the General Strike, if you remember.'

'I seem to recollect it only lasted a couple of days,' said Rosa drily. 'Dear Angus is such a romantic.'

Milly wondered what form this romanticism had taken with Rosa; was retrospective jealousy as useless an emotion as retrospective guilt? 'How is Felix?' she asked at an angle.

'Still unmarried.'

'How the girls chased him that holiday!'

Rosa grinned: 'There was an embarras de choix, the most choice your lovely Mabs and her friend.'

'Tashie?'

'Yes.'

'He put Cosmo and Hubert's noses out of joint; they were at the age when boys—'

'Lust,' said Rosa.

'I wouldn't put it that way exactly. I would say awaken.'

'I agree it sounds prettier. Are you sure you won't have another cake? Have an ice.'

'No, thank you.' Milly watched Rosa enjoy her cakes. No wonder she was fat and all five daughters huge. 'Rosa,' she said, 'is Felix your husband Jef's son?'

Munching, Rosa looked slantwise at Milly and as

she munched she smiled. Conscious of the enormity of her question Milly flushed salmon pink.

'No,' said Rosa, munching. 'He is not.'

And she is not going to tell me who the father is. It can't be Angus. Angus is heavily built and fair; Felix is slight and dark. What on earth possessed me? It just popped out! The question has been lurking for years. Oh my God and I am not even drunk!

'The Trevelyans' child had the makings of a beauty,' said Rosa. 'A wonderful mass of dark hair, generous mouth, sexy observant eyes and what eyelashes! How old was she?'

'About ten.' Milly gratefully seized on the switch of subject. 'She would be fifteen or so now. I suppose she is still at school. I believe she was to go to school.'

'I can get you her address, if you like. You could invite her to stay in the holidays. It would be a kindness.'

'Well—' Milly sensed a trap, attempted to reverse.

'Shed some retrospective guilt.' Rosa sipped her China tea. 'One wondered, seeing her parents, who her father was; they were both so fair. The man was almost an albino, was he not? Mr Trevelyan.'

'But they were utterly devoted. I mean one wondered how they ever managed to get out of bed. They – well!' Milly protested, laughing. 'You must remember that.'

'I do. Elizabeth thought they even did it during the famous picnic. The *garde champêtre* might have had a genuine case to arrest, instead of accusing poor Freddy of indecent exposure!' Both women laughed in reminiscence at Freddy's discomfiture. Rosa wiped her mouth with her handkerchief. 'I will send you the child's address,' she said. 'Felix went to see her at her school a couple of years ago when he was in England. He took her out to lunch. He said she was very shy, hardly uttered. I will ask him for the address.'

'Felix?'

'Got her address from la Tarasova; they apparently keep in touch. She has no family in England, it seems.'

'That was kind of him.'

126

'Now you will be kind, too.' Rosa snapped her bag shut. 'She was in love with your Cosmo, with his friend Hubert, and Felix, *ça va sans dire*.'

'In love? At ten years old! Ridiculous!'

'I must go,' said Rosa, rising. 'My love to Angus and the children. Next time the tea is on me. I hear Rumplemeyers is still very good.' She kissed Milly on both cheeks. 'I will send you that address.'

'I don't even remember her Christian name.' Milly made a last feeble protest.

'Oh yes you do,' said Rosa.

Watching Rosa go, Milly thought angrily, She punished my tactlessness along with my retrospective jealousy. Oh damn, she thought, damn, damn and blast. She asked for the bill. Then, walking down towards Piccadilly, she thought, If she is fifteen she will be fat and spotty, fifteen is a terrible age for schoolgirls, and cheered up.

Nineteen

The surprise, when the headmistress sent for her and told her that she was to be taken out by a friend of her parents, a Baron Something, was so great that Flora's heart had given a mad jolt and not settled to its normal rhythm for several minutes. She had nodded in mute obedience when told to be ready, wearing her best uniform, at eleven-thirty on the following Sunday. She would be allowed to miss church but must be in by six. The headmistress did not show her Felix's letter, but said kindly: 'I am glad you have somebody to take you out. This friend of your parents appears to be Dutch, such an interesting responsible people. Perhaps you remember him?'

She had murmured that she did.

The headmistress looked at the envelope in her hand with interested disappointment. In recollection Flora realized that the envelope had been plain. The woman would have appreciated a crest; one of the girls had as guardian a minor peer who, when writing about his ward, wrote from the House of Lords, using its facilities of free writing paper and postage. These letters were always put on top of other correspondence in the headmistress's study. The headmistress opined that the outing would make a nice change for Flora; Flora nodded.

'It will give you something fresh to write to your parents about.'

Flora nodded again; she particularly detested this weekly chore.

In the intervening days Flora walked on air, or

lay awake in her dormitory rehearsing the things she would tell Felix. She would make him laugh about compulsory games, the boredom of obligatory church, about the other girls' inexplicable joy when they received their parents' letters from Delhi, Bombay, Calcutta, Lahore, Peshawar, Hyderabad or Simla; how they counted the days until they came home on leave and when they had been, how inconsolably they wept at the renewed parting. Perhaps she could make her schoolmates interesting?

Then she thought, Perhaps I can tell him about Pietro, the stud groom my mother arranged I should visit in the afternoons that summer before I came to school, so that I could converse in Italian with him and his sister, keep up my Italian. No, she thought, Felix might ask what the man actually did. He might not understand that he frightened me; that he was like the man Cosmo bought the revolver from, although he did not actually smell, or that I let my mother send him money for my visits when I had only been there once. If I could not tell my mother how the man had disgusted me, I could not tell Felix. Perhaps, Flora thought, I just feel guilty at letting my mother pay the man money for nothing. Then she thought, How clever of Felix to say that he was a friend of my parents. In all her recollections of Felix there were none of him exchanging a single word with them, though he must have done, out of common politeness. Had he searched long and hard for her? Her heart swelled with excitement; the dream she had cherished since Dinard was about to come true: she was going to see Felix.

By the Saturday evening she had started a cold. By Sunday morning she was running a temperature. She was ready waiting in the hall before eleven; he might come earlier than he had said. Her stomach was a ball of nervous excitement; she alternated between bouts of shivering and feeling too hot. By eleven-forty she despaired of his coming. When he arrived at a quarter past twelve her handkerchiefs were soaked, her nose raw, her head aching. Felix was much shorter than she remembered. He had had his hair cut so that it was unruffled and neat. She remembered his smile.

He said, 'Hop in.' He had come by car, a different car from the one he had had at Dinard; that had been a red open two-seater. Today he drove a black saloon. 'I am sorry to be late,' he said. 'I didn't allow enough time.'

Flora said that it did not matter.

He said, 'I thought we'd have lunch out in the country; there's a hotel under the downs which has a good restaurant. Would you like that?'

Flora said, 'That would be lovely.' Her tonsils had begun to swell at the back of her throat, which made swallowing painful.

Felix drove down the hill and along the promenade. 'I imagine you walk along here in a school crocodile.' He was amused by the thought.

Flora had meant to tell him how she loathed walking in pairs along the concrete prom beside the angry sea, to describe how the girls eyed passers-by with critical appraisement, speculating as to whether they were 'gents' or 'common', their clinical eyes deducing from the cut of a person's garments his or her social status; how they played a game called 'Sahib', awarding themselves points for sightings, the highest being an old Etonian tie or that of the Brigade of Guards, rare sights fiercely espied. But now, with her blocked nose and sore throat, she did not think Felix would find her schoolmates' obsession with class amusing so much as distasteful, as she did herself.

'Do you like this place?' Felix asked.

'I loathe it.'

'Do you like the other girls? Have you made many friends?'

Flora said, 'No.'

Felix said, 'My sisters were lucky at school. Since there were five of them they could do without friends if necessary, and contrariwise this made friendship easier. Of course we were all at day schools in our country. Ah,' he said, 'we are leaving the town, getting

130

into the country. It is lovely at this time of year, is it not?'

Flora said, 'Yes.'

Felix said, 'If there is too much air, close the window; myself I like to feel it blowing in.'

Flora left it as it was; her cold was making her deaf in the ear next the window. Later she would imagine she could smell the autumn leaves rotting on the road.

Felix drove in silence until they reached the hotel where he proposed to lunch. 'You've got a nasty cold,' he said as they got out of the car.

'It's nothing,' said Flora.

'I hope I don't catch it,' said Felix.

Flora did not answer.

'Would you like to eat straight away?' asked Felix. 'I know I would, I am starving. And schoolgirls are always hungry.' He led the way into the restaurant. 'I reserved a table,' he said. 'If we run out of conversation we can look at the view.' He remembered how monosyllabic Flora had been in France. I should have brought a friend, he thought, to make a third.

They sat at a table in the window; the view was pastoral, rolling fields, sheep gently grazing, distant downland. The waiter spread a napkin across Flora's knees, presented the menu. Felix ordered himself a martini and asked for the wine list. 'A glass of wine will do your cold good,' he said and, 'Why don't you go to the ladies and have a good blow before we eat. Here, take my handkerchief, it's dry.'

Flora took the handkerchief. In the ladies she blew profusely into a paper towel. The flow from her nose seemed inexhaustible; she thought if she sniffed very hard she could stem it; she would keep Felix's handkerchief. When she got back to their table Felix said, 'I have ordered for us both: roast pheasant, red currant jelly, brussels sprouts and thin chips. I am starting with oysters. What about you?'

Flora shook her head, refusing a first course, mindful of his remark about schoolgirls' appetites; also, she had never eaten an oyster. But when, presently, Felix offered her his last, she accepted it and thought she had never tasted anything so delicious, fiercely regretting her lost opportunity.

Felix chatted cheerfully as he ate. He was visiting friends, he told her. He had left university, had gone into business; his sister Anne was married, Elizabeth had finished her thesis and was working on a dig in Asia Minor. She was engaged to a fellow archaeologist. All three of his other married sisters had at least one or two babies; his mother was in splendid form. 'And how are your parents?' he asked.

'All right,' said Flora dubiously.

'They come home from India every year to be with you?'

'No.'

'I believe I had heard that. Irena Tarasova told me. It was she who gave me your address.' (So that was it.) 'She is happy in London. You write to her, I think? She much prefers it to Dinard.' (What was she doing in London? Why had she left Dinard? How long was it since she had written? Six months?) 'You knew she had come to London?'

'No.'

'I expect she has not had time to tell you. She has parted company with her husband, you know. The pheasant is good, isn't it?'

'No.' Slowly Flora chewed her pheasant as she thought of Alexis. Did he still drive a taxi in Paris? 'I didn't know.'

'They lived more or less apart even when we first met them in Dinard. Bit of a gambler.'

'He drove a taxi.'

'Still does.' Felix laughed.

Flora sniffed, drawing air in through her clotted nose, releasing it through a mouthful of pheasant.

'You are not drinking your wine; it will do your cold good,' said Felix, watching her. Irena had said, Spare the time, take the child out, bring me news of her. Tell her I will write to her soon. 'Irena told me to tell you she will write to you soon.'

132

'He played terrific backgammon.' Flora's mind was on Alexis. 'Please thank her.' She reached for her glass and gulped some wine; it stung her tonsils as it went down but warmed her insides.

'How old are you now?' asked Felix.

'Fourteen.' She would be fourteen in six months; she was in her fourteenth year.

'You have grown a lot.'

(At least a foot. I get the curse now. I have got pubic hair, and hair under my arms.) 'Yes,' she said.

'Nearly four years since Dinard.' Felix impaled a brussels sprout and forked it into his mouth. 'How fast time—'

'Crawls.' The wine, while consoling her gut, was making her head throb. 'It crawls.' Flora gulped again at her wine.

'Where do you spend your holidays?' Felix ate the last bit of pheasant and ranged his knife and fork together.

'Here. At school. All the children have parents in India. If you have no relations to go to you can spend the holidays in the school. It's what's called a Home School.' The wine had freed her tongue. 'They talk about India all the time. About how many servants their parents have. Polo. Tigers. Dances at the Club. Leave in the hills. Simla. Kashmir. They call breakfast Chota Hazri and lunch Tiffin; they say Mahatma Gandhi is turning the natives into Communists; they call the Indians natives. They make a difference as to whether their fathers are Political, Indian Civil, Army, or Police. They can't wait to get back and get married.'

'It's their background,' said Felix, laughing, 'and for that matter it's yours, too, is it not?' Flora was restraining her sniffles rather well; her face had flushed with the wine. (I must not get a schoolgirl drunk.) 'Don't you look forward to growing up and returning to India, to your parents?'

'They all do.'

'And you don't?'

Flora shook her head. How to explain to Felix, so

133

devoted to his mother and sisters, that she dreaded such a reunion? 'I may have to,' she said, her voice rising.

'Oh,' said Felix, startled by a note of desperation not necessarily due to the wine. 'Oh.' Then, 'Would you like some pudding?'

'No, thank you.'

'Sure?'

'Yes.'

'I shall have some cheese. We don't get your delicious stilton in Holland.' Felix asked the waiter for the cheeseboard.

Flora watched Felix eat. She felt sore, sodden, heavy. Surreptitiously she looked at her watch. It would be wonderful to crawl into bed, to ask Matron for an aspirin. Felix filled his glass and poured the last of the wine into Flora's. 'Oh, by the way, I almost forgot. I spent a few days with the Leighs, d'you remember them?'

'Cosmo?'

'Yes, he was there, and his friend Hubert. Everybody called him Blanco. I can't remember why. They are both at Oxford.'

'His name was Wyndeatt-Whyte, it equals Blanco — a sort of joke.'

'So it was, so it is.' The girl's cold makes jolly heavy going. I can't think why I let myself in for this. I should have made Irena come with me. 'Cosmo's sister Mabs is prettier than ever. D'you remember her?'

'Yes.'

'I'm taking her out next week; we are going to a play. She's attractive; I remembered her as rather tiresome and silly at Dinard.'

Flora tossed back the last of her wine; if it anaesthetized her tonsils, it made her nose race. 'Excuse me, I must—' she stood up.

'Of course.' Felix pulled back her chair. 'I'll ask for the bill,' he said. 'I should be thinking of—' He thought that his intention of taking her for a walk on the downs and ending up somewhere for a cream tea was altogether too much. 'My bill, please,' he said to the waiter. Memory had tricked him. The expedition was a mistake.

In the car Flora remained silent; all she wanted now was to get back to school and to bed. In the cloakroom she had unbuttoned her shirt – the wine had made her feel hot – and made the discovery that her chest was covered by a rash. She looked forward to covering her head with the sheet and letting the agony of disappointment wash over her. When the car crunched to a stop outside the school, she scrambled out. 'Thank you, thank you very much,' she said.

Felix caught her by the hand: 'I have just remembered something,' he said. 'We were talking at the Leighs about Dinard, that time we all met. Cosmo said that you were the prettiest girl in Dinard.'

'Cosmo?'

'And Hubert said of course you were.'

'Hubert?'

'She has the most extraordinary eyes,' Felix said to somebody later. 'There she was with the most disgusting head cold, totally stewed with it, a little stewed perhaps with the wine I'd given her at lunch. I'd been wondering what possessed me, why I had taken the trouble to take her out; there are plenty of other miserable schoolgirls, after all. Then, just as we parted, she flashed me this look and—'

'What?'

'It almost made the day worthwhile.'

In the san Flora shivered and shook, snuffled and streamed; her head ached, her body burned. Matron brought her bitter lemonade. 'What a silly girl,' she said reproachfully. 'I hope nobody else catches it. Why should you, who never go away for the holidays, catch measles?'

'I don't know, Matron. Can I have some dry handkerchiefs, please?' She pushed Felix's handkerchief, unused, pristine, further out of sight.

'In a moment.' Matron drew the curtains. 'You

135

mustn't read,' she said, confiscating *Kidnapped* and *Wuthering Heights*. 'Measles can affect the eyes. Doctor will be here tomorrow.'

'Can I have my writing case, please, it's got—'

'And you mustn't write, either; you must lie in the dark, my girl.'

'Just my writing case. I promise I won't write.'

'When I've time. I'm too busy at the moment.' Matron went away to eat her supper.

Flora felt both hot and cold. I hate that woman, she thought; I'm not her girl. I want my writing case.

The postcard was in the writing case framed in leather; it blotted out the legitimate occupants, Denys and Vita, posing side by side on a photographer's sofa. All the girls kept photographs of their parents perched prominently on the lockers by their beds. Flora was the exception. 'Why don't you have a photograph of your parents, Flora?' I can see them better in my mind (and smell them, too).

If I lay against Felix as the marble girl does I would be cool, she thought. Sometimes she lay against Felix; at other times it was Blanco or Cosmo who held her in that tender embrace. Since she was in love with all three, she lay in rotation in their marble arms: Monday Felix, Tuesday Cosmo, Wednesday Blanco; today, Sunday, was Felix's turn. Tossing hotly, she pulled the pillow round and stuffed it along her back, but marble Felix became confused with Felix eating oysters, lending her his handkerchief, driving away relieved.

He had looked relieved. Flora blew her nose into the pristine handkerchief, scrunched it into a ball and threw it onto the linoleum floor.

Returning from supper, Matron said, 'Here's your writing case. What have you done with your pillow? This won't do, my girl. You'll never get well if you don't keep tidy. Look at that hankie chucked on the floor. There's no need to be untidy just because you have measles.' She removed the pillow from Flora's back. 'I'll get you some more lemonade. D'you

136

want to go to the WC? You'd better use the pot, the passage is chilly. Hurry up, I can't stand here all night.'

'Please don't.' (Verging on insolence.)

Flora crouched on the pot. Matron smoothed the sheets and plumped the pillow. 'What *are* you doing, tearing up your Mummy's photograph? You must have a temperature.'

'It's not my mother, but while I'm at it I might as well.' Flora ripped Denys and Vita from the frame and tore, ripping Denys diagonally from Vita. She dropped the pieces on the floor to join the scattered shreds of the postcard from the Thorwaldsen Museum.

'You'll be sorry you did that, my girl,' said Matron. 'If you weren't ill I'd make you pick up that mess yourself.'

'I won't be sorry and I am not your girl.'

'Amen to that,' said Matron, bending to pick up the scattered bits. 'Get back into bed and go to sleep.'

'Alone?'

'What d'you mean, alone?' Matron tucked in Flora's bedclothes.

Flora did not answer.

'Goodnight, then,' said Matron. 'Sleep tight.'

Flora kicked the bedclothes loose as Matron left the room, closing the door with a snap.

Listening to Matron's footsteps squeaking along the corridor, Flora gulped with rage and mortification. Never again would she take out the postcard and imagine herself as the girl, tenderly cherished. It stood to reason, *ipso facto*, that if Felix looked relieved at parting so would the other two. She could not trust them, would not think of them again. She would blot them out. Daydreaming about Felix, Cosmo and Blanco was as silly and childish as sucking your thumb or wetting the bed, things small children recently left at the school by parents from India frequently did. Felix had been nice, of course, very kind.

She did not want kindness.

He had looked bored, eating his pheasant, sticking

137

his fork into the brussels sprouts, and relieved as he drove away.

'Oh.' Flora tossed and turned. 'Ach!' She was miserable and sweaty. He only said that about Cosmo thinking me pretty as a sop, she thought. 'A sop!' she cried out loud, yelling in the school sanatorium. 'A sop. Nothing but a sop.'

Eventually asleep, she had nightmares and screamed because Matron, of all people, had turned into a marble bust which yet incomprehensibly and terrifyingly had arms, hands which held her in a throttling grip, shaking her awake. 'You stupid girl, look what you've done to your bedclothes, all tangled up and all over the floor. No wonder you are shivering.'

'Sorry, Matron, I was—'

'I'll get you a hot drink. Doctor will be here in the morning.'

'Is he marble?'

'What d'you mean, marble? Been dreaming you dwelt in marble halls?' Matron straightened the sheets and blankets.

'Marble arms—'

'Not arms, halls. I dreamt I dwelt in marble *halls*, is how it goes. I'm not totally uneducated, my girl.'

'And I am not your girl.'

Twenty

Flora stood on the platform, her suitcase at her feet, gripping her tennis racquet and the book she had not read in the train. All round the small station were green fields and rolling hills. The letter in her bag said, 'Get out at Coppermalt Halt'. This name was written large in black letters on a white board; she had obeyed instructions.

The train which had deposited her responded to the guard's whistle and started chuntering noisily off. The guard tucked his flag under his arm, swung himself into the van and slammed the door. Far down the platform a porter rolled milk-churns out of the sun into the shade. The train, dwindling down the track, shrieked as it sighted a tunnel in the side of a hill. The platform was long and empty, the afternoon hot; Flora wished fervently that she was still on the train.

'There she is.' Mabs appeared, running through the gate marked Exit. She was wearing a pale green cotton dress; Flora could see shadowy legs scissoring under the thin skirt as she ran. Behind her a figure in pink followed at a canter. They came to a halt beside Flora. 'There you are! It is Flora, isn't it?' Mabs was flushed with running. 'Gosh, how you've grown! Look, Tash, she's as tall as us. Is this all you've brought? You do travel light. I saw you get out of the train as we came over the bridge, then stand alone and forlorn on the platform as we jostled past Mr Ticket Collector and here we are. I bet you were wishing you'd stayed on the train, never got out, never got in, perhaps?' Mabs wore a large smile. She was hatless, beautiful, elegant,

139

confident. 'You *were* thinking better of it,' she said.

Flora found herself smiling.

'She *was* thinking better of it, she *was*,' exclaimed Tashie, smiling too. 'I can see it, look, she's blushing. We've caught you out, you are a recalcitrant visitor. We shall have to cure your recalcitrance, shan't we? We'll make her enjoy herself, won't we, Mabs?' Mabs and Tashie stood beaming at Flora.

The porter, advancing with leisurely tread, picked up Flora's suitcase. 'In the back of the car, Missie?' he addressed Mabs.

'Yes, please,' said Mabs. 'Got your ticket, Flora? He's ticket collector, too. We can't get out of here unless you surrender your ticket. He's dreadfully strict.'

Flora, walking between Mabs and Tashie, followed the porter down the platform and into the station yard. As she walked she felt in her purse for a shilling. The porter put the suitcase onto the back seat of an open tourer. Flora handed him her ticket, which he punched and returned with a grin. As Flora got ready with her shilling he said, 'You got platform tickets, Miss and Miss?'

'How strict you are, what a bully.' Mabs handed him a shilling. 'No, Flora, no, I've done it. You haven't seen us, Mr Ticket Collector,' she said.

'Then I can't give you the box the General was expecting off the train, can I?' said the porter, straight-faced. 'That will be fourpence each.'

'What a tease you are.' Mabs produced the money. 'There. Father would skin me alive if I forgot it; it's his port. Is that it over there?' She gestured towards a wooden case. 'Can we get it onto the back seat, I wonder?'

'Put that away.' Tashie indicated the shilling Flora was holding. 'One of Mrs Leigh's rules is that no visitors are allowed to tip.' Then, as Flora looked doubtful, 'Really, it's true.'

Flora stood with Tashie watching the porter manoeuvre the box onto the back seat of the car, while Mabs re-stacked a collection of parcels.

140

'Right we are,' said Mabs. 'There's room for us all on the front seat. In you get, girls. I say, Tash, look at her narrow, narrow hips. Aren't you lucky, Flora, with your gorgeous figure. Off we go then.' She started the engine and put the car in gear. 'With Father's port in the back I mustn't drive too fast or I'll joggle it, so easy does it, no Brands Hatchery.'

'It's five years, isn't it? We worked it out at dinner last night.' Tashie sat sideways so that she could look at Flora. 'I recognized you at once. Bet you thought we never noticed anybody except ourselves,' she said, 'and it's more or less true but we remembered *you*. We saw you watching us buy hats in St Malo, little sly boots. We thought they were terrific, cloche hats worn low over our noses—'

'D'you know how we found you?' asked Mabs. 'Felix, of all people, told Mother where you are at school. He found you via la Tarasova; she said you kept in touch, that you wrote. You know she's in London now? She makes my clothes and Tashie's. We've told all our friends about her, she's marvellous. She made this frock. D'you like it? No, I'm wrong, Felix told *his* mother, who told mine, so *that's* how Mother was able to invite you to stay. I can't tell you how pleased we all are. What did you think when you got her letter? Father has never forgotten the *langoustes* you produced for the picnic and Cosmo and Hubert are absolutely delighted that you are coming, as you will see presently. We don't call Hubert Blanco quite as much as we did now he's at Oxford, and only occasionally Lord Fauntleroy, your clever name for him. Have you seen Madame Tarasova since she came to London?' Flora shook her head. 'Well, you must, she's dying to see you like everyone else. By the way, have you brought your bathing suit? When we've deposited our junk, we are joining the others; they've gone ahead with the picnic tea to the river. It's so hot, we thought swimming – you can swim, can't you?'

'Yes,' said Flora.

'Golly, she can speak!' exclaimed Tashie. 'She's got

141

a word in, Mabs. Well done, Flora, that's quite a feat.'
Tashie and Mabs laughed joyfully.

'Isn't this fun,' said Tashie. 'Isn't Mabs a rattle?'

Mabs and Tashie then began to speak about two
people called Nigel and Henry. Flora gathered that
Mabs and Tashie were engaged to these two, Mabs to
Nigel, Tashie to Henry (later she would know them as
Nigel Foukes and Henry March). The conversation was
about clothes for both girls' trousseaux, some of which
would be made by Madame Tarasova. She would meet
these two characters shortly, Tashie said. They had
gone ahead to swim with Cosmo and Hubert. Stunned
by the volume of talk, Flora would have been content
to remain silent but neither Mabs nor Tashie allowed
this; they interrupted their discussion of clothes to
shoot questions at her. Did she like their engagement
rings? They held out their hands for her to admire dia-
mond and sapphire clusters. Did she like school? Was
she happy there? Was this the first time she had been
away in the holidays? Had she seen Felix again? Was
she fond of tennis? Could she ride? Did she still like
dancing? They remembered that she had danced at the
picnic. Did she still love dogs? They remembered that
comical dog on the beach. Did she like the way they
had their hair cut now? It was better than the shingle
of five years ago, wasn't it? Softer than a shingle. Hers,
they exclaimed, was looking wonderful, so thick, they
said enviously, it made theirs look positively scrappy.
Would she have recognized them if they hadn't shouted
her name? Did she think she would know Cosmo and
Hubert? Had she recognized Felix that time he came
and took her out? They had been quite jealous when
they heard about it; it was before Nigel and Henry, of
course. Several years ago, two at least.

While they chatted and questioned they exchanged
amused looks as Flora answered, 'Yes' and 'No'. She
was not to know that, remembering that if she spoke
at all it was in monosyllables, someone at dinner the
night before, probably Cosmo, had proposed a compe-
tition to make Flora talk freely. Tashie and Mabs had

142

betted that they would turn her into a chatterer like themselves. General Leigh had said, 'God forbid. Two of you is more than enough.'

'I have counted eight yesses and three no's. I am keeping score,' cried Tashie exultantly.

'We are having a party; have you brought your party dress?' asked Mabs.

'No,' shouted Flora, 'I have not.'

'Stop the car,' exclaimed Tashie, 'she's crying!'

Mabs jammed on the brakes.

'I haven't got a party dress. I've never needed one. I'd like to go back to school. Please take me back to the station,' Flora screamed. She felt she would choke. Her nose had begun to run with her tears. She wished herself back at school. However boring and horrible, she could cope with its drear familiarity.

Mabs drew up beside the road and pulled on the handbrake. The road stretched ahead, swerving gently up a hill through fields bounded by stone walls. In the crevasses of the walls there were ferns and cushions of pink and yellow stonecrop; in the grass verge beside the road pink campion and blue scabious and the loud sound of grasshoppers.

Mabs said conversationally: 'What a wonderful opportunity, Tashie. If you will let us, Flora, we would like to lend you a dress. You could choose. We are the same size as you. We would so love it if you would borrow a dress or two, wouldn't we, Tash?'

'Absolutely,' said Tashie. 'It would be doing us a kindness.' Mabs and Tashie's voices had dropped an octave; they were quiet now, sitting on either side of her, serious.

'I couldn't,' said Flora through gritted teeth, 'possibly.' She sat with her hands clenched in her lap, enraged as tears plopped off her cheeks onto her chest.

'Of course you may not like our frocks,' said Tashie. 'It isn't everybody who approves of our taste.'

'Well, I don't know, she might find something,' said Mabs hopefully, 'which would pass muster.'

Flora made a sound between a grunt and a hiccough.

'Mabs and I swap clothes the whole time,' said Tashie. 'It's between friends.'

'And you *are* our friend,' said Mabs reasonably, 'so—'

'I am not,' said Flora.

'Then please be, start at once.' Mabs was brisk.

'Absolutely,' said Tashie, equally brisk. 'Give it a try.'

'Oh.' Flora looked from one to the other.

'I do wish I had your eyes.' Mabs produced a handkerchief.

'I would be content with her mouth or her nose.' Tashie took the handkerchief and dabbed at Flora's cheeks. 'The trouble is, Mabs, she will look far better in our things than we ever shall.'

'Can't be helped,' said Mabs. 'We shall have to put up with it, won't we?' Then she said, 'I think your mother is the most Goddam awful, selfish, thoughtless *bitch* I have ever heard of.'

'And I,' said Tashie, 'can't wait for something really mean, humiliating and awful, something really *sordid* to happen to her, the bloody cow.'

'There!' said Mabs and Tashie. They had grown red in the face and looked much younger than they were. They sat staring at Flora, gulping their breath as they prepared to apologize.

Thinking of that moment in later years, Flora would remember the sensation of coming out of a long, lonely, foggy tunnel into an atmosphere of affectionate delight, but at the time, sitting on the front seat of the car beside an empty country road between the two girls, all she could do was burst into delighted laughter.

Twenty-one

While Flora, in a state of anguished delight, was trying on Mabs' and Tashie's frocks, Felix in London lay on the *chaise longue* in Irena Tarasova's workroom in Beauchamp Place. It was a hot afternoon; he had taken off his shoes and his jacket hung over the back of a chair. The rooms, reached up an early Victorian staircase with a mahogany rail, the treads carpeted in powder blue, were agreeably cool, the decor elegant. The contrast between this new establishment and the small stuffy room over the horse butcher in Dinard was sharp. Both the back room, where she worked, and the front room overlooking the street, where she received her clients, had plain white walls, blue and white striped curtains matching the covers of the *chaise* and the small sofa and armchairs in the fitting room. There was a vase of roses on a low table, a copy of *Vogue*, a bolt of yellow silk on an upright chair.

In the back room Irena sat with her back to the light tacking a sleeve into the armhole of a taffeta dress. The taffeta rustled as it received the pricking needle, hissed as she pulled the thread through; out of sight pigeons chortled and cooed on the roof. Sun, slanting through the open window, lit the colours on bolts of silks and velvets stacked on shelves along one wall and highlighted the white strands in Irena's hair. She stitched, her mouth full of pins, lips pursed in concentration.

'I am only in London for three days,' said Felix, answering a question. 'I was invited, but it is too big a rush to travel up north for one night. I am

145

not sufficiently interested. I have been once. The girls have changed. They are grown up, both engaged to be married, did you know?'

Irena said, 'M-m-m—' nodding, 'and Cosmo?' letting the name Cosmo escape through a gap in the pins.

Felix ignored the reference to Cosmo. 'Is this the *chaise* you had in Dinard?'

'I bought it in the Portobello Road.'

'I thought it was more comfortable.' Felix stretched, arching his back. 'And Alexis? Your husband, still in Paris?' Irena nodded, her eyes on her work. 'I have a hole in my sock.' Felix spied along the length of his leg at the sock.

Irena removed the pins from her mouth. 'I will mend it for you presently. If you had joined the house party, you would have found Flora Trevelyan staying there.'

'Oh?'

'Your mother persuaded Mrs Leigh to invite her, I heard from Mabs and Tashie. I make some of their dresses. Were you thinking of taking her out from school again?'

'No-o-o.'

'Was it a solitary impulse?'

'It was not a successful outing.'

'From what you told me she was unwell.'

'A disgusting cold.'

'She writes to me, too. I understand it developed into measles.'

'My God, I might have caught it. I have never had measles,' said Felix, shocked.

'Give me the sock.'

Felix leaned forward and removed the sock. 'My elegant toes poke through all my socks.' He handed the sock to Irena, then lay back contemplating his feet. I have very white skin, he thought, for a man with dark hair. He arched his instep, admiring a blue vein. Sunlight, slanting through the green taffeta Irena was working and reflecting onto his skin, made his foot appear drowning in an arctic sea.

146

'You should wear yellow socks.' Irena searched for a matching colour to the sock.

'Yellow? A little *outré*, dear Irena.'

'Narcissi are frequently yellow.' Irena stuffed her fist into the sock, preparing to darn.

Felix stood up and wandered round the room, placing his feet with care to avoid pins lurking invisibly in the blue carpet, fingering the texture of materials, draping a length of velvet over the headless, armless, legless dressmaker's dummy which Irena used for her work, letting his fingers trail across the cold wheel of her sewing machine. Then he stood at the window, staring at the backs of the houses in the parallel street.

'Don't stand in my light,' said Irena, darning. Felix returned to the *chaise longue*.

'They were amusing as adolescents five years ago, and the child had a curious quality.'

'Love.'

'Love?' Felix frowned.

Irena's needle darned intricately across the hole in the sock. 'Silk socks are all very well,' she said, 'but not strong.'

'Did the beautiful officers and noble nobles of St Petersburg and Moscow not wear silk socks?' Who was it at Dinard who had—'

'I know nothing about their socks.' Irena was unsmiling. 'But I hear King George wears wool, the finest wool.'

'Of course,' said Felix, 'it would be the finest. They go into almost instant holes, but it would not matter for the King, would it? How d'you learn these fascinating details?' He was laughing.

Irena smiled. 'People talk. He is, after all, cousin to the murdered Tsar, and I hope to become English.' Then, since memories of five years ago still came haunting, she said, 'You must know that each of those girls dreamed of marrying you.'

'Ah,' said Felix sombrely. 'Marriage. I get a surplus of hints from my mother. Don't you start. In any case, the Misses Leigh and Quayle are bespoke. Is that the

147

right word?' Of course, he thought, it was Flora who had told him about Irena's father being the court tailor; he remembered the little girl skipping up the street, her hand in his. 'Do you write to the Trevelyan child?' he asked.

'When I have time. Every few months perhaps.'

'And you have not much time?'

Irena shrugged: 'Less than you. She writes to me about her school, the dressmaking class; I shudder to think what the clothes the poor child makes must be like.' Some day, thought Irena, the child might become a client, as Mabs and Tashie had done. The occasional letter was not only a kindness but an investment; she must write again.

'You should visit her,' said Felix. 'I did.'

'It would take me a whole day,' Irena prevaricated.

Irena is just as selfish as I, thought Felix, watching, but why not take her down to that awful boring place in the car, take the child out to lunch? With Irena there things would go well. But no. He lay back, relieved. She is staying with the Leighs so the question does not arise.

'She must be fifteen by now,' said Irena. 'She might suit you very well in two or three years' time.'

'Ach.'

'No dot, of course, there is that disadvantage.' Irena had finished the darn. She cut the thread, replaced the needle, poking it into a cushion and handed the sock to Felix. 'Voilà! How hard does your mother press?'

'Hard enough; gentle, remorseless, systematic. I am twenty-five, the correct age, apparently, for matrimony.'

'Aie!'

'Thank you, that is a beautiful darn.' Felix put the sock on. 'I wish I could make as good a job of my nature.' He glanced at Irena sitting now, looking down at hands loosely clasped in her lap, unresponsive. 'It must be nice working with all these lovely materials.' He picked up a length of velvet and, throwing it across his shoulder, admired himself in the cheval glass. I

148

wonder, he thought, whether I am like my father?

Catching his eye in the glass, Irena said, 'Mrs Leigh asked your mother whether her husband Jef was your father; they were having tea at Gunters. Your mother said no. I could see what you are thinking,' she said.

'How do you know?' asked Felix, staring at Irena's reflection, 'that Mrs Leigh—'

'Women sometimes develop an intimacy with their dressmakers, as they do with their hairdresser. It is like talking to animals. English women tell everything to their dogs, and quite a lot to their dressmakers. Mrs Leigh was appalled at what she had asked your mother. She said it "just popped out". Apparently,' Irena was smiling now, 'Mrs Leigh was paying for the tea and your mother kept offering her cakes as though she was the hostess; it is these little things which create chaos in life.'

'Yes.' Felix was amused. 'I can see the scene. Do you believe my mother was being truthful or did she only wish to épater?'

'If Mrs Leigh had irritated her she might have been truthful. Who knows? She would not have expected to be believed. On the other hand it is well known that extremely masculine men breed only daughters; your mother may have acted for the best, after bearing five girls. I have heard that in Holy Russia this was often done.'

Felix was intrigued. 'Did the husbands connive at these surrogate fathers?'

'Probably.'

'My mother is a woman of courage; I wish I could believe I had inherited it.'

'You have, my dear.' She was serious.

'I don't know, I don't know, I—'

'It was after Mrs Leigh's gaffe that your mother suggested – it sounded quite a strong suggestion – that Mrs Leigh should invite Flora to stay.'

'Aha.'

'I had this from Mabs and Tashie; they were delighted, because they'd guessed Mrs Leigh was consoling

149

herself with the thought that the girl would have grown fat and spotty, as most English schoolgirls do. No threat to Cosmo.'

'She was neither fat nor spotty when I took her out to lunch, but the waif-like appeal was drowned in mucus.'

'You are disgusting. You must go now, I have to work out the measurements for some new clients; fat schoolgirls who have turned into Grenadiers. Look at this, nearly six feet tall, and this one has hips which are forty-eight inches and a bust of thirty-two.' Irena tapped a looseleaf notebook. 'So unfashionable.'

'You should have come to Holland, where everything bulges in proportion. But you must know that, you work for my sisters.'

'In a year or two I shall be British. The Home Office moves like a snail, but the idea of British citizenship gives me patience.'

'All bureaucracies do. It's getting late, Irena, why don't you leave your work and come out to dinner? We could go on talking about Dinard and the girls, if you must. Come on, join us.'

'Thank you. I do not care for dinner à trois.'

'He would not mind,' said Felix.

'No?'

'Well, perhaps.' Felix hesitated. 'Do come, we could talk about me. I came to see you to talk about myself. And you too, of course.'

'Of course.'

'And we have wasted the afternoon talking about girls of no particular—'

'A particular trio.'

Felix, hesitating, said: 'Ah.'

'Go away, Felix, I must work. I have to contrive a dress for a Miss Hippisley-Smith who has a thirty-one-inch bust and forty-six-inch hips. She wants it for a ball, this poor unbalanced girl. Go away, you distract me. She is coming tomorrow for a fitting and I have not even started.'

'Irena. I ask for help, please.'

'Yes?' Was that fear in his voice?

Standing with his back to the light, Felix raised his hands distractedly, dropped them, shouted very loud: 'I like girls, too.'

Quickly, she said: 'I know you do.' Then, catching his eye, she burst out laughing as she remembered an afternoon five years before, their shoes ranged side by side on the floor of the room above the *boucherie chevaline* in the Rue de Tours in Dinard. 'She was so innocent,' she said, chuckling, 'and you so clever. Now, off you go, you have kept him waiting long enough. Any longer and he will turn sour.'

'All right.' Calm again, Felix shrugged into his coat, bent to kiss first one cheek then the other. 'So I am to sort out my ambivalence on my own?'

'Teach yourself to be ambidextrous.' She edged him towards the door. 'How well we foreigners speak English.' She gave him a little push, using the tips of her fingers, and waited to hear his steps diminish and the street door slam.

Twenty-two

'I suggest we have swum far enough.' Cosmo turned towards his friend. 'Ready to give in?'

'I certainly am.' Hubert followed Cosmo towards the bank. 'Do you do this often?'

'I've never swum so far up river.' Cosmo pulled himself out of the water and collapsed, panting, on the grass. 'I wanted to see,' he gasped, 'how far we'd have to swim before you gave in. Then my legs gave out; they are trembling.'

'Mine, too.' Hubert stretched out beside his friend. 'My heart, my heart goes bang, bang, bang. Oh, lovely England, hot sun, sweet fresh water, it's surprisingly warm by the way, soft grass, the sound of grasshoppers – paradise.'

'It doesn't happen often.'

'The more wonderful when it does.' Hubert closed his eyes and breathed in the scent of the country. 'That was quite a test,' he murmured, 'the current is deceptive.'

'It's the depth of the river: going back, the current will carry us down.'

'That will be nice.' Hubert listened to the hum of insects, a woodpecker tapping somewhere near, and stretched his legs. 'We must not forget to collect our bathers as we go. Mustn't shock your mother's house party.'

'That would never do.' Eyes shut against the sun, Cosmo yawned and ran his hand down his naked body, wiping away surplus water. 'This is the only way to swim.' They had shed their swimming trunks further downstream.

'It's nice to be on our own for a bit. Your future brother-in-law rather holds forth.'

'Um, yes, he'll meet his match in Mabs.'

'Do you like him?'

'He's what one has been brought up to expect.'

Hubert said: 'Ah,' keeping his eyes closed; then, 'Is she in love with Nigel?'

'I suppose so. Why? Doesn't she seem to be?'

'Well – not quite enough.'

'Oh?'

'I may be wrong, of course.'

'I hope you are, Blanco.'

'Do call me Hubert.'

'What d'you mean by "not quite enough", Hubert?' Cosmo raised himself on his elbow. 'I've always been led to believe that *l'appétit vient en mangeant*, or words to that effect. What d'you mean?' He stared down at his friend.

'She's such a sexy little thing.'

'And Nigel isn't?'

'Keeps it pretty dark if he is.'

'What makes you think Mabs—'

'I've danced with her.'

'So have I.'

'You're her brother.'

'Of course I am, and she's known you such a long time you're a sort of surrogate. What's this about, Hubert?' Cosmo stared curiously at Hubert. 'What's this element of doubt?'

Hubert, pretending to be asleep, let his head fall away from his friend, kept his eyes closed and decided it would do harm if he told Cosmo that, dancing with him the night before, she had let her hand stray with inquisitive fingers across his flies; that she had been knowingly amused when he slapped the hand away. He turned on his side. Cosmo contemplated Hubert's back, watched a horsefly settle, waited for it to bite, then smacked hard: 'Killed it.'

'Bugger you!' Hubert rolled over towards him.

'It bit you. I have your blood on my hand, blood and squashed fly.' He wiped his hand on the grass. 'What's this doubt?'

Hubert, eyes open now, said, 'This isn't quite such a paradise after all.' Then, 'I've danced with Tashie too; she hasn't quite the sexy rhythm of your sister.' He said this hoping Cosmo, who had a nicer nature than his, would not observe his guile. He sat up, hugging his knees, contemplating the view. 'Nice cows,' he said, watching two stately ruminants sashay through the long grass across the river and sway lazily down to drink.

'I think Tash is pretty good. Light on her feet.' Cosmo, too, watched the cows' ponderous progress. 'I think both Nigel and Henry are lucky,' he said.

'So do I,' agreed Hubert. 'Nice chaps both, good prospects, good jobs, houses in the country to inherit, plenty of money, suitable.' He made the word sound ludicrous and Cosmo laughed with him albeit reluctantly, feeling that he was in some way betraying someone or something.

'In half a minute you will be onto Cousin Thing and Pengappah Abbey.'

'I don't believe it's an abbey,' said Hubert, pretending to rise to the bait. 'At most a manor, more likely a plain house, don't you think?' he joked, not wishing to suggest that his friend's sister might be marrying for money or be putting Nigel's worldly goods before love. 'Should we not go back?' he said. 'Were not Mabs and Tashie meeting Flora at the station? Why didn't they let us go?'

'They wanted to be the first to see what she's like.' Cosmo stressed words in the manner of his sister and her friend's affectation. 'Whether she will be worth taking up.'

It was Hubert's turn to be surprised: 'Oh?'

'That's how people are,' said Cosmo, 'even Mabs and Tash.'

Particularly Mabs and Tash, thought Hubert.

'Let's go back.' Cosmo stood and dived into the river.

The cows, standing hock deep in mud, jostled in alarm. Cosmo shook the water from his hair and trod water until Hubert joined him. 'You may not realize it,' he said, as they let the current sweep them downstream, 'but both Mabs and Tashie have been brought up to make suitable friends; they wouldn't know what to do with an unsuitable one, and that particularly goes for marriageable men.'

'Is that so?' Hubert drifted beside his friend, and as he drifted, remembering the straying fingers of the night before, he thought that he could guess the role in store for the 'unsuitable'. 'Do you suppose they have slept with Nigel and Henry? Tried it out?'

'Oh, no, no. They wouldn't know how to set about it, not those two.'

'Really?'

'I mean they are quite interested, or I take it they are, but they are like us, Hubert. Virginal.'

'I seem to remember you full of passionate zest in our spotty teens—'

'Of course. Dead keen. Still am, but who does one start with? I simply can't fancy what's offered so far.'

'No hurry,' said Hubert. 'Oxford inclines to chastity regarding girls. The inclination seems to carry on from school, stick to what you know – boys.'

'That's no help. I don't like boys.'

'Me neither,' said Hubert. 'Time enough. I say, didn't we leave our bathers behind that rock?' Paddling towards the shore, Hubert regretted an exploratory plunge into sex recently made. It had been an expensive experiment; he had learned nothing he was not already aware of, and lost something he could not retrieve. Watching Cosmo climb nimbly up the bank, he felt envious of his friend's inexperience. 'I should have thought,' he said, 'that by now you would know all about it.'

'All about what?' Cosmo was searching for the bathing trunks. 'Here they are.'

'Girls, women. You used to say you couldn't wait.' Hubert pulled on the trunks Cosmo handed him.

'The trouble is, girls can,' said Cosmo. 'The girls who attract me are great little waiters. Kisses, yes, but anything more there's nothing doing, the shop's shut.'

'Suitable girls,' murmured Hubert. Then, remembering Mabs, 'Do you really believe—'

'Listen.' Cosmo held up his hand. Round the bend in the river there was the sound of splashing, girls' voices, a man's laugh. Cosmo hitched on his trunks. 'Let's creep up on them.' He slipped back into the water and Hubert followed; keeping close to the bank they swam to the bend. In a large pool Mabs and Tashie swam. Mabs wore a red bathing dress, Tashie a blue; both wore white rubber caps. They were encouraging Nigel and Henry with cheerful cries. On the opposite bank Nigel and Henry debated whether it would be possible to climb along the overhanging branch of a beech tree and dive.

'Easy if they knew their way.' Cosmo trod water. 'Ah, Henry's found the way up.' They watched the two men climb the tree and set off hesitantly along the branch. Nigel, the least agile, wobbled and dived clumsily into the pool; Henry followed with a neat dive.

'Spectacular,' shouted Mabs. 'Do it again!'

Hubert gripped Cosmo's arm and pointed.

Above them on the bank Flora was undressing. 'Come on, Flora, it's wonderful,' shouted Mabs. 'Do hurry.'

Flora had taken off her frock and stood with her back to Cosmo and Hubert, dressed only in knickers. She held the end of a large towel with her teeth. Protecting her body from view of the bathers, she stepped out of her knickers and stood screened by the towel. She pulled on her bathing suit; she did this slowly as she watched the capering bathers, then let the towel drop, tied her hair back, took three steps towards the water and dived.

Cosmo and Hubert let out their breath. 'We'd better wait a minute,' said Cosmo, 'she might guess we'd seen her.' Hubert, clinging to the river bank, nodded.

Twenty-three

It was relatively easy for Flora, sitting at the bottom of the Leighs' dining-table, to keep quiet, eat what was offered, and deduce by watching her neighbours the correct order of knives and forks. She was relieved to find that it differed little from recollections of her parents' dining table in India.

Sitting between Nigel and Henry, who either talked to each other across her or to Mabs and Tashie on their other sides, she was saved by their absence of manners from the necessity of speech. She hoped to get through the meal without spilling food on the dress Mabs had lent her, or catching the eye of Cosmo or Hubert, who sat across the table. She was content to stay quiet and assimilate the pleasurable shocks her system had received since Mabs and Tashie had pounced on her at the station.

In India she had kept out of her parents' way and lived with the servants; her period with governesses in Italy and France had been dull; the last five years at school had been of stultifying mediocrity, spent with people she often actively disliked. She knew nothing of the outside world. The brief glimpse of family lives during the Easter holidays at Dinard had shrivelled into a dream. She was unprepared to meet the people she had dreamed of in the flesh, and astonished by the quality of love and good-humoured affection they seemed to feel for each other, and the manner in which they quite naturally appeared to include her.

Sipping her wine, she was careful not to look across the table and meet Cosmo or Hubert's eye, fearing that if she did she might blush or look confused. Although she had been expecting to meet Cosmo and possibly Hubert, she had not bargained for their sudden appearance in the river. They had surprised her coming up from her second dive by grasping hold of her, having swum underwater round the bend, and bobbed up gripping her tightly between them. 'Bags I' and 'She's mine!' Whether it was Cosmo who had said, 'Bags I,' or Hubert who said, 'She's mine,' she did not know, but their hard bodies encasing hers in watery intimacy had been both frightening and exciting as her breasts and thighs bumped against them. Cosmo had kissed her mouth as she opened it to cry out and Hubert her throat, bumping it with his teeth. Flora hoped, as she ate her dinner, that they had not noticed that her immediate reaction had been to return the kisses. Instead she had vigorously kicked free.

Swimming to the bank, she had joined Mabs and Tashie to unpack the thermoses and sandwiches for the picnic. Eating her sandwiches and drinking her tea she had noted the change in Cosmo and Hubert. Just as Felix had seemed smaller when he took her out to lunch, so Cosmo and Hubert, changed from boys into men, had grown larger. Hubert's nose was dominant; his eyebrows, nearly meeting above it, combined with his black eyes to give him an almost sinister air. Cosmo's face had thinned, his fair hair coarsened; his chin was bristly when he kissed her and his mouth formed a tighter line when shut. They had not meant anything particular, she decided as she listened to the talk; their behaviour was commensurate with the general good-humoured atmosphere of this beautiful place.

From the moment Mabs and Tashie had hailed her at the station she had encountered friendliness. If the two girls had overwhelmed her by their kindness, so had meeting her hosts been a surprise. Milly, kissing her, had exclaimed: 'My dear, you've grown up pretty,' as though this gave her personal pleasure and put her in the charge of Molly, a smiling housemaid. Molly took her to her room, unpacked her suitcase, ran her bath when she returned from swimming, helped her into the dress she now wore, brushed her hair and sent her down to the drawing-room.

Angus, grown greyer, had come forward with apparent delight, pouting out his moustache, reminded her of her *langoustes* at the picnic, enquired after her parents and introduced her to fellow guests, none of whose names she now remembered except a very thin Miss Green. 'And *this* is Miss Green.' Offered her sherry. She had refused the sherry but was put almost at ease, sufficiently so at least to watch the arrival of other guests, all of whom were greeted with great largeness of heart by Angus and Milly.

It was a big party: nine in the house, another eleven to dinner. 'I expect you will enjoy playing Sardines or Murder after dinner; that's what seems the mode at the moment,' said Milly. 'Or perhaps they will want to dance. Angus doesn't mind what they do as long as there isn't too much noise. We keep the drawing-room out of bounds. If you want to escape you will know where to run to. You don't look as though you will, though—'

She was not really talking to me, thought Flora. The butler was announcing dinner. She was looking over my head. She had never played Murder or Sardines, but she was ready to chance her arm; at school girls talked of these games. This was the first time she had been on a visit or stayed in a country house; the contrast with school and its inmates was intoxicating. She did not wish to miss a moment. Eating her dinner, she listened to the talk.

Mabs and Tashie's contribution seemed to consist of amiably teasing Nigel and Henry. There was talk of farming further along the table, and discussion of a law case. A man said, 'The report in *The Times* was excellent, I thought, absolutely fair. Does anyone know who wrote it? One should keep track of these journalists, one never knows—'

'Do you read the papers?' Nigel, remembering his

manners, turned a benign gaze on Flora. 'Do you keep track of what's going on?'

Flora said: 'We never see the papers at school. We do something called "current affairs", but it's so dull I never listen.'

'I suppose you bone up on the news in the holidays?' said Nigel kindly.

'I spend the holidays at school.'

Nigel said, 'Oh,' nonplussed. 'Ah.'

Flora felt she should apologize for her oddity but Nigel said, 'One way to get round that would be to take a newspaper of your own. When I was at Eton I read *The Times* so that I wouldn't look silly in the holidays.'

Flora said: 'I feel rather silly now.'

Nigel said: 'Actually, my interest was racing. I say, what's going on over there?' Flora followed Nigel's glance to where at the head of the table Angus Leigh had been holding forth to the lady on his right. Now he had turned his attention to Miss Green on his left. Miss Green had, like Flora, hoped to get through dinner without talking much; she was cursed with a stammer, unmarried, but far from stupid. She was a friend of the Wards and was staying with them.

Introduced to Hubert before dinner, she had said in Flora's earshot: 'F-Freddy s-says I shall have to s-sit next to our host. W-what s-shall I talk about? Can you s-suggest a t-topic? I hate t-talking.'

'Try the League of Nations and Stanley Baldwin,' said Hubert. 'That usually works wonders.'

Now there was the kind of silence one gets in the middle of a windy night before an increase to gale force. Miss Green, having taken Hubert's advice, looked up at her host.

Flora, sensing that nobody would be looking her way, risked looking up. All around fellow diners hushed. Across the table Hubert looked bland. Behind his master's chair the butler raised his eyes to the ceiling. General Leigh, face flushed red, said, '*What?*', glaring at Miss Green, who in an almost inaudible voice was heard to repeat her remark. 'D-don't you think the L-League of N-Nations wonderful, General Leigh? W-what do you think of it vis-à-vis B-Baldwin?'

'It is a club for Frogs and Wogs,' said Angus loudly. 'It bodes nothing but ill, it will bring disaster. That bugger Baldwin pretends to go along with it, but he secretly despises it, as I do openly. The League of so-called Nations is an international mafia of ill repute artfully concocted by political lounge lizards and communists at somebody else's expense. Who is going to pick up the bill for all their tommy rot and skulduggery, Miss Green? Tell me that.'

'Angus darling,' said Milly, from her place half-way down the table next to Freddy Ward, 'please.'

'The British taxpayer pays. You and I.' Angus ignored his wife. 'I take it you pay taxes, Miss Green?'

'Certainly,' replied Miss Green.

'Then vote, Miss Green; denounce as I do these impossible Bolshie foreigners building palaces of peace in Geneva with your money, or never come to my house again.'

'I shan't,' said Miss Green quietly.

'Angus! Apologize,' Milly's voice cut through the gale. 'At once!'

'I apologize,' said Angus unapologetically.

'You must know one of the children will have put her up to it. Look at their faces!' cried Milly. 'Miss Green is our guest; you have insulted her, this is a tease, darling.'

Angus glared at his wife. 'One of the children? They look pretty grown-up to me. Bolshies, are they? All Bolshies leave the room.'

Cosmo and Hubert pushed back their chairs and stood up. Mabs, Tashie, Henry, Nigel and Flora stood too. The girl sitting between Cosmo and Hubert looked bewildered. The butler signalled to the parlourmaid to open the door.

'Have you heard of Adolf Hitler?' Miss Green's voice was stammerless.

'No. Does he belong to the League of Nations?' Angus was still suspicious.

'No, he doesn't. He's German.'

'Then tell me about this sensible fellow. Oh, come back, all of you, try not to be so ridiculous,' Angus shouted after the departing young, then turned to Miss Green. 'You must forgive me, Miss Green.'

'What a performance,' said the girl sitting between Cosmo and Hubert as they regained their seats.

Hubert caught Flora's eye and smiled. Nigel and Henry leaned towards her and said, 'And what do you think of the League of Nations, Flora?' But Flora was smiling back at Hubert, remembering the incident in the river.

'Is this Hitler chap the sort of fellow we will get to hear of?' Angus enquired of Miss Green.

'Quite possibly,' said Miss Green.

Twenty-four

'Are you getting the feel of Coppermalt?' Mabs and Flora lay under a fourposter bed. The young of the party had chosen to play Sardines while their elders played bridge. Mabs wriggled herself into a comfortable position. 'Lie between me and the outside world, then if Nigel finds us he can't—' Her voice was inaudible.

'What?' Flora whispered.

'He's a bit of a fumbler, that's all. Now come on, tell me what—'

'This isn't going to do this dress much good.' Flora had been doubtful of joining Mabs.

'Never mind the dress. Keep still, hush.'

Flora lay still as told.

Another person who it was not possible to see in the dark opened the door, prowled round the room, muttered, 'Not in here,' and closed the door. Flora, who had tensed, relaxed.

'I was asking about your first impressions,' Mabs resumed. 'What were they?'

'Oh, love, kindness, affection, generosity; everyone is so—'

'Who's that?' Mabs jumped. Somebody had laughed.

'Only me; I was behind the curtains. Budge over, Mabsy.' Hubert crawled past her feet to lie beside her. 'Who have you got there?' He stretched across Mabs and touched Flora's head, letting his fingers explore her hair. 'I do believe it's Flora.'

'Of course it's Flora. Shut up, Hubert; go on, Flora. Everyone is so – so what? What are we besides loving, kind, affectionate and generous? Go on.'

163

'Then your father at dinner—'

'I thought you might be here.' Cosmo lifted the valance and slid in to join them. 'I didn't go out when I shut the door.'

'Crafty beast,' said his sister. 'That's cheating.'

'I might have gone away if you hadn't started talking. Move over,' said Cosmo. 'Let's get on with your first impressions, Flora. What were you going to say about Father?'

'Go on,' said Mabs, 'tell.'

Flora said hesitantly, 'He seemed so – um – angry about the League of Nations. He sort of exploded.'

'Hubert, you'll get stick from Mother,' said Mabs. 'She worries about his blood pressure; foreigners are bad for it.'

'I have already apologized,' said Hubert. 'I expressed suitable penitence. Miss Green – who is she, by the way? – looked sceptical.'

Flora, puzzled, said, 'But—'

'Foreigners,' Cosmo explained, 'are people to be fought. Leagues of them don't tally in father's book; he is not kind or loving or affectionate about foreigners.' Cosmo slid his arm under Flora's neck and pulled her head onto his shoulder. 'He is only generous to rare exceptions, and even they have been suspected of blotting their—'

'I believe she was quite shocked by Father's rage,' said Mabs quickly. 'We Leighs of Coppermalt are not all we appear at first sight, are we, Cosmo?'

Flora wondered what Cosmo had been going to say, whether he would have mentioned Felix.

'When you were in France,' she said hesitantly, 'your father got on all right with people, didn't he?'

'That would be the hotel servants or the waiters or shopkeepers,' said Hubert.

Beside her Cosmo chuckled.

'But he was very friendly with the Shovehalfpennies,' Flora protested. 'You shared their table.'

'Titled exceptions to his rule,' said Hubert.

Cosmo laughed outright.

Mabs said, 'Honestly, Blanco, must you?' rather crossly.

The door opened again and a girl came in.

'Has anyone looked under that bed, Nigel? Mabs had a thing about hiding under beds when she was little.'

'There's more to do on top of them.' Nigel followed the girl into the room.

'Let's have a look,' said the girl as she lifted the valance. 'I'm right, I spy feet. I recognize Mabs' shoes.'

'No room, no room,' said Cosmo.

'Let's lie on top then, under the eiderdown,' said the girl. 'Or will it make you jealous, Mabs?'

'No,' said Mabs. 'Feel free.'

Nigel and the girl climbed onto the bed, giggling. 'Got a chamber pot under there?' asked Nigel. 'The Coppermalt jerries are famous. My future father-in-law has a silver one, a collector's item, did you know?' The girl giggled. 'D'you think he would give it to us as a wedding present, darling?'

Mabs said, 'He's not your father-in-law, yet.'

'Oho – listen to that.' Nigel bounced on the bed.

Neither Mabs nor Nigel sounded particularly loving. Cosmo whispered in Flora's ear, 'Abysmal humour.'

'Come out, come out. You were talking so loud we could hear you in the passage.' Henry opened the door and switched on the light while the rest of the searchers stampeded in behind him.

'I vote we have one more game,' said Tashie, 'only play fair this time, keep separate and keep quiet. I'm glad you are wearing one of Mabs' dresses, not one of mine,' she said as Flora crawled from under the bed. 'Now, everybody, no cheating this time; let's start from the hall, no going about in twos, and absolute dark.'

'Tash is a great one for the proprieties,' said Henry.

'My turn to hide,' said Hubert.

'Oh, is it?'

'No, it isn't,' they said.

'Yes, it is.' Hubert over-rode them.

Unused to the house, Flora thought she would

stay on the ground floor. She felt her way cautiously round the hall. She thought if she found the stairs, she might cheat and latch onto another player coming up or down, or perhaps just sit on the stairs. Carefully she felt her way past an oak chest. She remembered that there were two and on each an important-looking vase; she must not break them. It was amazingly dark and silent. Tashie had made everyone take off their shoes and promise not to talk or even whisper. Trying to orientate herself, Flora stood still and listened. Against her cheek she felt the occasional whisper of a draught as somebody somewhere opened or closed a door. There was the murmur of voices from the drawing-room, where the older generation played bridge, then close by the clink of glass on glass, the squirt of a syphon and Angus' voice: 'What did you say, darling? I couldn't hear.'

'I said, she is pretty. I was expecting fat legs and pimples.'

Flora, calculating her whereabouts, started moving away along the wall.

Angus said: 'So you had convinced yourself, my love. Want a drink?'

'No, thanks. Freddy would like a whisky. It was your chum, Rosa, who persuaded me. I do hope Cosmo—'

'Ordered, more like.' Angus snorted with laughter. 'Is Miss Green having anything? Just lemonade? Very well. Good old Rosa. You needn't issue another invitation, let it drop.'

'I'll feel so mean,' said Milly's voice, quite close now. 'Is that for Miss Green? I'll take it to her. Thank you, darling.'

'You'll recover.' Angus sounded rather jolly, Flora thought. She now knew where she was; if she felt along the wall to the right, she would reach the stairs and be able to sit, but she must mind the second oak dresser. Milly's voice followed her. 'After what nearly happened with Felix that time—'

'That was your imagination.' Angus had moved away. 'Nothing came of it.'

166

'But I don't want Cosmo to—'

At the mention of Felix's name Flora pricked up her ears and was tempted to move back towards the drawing-room door, but an arm was put round her, someone whispered, 'Shh,' she was drawn into the recess of a deep cupboard and, still holding her, her captor shut the door.

Hubert murmured, 'Stand well back. There, just keep still while I rearrange all these—'

It was inky black, far darker than the hall. Hubert held her with one hand while he rearranged a cluster of coats and mackintoshes between them and the door. 'Nobody will find us now.' He leaned back, holding her against him, hands circling her waist.

'Hubert, Blanco.'

'Yes?'

'You made me jump.' Indeed her heart thumped with fright. She wanted to ask what the Leighs were talking about, but did not want him to think she had eavesdropped. Then she forgot the Leighs as Hubert began stroking her back. It was damply stuffy in the cupboard; the coats hanging round them smelled of horse and earth, tobacco, whisky, hair oil, fish and dogs. A Wellington boot leaned against her leg; when she put out a hand to steady herself she felt the mesh of a landing net. Hubert murmured, stroking her back, 'I saw you undressing by the river. I wanted to do this then.' He rubbed his chin over the top of her head, holding her close.

Flora said: 'I heard them talking in the drawing-room, something about Felix. Mrs Leigh seemed — Hubert, what happened?' She was consumed with curiosity.

'Oh, that's old stuff. He was invited to stay. Mabs made a dead set at him. You may not remember she and Tashie chased him like crazy that holiday we were all in Dinard.'

'I remember.'

'Oh? Yes, perhaps you would. Anyway, the General asked him to stay. Mabs made a dead set, made rather

167

a fool of herself actually and Mrs Leigh took fright.'

'Why?'

'Foreigners again. Better to have the Channel between your daughter and foreigners; no amount of money and nice titles makes up for the Channel.'

'Oh.'

'She need not have worried, Felix was not reciprocating and spent almost his whole time fishing with Cosmo and me. I like Felix.'

'So do I.'

'Why are we talking about Felix? We are playing Sardines. Squash up, Flora, that's the point of the game.'

Flora pulled away. 'It's an awfully silly game. What is it for? Didn't Felix want to marry her?'

'Not so that you'd notice. Funny fellow, Felix.' Hubert pulled her back. 'Sardines is a game. Somebody hides, then everybody looks for that person and, when they find them, they squash in with them. In a way it's a better game than Murder.'

'Murder?'

'With Murder you all wander about until the murderer takes somebody by the throat. Like this,' Hubert put his hands round Flora's neck, 'then the person screams. Don't scream now, stupid' – for Flora had gasped – 'just keep still. I want to put my thumbs in these hollows, these little salt cellars.' Flora stood still; she was beginning to feel frightened. 'Don't be afraid, I won't hurt you.' Hubert let go of her neck and put his hands back round her waist.

'I'm not afraid.' His hands round her throat had felt huge. Then Hubert did something she did not expect: he pulled up her dress and put his hand down across her bottom, letting his middle finger trace the cleft between her buttocks. 'When I saw you by the river I wanted to do this too,' he said, 'badly.'

But Flora was pulling away. 'No, no, no, don't – please don't – my mother, my mother, my—' Gasping and weeping, she remembered looking down from the top of the cliff in Brittany and seeing her father pull up her mother's dress at the back; her mother had pulled it over her head and lain down on the sand and opened her legs—

'You poor little thing. Here, let me mop.' Hubert fumbled for a handkerchief. 'The last thing I want to do is make you cry. I thought your mother a disaster. Mabs and Tash were only saying earlier what a cow she is, giving you no clothes.'

'Oh, she is,' Flora hiccoughed, 'she is. I hate her. It's just, oh, Blanco, I can't explain.'

'Then don't try.' Hubert remembered Denys and Vita wrapped up in each other, aloof, unlike the ordinary run of parent. He held Flora gently with one arm and applied his handkerchief with his free hand.

Flora leaned against him, regretted pulling away. She whispered, 'Put it back.'

'What?'

She reached for his hand, replaced it round her waist. 'It was because I remembered my mother,' she said.

'And?'

'And my father. They were, they are so – then at the picnic, when you were all swimming and things and—'

'Yes?'

Flora told him, whispering how she had seen her parents from her perch at the top of the cliff. 'I thought they'd gone mad,' she said. 'They looked so ridiculous. I thought if people saw them they would laugh. What do you suppose they were doing?'

With his arms round Flora, Hubert shook with laughter. 'Oh, Flora! Oh-ho-ho-ho oh ha-ha-ha.' He swallowed his laughter in her hair. 'Oh, Flora, oh.'

'That's what I thought would happen. You *are* laughing. That's what I remembered when you—' She was furious.

'I wasn't laughing at your parents, I promise.'

'Yes, you were.'

'Only a little, I swear. I guessed they were a bit randy. I was laughing at their choice of venue, such

169

a chilly locale.' (And I was laughing because I am a bit shocked, he thought. Well, more than a bit, quite a lot.)

'Doing what? What's "randy"? What's "locale"?'

'One is a word you shouldn't use, and locale is, well, this coat cupboard is a locale, our present locale.' Hubert nuzzled Flora's neck. 'You smell delicious, like unsalted butter. What are you doing? Why are you wriggling?'

'I am easing my knickers up. You pushed them half-way down. They are uncomfortable.' Hubert was laughing again. 'And this cupboard stinks,' said Flora huffily, as she readjusted her dress.

'You're right, it does. Perhaps we had better get back to the game, rejoin the others.'

'All right.' Flora felt she had put a foot wrong in some way, got out of touch. 'How is your mother?' she asked, groping for conventional ground.

'My mother re-married.'

'Gosh. Someone nice?'

'He's all right. He has enough money, he cares for her and she for him. We have nothing in common.'

'I had imagined your mother caring for Pengappah for you.'

'Fancy you remembering. I haven't got it yet. When I do, I shall put you in charge. What a memory you have.'

(Of course I remember. I remember everything, she thought, I always shall.)

'Has anybody ever kissed you?' Hubert was asking.

'Yes,' she said. Had not Cosmo kissed her that day by the river?

'Properly?'

'What's properly?'

'Like this.' Hubert held her face between his hands and bent to kiss her mouth. What Flora remembered in old age of this, her first proper kiss, was that the smells of the cupboard finally got to her and that she smothered Hubert's kiss with a violent sneeze, and Hubert called her an inept bitch.

170

Twenty-five

Flora was to learn from other games of Sardines that there was nothing unusual about being fondled in the dark and that it was more pleasurable with some than with others. Nigel and Henry were early discouraged, should they pretend to mistake her for Mabs or Tashie. Unwilling to invite for herself in games of Murder the role of murderee, a role coveted by Tashie (who had perfected a shriek which distinguished her from other victims), she cheated, hiding in the hall cupboard until she heard a yell, for after her brush with Hubert she had the cupboard to herself.

She was happiest on the nights when they danced, rolling up the rugs in the hall and foxtrotting to bands on the wireless. She liked being partnered by Henry or Nigel, for with them she was not harassed by love, a love which with Cosmo or Hubert could make her stiff and shy in their live presence after years of lying in their imaginary arms. 'Relax,' they said, and, 'What are you laughing at? Share the joke, do.' There was no tension with Nigel or Henry; they were indistinguishable young men engaged to marry Mabs and Tashie.

By day the party played tennis, swam in the river, rode or walked in the hills. If it rained they lolled in the library, playing cards and backgammon. Flora watched and listened, for she was unused to life other than that of school. It was vital, she felt, that she too learned to be as buoyant, confident and gregarious as the Coppermalt young and the friends who came to play tennis or dine and dance.

Particularly she watched Mabs and Tashie with Henry and Nigel; these two surely knew how to manage being in love? Tashie and Henry sat next to each other at meals, and frequently held hands; they disappeared for hours at a time to reappear sleepy and flushed, Henry with ruffled hair, Tashie with smeared lipstick. When they danced Henry held her close, pressing his chin on the top of her head. If they sat on a sofa, they sat close together; often they shared an armchair.

While Mabs and Nigel did this, too, Mabs could turn suddenly aloof, contradictory and sharp, complaining when they danced that Nigel trod on her toes, that she would sooner dance with Hubert, one of the other men or Wellington, her father's labrador. 'If Wellington were human, I would marry him,' she said. 'He is perfection.' And Nigel, patient: 'You love dogs because they do not answer back.' Then he would look unhappy, watching Mabs pull Wellington up onto the sofa to sprawl, leaving room for no one else.

Then Mabs would spring up, fling her arms round Nigel, hug and kiss him in front of everybody so that he looked a fool and pushed her off, and Mabs, angry, would flounce away to vanish for hours without even Wellington for company.

One afternoon Flora overheard two guests who, coming to play tennis, had witnessed some such scene; they were coming out of the downstairs lavatory and did not notice her on the stair. One said to the other, 'What Mabs needs is a jolly good rogering,' and the other said, 'One wonders whether old Nigel is capable of delivery,' and as they walked away the first man said, 'I would be more than willing to take old Nig's place, she's so—' and the second, interrupting, agreed. 'Ah, yes, isn't she?'

Mystified, Flora looked up 'roger' in the dictionary and read: (1) copulation and (2) 'message received', and was none the wiser.

One lazy afternoon they congregated in Mabs' room, where she and Tashie were discussing their trousseaux with repetitive intensity as they studied the autumn issue of Vogue and fingered swatches of materials sent up by Madame Tarasova. Mabs' and Tashie's enthusiasm for clothes continually amazed Flora. They displayed the same affection towards dresses and frocks that they showed towards her, the same love that they lavished on their family, friends and household dogs. As they continued to lend her their frocks, so they included her in their chat.

Cosmo and Hubert came to sprawl on the floor or loll on the bed and teased the girls. 'What part does Henry play in all this?' asked Hubert.

'And what does Nigel wear?' enquired Cosmo.

'Henry wears the trousers,' Hubert answered him and said, 'Oh?' in mock surprise when Mabs snapped, 'Nigel will wear the clothes I choose for him. He has no dress sense; I shall make him change his tailor.'

'Does he know?' whispered Cosmo, awed.

'He soon will,' Hubert whispered back mockingly.

But Mabs, refusing to rise, said, 'Look, Flora, you'd look lovely in this,' showing her a design. 'Or this. You've a lovely figure; you could get away with it. You could be a mannequin, then there would be no need for you to go to India.'

The prospect of India had come up when Flora, asked about life at school, had made them laugh at a description of her fellow pupils happily anticipating rejoining their parents at the age of seventeen or eighteen in Delhi, Calcutta, Bombay, Poona or Peshawar. There they would watch polo, dance at Vice-regal balls and the club and meet their future husbands – who would be in the Army, the Indian Army, the Police, or the Political Service – marry and live happily ever after in large bungalows with hordes of servants. They would spend the hot weather in the hills or Kashmir. It was Hubert who referred to the girls as the Fishing Fleet.

'Every October a fleet of nubile girls charged with sexual abandon are loaded into P & O liners to traverse the Mediterranean, the Red Sea and the Indian Ocean. Arrived in Bombay they entrain and travel up

173

the far-flung Raj to be snapped up by sex-starved subalterns, District Commissioners and Political Officers.
That is what happens, that is how the Empire is per-
petuated, pristine virgins fed into its maw to breed
more.'

'Hubert, don't pun,' they cried.

'Aren't you looking forward to it, Flora?' Hubert
teased her, and when Flora shook her head, 'She is
not looking forward to it, she will sneeze in their
faces,' (I think I hate him) 'refuse her contribution to
the perpetuation of the Raj, wear defiant red knickers
to shock the memsahibs, sneeze defiance of the norm,
betray the Empire, go on strike, sneeze, sneeze, what
a good wheeze.' (I do not like him at all.)

'And you are to go when you are seventeen?' asked
Cosmo seriously.

'Yes.'

'Oh,' then, 'Really?' and 'Must you?' they asked.

'When I am seventeen,' said Flora flatly, 'they will
send me money to kit myself out.'

'We will help you choose your dresses!' interrupted
Tashie.

Flora went on, 'And a ticket to Bombay where I
shall be met by my father's bearer and travel by train
to wherever they are at that time.'

'And then?' Cosmo frowned.

'Then she meets all these marriageable chaps. I
hear there is a huge choice,' said Hubert.

'How come you are so well informed?'

'My step-father was an Empire Builder in Singapore.
It's the same system.'

'And you don't like him,' said Mabs.

'Nor does Flora like her parents.'

'That is neither here nor there,' said Flora. Her
quiet voice caused a temporary silence in which Tashie
sighed, murmuring, 'A pity about the clothes.'

It was Hubert who, having teased, now eased by
suggesting a 'Save Flora from the maw of the Raj'
campaign. Flora must get herself a job, he said, then
she would not have to go to India.

'We girls are not brought up to do jobs,' said Tashie.
'We are brought up to marry.'

'So one observes,' said Cosmo.

'Come the revolution both sexes will work and marriage will lapse,' said Hubert.

Cosmo said: 'Oh, Blanco, you haven't rolled out the revolution for weeks.'

'Under your roof I am tender towards your papa's feelings.'

'Not noticeably so—'

'Your revolution will not come in time to save Flora,' said Mabs.

'She could find a job as a housemaid, sneeze away the dust,' said Hubert, staring at Flora. 'Become a serf until it starts.'

'Pig,' said Flora, wishing that she had sneezed worse, more messily. 'Swine.'

At this point Milly Leigh came into the room. 'Really, my dears! All cooped up with the windows closed! It's a beautiful day. Why aren't you all out of doors getting some exercise?' She stepped across the tangle of young people on the floor, half-slipped on the shiny cover of Vogue, recovered her balance and threw the window open. 'There!'

'How I deplore this upperclass mania for fresh air,' Hubert muttered, uncoiling his legs.

'Come on, let's catch the evening rise on the river,' said Cosmo. 'See you later, girls.'

'I am sure Nigel and Henry would love a game of tennis,' said Milly, fixing Mabs with her clear eye as she left the room.

'We might just as well be in India,' exclaimed Mabs.

Tashie gave her a slantwise look and said, 'Come on, come on – try.'

'You two go. I think I shall take the dogs for a walk,' said Mabs.

Flora lay awake a long time that night and was heavily asleep when Mabs woke her in the early morning.

'Will you come with me for a ride? I can't sleep.'

They crept out of the sleeping house, caught and saddled their horses and jogged up to the high grass moorland along the Roman Wall. Flora listened as she rode to the bits jingling, the creak of leather, the brush-brush of the horses' hooves through the grass, the croak of a carrion crow in the valley. As the sun rose and the wind stroking the yellow grasses dropped, they reined in their horses, let them crop the turf and sat watching the view.

'One morning just like this,' Mabs said, 'I brought Felix up here. He looks right on a horse. He liked the view, he said. He thought it was fine. I think he said historic. But he said he liked Holland better, that he liked looking at views by himself. He was awfully courteous, I think would be the right word, but he liked flat country best. Then I knew. Of course Mother was relieved; very pleased, really. I thought I'd tell you. Life at Coppermalt isn't all love, kindness, affection and generosity.' Mabs picked up her reins, pulled her horse's head up and said, 'Shall we canter up to the top?'

Watching her canter away Flora felt absolute fury. How could Mabs, who had everything, lay claim to Felix? It was immaterial that he had rejected her; she had possessed him in thought, wanted to marry him. Choking with rage Flora kicked her horse into a canter. The horse, infected by her passion, put its head down, humped its back and performed a series of bucks. Flora survived the first two but fell off at the third. The horse, running loose, stopped beside Mabs, who had reached the top of the hill; she caught its dangling reins.

'Why did you let go of the reins? What did you do to upset him? He's as quiet as a mouse,' Mabs shouted. 'Are you hurt?'

'No,' Flora called back.

Mabs led the animal back to her; Flora remounted. 'He's normally so docile,' said Mabs, puzzled.

'I am a docile girl.' Flora patted the animal's neck.

'Don't make me laugh,' said Mabs. 'We all suspect you are a sleeping volcano.'

Flora smiled. 'I landed on my bottom; your jodhpurs are stained with grass.' (She is so kind, she even lends me riding clothes; it makes my jealousy worse.) 'Will it wash off?'

'Of course.'

They jogged slowly down the hill.

'Did Felix ride this horse?'

'Yes. He didn't get bucked off.'

(So he had sat astride this horse, in this saddle.)

'Did you want to marry him?'

Mabs stared ahead: 'Yes, I did. You wouldn't know, you were so small when we all met in France; you wouldn't have noticed but Tashie and I adored him. We did everything to attract his attention.' (Those silly hats!) 'Then later, when he came to England, he took me out a few times. He was friends with Cosmo, too. Then Tash met Henry and fell in love and forgot about him; I met Nigel and he fell for me. I still fancied Felix but I knew, as you know when you are grown up, that there was no future in it and my parents weren't keen so I got engaged to Nigel. That's about it.'

Flora said: 'I see,' keeping to herself the years she had lain in Felix's arms – Cosmo's and Hubert's too, of course. Never in a million years could she possibly speak of them to Mabs. Her jealous rage subsided; she stroked the horse's neck. He relaxed between her knees. 'Are you glad now?' she asked.

'I suppose so. Parents know best.'

(Parents? What did parents know of love?) 'So you are happy?' she said.

'Mostly.' Mabs' reply was ambiguous. 'We'd better trot on,' she said, 'or we'll be late for breakfast.' Presently she said, 'The thing is both Nigel and I like hilly country. We have that in common.'

Flora cherished to herself that what she had in common with Mabs was that she too had been rejected by Felix.

Twenty-six

Angus enjoyed visiting his wife after breakfast. Seeing her propped by pillows, breakfast tray across her knees, shoulders covered by a white shawl, satin nightdress revealing the swell of breasts grown plump in middle age, spectacles perched on shiny nose, one hand holding her coffee cup, the other *The Times* newspaper, filled him with affection and pride. She would look up as he came into the room and say, as though he had not left their bed barely an hour before, 'How are you? Had a good breakfast?'

And he, pouting out his moustache, would bend to kiss her, saying, 'Aah, that's nice, very nice,' kissing each smooth cheek in turn, inhaling her womanly smell before settling in the chintz-covered chair by the bed, asking, 'And how is Bootsie?' in a growly voice. Bootsie, a quasi-Cairn terrier of doubtful temper devoted solely to Milly, would at the sound of his voice scrunch herself into a tighter ball at Milly's feet, growling through clenched teeth while Milly, smiling at her husband, asked: 'Any news?' and 'What are your plans for today?'

'I shall take Nigel and Henry out with a gun, see what we can bring back for the pot.'

'Not Cosmo or Hubert?'

'They seem to have gone off shooting. They fish. Can lack of interest in shooting be something to do with Hubert's political views? He's practically a pacifist. He tells me Oxford is boiling with lefties; I presume he is one.'

'He only tells you that to tease. His politics should

178

not prevent him shooting.'

'He bothers me. He niggles on about the unemployed and says the streets of London are full of down-and-out miners.'

'So they are.'

'Milly.'

'They are, darling. I've seen them, you've seen them. I know how you admire the miners. What's your worry? Are you afraid he will make Cosmo join the Labour Party?'

'God forbid.'

'Cosmo is not going to turn red, darling, he isn't interested. I am more worried about him than you are.'

'What's he done? Got into debt? Being dunned?'

'It's not money, it's Flora Trevelyan. I see him watching her.'

'She's a child.'

'Not any more. He watched her when we were in Dinard and he watches her now.'

'She was a child then.'

'I know.'

'You invited her to stay.'

'I was tricked by Rosa.'

'Ah, Rosa, m-m-m. We haven't seen that son of hers lately.'

'You frightened him off.'

'Not I. If you'd been watching, you'd have seen that he turned Mabs down. Cosmo tells me that he invited him up this summer but he said he was too busy. A pity. I'd have liked him to come.'

'You can't have it both ways. You were terrified he'd encourage Mabs.' Milly sighed. 'Anyway, it's all right now, she's got Nigel.'

'Hum.' Angus sat with his hands on his knees, legs apart. 'How long did you invite her for? The little Trevelyan.'

'That's just it. I've forgotten. I probably said come and stay for a few days, as one does. To be honest, it never occurred to me she'd accept. She's been here

179

three weeks. Mabs and Tashie have taken her up and all the men – well.'

'Well?'

'Oh, Angus, I thought she'd be spotty and plain, but she isn't; she dances marvellously, and she makes them laugh.'

'Now that is dangerous.'

'Don't joke. Just suppose Cosmo—'

'She seems as interested or not in Hubert; doesn't show much interest, actually. A shy sort of girl, reserved.'

'Hubert is not our son, we are not responsible.'

'What you mean is that she has no money and is not the sort of girl you want for him.'

'Exactly.'

'Then don't invite her again.' Angus smiled at his wife. 'Who would have thought, when I picked you out of the schoolroom, that you'd develop such worldly wisdom?'

'Don't, Angus. Oh dear. If only she would leave.'

'Presumably she has to go back to school sometime. If you are fussed, drop a hint or two or ask Mabs.'

'Mabs wouldn't.'

'Then stick it out. As I say, don't ask her again. Aren't you exaggerating? She's only fifteen. At twenty, Cosmo isn't going to be interested in any girl for long; I wasn't.'

Milly looked at her husband; he's leaving it all to me, she thought. 'I must do the polite thing,' she said, 'and write to Flora's mother. She will be pleased to hear from someone other than the child's school.'

'I don't remember liking the woman, or the man. They weren't interested in the child; I remember them quite absorbed in each other. In consequence she is ignorant as hell, unsophisticated, barely knows who the Prime Minister is. Nice manners, though.'

'She will fit in very well in India.' Milly looked down at her hands.

Angus looked up sharply. 'You used not to fuss like this.'

'The children were younger, darling. Now I worry. Since Mabs nearly – well, that's over. I want the best for them.'

'Life was less complicated when they were small.' Angus stood up. Then, taking his wife's hand, he bent to kiss her breasts, murmuring, *Ces belles choses.*'

'Your moustache prickles and tickles.' Milly stroked his head.

Angus drew the shawl gently across his wife's chest. 'You're a wonderful wife and a good mother,' he said. 'A wife above rubies. Hear that, Bootsie?' He poked the little dog, who growled shrilly.

'Don't tease her, darling,' said Milly, as she did every morning. 'Could you please pass me my writing things? I'll scratch a few letters before I get up.'

Angus went downstairs whistling.

It was true that Cosmo watched Flora. When he and Hubert had held her between them in the river and he had kissed her, he had wanted to do it again. During those seconds while he kissed her mouth and Hubert her throat she had kicked out to free herself and her feet had pushed hard along his belly and across his genitals in a way that was sexually exciting; the weight of the water turned what might have been a painful kick into something in the nature of a caress, the more interesting because unpremeditated and unconscious.

When they had shouted, 'Bags I' and 'She's mine,' it had been a joke, the kind of thing they did to Mabs or Tashie. But after the kiss and the kick he felt differently. He resolved to get Flora to himself, but found it difficult. First playing Sardines his sister was present, and Hubert, so that all he managed was to put an arm round Flora's neck and her head on his shoulder; she had moved it off. Later something had gone wrong with Hubert to sour the atmosphere and his hopes of cornering her came to nothing. He fumbled about in the dark but could not find her. It was years later that she confessed to cheating and hiding in the hall cupboard.

It was too public to kiss her when they danced; she seemed more relaxed dancing with Nigel or Henry than with himself or Hubert. He suspected Hubert had erred in some way, but did not care to ask. Slightly puzzled, he decided to wait for the perfect opportunity.

So he took to the river with his rod and, as he followed its twists and turns and cast his fly, he visualized Flora in a succession of erotic situations which began with her long eyelashes brushing his cheek and ended with her clasped warmly naked in his arms in a paroxysm of delicious lust. Adept at sexual fantasy Cosmo was, as were most of his contemporaries, an innocent, given to masturbation which left him frustrated.

Another block was Mabs who, with Tashie, spent much time with Flora, so much indeed that it crossed his mind that Flora was being used as a shield. Should Tashie disappear with Henry on a romantic ramble, rather than follow suit with Nigel Mabs kept Flora by her, so that she was constantly part of a threesome, as intimately inaccessible as though she'd been strung up in a cage like a canary.

When, one afternoon, he rounded a bend in the river and saw Flora sitting staring at the water with her arms hugging her knees, he stopped and watched to make sure she was alone before sitting beside her. She gave him a startled glance. He said, 'I'll go away if you want to be alone.'

She said, 'No.'

There was a trout in the pool well known to Cosmo; he had hooked it twice in the past. It had grown old and wily. He wondered whether to point the fish out but thought that if she had seen it this would be a waste of breath, and if she had not she might betray a lack of interest. He sat listening to the sound of the river, the rustle of swallows swooping across the water and distant sounds of harvesting.

Flora said, 'It's very difficult for me.'

Not knowing her train of thought Cosmo asked,

without turning his head, still watching the fish, 'What's difficult?'

Flora said: 'At school the other girls whine and moan for their parents. They cry for their mothers. They sob. I never know how real it is because, when one starts, the others join in. Sometimes the whole dormitory is in tears. I didn't tell you this the other day when I made you all laugh. I wonder whether I am odd. I don't cry. I tried once, I lay in the dark and worked myself up. "I want my mother, I want my mother," I said to myself, but I didn't want her. I couldn't squeeze out a tear. I felt ashamed.'

Cosmo gripped his knees and stared at the trout a foot down in water the colour of beer. Its tail and fins moved as it positioned itself against a rock.

Flora went on: 'Of course I've always known, but coming here to Coppermalt and seeing how you all love your father and mother and how they love you makes me sure. I dislike my mother and my father; there have been times when I hate them.' Cosmo remembered Hubert's description of Flora walking into the sea. 'And yet,' she said, 'you are not all perfectly happy. I can't make it out.'

Cosmo looked at Flora in surprise. She was right, he thought, but any lack of happiness could not be blamed on his parents.

'I was wondering, when you came along,' Flora said, 'whether there is all that difference between love and hate, between doing things to please your parents, as you and Mabs do, or because you must, as I must.'

Cosmo said, 'Why did you keep your eyes shut when you walked into the sea at Dinard?' (Was it hate? he wondered.)

'It was because I couldn't swim. I suppose Blanco told you.'

'You bit and kicked him.'

'He interfered.'

'They would not have minded you dead. It would have done them a favour,' said Cosmo.

'From hate?'

'From whatever.'

'There you are!' She was looking at him now. She did not look like the girl he fantasized about at night – by day, too.

Cosmo said: 'If you are really unhappy about going to India when the time comes, don't. I'll help you.'

'How?' She looked at him fiercely.

'I'll think of something.'

Flora laughed. She did not laugh nicely. She sounded older than fifteen. Cosmo was annoyed. He should have said, 'I'll marry you,' or 'You must live with me,' or, 'I will look after you, save you from the suitable subalterns,' anything rather than, 'I'll think of something,' which in its ineptitude meant nothing. He picked up a pebble and aimed it at the trout; the trout, who had endured worse, did not disturb itself. Flora whispered: 'You wouldn't dare.' Then she said, 'Mabs tells me that life at Coppermalt is not all kindness, affection and generosity. I had to be told. Mabs knows. She isn't happy.'

'Of course she is. She is going to marry Nigel.'

Flora raised her eyebrows, fluttered her eyelashes and said, 'True,' pursing her lips.

Remembering various scenes of doubt, hesitation and his parents' worried faces, Cosmo could gladly have hit Flora, but he said: 'It's all fixed, you know. She's having a great time shopping. I am to be chief usher and Henry will be best man at the wedding.'

Flora said: 'She wanted to marry Felix.'

'How d'you know?' Cosmo was startled, 'Felix?'

'Because she told me.' (Because I too love Felix.)

'My parents—'

'It wasn't them. He didn't, Felix didn't want to.'

'She told you that?' Cosmo was amazed.

'Yes.'

'Poor old Mabs.' (I must be blind as a bat.)

They sat staring at the river. Flora said: 'Life must be a lot simpler for that big trout half-hidden by that stone.'

Cosmo said: 'I've hooked him twice. He got off each time, he's wily.'

'Bully for him. The only sort of person who would help me,' said Flora, 'is someone like Alexis Tarasov, if he still exists.' (I do not love Alexis, I never would.)

'Oh, he does,' said Cosmo. 'By chance Hubert and I met him in Paris. He's still driving a taxi; he drove us from the Gare de Lyon to the Gare de l'Est. We recognized him. I've got his address somewhere. He's grown fat and jowly.'

'Give it to me.'

'We had time for a game of backgammon in a café frequented by White Russians. He beat us both. He wouldn't be of any use to you.'

'I'd still like his address.'

'All right, I'll find it for you. We should go back, we'll be late for dinner.' Cosmo stood up and held out his hand. Flora took it and let him pull her up. 'I will help you if you ever need it,' he said. 'I promise.' Flora did not answer for, with a percipience beyond her years, she knew that he did not want to be tied, that in this sense he was like Felix.

Walking up to the house, Cosmo felt he had been closer to Flora when she was a child and he fifteen, when they sat on the floor in Madame Tarasova's room above the horse butcher and played backgammon in the shadow of Elizabeth Shovehalfpenny's breasts. He had tweaked her eyelashes. He had been happy. He said: 'Oh hell, we'd better hurry, I'd forgotten; there are people coming to dinner, Miss Green and Joyce. Do you remember Joyce? A very agile girl. She's arriving to stay.'

'Sticking-out teeth and white eyelashes?'

'That's the one. The teeth are straight now; she looks like a rather wonderful chestnut horse. She darkens her eyelashes; she's really rather beautiful. She has the most stunning figure, gorgeous long legs and her breasts are terrific.'

'How nice.'

185

'We all stay at the place her step-father takes for the grouse shooting. We go next week, I think. It's near Perth.'

'I thought you did not shoot.'

'I get a bit bored with Father, but Scotland's different. We go most years. Why are you running?' For Flora had broken into a trot.

'I'm cold.' She ran faster.

Oh damn, thought Cosmo, watching her race ahead, why didn't I kiss her by the river? When she took my hand and I pulled her up I could have kissed her. We were alone, it was a perfect opportunity. I could have had a go, raped her even. Visualizing the imaginary scene Cosmo broke into laughter. Seen from behind Flora looked childish, he thought; she lacked the fluidity of movement which graced Joyce. Looking forward to Joyce he too broke into a trot.

Twenty-seven

Vita and Denys sat on the Club verandah watching a game of tennis played in the near distance between two girls freshly arrived from England, partnered respectively by a captain in a Gurkha regiment and the Governor's A.D.C. A dachshund belonging to the Colonel of one of the Sikh regiments romped with Denys' Airedale bitch Tara on the lawn between the clubhouse and the tennis court. Watching the dogs circling crazily, Denys said: 'That obviates the necessity of exercising her; we should be grateful to the Colonel.'

'So long as they don't destroy the flowerbeds,' said Vita, as the animals doubled away from a bank of Canna lilies. 'I rather hate that colour red. It's evil.'

It was Sunday. Denys and Vita had been to church; they sat waiting for drinks to be brought them. The day was agreeably warm after the cool night of northern India; people sat around in twos and threes, gossiping as they drank their Pimms, pink gins or Martinis, and idly watched the tennis. A few sat apart, reading month-old *Tatlers* or *Country Life*. The men looked appreciatively at Vita; their women waved and noted her peach-coloured crêpe-de-chine dress, white cardigan, silk-stockinged legs and co-respondent shoes. Denys complemented his wife's chic in a pale grey suit, cream silk shirt, old school tie and suède shoes. 'I don't know how she does it,' said a woman to a friend. 'How does she keep that incredible complexion in this climate? They never go home. Just look at her hair, it's as glossy as a child's. She must be nearly forty. It makes one sick.'

'We all know what they say,' said her friend.

'They look jolly well on it.' Both women shook with laughter.

A pair of kites circling the sky spiralled down to perch on the Club roof and stare with malevolent eyes.

'I ordered stout,' said Denys, pulling up his trousers at the knee and crossing his legs. 'The first of the season's oysters have arrived from Bombay.'

'Delicious,' said Vita.

'Just what we need.'

'We need no spur.' Vita smiled the smile her husband loved. 'Did you order brown bread and butter?'

'Of course. That girl plays a good game. Who is she staying with? What's her name? She's new.'

'I don't know yet. She's the niece of the Colonel of the 1st/11th Sikhs. A bit on the dumpy side, but she's off on the right foot with the Governor's A.D.C. No messing about there.' Vita laughed.

'Let's hope when our turn comes that we can manoeuvre an equally effective launch.'

'Don't talk about it! We have two years yet.' Vita frowned. Then, looking up as two men went by carrying squash rackets, she said, 'Hello. Come and join us after your game.'

'Thanks, we'd love to,' said one of the men.

Vita said, 'One of those might do if he hasn't been snapped up.'

'Early days,' said Denys. 'Ah, here are our drinks, and I nearly forgot, a letter for you addressed care of the Club.' Vita took the letter as a servant in Club uniform set oysters, tankards of stout and a plate of bread and butter on the table between them.

'I don't know this writing.' Vita turned the letter over. 'Nice paper. Oysters first.' She put the letter down and impaled an oyster on a toothpick. 'Delicious,' she breathed.

Denys watched her swallow; the slight movement in her throat stirred him.

'My word, you two take risks,' said a woman as she

passed their table. 'Oysters in barrels from Bombay! Smacks of suicide to me!'

'Perfectly fresh,' said Vita sweetly. 'We know what we are doing.'

'I should say you risk the trots, if not dysentery,' said the woman.

Vita spiked another oyster, murmured, 'Busybody, interfering bitch,' as the woman receded.

Denys grinned; his wife's relations with other women never failed to delight him. He watched his dog circle crazily round the dachshund. 'She'll give it a heart attack,' he said, helping himself to bread and butter, gulping his stout. 'Look at its wretched little legs. Who is the letter from?'

Vita tore open the envelope, spread out the letter and peered at the signature. 'Milly Leigh. Who is Milly Leigh? Oh, I remember – Dinard.'

'Married to a retired old buffer General, one son, one daughter. Friends of that Dutch family. What does she want?' The dogs were now lying exhausted, facing each other, tongues lolling. 'I think I'd better get her clipped.'

'Who?'

'Tara, darling. Why should Mrs Leigh write to you?'

Vita was reading the letter. 'They seem to have had Flora to stay. How curious. Thought we'd like news of her which does not come from the school. Grown quite pretty – that's a relief, I suppose. Dances well, tennis, swims, rides. Of course she does, she has two legs. Something about "a dry school report". Do we ever read them?'

'I skim through when I pay the bill; she's average.'

'Above average would not do out here. It's a bit of a cheek; is she hinting at something? I wonder why she invited her? Nice of her, I suppose.' Vita read the address. 'Coppermalt House, Northumberland.'

On the tennis court the dumpy girl screamed, 'Out, it was out!'

'If you say so,' said the Governor's A.D.C. 'Change ends, my serve.'

189

'Silly girl, it was in,' said Denys.

Above their heads the kites moved with a rustle of wings from the Club roof to the branch of a tree.

Vita went back to the letter. 'Rather awful handwriting, what sheets. Quite a newsy lady. The son is at Oxford and so is his friend, who I may remember as Blanco. "But we now call him Hubert, of course." Fancy that.'

'I recollect two rather offensive boys.'

'I don't. Oh, the girl is getting married and so is her friend, Tashie. Why should we be interested? Ah, wait, there's more; they were both presented at Court and have done three seasons. Think what that must have cost. Not very fast off the mark, were they, those two? Flora will have to do better than that. I'm not putting up with her hanging around for years. I think Mrs Leigh rather interfering, Denys. Is she suggesting we should have Flora presented? What an absurd suggestion.'

Denys laughed. 'She's the sort that takes it as a matter of course.'

'Well, it's not on,' said Vita angrily. 'It's quite unnecessary.'

Denys smiled; he loved seeing his wife get angry about something unimportant. 'Did you see a lot of her when I left you in France? Were you friends?'

'Not really. She's not my type. I was too busy.'

'Doing what?' What had she done all that July, August and September? She had hardly talked about it. He repeated his question, 'Busy doing what?'

'I was looking after Flora. Getting a new outfit. I spent hours having fittings, hours. That Russian dressmaker was terribly slow. Only worth it because she was cheap.'

'And what else?'

'I was bored and lonely without you.'

'Were you?'

'And then—'

'And then?' He leaned forward; her nose had sharpened as it did when she told a lie. 'And then?' he persisted.

'Denys, you're not jealous?' Her pale grey eyes were bright, the whites very white.

'I am.'

The kite which had been watching them with clinical interest chose its moment and swooped to snatch the oyster Vita held impaled on a toothpick. Flapping as it reversed upwards with its prize, it struck Vita's face. She screamed.

Several people sitting nearby on the verandah laughed as Vita, lashing out at the bird, upset her drink so that brown foam ran down her legs. Denys exclaimed: 'It's scratched your face, you're bleeding,' in a high anxious voice. 'Come home, sweetie, we must get some disinfectant on it; they are scavengers.'

Vita put her hand to her face and brought it away covered in blood. 'It might have blinded me.' She began to sob. 'Oh, Denys, my face.'

'Come on, let's get you home.' He put his arms round her. 'Here's my handkerchief.'

Vita held it to her face.

'Wasn't that bird neat! Do they do that often?' The dumpy girl had finished playing tennis.

'I say, Denys,' a man shouted after Denys as he led Vita to their car, 'the Colonel's Kraut has got your bitch in a clinch. Is she on heat?'

'Not due yet, but must be. Damn and blast, could somebody bring her back for me? I must get Vita home.'

'You would think he'd have the sense to know when his dog's on heat,' said the woman who had doubted the oysters.

'With a wife who's in that state en permanence? Not Denys,' said her friend.

'They are stuck together, you won't pry them apart,' said the dumpy girl. 'I know about dogs. The bitch lay down for him.'

'Really! Some people,' said the oyster-doubter.

The Governor's A.D.C. uttered orders in Urdu and disapproving Club servants brought buckets of water to douse the dogs. 'Puts one off one's lunch,' said a woman who had not spoken before.

Denys bathed Vita's face. She was crying now from shock. 'It's all right now, darling, don't cry.' He held her tenderly, stroked her hair.

'Shall I have a scar?'

'No, no, of course you won't. Keep still while I put this dressing on.'

'I was trying to tell you when that thing hit me that there is no need for you to be jealous. Nothing happened that summer, nothing. I had beastly rows with Flora. She was impossible. I never told you because I felt guilty. I should have done what you wanted and come back to India with you, left her at the school instead of paying attention to what other people said. As it was, I was bored to tears and made to feel guilty by people like that Leigh woman. Look what I've done to my dress; it's ruined.'

'I'll give it to the servants to give to the *dhobi*. Let me help you out of it.' Denys lifted the dress over Vita's head. 'Mind your face.'

Vita wrapped herself in a dressing-gown. 'There's someone arriving.'

'Lie down, sweetie, rest for a bit. It will be some kind fellow with Tara. I will see she is shut in the stables.'

'You said we should be grateful to the Colonel.' Vita began to laugh. 'Ha-ha-ha. Oh, my God, she will have the most ghastly puppies.' She stopped laughing. 'Bang goes her pedigree.'

'They will be drowned,' said Denys. 'Now rest.'

Vita lay back on her bed. She could hear Denys being polite, a sharp yelp from Tara, Denys giving orders to have her shut away, men's voices, then the sound of a tonga driving off. The horse, like so many tonga horses, was lame.

How had that dreadful row with the child started?

'Is he in love with you?' Flora had asked in July 1926 in the flat at Dinard.

She had snapped the child's head off. 'Why on earth should you ask that?'

'He looks at you as Jules looks at Madame Jules, that's all. Jules is in love. I only wondered.'

192

She should have made a joke of it, but she had said, 'Don't be idiotic,' and, 'Who may Jules be?'

The child had said, 'He's a friend. He keeps a café in St Malo.'

'You cannot be friends with people of that sort.'

Flora had shouted, surprisingly and very loudly, 'He *is* my friend. There is nobody left except Tonton.'

Unwisely she saw now, she had said, 'And who may he be?'

'A dog,' the child had yelled. 'A dog I meet on the beach. I suppose,' she had shouted, 'I cannot have a dog friend while you are friends with someone you met on the train from Marseilles when my father had gone away in the ship.'

She had smacked Flora's face and Flora had yelled, 'I wish I had drowned,' her mouth ugly with passion.

She had yelled back, 'I wish you had,' with equal passion though, thinking of it now years later, she couldn't see how the subject of drowning had arisen.

It had jolted her, though. She had sent the young man on his way and nothing whatever that anybody, even Denys, could take exception to had happened. She had not even seen him off on the launch to St Malo. She had not mentioned meeting this amusing man to Denys in her letters. I can't even remember what he looked like, she thought, as gingerly she touched her cheek which was throbbing less, thank God.

But that summer! The boredom. The child out all the time supposedly doing her lessons – Italian conversation, maths and Russian – with the dressmaker. Vita remembered long weeks wandering about the town looking at the shops, lying on the sofa reading novels, writing to Denys and counting the days when she could get shot of the child and back to India. She had taken to thinking of Flora as 'the awful warning', which was exactly what Flora was; a reminder of an evening spent with a traveller passing through the hill station en route to the Himalayas, someone she had never seen again. Too much to drink when she was not used to it, heavy petting which went too far, and the discovery some weeks after Denys had joined her for his leave that she was pregnant. There had never been a whisper of gossip. When Flora was born and Denys suggested adoption she had vigorously refused, fearing that if she agreed, as she longed to, Denys would suspect, if not immediately then at some later date. That summer in France she had often wished she had taken the risk. How the days had dragged and the company of the child sickened her, reminding her of that one slip which she had not even enjoyed. The man had been rough and selfish, not in the least like Denys. Vita called out, 'Darling, are you there? I need you.'

Denys came into the room. 'What is it, sweetie?'

'Is poor Tara all right?'

'Yes, of course.'

'Must you drown—'

'The only thing to do; we can't be lumbered with a pack of mongrels. We'd be a laughing stock. We'd never be rid of them. You are too soft-hearted.'

'I'm silly, I know. That stupid letter upset me, although I suppose she meant well.'

'To mean well can prove fatal,' said Denys. 'It's not a state of mind I condone.' He sat on the side of the bed and took her hand. 'How is the poor face?'

'Miles better.'

'Well enough for a stiff drink and some lunch?'

'I think so.'

'Good. I trust that bloody kite hasn't put paid to our Sunday siesta.'

'Certainly not,' said Vita, 'it would take more than that.'

Alec, the Governor's A.D.C., and the captain in the Gurkhas who had brought Tara back discussed the girls they had played tennis with as they drove away. 'The smaller one played a good game,' said the Gurkha captain.

'I am sure that ball was in,' said Alec.

'So you didn't find her attractive?'

'Not really, no.'

'Ah.'

'I am handicapped *vis-à-vis* girls,' said Alec. 'I measure them against Vita Trevelyan.'

'Really?' The Gurkha captain expressed intrigue.

'Theirs is a perfect marriage,' said Alec. 'She is beautiful; they are inseparable. She never leaves him to go home. They adore each other.'

'Not all that popular with other women, I note.'

'Jealous, I expect. They'd probably like a crack at Denys.'

'You have such high standards,' said the Gurkha captain. 'I am not against a spot of separation. I shall ask the cheater to the next Club dance. I like a trace of fallibility.'

Twenty-eight

The chill which struck Flora with Cosmo by the river
and made her run was the realization that her visit was
almost over; she was due back at school in three days.
When Cosmo and Hubert were in Perthshire she would
be back in the ambience she detested. Still, there were
three more days.

'Hi, stop,' said Nigel, who had watched her running
towards the house. 'Come here a minute, spare me a
mo.' He caught her wrist.

Nigel was sitting on the terrace in the evening sun
with The Times newspaper on his lap, a half-empty
glass of whisky on the table beside him. He looked
glum. 'Sit down.' He pulled her down onto the seat.
'I want to show you something.'

'What?' She was impatient to go up to her room
and change into evening dress, wallowing first in a
hot bath. Too soon this luxury would be lost; she
would be forced to share a bath with another girl,
have only three a week. She tried to jerk his wrist
free. Nigel held on.

'Wait a minute, this is important.' He held her
with his left hand, the tumbler of whisky in his right.
The smell of whisky mingled with the scent of jasmine
growing against the house. 'Watched you run,' Nigel
said. 'Good legs, not knock-kneed like Mabs. Mabs is
knock-kneed, have you noticed?'

'No.' She twisted her wrist in his grip.

'Look,' said Nigel. 'I've got The Times newspaper
here.'

'So?'

'So I am going to do you a kindness, teach you how to read it. No, don't run away. This is important, young Flora. If you want to understand what makes people tick, you read this paper.'

'What people?'

'The Leighs, stupid, and their ilk. You are not of their ilk so you had better understand them.'

'Are you of their ilk?' she asked on a rising note.

'I am. The "ilk" is financial, dear girl. I am also a bit drunk. Where was I? Oh yes, you had better take this opportunity while it lasts, as they say in the advertisements. Are you ready?'

'If it doesn't take too long.' She was grudging.

'The rudiments won't take long, the actual experience takes a lifetime. Right. Don't run away, promise?'

'I promise.' (Whose dress shall I borrow tonight, Mabs' green or Tashie's blue?)

'Right, then.' Nigel released her hand and picked up the paper. 'Here we are, pay attention. This is the hatch, match and despatch column. Births, deaths, marriages, right?'

'Right.'

'Imagine you are pleased to read here that, let's see, Admiral Bowing has died. He may be your uncle, see, and with luck he has left you a packet in his will. Always look at the deaths first, they can cheer you up no end. Got that? Now the births. Some foolish friend has started a family, or added to one. You write and congratulate or condone, must do that, that's what friends are for. You with me?'

'Yes.'

'Well then, turn over to the Court page, engagements. Miss Mabs Leigh is engaged to, oh dear,' Nigel drained his glass, 'Nigel Foukes. And from time to time the engagement is broken off. You keep a weather eye on that little lot otherwise you may drop a social brick and nobody, Flora, forgets a social brick. It hangs around your neck like a – oh dear, no more whisky.' Nigel put his glass carefully onto the table. 'Where was I? Yes. Note, here are reports of the weddings which come off, bloody lists of all the people who went to the ceremony. They like to see their names sandwiched between a Lord and a General, for instance. Makes them feel they exist, poor sods.'

'Shall I read about you and Mabs?'

'Who knows? It's possible.' Nigel squinted into the middle distance. 'Who bloody knows?' He sighed gustily. Flora flinched from his whiskied breath. 'Sometimes you read the joyful news that a marriage has been dissolved. Well, it's joyful for some, presumably. Aah—' Nigel sighed again.

'Is that the lot?' She was anxious to get to the lovely steamy water with bath salts.

'No. It – is – not. You must read the leaders here and here; this one, the third, is witty quite often. Then read the letters; they tell you what the current obsession may be. You get a grip on opinion. Now here are the parliamentary reports; once you've found out who is who in government, you'll pick it up as you go. You'll follow those with glee. Racing page? Interested in racing? You may marry a racing man. Then, for light relief, this page: murder and murder trials. You'll enjoy those. By now, Flora, you are *au fait* with what's going on in the world, however garbled the report may be. You don't have to believe it, but it looks good if you can pretend to hold an opinion. Look at Hubert, everybody thinks he's clever and deluded because he talks socialist. He maddens people, makes them talk; they love it. Think you can manage?'

'I'll have a bash.'

Nigel laughed. 'You do that, Flora, and I swear you will begin to understand what makes the Leighs of Coppermalt tick.'

'I'd like that.'

'And again you may not.' Nigel stared at her, then said, 'Well, it's a start. If half the parents of people like yourself persuaded their daughters to read *The Times*, they'd save a lot on school fees, finishing schools in particular.' Nigel belched. 'Sorry.' He lurched to his feet. 'I must change for dinner. Mustn't blot my copybook by being late. Need another drink first, though.'

Flora said, 'Thank you very much. I shall remember what you say.'

'And act on it?'

'Certainly.'

'You are an intelligent girl. Contrary to general belief, chaps like a girl with brains.'

'Thank you.'

'I might even ask you to marry me.' Nigel had hold of her hand again. 'You've got jolly decent legs and the rest of you's a bit of all right; how about it?'

'You are marrying Mabs,' said Flora, laughing.

'That's what you think.' Nigel shambled away into the house, carrying his empty glass. As he went he pulled a handkerchief out of his trouser pocket. If it had been anyone else, Flora would have thought he was crying.

Entering the house through the French windows in the drawing-room, Flora heard voices in the hall.

'Ah, Flora,' said Milly, 'here you are. You remember Miss Green? She is here for the night on her way south. And Joyce, you remember Joyce?'

'I remember Flora.' Joyce came forward. 'A silent and mysterious child, a watcher.'

Flora said, 'Hello.' Joyce with straightened teeth was not at all like a horse; she shook hands with Miss Green who said, 'H-how d'you do,' in a quasi-whisper. She looked into Flora's eyes as she shook hands; she had a small dry hand which clasped Flora's as though pleased to. Flora returned the smile. Nigel's hand, clasping her wrist, had been damp.

Milly was speaking. 'As Miss Green is motoring south tomorrow, Flora, we thought you would like to go with her. I was worried, thinking of you travelling so far alone in the train. Miss Green lives only twenty miles from your school. Isn't that a piece of luck? She will be glad of your company.'

'V-v-very glad,' said Miss Green. 'F-fortunate coincidence.'

Flora heard herself saying, 'How terribly kind, that will be absolutely marvellous,' in a steady voice. Part of her congratulated herself on the response of a lifelong *Times* reader, while the other part felt she had been hit in the solar plexus. 'I must change for dinner,' she said, 'or I shall be late.'

The visit, which had started as a sort of joyous balloon when the girls had met her at the station, had begun to shrivel while talking to Cosmo by the river, and made a small spurt upwards while sitting with Nigel, was now almost burst. But Joyce was speaking. 'Back to school, you poor thing. It would have been such fun if you could have come on to Scotland with us, wouldn't it, Mrs Leigh?'

Milly said, 'Well—' smiling, and, 'Of course, it would have—'

And Miss Green said, 'G-g-goodness, is that the time? I must change. And I s-say, w-what apart from the L-League of Nations and p-politics do I avoid at dinner?'

Milly, laughing, said, 'The old disgrace—'

'Steer clear of religion,' said Joyce, 'and sex.'

'Hush, Joyce,' said Milly. 'Really, dear!'

Miss Green murmured, 'That doesn't leave us much,' and set off up the stairs.

'It's lovely to see you, you naughty thing.' Milly put her arm round Joyce. 'You are a breath of fresh air.'

'I shall try not to cause a draught.' Joyce followed Miss Green upstairs.

'Well, then,' Milly turned smiling to Flora. 'Isn't that a happy arrangement? Now, what shall you wear tonight? Make yourself pretty.'

Lying in the bath, Flora looked at her legs, glad that they passed muster. She stretched to manipulate the hot tap with her toe. The baths at Coppermalt were sized generously for tall men; school baths, she thought resentfully, were economically short. She soaped her neck and armpits, scrubbed her back with a loofah and bathed her face. Whenever she bathed her face she heard her mother's sneer, 'Blackheads'. Shaking off the memory, she stood up and soaped her bush.

Tashie shouted outside the door, 'Which dress would you like tonight? Joyce has a gorgeous red job; would you like my little blue number or Mabs' green? You could try the yellow tomorrow.'

'I won't be here tomorrow.'

'What?'

'Miss Green is giving me a lift back to school.'

'No!'

'Yes.' Flora got out of the bath and wrapped herself in a towel. School towels, she thought, were skimpy beyond belief. Outside the door Tashie called, 'Can I come in?' Flora unbolted the door. 'Who arranged this lift?'

'Mrs Leigh.'

'The *cow*.'

'Tashie.'

'Well, she *is*.'

'Not really, I am sure she—'

'So which dress will you wear? Blue? Green? Yellow?'

'I'd like to wear black,' said Flora.

Twenty-nine

'D'you think it kind to send the girl away?' Angus came into Milly's room from his dressing-room. 'Tie my tie.' He stood in front of his wife in dinner jacket and trousers, black tie dangling. 'You do it much better than I can.'

'You manage well enough when you are on your own.' She reached up to tie the bow.

'Was it kind?' Their faces were close; she could see the white stubble on his cheeks and smell the soap from his bath. 'There are several more days before her term starts,' he said.

'Dearest, it is politic. There.' She had tied the bow. 'She has been here long enough. When the chance of a lift with Miss Green came up, it seemed a God-sent opportunity.'

'Personally, I would leave the Almighty out of it.' Angus sat on the edge of his wife's bed. Although he too slept in the bed, he thought of it as his wife's; his own single bed was in his dressing-room, seldom used. 'I do not think God had a finger in this pie,' he said. He watched Milly, still in her slip, brush her hair. There were white hairs a-plenty, but since she was fair they did not show in artificial light; his formerly brown hair was white, his moustache brindled. He watched her reflection. 'Well?'

Milly stood to put on her shoes; she felt more confident in high heels. 'I told you, darling, the men are looking at her. It wouldn't do if Cosmo— I saw her this evening with Nigel on the terrace. He caught hold of her hand. It probably meant nothing, but—' Angus watched his wife move to a cupboard and take out a dress. She had thickened, but her figure was still excellent, he thought, and hoped as he often did that she would not go in for this banting which was so popular. As she put the dress over her head her voice was muffled. 'Remember how worried we were about Mabs and Felix?'

'Nothing came of it.'

'Thank God it didn't.'

'Not so sure about it now; his father was a great friend. I can't stand Nigel's father; the fellow's a Liberal.'

'But Jef *wasn't* his father.' Milly's head appeared through the neck of the dress. She shrugged it down. 'Do me up, darling. Rosa admitted it.'

Angus left the bed to hook his wife's dress. 'Wish someone would invent something easier than these fiddly things. Stand still. Rosa, you should remember, is an inveterate joker. She was pulling your leg. You should not have asked her whether Jef was the father, it was begging for trouble.'

'But I *did* and she said he *wasn't*!'

'And it's drifted across Europe. One wonders how—' Angus hooked hook to eye.

'Not spread by me,' said Milly (too quickly?).

'Probably Rosa herself and Felix, too, I shouldn't be surprised. Bloody things, these fasteners, stand still.'

'You are tickling my back.'

'I've never told you, since you are sensitive about *faux pas*, but Felix is the spit of Rosa's brothers. Perhaps I should have. There is both fair and dark on her side, quite pronounced.'

'You mean?'

'Same nose, too. He has his uncle's nose.'

'Then I have made a fool of myself?'

'Yes, darling. There, all done.' Angus put his hands on Milly's shoulders and kissed the back of her neck. 'And while we are about it, I'd better tell you another rumour. It is said that he likes boys.'

'How appalling.' Milly looked horrified.

'I have a hunch that there isn't a word of truth in that either, but it's a wonderful out if you don't want to get tied. Rosa wants him to marry; he enjoys being a bachelor. What better alibi could he have?' Angus grinned. 'Fellow has his mother's humour.'

'Extremely dangerous.' Milly put on her rings, reached for her pearls. 'And stupid.'

'Which brings us back to the Trevelyan girl.'

'No, it doesn't.' Milly ran a comb through her hair, smoothed her eyebrows.

'Yes, it does. Parents should stand back and not manipulate.'

'Are you suggesting I interfere?'

'Yes, I am. We all do. I don't wish to labour the point but it would have done no harm to let the girl stay another few days. She has never been anywhere, stuck in a school by her parents all the year round. She is so ignorant of life, she might be a visitor from Mars. What possible harm could she—'

'Oh, Angus, shut up. It's done now. I'm sorry. Let's drop the subject. I have written a friendly letter to her mother that should help. Shall we go down and have a drink before dinner?'

'Very well, Millicent.'

Milly looked at her husband with annoyance; he never called her Millicent unless he was angry. She looked round her familiar room, the bedroom of their marriage. Mabs had been born here, Cosmo too. It was redolent with cherished intimacy. The door of the dressing-room was open; Angus' discarded day clothes lay scattered about, among them socks she had knitted him, as she had countless others of the same pattern all the years of their marriage: wool socks with cable stitch. She had been knitting a similar pair when she sat chatting with Rosa in Dinard. Rosa had said something which shocked her – she forgot the words, remembered the shock. She closed the dressing-room door. The servants would come up and tidy. Angus was waiting. She would put Miss Green on his right

at dinner, dear jolly Joyce on his left; this time
tomorrow the source of Angus' annoyance would
have left.

Thirty

Felicity Green did not take long changing for dinner; she washed her face and armpits, put on clean knickers and slip, and shrugged into a rust-coloured dress. The colour did not enhance her complexion, but what the hell, she thought, brushing her bobbed hair, I'll never improve on God's off day. She glared at her froglike face in the glass, meeting black intelligent eyes. She applied lipstick, patted on powder, bared her teeth in a snarl to make sure no red had strayed, transferred flapjack, comb and handkerchief to an evening bag and set off. She was anxious to get to the drawing-room before the rest of the house party and have a look round on her own. She was planning a novel; it had struck her on her previous visit that the Coppermalt drawing-room was worth scrutiny. The room was empty except for Nigel, standing irresolute by the drinks tray. He said: 'Hello.' He had not yet changed for dinner.

'We met the other day.' Felicity held out her hand.

'So we did.' Nigel stared, trying to remember.

'League of Nations,' Felicity prompted.

'Right.' Nigel pumped her hand up and down. 'Right. Try him on that German chap again. Want a drink?' He released her hand.

'I'll help myself.' Felicity poured herself a small tot of whisky. 'Somebody's been at the decanter.'

'I have,' said Nigel, nodding. 'Poor old decanter.'

Felicity said: 'Um,' and watched him rock on his heels. It was not for her to interfere. 'Suppose you went and changed for dinner?' she said, interfering.

Nigel said 'What?', affronted and loud.

Gage the butler came in. He walked softly to the fireplace, swept ash, plumped a cushion on a sofa, came to inspect the drinks tray and pursed his lips. 'Tsk, tsk. Dinner in a quarter of an hour, sir.' He picked up the whisky decanter and Nigel's glass and left.

Nigel followed the butler.

Felicity explored the room. Admirable flower arrangements, *Vogue*, *Tatler*, *Blackwoods Magazine*, *Royal Geographical* and *The Field* ranged on a sofa table. Pot-pourri in bowls. The view from the French windows pastoral: lawn sloping to a haha, fields dipping to the river, various trees strategically planted, a cedar on the lawn to the right of the house and, further away, beech, oak and lime.

The butler returned with the replenished decanter, glanced round, went to close the French windows and left.

Felicity re-opened the French windows. There remained a sniff of Nigel. What I need, she thought, are photographs on the piano – dogs, débutantes, royalty, or a peer in coronation robes. She was unrewarded, except for a few badly focused snapshots under a paperweight: Mabs aged about twelve with a dog; Cosmo in baggy shorts, a tooth missing, both knees bandaged, with another dog; several snaps of yet more dogs. She opened a sofa table drawer. There they were: the silver frames, Edwardian ladies, hair heaped high, bulging busts over minimal waists. Angus and Milly's pre-war wedding, Mabs in débutante feathers and train looking sulky, Angus in staff officer's uniform with rows of medals. And, at the back of the drawer, a person she recognized as minor royalty. But no peers. Felicity shut the drawer and crossed to examine the contents of a glass-fronted bookcase.

'Pretty dull,' said Cosmo, who had come in unobserved. 'My family aren't great readers. Are you looking for something?'

Felicity said, 'Yes, country house atmosphere. I am plotting a novel.'

Cosmo said, 'Nothing much happens here.'

'No?'

'Nothing out of the ordinary. No rows, no scandals—'

'Your father?'

'Retired generals are expected to be peppery.'

Somewhere in the house a girl shouted, 'Cosmo, where are you?'

Cosmo said, 'Excuse me,' and left. Felicity moved to a writing table. Someone had recently used fresh blotting paper. Above the table was a Regency mirror; she held the blotter to it. 'Expect me sooner or later.' 'I shall be coming your way.'

'One of the messages is in Russian,' said Hubert, as he came in. 'I'm not really sure what it says. Can Flora be trusted? There are others in German, French, Italian and so on.'

'A game?' (When caught in an anti-social act, be brazen.) 'I am snooping,' she said.

It was Hubert who looked embarrassed. 'Sort of, a bit silly, really. I am thinking of dropping it. I don't do it often,' he excused himself.

From upstairs Joyce shouted, 'Hubert, where are you? Buck up and bring it, if you're going to.'

'Oh, sorry, I must go. Fetching them a bottle of this.' He held up a bottle of champagne. 'Joyce's idea; it's for the girls. I must—'

'Rush,' suggested Felicity.

'Yes.' Hubert hurried away.

Felicity replaced the blotter and strolled out onto the terrace. From open windows there came the sound of girls' voices. 'You look *wonderful*, nobody will – ah, *here's* Blanco. What an *age*. Come on, come on, open it.' The sound of a champagne cork. 'Flora first, it's Flora's gala. Drink up. No, no, you like it really. Oh, Nigel, what a sponge you are, there'll be none left for— No, *no*, Flora, you *cannot* wear those, it spoils the *line*, *la ligne*! The whole idea is to look slinky. Stand still a minute while I – that's better. Oh, delicious.'

Felicity sniffed the jasmine, hoped the Trevelyan child would not chatter in the car; she would plot her chapter as she drove, spend the night in Lincoln perhaps, make London the next day. She could put the girl on a train from there if she was bored with her. Had Mrs Leigh the faintest idea what an imposition it was? She would tell the General at dinner about the Germans' plans for new roads; he was the sort of man who would approve, as he probably did of Mussolini's trains. Had these *anciens militaires* the remotest notion of the danger of dictators? There must be no indigestible row this evening. This sleepy atmosphere was just what she needed.

'Oh good, you have given yourself a drink,' said Milly, coming through the drawing-room onto the terrace. 'What a lovely evening. May I give you a refill? It was sherry, wasn't it?'

'Whisky, actually. Neat.'

'Oh.'

'No thanks.'

'Oh? Well, I shall have a small sherry. I must admit to enjoying the end of the summer holiday. We are off to Perthshire in a few days to rally our strength for Mabs' wedding. Such fun. I shall put you on Angus' right, and he can have jolly Joyce on his other side.'

Milly was looking smug, Felicity observed. 'I will steer clear of controversial topics,' she said.

'Oh, that. Wasn't he absurd?'

Felicity positioned herself near the fireplace, from where she could watch Angus come in smiling jovially, then Cosmo with Hubert, followed by Nigel and Henry who stood near the drinks table but did not drink. Hubert came up to her and began explaining a complex relationship with an elderly relation which had to do with the writing on the blotter. There was a stinginess which had turned him into a gambler. 'I bolster my allowance at Oxford with bridge and backgammon. I don't somehow trust the horses or dogs, do you?'

'I thought all country people trusted horses and dogs.' Felicity was barely listening.

'Oh, we do,' said Hubert. 'But not—' Damn the woman, plain as a currant bun, not even pretending to listen.

209

'Is it Henry who is engaged to Mabs, or Nigel?'
Felicity was watching Nigel. 'They are so alike.'

'Henry is engaged to Tashie, Nigel to Mabs. They look alike because they were at the same school, work in the same merchant bank and have the same tailor and the same political opinions.'

'But one is drunk, the other sober,' said Felicity.

'They can't be. There was only one bottle of champagne between eight of us—'

'Whisky and champagne don't mix.'

Hubert stared at Nigel. 'Oh my,' he said. 'Dear, dear.'

The butler opened the drawing-room door and announced dinner.

'What can the girls be up to?' said Milly.

Angus looked at his pocket watch. 'Don't they know what time we have dinner? When have we ever had it at any time other than half-past eight?' He closed the watch with a snap.

Cosmo muttered something in his mother's ear.

'Apparently it's Flora's last night,' said Milly, looking around.

'As if you didn't know,' grumped Angus.

Milly paid no attention. 'The girls are dressing her up to look especially – er – they've been lending her their frocks.' She turned to Felicity. 'She has nothing much of her own. I wondered, Miss Green—'

'Do call me Felicity,' said Felicity.

'– Felicity,' Milly raised her voice, 'whether, as you pass through London, you would stop a moment at our little dressmaker in Beauchamp Place? It wouldn't take more than a few minutes and wouldn't be out of your way. Angus and I want to give her a party dress of her own—'

'Do we?' said Angus. 'First I've—'

'Yes,' said Milly, 'we do.'

'Hum,' said Angus. 'Blood money.'

She's got a nerve, thought Felicity. She began counting the threads of various emotions at large in the room. The butler in the doorway, a prey to suppressed irritation; Milly, now a little fearful, obstinate, placatory;

210

Angus suspicious; Nigel straining to appear sober; Cosmo and Hubert expectant. Expectant of what? (Cancel the peaceful country house.)

Milly, speaking in the room where talk had dwindled, said: 'Ah, I think I hear them at last. We'll go in, Gage,' she said to the butler, 'as soon as they've made their "entrance". The girls have done all they can to give Flora a good time,' she said to Felicity. 'She's such a child.'

'If that's a child,' said Nigel thickly, as the girls came into the room, 'you could fool me.'

It was the cut of the dress which caused the effect. Long enough to cover her feet, demurely high at the neck, it had sleeves which reached the elbow. The heavy black silk clung to Flora's body faithfully, outlining curve of breasts and buttocks, hinting at the dimple of navel and V-shaped mound above long thighs; a simple dress, its matt sheen complemented Flora's pale skin. She wore no makeup or jewelry. It was, too, obvious that she wore nothing else. Felicity Green whispered, 'La ligne,' sighing with pleasure as she looked round.

Nigel staring, Henry with mouth open as though about to shout; Angus pursing his lips in a silent whistle, Cosmo's eyes shining, Hubert gulping with sudden emotion, Milly flushing an unkind red.

Mabs, Tashie and Joyce bustled in behind Flora, fluting through lipsticked lips:

'So sorry to be late, Mother.'

'Do forgive us, Mrs Leigh.'

'We are terribly sorry, Milly, dear Milly,' in what sounded like a rehearsed chorus. They closed protectively round Flora in their red, green and blue dresses. Flora did not speak.

The 'entrance' lasted a few seconds, searing itself like a car crash on Milly's memory. 'Shall we go in?' she said. 'You know what cook is like when she's made a soufflé.'

Angus offered Felicity his arm and led the way into the dining-room, seating her on his right while Joyce took the chair on his left. Nigel and Henry, Felicity observed, sequestered places on either side of Flora. Hubert and Cosmo sat opposite with Mabs and Tashie, leaving Milly slightly apart, looking forlorn.

'Shall I tell you about the master plan for roads in Germany?' Felicity helped herself to soufflé.

I wish I was as young as that lot, thought Angus; one wouldn't have hesitated. 'I thought you spoke with a stammer. Forgive me for drawing attention to it.' What the hell is Mabs up to? It never bodes good when she looks like that; she's using the girl as a stalking horse. Somebody's in for a tumble. Angus glanced along the table at his wife sitting with eyes downcast. Flora's eyes were downcast too; they usually were. 'Your stammer,' he said, 'is rather fetching. Did you say roads?'

'My stammer is a social convenience,' said Felicity. 'It gives me time to answer a question with an appropriate quip. It is not often uncontrollable.' She swallowed a feathery mouthful of soufflé.

Angus said, 'Aha, I see,' helping himself to soufflé. 'Hurry up with the wine,' he murmured to the butler.

He does not know how much has already flowed, surmised Felicity. 'Delicious soufflé,' she said. 'Your cook is a paragon.'

'A little vino loosens the conversation, does it not?' Angus beamed at Felicity.

'So long as it does not loosen too much.' No, he has no idea. Joyce, hitherto silent, snorted. 'Do you want to hear about the roads or not?' Felicity asked.

'Ah yes, the German roads. Do you imagine that child is wearing knickers?' Angus lowered his voice.

'Imaginary ones, I'd say.'

'Has she the remotest idea of the electrifying shock she has dealt our male senses? She might to all intents and purposes be naked.'

'She would look less indecent,' murmured Joyce, overhearing.

'I am sure no idea – or perhaps half,' said Felicity.

'It's my dress,' said Joyce. 'Tash stripped her knickers off; you should have seen Hubert and Cosmo's faces.

212

The line of the knickers showing through made the dress look common.'

'C-c-common.' Felicity tried not to laugh. 'Shall I keep the roads of Germany for another time? They have military potential.'

'What we require at this moment is some form of suppressant,' said Angus. 'I think my daughter is about to bolt.'

'He's given to horsey turns of phrase,' said Joyce, who seemed to be enjoying herself. 'He's right, though, the old darling. Hark, I hear a warning note.'

'Your speech impediment—' Angus strove to ignore an eruption further down the table. Then: 'Oh I *say*!' He gave up polite conversation to glare down the table at his daughter. 'What?' Felicity watched with interest. In a novel, she thought, trouble would have been brewing for a long time; was it possible Flora was responsible? Were those velvety brown eyes the cause of Mabs' raised voice? 'What's going on?' Angus asked loudly.

Mabs shouted: 'I'm breaking off my engagement, Father, that's what's going on.'

(Quiet country house atmosphere, my foot, thought Felicity.)

'During dinner?' enquired Angus, forking soufflé into his mouth.

'For ever,' shouted Mabs.

'Don't shout, darling. We are not deaf,' said Milly.

'Why?' asked Angus, as the parlourmaid removed his plate.

(I couldn't possibly write it down as it's happening, thought Felicity.)

'He's *boring*, I can't stand his clothes, he drinks, he gambles, I can't stand his conversation, he doesn't *wash*, he smells of old sweat and number two.'

'Steady on, old girl,' said Nigel.

'And I can't stand the thought of going to bed with him. He's got short legs.'

'A long whatsit,' countered Nigel, beginning to bristle. 'You wait and see.'

'Oh *dear*,' said Milly. 'Stop it, Mabs, this isn't—'

'And he's not "my dear", nor will he ever be.' Mabs in spate seemed unable to stop. 'You stopped me getting off with Felix, you—'

'Felix got off with my brother *and* his girlfriend.' Joyce, elbows on the table, leaned towards Mabs. 'Felix likes everything and everyone. He's the greatest all-rounder of all time.'

'What are you talking about?' exclaimed Milly. 'Joyce, please!'

'You only want me to marry Nigel because he's got money, makes money and is inheriting a house; all you think of is class and security.'

'Not all that again,' said Cosmo.

'Give me back the ring then,' said Nigel. 'I'll give it to Flora. Flora will marry me like a shot, won't you, Flora?'

'No, I won't,' said Flora.

'Flora's too young for you,' shouted Cosmo. 'Anyway, she belongs to Blanco and me.'

'You keep out of this,' shrieked Mabs. 'Flora is too good for you, she'll go far.'

'I wouldn't doubt that,' said Angus under his breath.

'She's much too good, just look at her, lovely, demure, virgin—' Tashie was not to be left out.

'I'd hardly say—' began Henry.

'Who asked you to say anything,' snarled Nigel. 'This is between my fiancée and myself.'

'I'm not your fiancée – I've broken—'

'Mabs, darling, please—' said Milly.

'Shall I ask cook to delay the duck, madam?' asked the butler at Milly's elbow.

'Yes, no, no.'

Angus stood up. 'Shut up and get out, all of you. I will not have this behaviour at my dinner table.'

'You often do,' said Joyce pertly.

(That's interesting, thought Felicity.)

'Out,' said Angus.

'I don't know what all this is in aid of. Do you want to break *our* engagement, Tashie?' Henry tried to lower the temperature. 'Be *à la mode*?' he asked conversationally.

'This is not a joke.' Tashie's voice rose several decibels. 'Henry, you mustn't *joke*.'

'Will you get out?' Angus roared. 'I mean it. All of you. Not you, Miss Green.'

'Felicity. Do call me Felicity.'

'All right, Felicity, you stay and don't you go, Flora, you haven't done anything. And you, Henry, stay to keep me company.'

'Sir,' said Henry, looking unhappily at Tashie.

'Stay,' said Angus. Henry stayed.

Mabs, Tashie, Cosmo and Hubert pushed back their chairs and trooped out. Nigel gulped the last of his wine and followed them.

'Perhaps we could get on with our dinner,' said Angus, 'while your daughter comes to her senses.'

'Our daughter,' said Milly, exasperated, then, 'What's it like to have your first proposal?' she asked Flora.

Flora put her napkin on the table and left the room. Henry got up and followed her.

'Was that necessary?' Angus glared at his wife.

'She started it,' said Milly, meeting his eye.

'Duck, Miss?' said the butler, proffering the *entrée* dish.

Thirty-one

Angus, Milly, Tashie, Henry and Joyce came out to watch Gage stow suitcases in the boot of Felicity's car. Mabs, Nigel, Cosmo and Hubert were noticeable by their absence. The family dogs grouped languidly around the front door, mouths slightly agape, benevolent tails wagging.

'Please say goodbye to the others for me,' said Felicity, in the role of departing guest. 'I am so sorry to miss them.'

Milly stood beside her husband, legs slightly apart, like a boxer preparing to parry a blow. She held the dog Bootsie against her chest. 'Of course I will,' she said. 'I apologize for their lack of manners. They must still be snoring. It takes something they think really important to rouse them in the mornings.' Milly let her eye pass over Flora waiting quietly near Tashie and Joyce.

Sensing the maggot jealousy Felicity turned to Angus. 'I meant to explain, General Leigh. Those ideas about roads; none have been built yet. Hitler wrote this book, *Mein Kampf*. It's all in that—'

'I don't read German.' Angus' eyes rested appraisingly on Flora.

'It is bound to be translated.' Felicity wished the butler would make haste with the luggage; he had earlier loftily refused her proffered tip. 'It would be worth your while,' she said, wishing she had the nerve to add, 'you old fool.' (Somebody might have told her not to tip the servants, that it was against house rules.)

'Isn't it time someone taught that child the facts of life?' Angus spoke thoughtfully.

'I assumed, after last night's exhibition, that she knew them,' Milly answered. 'Or were you about to volunteer?' she gritted between her teeth. She had dressed, Felicity noted, in tweeds, as though in response to an unwelcome breeze, yet the day was warm. 'When Miss Green has gone,' she said to the butler, 'see that somebody wakes Mr Cosmo and his friend.'

The butler raised a shoulder and gave a half-nod towards Tashie and Joyce, who stood attentively smiling.

'I can't thank you enough for putting me up.' Felicity abandoned *Mein Kampf* and, hoping to speed departure, began shaking hands and moving towards her car. 'It's been lovely to break my journey, goodbye,' she said. 'Goodbye, goodbye,' she said to Tashie, Joyce and Henry. 'I have so enjoyed meeting you.'

Flora extended her hand to Milly. 'Thank you, Mrs Leigh, for having me; it's been a wonderful—'

'You must come again, my dear. I'll write.' Milly pecked towards Flora's cheek. In her arms Bootsie growled.

'I know you won't,' Flora said quietly as she turned towards Angus. 'Goodbye,' she said, 'and thank you for your kindness.'

'Won't you give an old man a kiss?' Angus put an arm round Flora, drew her to him and kissed her. 'Tell you what, when I'm down in London I'll invite you to lunch at my club. How would that be?'

Flora did not answer and was immediately surrounded by Tashie, Joyce and Henry who hugged and kissed her as she walked towards the car, crying: 'Goodbye, safe journey, write to us, see you soon, don't forget,' so that the attendant dogs, infected by their enthusiasm, began barking hysterically.

Flora did not look back as Felicity drove down the drive. She exposed only a slight profile under her school panama. In blouse and skirt, lisle stockings and clumpy shoes she looked a typical schoolgirl. Felicity wondered whether to break the silence enclosing

217

them. 'Mind the dog,' said Flora, looking out of the car window.

'What dog?' Felicity braked nervously.

'Bootsie, Mrs Leigh's treasure. She's on your side now. She chases cars, does Bootsie.'

'Damn.' Felicity, who disliked dogs, accelerated past the scuttling animal.

'Missed her,' Flora sat back and crossed her legs. 'Just.'

Two miles down the valley Cosmo and Hubert barred the way. Felicity stopped abruptly. They opened the car door and pulled Flora out and, holding her between them, kissed and caressed her, nuzzled her neck, stroked her hair, tipped the panama onto the road. Felicity watched, astonished. Flora freed herself, bent to retrieve her hat and scrambled back into the car, shutting the door. She was very pale. She waved a hand, indicating that Felicity should drive on.

Looking back in the mirror, Felicity Green saw Cosmo and Hubert watching until a bend in the road hid them from sight. Yet, rounding the bend, her novelist's imagination registered Cosmo striking Hubert violently in the face. Beside her Flora, face hidden by the panama, sat in silence.

After a while Felicity let out her breath and said: 'Well!'

Flora did not respond.

Felicity wished her passenger would say something, do something; weep, for instance? As the miles flew past she started to feel angry. 'I did not notice Mabs and Nigel troubling to see you off,' she observed. 'Or shall we find them, too, lying in wait to give me a coronary?' She spoke spitefully. Flora had been imposed on her; with the girl beside her she could not possibly compose her chapter.

'They are too busy,' Flora sounded jubilant, not weepy. She slapped her knees as an old man might, tipped up the brim of her hat and laughed a long chuckling laugh. 'Nigel said to look in *The Times* in nine months' time.' Her laughter escaped in little gusts

218

and rushes. 'They are all *right*,' she said, 'all *right*!'

Felicity said, 'Oh,' and 'I see,' glancing sideways at Flora. She desperately wanted to ask what had happened after the row at dinner. The house had been strangely quiet. She had played three-handed bridge with Angus and Milly; it was still quiet when they had gone to bed. The young people had disappeared. Looking at the upturned brim of Flora's panama she decided not to ask.

Then, puzzled as to why she would not ask – Flora was after all only a child – she was faced with the uneasy answer: the girl was not a child. There was no question of it in the way Cosmo and Hubert behaved, murmuring endearments, holding her intimately. Words she used sparingly or not at all in her novels filtered into her reluctant mind: lust, passion, loins? She felt a pang of retrospective sympathy for Milly, found herself flushing. The previous evening Flora had looked shockingly innocent in the black dress; now in the unbecoming school uniform she was sensual and desirable. The blow she had seen Cosmo deal Hubert was not imaginary. Felicity Green, who prided herself on her breadth of mind, was shocked.

PART THREE

Thirty-two

'You are early!' said the receptionist.

'I don't mind waiting.' Flora shuffled through a pile of magazines to find *The Tatler*. 'If I am cluttering up your waiting-room, I'll wait in the hall.'

The receptionist was new. Her predecessor would have known that she came early, that sometimes she lingered in the waiting-room after her appointment; that she came every holiday before the start of term.

Flora sat with her back to the window beyond which a melancholy sea ground shingle against the wall of the promenade. Opposite her an old gentleman sat reading *The Field*. 'When you have finished with that,' Flora said, 'might I have a look?'

'Have it now,' said the old man. 'There is an excellent article on wild geese.'

'I am not so much interested in wild geese as in tame humans,' Flora murmured. 'Please don't hurry,' she said. 'I'll skip through this first.' She raised *The Tatler* for him to see.

'You can have *The Sketch* if you like,' said a grey-haired matron. 'I can't concentrate. I have an abscess.' She handed the magazine to Flora. The receptionist called her name and she hurried away. Flora laid *The Sketch* on her knee, ignoring a hungry look from a woman waiting with a fidgety child. The old man stopped reading *The Field* and took note of Flora. About seventeen, he surmised, still at school, vide the uniform, good legs, beautiful skin. Figure? Impossible to gauge under those garments. Nothing wrong with her teeth. He eased his denture with his tongue where

223

it pressed on his gums. Lovely hair and eyes. Strange the way she flicked through the magazine. 'I hope you find what you are looking for.' He was unable to control his curiosity.

'Sometimes I do, usually I don't.' She looked up briefly.

Could those eyelashes be real?

The receptionist called his name; he got stiffly to his feet and handed Flora *The Field* which, thanking him, she laid on top of *The Sketch* in her lap. The woman with the child hissed, 'Really!' It was possible Flora did not hear; she finished riffling through *The Tatler* and put it back on the centre table. The woman compressed her lips and resisted picking it up. Flora started on *The Sketch*.

A year ago her finger, sliding on the pages of a similar magazine, had evoked the memory of cool skin on Cosmo's inner arm and, her mind leaping, she remembered too the salty taste of Hubert's eyelids when they kissed on that last night at Coppermalt.

Banished by Angus from the dinner table, they had run from the house across the lawn. At the haha she had taken off her shoes to tread barefoot on the soft grass, reaching the river between Cosmo and Hubert, where Mabs, a little apart, was clinched in bitter argument with Nigel. Then Henry, loping along with Tashie and Joyce, brought champagne. They had raided the cellar; Gage, the butler, had connived. Hubert had laughed and said, 'He is a closet socialist.' Tracing her finger across the slippery page, Flora remembered that it was Joyce who suggested they should swim while the champagne cooled at the edge of the pool.

'I shall swim in my knickers and bra,' Joyce said. 'I've done it with my Irish cousins, it's perfectly decent.' She had taken off her dress and slip and hung them on the branch of a tree.

Tashie followed suit, and Mabs, whose argument had ground to a halt, undressed also, while the men divested themselves of dinner jackets, trousers and stiff shirts, hanging them among the dresses and slips in the moonlight until the tree became host to a band of ghostly dancers.

'And Flora? What about Flora?'

'Flora, you must swim.'

'Come on, Flora, try,' said Tashie.

'She can't,' said Mabs. 'She has nothing on underneath.'

'It's dark,' said Joyce (which was partly true).

Then Hubert and Cosmo took the hem of the black dress and peeled it up over her head. 'Now you look decent,' they said. 'Positively respectable. Infinitely more decent than dressed.'

Joyce said, 'If that's how things are, I'll keep my knickers dry,' and she hung her panties and bra on the tree and dived into the river, but not before it was noted that the hair of her head was no more orange than that between her legs. The others also draped their underclothes among the branches. Swimming naked in the peaty water, she had learned the feel of Cosmo's skin and Hubert's eyelids, cool in the water, cool as marble. Sitting in the dentist's waiting-room, Flora remembered. It was later on the riverbank, drinking champagne, wrapped in Hubert's dinner jacket, that Hubert leaned across her to speak to Cosmo: 'This is becoming serious. I don't want to fight, but I'll take you on at any game you like—' and Cosmo, also leaning across her, 'I thought you only gambled for money, not—' their faces practically touching. Then Hubert, fumbling in the pocket of his coat as though it hung on a hanger and not across Flora's shoulders, found dice and said harshly, nastily, 'Winner takes all.'

And she, alarmed, had leaned away from them, supporting herself on her hands while they stared at each other across her body. She said, 'No. No. You must not,' her voice sharp with a sense of loss. She remembered in the dentist's waiting-room her frisson of fear.

Mabs had called to them, 'What's going on? Listen, all of you, Nigel and I have made it up!' She sounded so happy, Flora remembered.

Nigel had popped another bottle and there had been a sense of relief and jollity which spread to Cosmo and Hubert, who renewed their discussion but on a jokey, amiable plane.

'I saw her first, she was on a beach in France with a dog,' claimed Cosmo. 'So she's mine.'

Wrapped in Hubert's jacket, Flora murmured, 'His name was Tonton.' She had had to move her legs, for there was a thistle in the grass. She remembered the thistle.

Hubert countered: 'I stopped her drowning. Technically she belongs to me, like salvage.'

'Make up your mind who you belong to.' Which of them had said that? They were both a little drunk (and I suppose I was too).

They had flanked her on that summer night, naked but not marble. She had answered lightly, to hide a confusion of feelings, that she could not, would not, decide and they, sensing her discomfort, had said: 'Very well, we will share,' and 'She is too young to decide,' 'Too young,' teasing her gently now, without passion. She had been happy lying between them on the river bank while Cosmo kissed her mouth and, nuzzling open the jacket, her breasts. Then Hubert, kissing her roughly, had pressed his hand over her pubic hair, muttering, 'I need to do that,' so that her sense of happiness was superseded by something startling and pleasurable.

Then Mabs, interrupting, her arms round Nigel, stood above them. 'You'll catch your deaths of cold, you licentious creatures.' And Nigel said, 'We are off to do a little premarital fornicating in bed. Not for us the great outdoors. Mabs has forgiven my short legs.'

And Joyce, searching round the tree with Tashie for her clothes, said: 'I can't find my things anywhere. This is worse than the January sales. Let's get back and find something to eat, I'm starving. Oh there they are, my poor dear knickers.' And Mabs again, laughing, calling over her shoulders as she left, 'But should you need a chaperone, Flora, we can stay.'

226

Turning the pages of the magazine Flora was retrospectively rueful. She had not fornicated (she had since learnt the meaning of the word from her English mistress's *OED*); such an act was impossible with Hubert with Cosmo present and vice versa. They had dressed and, on the way up to the house, one of them said: 'You don't know what Mabs and Nigel mean to do, do you?'

Barefoot, rather chilled now, holding up her skirt to avoid the dew, she had protested that of course she knew.

'No, you don't. You are still at the stage when you think the chap in the Old Testament who spilled his seed on the ground was a butter-fingered gardener.'

They had yelped with laughter, laughed so much they staggered about, gone off into hoots and toots.

There was no need for Milly Leigh to be so horrible the next day.

'Mr Smart is ready for you,' said the receptionist.

Flora lay back in the chair. 'I won't be coming to you any more, Mr Smart.'

'Leaving school? Joining your parents in India? Open, please. I'll just have a little look round. You must be counting the days.'

'Arrgh.'

'Nothing wrong that I can see. No doubt it will be wedding bells in no time.'

'Arrgh.'

'There we are. Remember to brush well round that little bit. Jolly good. Rinse.'

Flora spat. 'I shall miss your magazines.'

'Oh?'

'Source of information complementary to *The Times*.'

'Come again?'

'I look at the photographs.'

'Ah.'

They shook hands. 'Goodbye,' they said. 'Goodbye.'

'I shall be attending to your children's teeth in ten years. It happens, you know.'

Flora said, 'God forbid,' before she could stop herself.

She ran out into the wind. The tide was smashing at the stony beach, hurling cobbles high onto the prom; she wished she could cast off the prospect of India with similar power. She had learned little from her study of the dentist's magazines. There had been photographs of Mabs' wedding. They had all been there: Angus, Milly, Cosmo. Then Cosmo in a group at an Oxford ball with a girl; nothing of Hubert. Tashie's wedding, similar photographs, smaller bridesmaids and a back view of Cosmo, a front view of Hubert scowling. A letter in *The Field* about mayfly by Angus. A photograph of Milly at a point-to-point with Bootsie on a lead. Announcements in *The Times* of Mabs' baby, a bare eight months after the wedding, and Tashie, a son, a year after hers. Joyce had announced her engagement to a Hungarian, only to cancel it six weeks later. Once in *The Sketch* there had been a photograph of her own father at a shoot, wearing a topee, holding a rifle, standing by a dead tiger. It was a far cry from Coppermalt.

It would have been sensible to forget Coppermalt. She received no invitation to Mabs' wedding, nor had Milly written. Flora had not expected her to, not after Felicity Green had taken the trouble to deviate from her route across London to call in at Irena Tarasova's in Beauchamp Place to order a party dress for which Milly would pay.

Dodging the spray on the prom, Flora thought of her first sight of la Tarasova's London establishment. Less homely than the crowded room at Dinard, it smelt rich. Irena, become smart, had lost her timidity. There was no lingering whiff of Imperial Russia, no crystal ball, no backgammon, no cards, no Prince Igor. Instead a photograph by Lenare of an English duchess, lady-in-waiting to the Queen.

She had refused point blank to have the dress.

Flora recollected Irena's consternation with satisfaction and Felicity Green's irritation with glee. She had been so angry she had decanted her with her suitcase at Waterloo to finish her trek to school by train. There had since been a derogatory review of Felicity's novel in *The Times*. Perhaps the chief benison of Coppermalt had been Nigel's suggestion? While waiting for her train, after being dumped by Felicity, she had bought her first copy of the paper.

After this initial chill there was renewed contact with Irena. Allowed on day trips to London in the holidays to visit museums, she called instead of the V and A on Irena, in the hope of titbits of news which Mabs and Tashie might let drop, when they came for their fittings, of Hubert and Cosmo. And since Dolly, formerly Shovelhalfpenny, also had clothes made by Irena, might there not be news of Felix? She was not proud of these visits; it would have been better to forget Coppermalt, as its denizens had forgotten her. A few picture postcards casually sent could not be considered remembering in any serious sense.

There had been cards from Venice and Kitzbühl from Mabs and Tashie's honeymoons. A random card from Joyce from New York. A card from Paris signed 'love Hubert and Cosmo'. 'We remembered you wanted A. Tarasov's address; here it is.' And months later several cards in quick succession from Athens, Rome, Budapest, Berlin and Istanbul, always signed 'Cosmo and Hubert' or 'Hubert and Cosmo with love'. Love on a picture postcard was as worthless as a heart worn on a sleeve; people on holiday sat writing postcards while waiting for the waiter to bring them their espresso. She had seen her Italian governess do it. Her own cards sent in reply, picturing the pier or the downs behind the town, were of monumental insignificance. She would have liked to send some of the *louche* cards on sale in the summer season, full of *double-entendres*, but the mistresses watched what one bought and confiscated the unsuitable.

But now, with India inevitable and looming, her mother had written to Irena listing the clothes Flora must have. Three evening dresses, three day, one garden party, two tennis. She had chosen the colours, stipulating that each must be of different design so that they could be copied by cheap Indian fingers. Flora had not been consulted. She picked up a stone and hurled it at the sea. 'I hate my mother,' she shouted into the wind, and remembered Tashie that first day at Coppermalt wishing that something awful would happen to her mother.

Amazing, Irena had remarked during the fittings as she pinned and hitched, amazing that Flora's and Vita's measurements were so similar. 'Stand still, Flora, hold yourself up. Your posture is not as good as your mother's. You slouch.'

Flora had sneered, 'Posture,' filling the word with contempt. 'She wants the clothes for herself; in no time I shall be wearing the copies.'

'What a dreadful idea!' exclaimed Irena, to whom it had already occurred. 'What a mind you have.'

Flora had snorted. 'You know I'm right.'

'I made a dress like this for Mabs; she always asks after you. Turn round and stand still. I want to pin the hem.'

Flora was not deceived. Mabs knew her address. My address is 'out of sight, out of mind', she had thought, cruelly balancing it against the love and kindness of Coppermalt.

Gripping the cold rail of the promenade above the ugly sea, she wished with all her heart that she had never been to Coppermalt, never fallen in love with Felix, Cosmo and Hubert. If none of that part of her existed, she could face the trip to India to join her parents and conform to their mores; as it was she felt lost, alien, unnatural. Gripping the iron rail she yelled into the wind, 'I am unnatural,' and added for good effect, 'I am lost,' before breaking into a run along the prom, up the hill and past the playing fields to the school, where tomorrow the other girls who loved their parents and longed to rejoin them and get married to suitable people would be arriving back from their holidays.

She was sent for by the headmistress in her study.

'Sit down, Flora. I have a letter from your father.' (He writes such dry and boring letters. I have great

230

difficulty answering them. And my mother's are worse, all about parties at the Club and people I don't know; she can't find mine very fascinating about Latin, maths and hockey scores.) 'Flora, are you listening?'

'Yes, I am.'

'It is bad news, I'm afraid.'

'Oh?'

'Rather dreadful—'

'?'

'There is a letter for you, too.'

'Thanks.' Flora took the letter. (The stamps are nice, though Blanco would doubtless sneer at the Emperor's crown; why do I call him Blanco? He's Hubert.) 'What's—' The headmistress looked distressed. (A nice woman, I've always quite liked her. Well, like is a strong word, let's say she's a lot better than some.) 'What is it, Miss—' She gripped her father's letter.

'Your mother has been bitten by a rabid dog.' The headmistress leaned forward, kind myopic eyes full of sympathy. 'The dog had rabies.' She underlined the point as though Flora was stupid.

But I am not stupid, Flora thought, as she felt her throat constrict and blood thunder in her ears. I am not. She held her father's letter tightly between her fingers. 'The poor dog,' she whispered.

'Of course your mother will recover,' said the headmistress. 'I believe the treatment is rather awful, but—'

'Stomach injections.' Flora stared at the headmistress. Was this the sort of ignoble awfulness Tashie had visualized? 'Not the sort of thing one would wish on one's worst enemy.' She had begun to shout. 'I'm sorry,' she said. 'I was shouting.'

'It's understandable,' said the headmistress, who prided herself on this particular gift. 'I understand.' But she didn't understand Flora's expression at all; she had an air of pleasure, relief. Whatever next? I must not be so imaginative.

Thirty-three

On the maidan the Governor's A.D.C. reined his pony in beside Denys. 'How is Vita?'

Denys' mare laid back her ears. 'A lot better.' Denys pulled the mare's head up; she had been known to bite. 'One more injection and then it's over,' he said. 'Magnificent sunset.' He did not wish to discuss Vita's plight; it was an intrusion into their particular privacy.

'Dust in the atmosphere. Would Vita like a visit? Is she up to it?' Alec watched a blue jay streak across the improbable sunset.

'She's up to it.' Denys tilted his topee over his nose, reducing his view of the other man. 'Why don't you come and see her? She's pretty bored these days.' His tone implied that almost anyone would alleviate the boredom.

'I'll send my bearer with a chit to ask when it would be convenient. I have some books she might enjoy from the autumn list, sent out by Hatchards.' The Governor's A.D.C. was not easily deterred and quite able to upstage.

'You do that.' Denys turned his horse and headed towards his bungalow.

The other man called after him good-naturedly, 'Surly bugger.' If Vita had died, he thought, old Denys would have gone off his rocker.

As he dismounted and handed the reins to his saice Denys missed the greeting his dog Tara would have given him and felt a fresh pang. Why did it have to be his dog who caught rabies? In the bungalow it was quiet and still; he helped himself to whisky and thought of the Governor's A.D.C. Wasn't it time the fellow got married? Denys gulped his whisky. And time he stopped worshipping Vita? He was used to Vita's admirers, indeed he rather liked them; but some, worshipping longer than others, became a bore. He topped up his drink with soda water and carried it with him into the bedroom.

Vita was asleep on her back. Denys sat in a chair by the bed and observed her. Without make-up she looked young. He could count the crow's-feet at the corner of her eyes and the thin lines running from nose to mouth. He loved these tiny imperfections wrought by their joint lives, but knew that she, resenting any flaw in her looks, imagined he did too. She could not understand the distinction he made between the crow's-feet and the stretch marks on her stomach. Sipping his drink, he remembered with partial shame the occasion when he had chalked those traitorous lines in green. He had been drunk. He had said: 'I am jealous of who is responsible for these,' scoring the marks, pressing hard with the chalk. She had been afraid. She tried to laugh and called him kinky.

Since Tara had bitten her the line between nose and mouth was more pronounced; she had suffered, he thought tenderly, as much from the undignified treatment as from its pain. Hallucinating one night from the drugs the doctor had given her she had suddenly sat up, stared at him and said: 'I don't even know your name,' and, covering her face with her hands, turned away, thus proving, he thought wryly, something he had long suspected. Dotted the i's and crossed the t's, as it were.

It would be interesting to know, he thought, who the fellow was – one knew fairly well who he wasn't – although, after so long, the interest was academic. In this country with its interlocking society it was possible, indeed quite likely, that one had been introduced to the man. The idea amused Denys, as he sipped his drink and watched his sleeping wife; it consoled him a little for the loss of his dog, who would normally have

233

been sitting beside him with her jaw pressed on his knee trying to catch his eye. Tara had been jealous of Vita. She had bitten one of the soldiers at the barracks before they caught up with her and shot her, but she had gone for Vita first. Denys sighed, mourning his dog.

In the bed Vita stirred and turned on her side. She had been reading *Vogue* when she fell asleep; her finger still marked a page. He leaned forward to take her hand in his so that when she woke she would be reassured to know that he loved her, would give his love and all he possessed to make her happy.

At the height of his anxiety, when she was bitten, he had written to the girl; he had sent money and a list of luxuries to buck Vita up after this ghastly experience. Denys wondered what she looked like now; dreary school groups were no indication. Would he perhaps see a likeness? Catch a glimpse? Or was all this fruit of his imagination?

Vita opened her eyes. 'I was asleep. Have you been back long?' She smiled as he squeezed her hand. 'Nice.'

'Not long.' He bent to kiss her. 'Like a drink?'

'Not allowed.'

'A—'

'Not allowed!'

'Drink, then. Fruit juice? Tea?'

'Fruit juice.'

'I met your tame A.D.C.,' he said, bringing the drink. 'I thought he might do worse than marry your daughter.'

He always said 'your daughter'.

Vita smiled. 'What a suggestion.'

Denys lit a cigarette. 'Many men marry the daughters of mothers they lust after; I could quote you a dozen straight off.'

'Are you serious?'

'Why not? The fellow's got prospects.'

Vita sat up and propped her back with pillows. 'I don't care for the idea at all.'

'If you are going to discount all the men who want

to sleep with you, sweetie, you rather narrow the girl's field.'

Vita had long since stopped reminding him that Flora had a name. 'And you,' she said, 'what about you?' She drank her fruit juice, meeting his eye over the rim of the glass.

'What about me?' Denys teased. 'Jealous?'

'Of course. You will want to sleep with her if they do. It's logical,' she teased in turn.

Denys drained his glass. The thought of sleeping with Flora had not occurred to him. 'Don't put ideas into my head,' he said, watching her. They had always voiced their fears and thoughts – or Vita had. That was part of their charm for each other. 'Would that not be incest?' He was amused. 'I look forward to meeting her,' he said.

'It would be a very cruel thing to do to me, darling,' she said seriously.

Denys said, 'Yes, yes, it would. Perhaps after all I won't, but should I be tempted please remember it was you who planted the idea.'

Thirty-four

Rounding the corner of the square, Tashie saw that there was someone on her doorstep. Whoever it was had rung the bell and was waiting for the door to be opened. Anxious to get home, kick off shoes which pinched, relax on her sofa and have tea, Tashie slowed her pace; if she kept out of sight her maid would answer the bell and say she was out, and the caller would go away.

To make sure she was not seen Tashie took the right-hand pavement, putting the square garden between herself and the house; she could watch between the square railings.

As expected her maid opened the door, shook her head in answer to the caller, and closed it. The caller, a girl, went down the steps and walked away while Tashie complacently watched. Then she let out a yell and began running after the girl, shouting: 'Stop! Wait! I'm here! Wait, blast you, wait!'

The girl did not hear Tashie above the sound of traffic and walked on. In a moment she would round the corner into the busy street and be gone. Tashie kicked off her high-heeled shoes, put on a spurt and caught up as she was stepping onto a bus. 'Flora!'

Flora said: 'Oh, Tashie – your feet.'

Tashie said: 'You were coming to see me?'

'Yes.'

'Then come along, how lovely. What's the matter?' Something looked very much the matter.

'Do you remember you wished something really sordid would happen to my mother?'

'Of course I do.'

'Well, it has.'

'Oh good, what?'

'She's been bitten by a dog with rabies.'

'How splendid.'

'If you ladies are not getting on the bus, perhaps you'd allow other people to,' said a man who had been queueing.

'Oh do, do get on, oh please get onto the bus.' Tashie drew Flora aside.

'Your feet, Tashie—'

'I left my shoes on the pavement—'

'Wits, more like,' said the man, climbing onto the bus. 'I said wits.'

'Very witty,' said Tashie. 'Immensely humorous.' She had hold of Flora's arm. 'They pinched like blue murder. Oh, Flora, I haven't seen you for years. Come along, stockings laddered to shreds, we'll ask Molly to get us tea.' She led Flora back into the square. 'You remember Molly, she was under-housemaid at Coppermalt.'

'Your shoes? Yes, I do.'

'Darling, they were one of those fatal buys, a size too small. Sheer vanity, I'm always doing it. Here we are.' She put her latchkey into the lock. 'Safe home. Hello, Molly.'

'Look at your feet,' said Molly. 'Whatever happened?'

'I took them off. They are on the pavement across the square. You remember Flora, Molly?'

'Oh,' said Molly, 'yes, I thought – my sister takes that size, I'll just—' Molly scooted down the steps.

Tashie called after her. 'Will you get us tea when you come back?'

'Yes'm.'

'Not an utterly wasted buy, after all. She loves my clothes, does Molly. Come upstairs to the drawing-room and tell all. One of the arts of keeping servants is to wear clothes of the same size.'

'I don't know where to begin.'

'With the dog, of course.'

237

'Oh, the dog. It was my father's, an Airedale bitch. I believe he was very fond of her.'

'But a dog of taste and discernment even when her wits were affected.' Tashie sat on her sofa and massaged her feet.

'My mother might have died,' said Flora.

'You mean she *hasn't*? Oh Lord, what a disappointment. I thought from what you—'

'No.'

'The dog?'

'Yes.'

'Ah.'

Molly brought in tea which she put on a low table beside Tashie. 'Exactly my sister's size,' she said. 'She will be pleased. I thought you'd like crumpets.'

'Thank you, Molly. Delicious. Please remind me next time I set off to buy shoes what size I really take.'

'It would be against my nature, ma'am.' Molly left the room.

'Isn't she killing?' Tashie poured tea. 'She's in love with Jim. D'you remember the butler at Coppermalt? He's got a job in London now; he takes her to Communist meetings in King's Cross. He's joined the Party. Sugar?'

'One, please.'

Flora perched on a chair facing Tashie. Tashie looked smarter, more sophisticated and harder than when last seen; it had been folly to give in to the impulse to visit her. She sipped her tea. 'You've got a baby,' she said.

'Yes. Upstairs with Nanny. I'll take you to see him presently. How did you know?'

'I read it in *The Times*. I take it at school.'

'Nigel?'

'Yes.'

'Funny old Nigel. They are very happy, you know.'

'Good.' Flora put her cup aside, it tinkled in the saucer.

Tashie thought, This isn't a joke, I am at a loss. How long is it since we saw her? What's been going on? She's very pretty. Why has she come to me? She said: 'Please tell me what's the matter, Flora.'

Flora flushed. 'I don't want to be a bore.'

'Does this accident to your mother mean that India is off? Is that it?'

'No.'

'Oh.'

'I sail from Tilbury on Tuesday.'

(Tuesday. Tuesday. We won't be back from the week in Norfolk for the partridge shooting, thought Tashie.) She said: 'By P & O all the way?'

Flora nodded. 'I have the clothes my mother told me to get. Madame Tarasova made them.'

'That's nice. You should have let Mabs and me help you shop.' (Why should she?) 'But you are not all that keen on going, is that it?'

'Never was.'

Of course she wasn't. 'But now, do you have to?'

'Yes.' Flora opened her bag. 'This may explain better than I can.' She took her father's letter and handed it to Tashie. 'It came by the same post as the letter to the headmistress about my mother.' She handed the letter to Tashie.

Tashie began to read. ' "Twelve pairs of silk stockings, get advice as to colour, two pairs riding gloves (pigskin) size seven, six camiknickers satin or *crêpe-de-chine* white, from White House bust thirty-six, four thin nightdresses, white, box sandalwood soap Floris, two pairs tan shoes size four and a half Rayne, large bottle Mitsuko Fortnum's and her usual order at Elizabeth Arden." Gosh, this isn't a *letter*. What about dresses and a mink coat, while we're about it? Are you supposed, oh yes,' she said, reading, 'I see you are supposed to bring all these out with you. Do you want me to help you shop, is that it?'

'No. I've done the shopping.' How to explain that she just wanted to see, to catch a glimpse, to get some news perhaps, before she left. 'My father arranged about paying,' she said. 'It's over the page.'

Tashie looked over the page. 'Yes,' she said. 'I see.'

239

She handed the letter back. 'I remember your parents,' she said soberly.

'He does adore her.' Flora folded the letter and put it back in her bag. 'I really ought to go,' she said. 'There's a train at—'

'But you must see my baby and wait until Henry gets in. He'd love to see you.'

'I'd love to see the baby; what's he called?'

'John. We nearly called him Hubert, but there are too many Huberts and Cosmo, who is a godfather, well, Henry doesn't like Cosmo, not the person, just the name, so he's John, you can't go wrong with John. Come on up to the nursery and see him.' Tashie led the way out of the room.

Flora let John hold her finger; he looked quite an ordinary baby in Tashie's arms. John's Nanny shook hands when Tashie introduced her and said, 'We'd better wrap up warm this weekend, hadn't we, Mummy?' And Tashie said:

'Yes, we had, it's a very cold house.'

Flora felt John's Nanny was in no way interested in her. She made this clear when she said, 'And what time does Mr March want to leave tomorrow? I hope we start in good time so that baby's feeds are not interfered with.'

Tashie handed the baby back to the nurse. 'She's a fearful dragon but a wonderful nanny. She thinks I'm a hopeless mother,' she said as they went back to the drawing-room. 'The nanny where we are spending the week snobs her. She's nervous that John will cry if he doesn't get his feeds on time or if we arrive late and disgrace her.'

'I really should go,' said Flora uneasily.

'Won't you wait for Henry?'

'My train—'

'Oh.'

'Could I go to the lavatory first?'

'Of course.'

In the lavatory Flora shredded her father's shopping list and dropped the bits in the bowl. When she pulled the plug a lot were not washed away; she was tempted to retrieve a piece of the envelope with a stamp on it to give to the school gardener for his little boy's collection, but thinking the retrieval disgusting left matters as they were.

Tashie, who still had not put any shoes on, came with her to the door and kissed her. Flora walked away quickly. She had not asked for news of Mabs or Cosmo or Hubert; she had not even hinted that she remembered Felix. She could quite well have waited to see Henry, there was masses of time. 'Oh, why did I go?' she muttered as she walked along. 'There was nothing for me there, nothing.'

Later Henry complained to Tashie that some fool had been putting letters down the lavatory and Tashie burst out crying. Henry took her in his arms and said: 'What is it, darling, what's upset you?'

And Tashie said: 'It's Flora. There was a moment when I thought she was going to talk. I wanted to help but she clammed up. Oh, Henry, we should have done more for her. We should have had her to stay or something. We've never bothered.'

'Or Mabs should.'

'But we never *have*. I was dreadfully flippant about her ghastly mother, sorry she hadn't died and so on. I joked. I should have done something. Oh, God, I feel so bloody inadequate, a selfish tactless fool.'

'I don't see what you could have done,' said Henry. 'We are going away for the week.' A little later he said: 'Darling, you can't go interfering with other people's lives.'

'Whyever not? It wouldn't be interfering, it would be helping. We could—'

'She's under age,' said Henry reasonably. 'She's only seventeen. What she does is her parents' business, not ours. You really must stop crying; if you don't you'll look awful. You seem to forget we have the Meads coming to dinner.'

Tashie said, 'Damn the Meads,' but she stopped crying.

In the train Flora thought of all the things she had
bought her mother. She had not, as her father asked,
taken advice about the colour of the silk stockings,
but used her own judgment. She would have to buy
another suitcase for the day's shopping. She had
enjoyed the shopping; it had gone to her head. She
had fantasized that she was shopping for herself, that
she might meet Mabs or Tashie in one of the shops,
that they would be glad to see her. This had led to
her calling on Tashie. As the train clattered through
the suburbs Flora thought Tashie would have helped
her if it had been easy and enjoyable, as it had been to
lend her clothes on her visit to Coppermalt, when she
and Mabs made a game of it. They had got a lot of fun
out of it, especially so on the last night when the game
got out of hand. Older, married, and mother of a baby,
Tashie had lost none of her generosity; look at the way
she ceded her shoes to Molly, the maid. Flora thought
with disgust of how she had sat tongue-tied and mum
in Tashie's drawing-room. She had not even eaten a
delicious buttery crumpet. There will be no crumpets
in India, she thought morosely.

In London Tashie, telephoning Mabs, said: 'I just
thought I would tell you.'
    'What did she say, apart from the rabies and the
shopping list? Look, Tash, I'm in my bath. Can't you
ring me back?'
    'No, we've got people coming to dinner—'
    'Hurry up, then. I'm all wet. Ring me in the morn-
ing.'
    'Can't. We are off early for the partridge shoot.
Henry's friends in Norfolk, the Moberleys.'
    'Do bring me back a brace or two. What did she
say, then, Flora?'
    'Hardly anything, that's what upset me. It was
clear as mud she was unhappy, doesn't want to go to
India—'
    'She never did. Wasn't there something funny about

her parents? Don't you remember them in Dinard? But gosh, she'll like it when she gets there. My cousin Rachel had a hell of a good time in Delhi.'

'I daresay she did. Oh, God, Mabs, I felt I should have given her asylum. I felt so inadequate.'

'But she's in the charge of the school and you are going away. You just said so.'

'You sound like Henry.'

'She's under age. You can't interfere.'

'Henry said that, too. Are you still there?'

'Yes, I am. But look, Tashie, I'm all wet, I've got to change; we are going to a play.'

'Oh, what?'

'Noel Coward.'

'You'll love it. Henry and I went last week.'

'What do you propose to do about Flora, apart from telling me how rotten you feel?'

'I don't see what I can do. We shouldn't have been nice to her at Coppermalt. Or, if we were, we should have kept it up. It's like buying a puppy for Christmas and then neglecting it. That's why I feel so frightful, Mabs.'

'It was Felix's mother started it all, made my mother invite her—' said Mabs.

'Your mother thought she was carrying on with Cosmo, don't you remember?'

'I thought it was Hubert,' said Mabs.

'Or *both*! Oh Mabs, do you think she really—'

'She can't have, she was only fifteen. Not with both together. My ma was having one of her menopausal fits.'

'So what shall we do?' cried Tashie.

Mabs said: 'Knowing us, Tashie darling, we will do what comes easiest. I don't suppose we shall do anything. Sorry, love, I've got to go.' Mabs replaced the receiver and got back into her bath to find that the water had gone cold.

'You are looking very pleased with yourself.' Hubert joined Cosmo at the bar of their local pub.

'Am I? What shall you drink? Your usual? Shall we sit over there?'

'Don't tell me, let me guess.' Hubert watched Cosmo drink his beer. 'A married woman,' he suggested. 'You are not in love with her and she's not in love with you. You have fun in bed when her husband is away. It's extremely light-hearted and enjoyable and does nobody any harm. That's it, isn't it?'

Cosmo laughed. 'Don't be absurd. How is life treating you? What is it like working in a merchant bank?'

'So we don't discuss, we are discreet. My merchant bank, you ask. God, Cosmo, how can Nigel and Henry revel in it so? It's unbelievable. I hate it. I won't last, there are so many more appealing things to do in life.'

'Such as?'

'I don't know yet, but I intend to find out. And you, eating your dinners, do you still see yourself as a successful barrister?'

'Eventually.' Cosmo swallowed some beer.

'Did I tell you,' said Hubert, 'that after all the hooha about no money with it, a little has come with Pengappah?'

'No! How much is a little?'

'I have yet to find out. You know how solicitors are, very very slow, but apparently Cousin Thing felt some sort of remorse about the roof. He left enough to keep the rain out.'

'Have you been to see it yet?'

'No.'

'Why not?'

'It's been a myth for so long, I feel hesitant now I own it. To be honest, I don't want to be disappointed.'

'If it were mine,' said Cosmo, 'I'd rush—'

'Taking the married woman with you—' There was the hint of a sneer in Hubert's voice.

'Well—'

'She would not be the right person. Just think of the risk of taking Joyce. I speak metaphorically, of course. She'd prance and be jolly. She'd shatter the atmosphere.'

'How did you guess it was Joyce?' Cosmo looked ruffled.

'I saw you together,' said Hubert, which was untrue. Loving his friend, he was not going to divulge that he had smelled Joyce. Being married to a rich man Joyce had scent specially made for her in Paris. Its fragrance had lingered in Cosmo's flat, just as it had lingered in his own rooms during his last year at Oxford; he had sniffed it too in the rooms of other men of his acquaintance. Joyce was a girl who got around. 'Joyce has the knack of making life joyful,' he said.

'Oh, she has,' agreed Cosmo. 'Which is more than can be said for my sister Mabs and her chum Tashie.'

'What have they been up to? Those two have the makings of society matrons; in no time they will be presenting their daughters at court.'

'Oh, come,' said Cosmo, laughing. 'Their babies are boys.'

'They'll have girls next, just you wait. But what's troubling them?'

'They have seen, or Tashie has seen, Flora. The version I heard garbled by Mabs is that her mother has rabies and her father has made her buy up the contents of Fortnum's as consolation presents, which Flora has to escort to India where she sails by P & O.'

'When?' Hubert put down his glass, spilling some beer.

'Soon, I think. Mabs and Tashie feel they should have kept up with her, had her to stay and so on. They feel remorse at having let her slip from their busy little lives. In other words it's pangs of guilt.'

'Which we should have too,' said Hubert.

'What?'

'You seem to forget there was a time we both wanted Flora. We agreed to share her.'

'So we did. Bloody silly idea. One couldn't share a girl, could one? I mean, I can't see myself doing it.' (Hubert raised an eyebrow.) 'Of course, I saw her first,' said Cosmo.

'And I fished her out of the sea.'

'We sent her postcards, didn't we? I remember we sent postcards from—'

'Postcards!'

'The person she loved was Felix. Heavens, Blanco, d'you remember Felix at Dinard? How all the girls flocked—'

'Honeypot Joyce among them, snaggle teeth in those days, a little chrysalis of fun.' Hubert smiled in recollection of those infatuated months at Oxford. But for Joyce he would have got a first. 'Felix was adept at keeping disentangled; one couldn't help admiring him.'

'He's tangled now,' said Cosmo. 'Joke's over.'

'Has anyone seen him since his wedding?'

'It was a good party,' said Cosmo. 'Father had a great time, reminiscences and so on. You know how he is. Why weren't you there?'

'I was asked but couldn't make it. I wonder whether Flora knows. Was Joyce at the wedding?'

'Yes. That was where I – yes-er-um – where we—'

'Oh, all right, no need to be so discreet. But back to Flora; I think one of us should see her off.' Hubert felt obscurely that this would annoy Cosmo, whose sexual satisfaction was aggravating him.

'All right, let's all see her off. I'll bring Joyce. I'll ask her to find out the P & O sailings, check the passenger list. She's fearfully competent.' Cosmo, basking in his affair with Joyce, was in no way annoyed. 'Joyce has a good brain,' he said complacently.

'Not as active as her cunt,' said Hubert. 'Don't hit me,' he said, 'you did once and it hurt.'

'So I did,' said Cosmo. 'Over Flora. Your nose bled and I hurt my knuckles.'

Hubert resented Cosmo's laughter and his easy suggestion that they should all see Flora off. He was surprised to feel the hot rage he had felt once before. I can't be jealous, he thought, not of Flora and certainly not of Joyce.

Thirty-five

Miss Gillespie, escorting Flora from school to ship, had had enough. On former occasions with other girls she had sympathized with their eagerness to be off, down channel through the Bay of Biscay, into the Mediterranean, heading east to India and the delights of the Raj. Miss Gillespie was a romantic; she watched her charges note the young men boarding the ship with them: army officers, Political Officers, Indian police officers, officers returning from home leave, with straight backs, sunburned faces and trim moustaches. Potential husbands. Miss Gillespie, in her late, wistful and maiden thirties, envied the girls their chance.

Flora Trevelyan, remote and adult in her new clothes, was indifferent to the excitement of boarding. Her lack of appreciation maddened Miss Gillespie. She would leave her now, get back into London and spend the evening with her married sister. They'd go to the cinema, perhaps see Ronald Colman. 'Shall you be all right if I leave you now?' she enquired. She had fulfilled her duty.

'Yes, thank you, Miss Gillespie, I shall be all right,' said Flora.

'I have asked the Purser to keep an eye on you, and the Captain knows you are travelling alone. I think you will be comfortable in that cabin.' (Why must she repeat everything? I was with her when she spoke to the Purser and with her when she gave him the letter for the Captain. She was with me to inspect the cabin. I wish she would go.)

'You seem to have a nice steward. A family man, he

247

will keep an eye on you.' (All these eyes!) 'He said your cabin is on the starboard side, but it does not matter at this time of year. He will have your trunk brought out of the hold at Bombay and see that you meet your father's bearer.' (I was there, I heard you.) 'You will remember how much to tip the steward, won't you, dear? Not too little and not too much; one must keep their respect. And you will mind, won't you, how you behave in front of the crew; they are all natives. It's so important.'

'I wish, if you are going, Miss Gillespie, that you'd go,' said Flora pleasantly.

'Flora Trevelyan! Your manners! I shall have to tell—'

'The headmistress? I've left school, Miss Gillespie. You don't have to do anything any more.'

'Flora.'

'I am sorry, Miss Gillespie, but you repeat yourself. People get bored. I've longed to tell you for seven years,' said Flora kindly, 'that if we'd had to strain to hear what you said just once, we would all have learned a lot more.' Oh hell, I've hurt her feelings, reduced her to huff.

'Ungrateful, after all I—'

'Very sorry, Miss Gillespie.' Flora walked fast along the deck towards the gangway with Miss Gillespie keeping up. 'I hope you have a nice evening with your sister and Ronald Colman,' she said. Miss Gillespie did not reply; she had often suspected Flora's tone, never exactly pinned it. 'Do you write to Ronald Colman?' asked Flora, who knew from the school grapevine that she did. 'Next time you write, do ask him to shave off that moustache. None of the girls believe Beau Geste would have been allowed it in the Legion.' Flora felt, as she walked along the deck, that in spite of her parents waiting to trap her in India she could at least shake off school. She would be wonderfully, luxuriously alone on the ship for three weeks.

Awkwardly they said goodbye. Miss Gillespie hesitated before kissing Flora, but it was best to part on good terms and ignore her hurtful speech. Flora might some day have children, as other old girls had, and need a school for them. 'I wish I was going to India,' she said mournfully.

'Oh, Miss Gillespie, go instead of me! I'll give you my ticket, just say the word,' cried Flora. 'Swop.'

'What an idea,' said Miss Gillespie. 'What a fanciful girl you are, but generous. What would your parents say?' She had misjudged Flora.

'They'd find you a husband and fix you up,' said Flora, undoing her small good.

She watched Miss Gillespie's back, in her respectable coat and skirt, as she made her way down the gang-plank and walked away to find a taxi. The exact price of the taxi would be put on the bill and sent to her father c/o Cox & Kings, Pall Mall, SW1. She leaned over the rail and peered down the ship's side into the murky water of the dock. Far below in the filthy water she could see a rat painstakingly breasting through the rubbish, paper, straw, orange peel, cigarette stubs. Someone threw a bucket of soapy water from a port-hole and swamped the rat. As Flora watched, its head bobbed up; she imagined its whiskers and desperate paws. Oh, courageous rat. She craned her neck to see better.

'There she is. Flora! Flora! We've come to see you off. Isn't this fun? Aren't you thrilled, off on the long voyage into adulthood, fun and wickedness?' Joyce, Cosmo and Hubert were bearing down on her. Joyce strode forward, showing her teeth in her big smile, holding out expansive hands to grasp Flora. Cosmo followed, looking English and sheepish. Hubert looked angry.

Surrendering her hands, Flora recollected that Joyce had American connections which would account for this enthusiasm. She said, 'Hello.'

'Aren't you pleased to see us? You look surprised.' Joyce squeezed Flora's hands. 'We heard you were off from Mabs, who heard it from Tash. You are a funny one. Why didn't you tell us? Why did you never come

249

and stay? We've brought a bottle of champagne to drink you on your way. Oh, you've got it, Hubert. Let's ask a steward for glasses. I suppose you are travelling first class?'

'Second.'

'Much more fun. The old and married travel first, all the young and lovely men will be in the second. You're going to have such a marvellous time, Flora. I wish I was coming too. Shall we join the ship? Wouldn't that be a joke?' Joyce slipped her arm through Cosmo's, drawing him close.

Flora supposed later that she had said the right things. They had moved from the deck, where porters were still bringing on board trunks and suitcases banded with regimental colours, their owners' names painted large: Major this, Colonel that, Lieut. something else. In the saloon a steward brought glasses, uncorked the bottle and poured. Joyce sat close to Cosmo. 'My goodness, Flora, what a choice of appetizing men! Look at them! I bet you get engaged by the time you reach Bombay.'

Cosmo looked about at passengers milling to and fro, seasoned travellers. 'I suppose it's all army and civil service.'

'There will be some boxwallahs too, bound to be,' said Joyce. 'They've got more money so they'll join the ship at Marseilles. So don't lose your heart before Marseilles, Flora, keep some room for those—'

'Joyce knows it all,' said Cosmo drily.

'In two days she'll know everybody. She's by far the prettiest girl,' said Joyce.

'When does the ship reach Marseilles?' Hubert asked. It was the first time he had spoken.

'In a week, I think. Then Malta, Alexandria and Aden.'

'I see.' He watched her, frowning.

Cosmo and Joyce drank and refilled their glasses. Flora thought of the rat. Had it reached safety? 'What a beautiful suit.' She remembered at Coppermalt the girls always complimented one another on their clothes. Joyce's suit was banana yellow, nipped in at the waist.

Joyce sipped her drink and stretched her long legs. 'I had it made for Felix's wedding,' she said. 'I like yours. Did la Tarasova make it?'

It wasn't a mistake; she had heard right. 'I didn't see it in *The Times*.' She kept her voice flat. Felix married?

'It would not have been in *The Times*,' said Hubert. 'They were married in Holland.'

'Naturally.' Flora gulped champagne. It fizzed in her nose and made her eyes water. She put her glass down with a steady hand.

'Oh gosh, there's the bell, they want us to go ashore.' Sitting arm in arm with Cosmo, Joyce showed little sign of moving.

Hubert stood up. 'We'd better get a move on,' he said.

Cosmo pulled Joyce to her feet. People who had come to see friends off were making for the gangway.

Hubert walked beside Flora. 'You don't want to go to India, do you?'

'Yes, I do.'

'We had rather a lot to drink at lunch, that's why we are inept,' he said.

'I don't find you inept,' said Flora. 'Just ordinary.' He would hate to be called ordinary. Behind them Joyce and Cosmo strolled arm in arm; were they engaged? Who had Felix married? She must not, could not ask. 'There was a rat,' she said, 'swimming in the dock.'

'Rats are brave animals.'

'Someone threw a bucket of dirty water onto it.'

'It will survive.'

'Miss Gillespie, the English mistress, brought me to the ship. She asked the Purser and the steward and the Captain to keep an eye on me.'

'In case someone throws a bucket of slops over you.'

'Metaphorically.'

'Mind you survive.'

'There you are, we got separated. We must go, they are shooing us. Write to us, Flora, won't you? Give us a kiss. There. Come on, you two. They want to pull up the gangway.' Joyce kissed Flora; she smelt delicious. 'You know Mabs and Tash would have come if they could, and Ernest?'

'Who is Ernest?'

'My husband, silly. Didn't you know I was married? It was in all the papers. Come on, you two, we are being a nuisance.'

'You are drunk,' said Hubert, pushing Joyce along.

Cosmo said, 'Flora—' and bent awkwardly to kiss her cheek. 'Goodbye.' He hurried after Joyce.

Hubert took Flora's face between his hands, squeezing it, forcing her mouth open and kissed her so that she gasped. Half-way down the gangway he turned and came back.

'You don't want to go. Come ashore with me.'

'I must. I do. I can't.'

'You look like a caged bird.'

'For the moment I am free.'

'Not for long.'

'For the voyage, three weeks.'

'Sir – last visitors – visitors ashore, sir – please sir—'

Bells clanged and under her feet the deck vibrated. The wind coming up the Thames estuary smelled of the sea. Squawking gulls circled a giant crane. The ship's siren let out a blast. There was a gap between the ship and the dock as the ship's propellers churned the brown water, but no sign of the rat.

Thirty-six

Pacing along the dock Hubert looked up at the ship, black, shiny and dimly lit by harbour and dockyard lights. It would be dark for another hour; it was far too early to go on board. He was hungry. He turned about to find a café open for night workers, stevedores or police. As he moved away a taxi came along the dock and drew up by the gangway. A girl got out. In the half-light Hubert recognized Flora. She was in evening dress, a shawl held tightly round her shoulders.

Flora said to the driver: 'I have no francs. Will you take English money? I will give you more than your fare is worth in francs.'

Leaning from the cab, the driver said something Hubert could not hear. Flora stamped her foot and said, 'You must,' in a strained voice.

The driver replied to the effect that he was not in the habit of transporting seafaring English prostitutes back to their ships from respectable French bordellos; it was taking the food from the mouths of hard-working French girls. This was not the sort of thing he had fought for, up to his waist in mud from 1914 to 1918. Mademoiselle must pay in francs or he would go to the police.

Hubert stood at Flora's elbow. 'How much does the lady owe you?'

The driver, startled, named the price. Hubert stood tall in the half-light, his shoulders broad, his eyebrows meeting darkly above black eyes. 'You will wait,' he said, 'while this lady and I fetch some things she must

253

collect from her cabin. Then you will drive us back into town. We shall not be long.'

Flora noted the driver's meek response. 'Oui, monsieur, d'accord.'

Hubert took Flora's arm. 'Where's your cabin? You can't travel in that dress. While you change and pack a suitcase, I'll write a note for the Purser to give the Captain. You are coming,' Hubert said, walking her up the gangway, 'with me.'

Mimicking the taxi driver, Flora said, 'Oui, monsieur, d'accord,' but her voice quavered.

Hubert said: 'Don't try to talk; plenty of time later. And buck up, I am hungry and want my breakfast.' She had had some sort of shock, he thought, which was useful. It delayed prevarication.

In her cabin Flora changed into day clothes, filled a case with necessities and various garments which Hubert handed her. When the case was full he shut it and helped her into her coat, saying, 'Come on, then.' Carrying her case, he led her off the ship to where the taxi was waiting. 'Get in,' he said, and gave the driver directions. As he was about to join Flora in the cab a second taxi drove up to the gangway and disgorged three men, young, jolly, drunk and English. Flora shrank back into a corner. 'I left them there, I—'

Hubert said: 'Would you like me to chuck them into the dock? Better not, it would delay our breakfast. Drive on,' he said to the driver. 'You will feel better,' he said to Flora, crouched in the corner seat, 'when you have had some hot coffee and croissants.' It would be folly to touch her, he thought; she had not kicked his shins or bitten him yet.

As the taxi drove away Hubert, looking back, noted that an altercation had broken out between the second taxi driver and his fares. With luck, he thought, watching the three men staggering about, one or more would trip and fall into the dock. 'You keep charming company,' he said.

Flora did not answer. She turned away and looked out of her window.

Half-way into Marseilles Hubert stopped the taxi to buy a newspaper. 'I need to read the news,' he said, getting back in the cab. 'D'you remember frog-faced Miss Green trying to interest General Leigh in Hitler? He's much in the news now. She was ahead of her time; Hitler is Chancellor of Germany. Let's see what the French have to say.'

Flora said: 'I read *The Times*.' She continued to look out of the window.

'So you are *au fait*.' Hubert folded the paper, stretched his legs and glanced at the headline. 'But you are probably not aware – ' he risked a glance at her profile – 'of what Hitler plans. He is a tidy fellow.'

'Tidy?' She was only half-listening.

Keep up the chat, thought Hubert. 'If one ploughs through *Mein Kampf* the tidiness becomes apparent; he plans a perfect Germany, no less. He will eliminate blots like the Jews, gypsies, Jehovahs, half-wits, cripples and communists. Germany will become a nation of tall, blond, obedient Nordic giants.'

'An awful lot of Germans are dark,' said Flora, looking out of her side of the taxi.

'Indeed yes, as are French, English, Dutch and Belgians. Even General Leigh, who, by the way, has become an ardent supporter of the Nazis, remarked on that. He listed an array of dark Germans and pointed out that Felix, a representative Dutchman of high calibre, is dark.' (Did she not have a crush on Felix?) 'The master race, the General thinks, is a bit of a pipe dream, but since the Führer is anti-communist, he's pro.'

Flora said, 'Oh,' keeping interest out of her voice. 'Is he?'

'Oh yes, the General is scared stiff of the Bolshies, of communist rot among the working class; apparently in the General Strike in 1926 he thought there might be a revolution. He armed himself with a revolver to travel north to Coppermalt.'

'I remember.' Recollecting the man in the gunsmith's at St Malo, Flora winced.

How did she know? Her profile told him nothing. 'The General's anti-Bolshiness so turned his butler's stomach he gave notice and joined the Party. Mrs Leigh keeps on that Gage was "such a good butler". Cosmo, saying "*Ceci n'empêche cela*," only gets his head bitten off.'

Flora laughed.

Hubert glanced at her with relief. 'We'll have breakfast in that café,' he said. 'This street is called the Cannabiere. All Marseilles passes through it.' He told the driver to stop.

Flora drank scalding coffee sitting at a pavement table while Hubert hungrily demolished *œufs au plat* and croissants and watched Flora's face grow less pale.

Between mouthfuls he continued his desultory chat, telling her about his time and Cosmo's at Oxford, about trips abroad with Cosmo and other friends. 'We sent you postcards.' About London theatre, cinema, concerts. The rooms he had shared with a friend until he found a place of his own, it being more agreeable to be independent. That Cosmo, having opted for the law, would become a barrister; that he rarely saw Mabs and Tashie these days, their lives being so different from his, but that in the course of work he came across Nigel and Henry. Did she perhaps remember the great scene Mabs had made, breaking off her engagement? She was now the most devoted of wives. Since she had persuaded Nigel to change his tailor his legs appeared appreciably longer. It's all in the cut of the trousers. He was grateful, said Hubert, to that lot for showing him the sort of future he could expect if he remained with his merchant bank. It might well, he said, suit Nigel and Henry but the life was not for him. Glancing at Flora he thought she barely listened; her look of strain was less, but she looked exhausted. He did not tell her that he had been approached by some chucklehead trying to recruit him into secret intelligence, that this had climaxed his discontent. He had walked out of his job four days after seeing her off at Tilbury and caught the train to Dover. 'I stopped for a night in Paris,' he said, 'played a few rubbers of bridge, made us a few francs.' (A slip to say 'us'.) 'You might remember,' he went on, 'Alexis Tarasov? Married to the Russian Armenian dressmaker, the backgammon fiend? In the summer he stops driving his taxi and plays in bridge tournaments at Le Touquet and Biarritz. I play for money when I'm short, but I can't take it seriously like Alexis. There is nothing more boring than a bridge fiend, my mother's one and my step-father, and Joyce, who you saw with us the other day, is turning into another. She took to it when she married her tycoon Ernest, had to find something to do, I suppose.' (Besides fucking with Cosmo and me and all and sundry.) 'Jolly girl, Joyce,' said Hubert. 'Flits from flower to flower, brightens people's lives.'

Flora had finished her coffee and eaten a croissant. She sat now almost relaxed, watching the passers-by. She barely listened, Hubert thought, to his burbling; she was not ready to talk. 'Well,' he said, 'right, then. We'll be on our way.' He signalled the waiter and paid the bill. 'I left my bag at the station,' he said. 'We'll collect it and catch the bus. It's only a short way, we can walk.' He picked up Flora's case.

Walking beside Hubert, Flora did not ask where they were going. At the station Hubert retrieved his bag and led her to a waiting bus. Looking up at the station clock, Flora noted the time. 'The ship will have sailed,' she said. 'They will be gone.'

Hubert said, 'Yes.'

In old age they would wonder whether they had really heard the blast of the ship's siren above the noise of the Marseilles traffic and exchanged a smile as they boarded the bus. The smile, yes, but the siren?

Rattling out of Marseilles Flora fell asleep, letting her head drop against Hubert's shoulder. Hubert, who had had no sleep since leaving London, began to doze, and dozing was presently aware that Flora was talking.

'I didn't talk to anyone for the first part of the voyage. I was frightfully seasick and stayed in my cabin. Then when I was better I met them at meals –

they seemed quite nice – asked me to dance – shuffled their places at meals so they were all at my table – to be honest, I rather liked it, they paid more attention to me than to other – a bit boring trying to kiss – it wasn't like Coppermalt, they were different, somehow – or I was? I don't know. At Gibraltar I went ashore with them; we swam in a cove, that was lovely – one night two of them tried to force their way into my cabin – pretty stupid really. Then when we got to Marseilles I thought it would be all right to go with them to a nightclub. I'd never been to a nightclub, I wanted to see what it's like – I thought a French nightclub would be— It was not what I expected, no band and no glitter – disappointing, actually – very made-up girls sitting about urging people to order drinks – none of the men spoke French so they looked pretty silly and the girls didn't speak English – after a lot of boring sitting about we went into another room – I thought we were going to dance but there was no band – I do love dancing – it was a sort of cinema and when the film came on, it was people with nothing on doing – it wasn't funny, I supposed it was meant – I thought it, well, ugly – then in the middle of this film, the most extraordinary contortions, I remembered when I was very small, I'd practically forgotten but it all came rushing back – going into my parents' room in India and they were doing – and there was this *smell* and they yelled at me, scared me to bits – they were hating me, *hating* – I've been puzzling for years why I didn't want to go to India – the people are wonderful, the country is lovely, there's this marvellous scent in the air of dust and spice and dung – well, those people on the screen – some of it was comical, I suppose, but nobody – well, it wasn't like lying in marble arms – I whizzed out of that place, found the taxi and he, of course, the taximan, thought I knew it was a brothel, not a nightclub and that I was a prostitute. Honestly, Blanco, I've never felt such a fool in my life. Sorry, Hubert.'

Hubert, who had been holding his breath, let it out in a long sigh.

Flora said, 'You must let me know what I owe you for the taxi.'

Hubert said, 'What are marble arms?'

Flora said, 'Just something.'

Thirty-seven

'It is a wonderful invitation, we may never get another
chance. We must go, darling. It's not as though he was
one of the minor Maharajahs who ask just anybody.'
Vita fingered the letter, feeling the stiff paper with
pleasure. 'Everyone we know will go green with envy.'

Denys thought, as he so often had before, that ani-
mation made her sparkle. 'It would do you good,' he
said, 'to have some fun, a pick-up after all you've been
through.'

'But what a pity—' Vita drooped.

'What's a pity?'

'Those new frocks she's bringing with her. It would
have been nice to be able to borrow them for the trip.
And to have new shoes and a fresh bottle of scent.'

'You always look lovely; surely you have enough
clothes?'

'Not new ones, alas. But we will go?'

'Of course.'

'What about—?'

'Don't fuss. She can settle in by herself, she's not
a child. She'll be met and brought up here. She will
be all right with the servants. It won't be for long. I'll
ask one or two people to keep an eye on her. I believe
there's a niece coming out to stay with somebody, I'll
enquire. She can ride if she wants to. I'll tell the saice.'

'Not Robina?'

'No, no, one of the older ponies. I can't risk my
best polo—'

'Of course not.'

'Well, then,' Vita smiled. 'When we get back from

260

our visit I shan't feel let down by the humdrum. I shall have some new clothes then, won't I?'

'Speaking as your humdrum husband, I prefer you without,' said Denys. It was good to see her perking up. The injections had taken it out of her; she had been so brave.

'I brought you some magazines, Vita, which arrived today in the mail.' Alec, the Governor's A.D.C., appeared on the verandah. It was pleasant, he thought, not to be greeted by a snarling Airedale. He bent to kiss Vita's cheek.

Vita said, 'Oh Alec, thank you. How kind and thoughtful.'

Denys said, 'Hello, Alec. Sit down, have a drink,' and shouted an order to his bearer. Alec's hair, he noted, was greying at the temples, which added to his air of distinction.

'When you have finished with the *Geographical Magazine* may I have it back?' Alec settled in a chair. 'I usually pass it on to the missionaries. But please keep the others.'

Vita said, 'Those tiresome missionaries, how can you put up with them? I will skip through the geography while you talk to Denys. Tell him about the invitation, darling. It's so exciting.'

Denys said: 'We've been invited to stay – here, look at the invitation.' Denys passed the Maharajah's letter to Alec. 'Vita is more concerned about what she will wear than with geography. Geography is not her line.'

'Oh, I say, how grand. My word, he gets his writing paper from Cartier, like my grandmother. I do think you are lucky, hardly anyone gets asked. He must have heard of Vita's beauty.' Alec accepted a drink brought by the Trevelyans' bearer borne, he noted, with an inward sneer, on a salver won by Denys at polo in New Delhi. 'Gosh,' he said, 'I envy you.'

Denys, who had no titled grandmother who bought her writing paper at Cartier, said, keeping his voice bland, 'But you've been, you must let me pick your brains.'

'In the course of duty, not a proper visit. I attended my master.' Alec invariably referred to the Governor as his master. He sipped his drink as he sat in a chair from which he had a good view of Vita. She is lovely, he thought; lovely and unobtainable. Which suits me fine.

Conscious of being watched, Vita began turning the pages of the magazine as she listened to the men. The Maharajah's attitude to the British was excellent, said Alec; he had after all been educated at Eton and Oxford – no, not Balliol, Christ Church – and he kept up with English friends. His attitude to Congress? Well, you know how they are, totally aloof and yet and yet – in Europe. Of course, it was Monte Carlo and the Ritz in London for Ascot week. Yes, quite a gambler. Knows about horses, oh yes. And the usual restaurants and nightclubs. Fond of cars, too. Shoots with a couple of dukes, but it's not all money; he keeps up with school friends, there's an article there in the magazine Vita's reading about one of them, an explorer actually. 'May I borrow that for a minute?' Alec leaned forward and took the magazine from Vita, flipping through it. 'Ah, here we are. This chap. But I remember now, don't mention him, he blotted his copybook with His Highness, so steer clear—' Alec showed the magazine to Denys.

Denys said, 'Never heard of him. Should I have?'

'No. He writes travel books, known in those sort of circles. Not your line really, a bit superficial. He never stays long enough in one place to know it so one doubts the integrity of his writing. It is said that wherever he goes he – er – impregnates some woman and leaves a trail of unexplained infants. But on the other hand – ' Alec laughed – 'I did hear that the *froideur* with the Maharajah was over a boy, so Lord knows what's true, I imagine he is a man who creates legends; people who never stay in one place do.' Alec handed the magazine back to Vita.

262

Turning the pages, Vita was conscious of Alec's admiration; he had once, when dancing, muttered in her ear that he worshipped the ground she trod on. He had had a few drinks. Would Alec, Vita wondered, as she surreptitiously studied the photograph of the explorer, do for Flora? If he married Flora, she would retain a hold. 'Bought any rare and lovely rugs lately?' She handed him back the magazine. 'Nothing much to interest me in that,' she said, 'but thanks a lot.' (The man, if it was the man, was unrecognizable.)

'Rugs.' Alec's eyes lit up. 'Ah, yes. I have my eye on three, but the old devil is asking too much; he knows I collect. You will see some wonderful rugs in the Maharajah's palace, and many other treasures. Mouth-watering. He has a French chef, by the way. You'll get excellent food.'

'I shall like that,' said Vita. 'I love French food.'

'Tigers?' asked Denys. 'Does one go prepared? Nothing is said.'

'Oh, go prepared. It was mooted for my master but you know him, he hates killing things. I suspect His Highness was miffed, expecting him to be like his dukes. Now, my dears, I must go. Many thanks for the drink.' Alec stood up, bent down and kissed Vita's cheek. 'Have a good time.'

'Thank you, Alec.' Vita smiled and waved.

Did Alec by any chance like boys, Denys wondered, walking with him to his car? 'Vita's daughter will be arriving soon,' he said. 'You must meet her.'

'Shall look forward to it,' said Alec. Just one more effort to marry me off, he thought, getting into his car. 'No doubt all the chaps will swarm like bees,' he said.

Watching the Governor's A.D.C. drive away, Denys thought, Bees are of the feminine gender. What an old woman. Rejoining his wife, he said, 'If you fancy Alec as a son-in-law, darling, I think he is a non-starter.'

Vita laughed. 'Alec adores me,' she said. And Alec, driving back to Government house in the dusk, thought of how he loved Vita's apparent stupidity, her vanity, her passionate and tremendous selfishness, her terrifying sexual grip over Denys, her contempt for the opinion of other women. I utterly adore and admire her, he thought. Thank God for my celibate state.

Thirty-eight

'Try turning towards me,' said Hubert.

Flora felt rather muzzy, not sure how they had got here, in bed in a room at the back of an hotel in Aix-en-Provence overlooking a courtyard. Several floors down, a group of women on wooden chairs sat gossiping in the moonlight, their voices rising and falling, Provençal accents interspersed with claps of merriment filtering agreeably up through a trellis of vines.

She lay with her back to Hubert, as the marble girl in the postcard had done; as she had so often herself, dreamy and cool, in the arms of Felix, Cosmo, or Hubert. The difference was that this time she felt his warmth along her back, across her buttocks, down the backs of her thighs. Her heels rested on his shins just below his knees. The back of her head was against his chin. 'Try turning towards me,' he said.

They had laughed at dinner sitting at a table under the plane trees in the Cours Mirabeau. They had remembered together the picnic at Dinard, the singing, the tango, the bonfire and fireworks; spoken slightly of Coppermalt, closer in time, less safe. She had chattered like the women below in the courtyard, told him about school. For some reason he had not been bored. Rather, he was amused when she told him how she had stolen a look in the headmistress' study at the school reports, that hers variously said, 'She watches what goes on with detachment and seldom joins in.' 'One gets the impression that to her our curriculum is anathema.' 'She is better at weaving private dreams than sewing.'

'Has a marked preference for her nose in a book over activity on the hockey field.' And how the other girls, so unlike the girls of Coppermalt, were so obsessed with marriage and class, the majority sneering at the minority whose vowels betrayed them.

'And what had the dreams been about?' Hubert asked, refilling his glass.

'That Easter at Dinard and the visit to Coppermalt,' she had said. Just that really, because apart from those times she knew nothing of Real Life.

'Oh,' said Hubert. 'Real Life, yes. But was not the voyage from Tilbury to Marseilles real life?'

And she had said she hoped real life was not being seasick and propositioned by young officers with moustaches. And Hubert had said: 'What a lot of long words you know. Shall we eat some figs?'

So they had eaten figs. Before the figs there had been wonderful pongy cheese, and before that green salad, and before the salad *cervelles au beurre noir*, and before that they had nibbled crisp radishes while they waited for the *cervelles* and sipped cool white wine. Lying against Hubert, Flora pleasurably reviewed the meal.

When they had finished and sat drinking black and bitter coffee he had said, 'Tomorrow I will feed you on wonderful fish with *aïoli* and, if it is not too late in the season, artichokes and, of course, *bouillabaisse*, and more delicious figs.' And she, watching the people drift along the pavement of the Cours Mirabeau in the dark, for since it was October the sun had set long ago, had said that he seemed very fond of food. He had said: 'Yes, very fond, and very fond—'

And she was happy watching the people stroll along by the light of the moon, the street lights and the lights from bars and cafés; old people with their old dogs, lovers in twos, families in groups, all their voices rising and falling in cadence.

Hubert said again, 'Try turning towards me,' and his breath ruffled the hair at the back of her neck.

*

He had not been prepared for her response, Hubert thought, as she slept beside him. It was really miraculously lucky that things had gone so right. He had been afraid of hurting her. He had heard how easy it was to put girls off, that they got hurt and took against it, especially if they were virgin, as Flora undoubtedly was or had been. Thank God for Joyce, he thought. My word, if it hadn't been for Joyce, I would have got it all wrong. Amazing girl, Joyce, and jolly unselfish to teach so much, to pass on those tips she had gleaned from her husband (looking at Ernest one would not in one's wildest dreams imagine he could—) and of course others, for Joyce was nothing if not promiscuous. In the dark, with Flora curled asleep beside him, Hubert supposed that perhaps even at this moment friend Cosmo was gaining enlightenment under Joyce's able tutelage, and good luck to him, good luck.

But he had not been prepared for what had happened. He had been careful, tried not to be hasty and brutish, tried not to get carried away, but when quiet little, shy little Flora let out that shout of 'Whoops, how wonderful!' it had been a surprise.

Had she noticed, Hubert wondered, that three floors below in the courtyard the chattering ladies had hushed and that one of them called out, 'Bravo!'

As Hubert shook with laughter he saw by the light of the moon shining through the shutters that Flora had opened an eye, that her lips moved. 'What is it?' he whispered.

She said, 'We did what I saw my mother and father do, and the people in the film in the brothel; so ugly and ridiculous.'

'It is not ugly or ridiculous if you cannot see yourself doing it,' he said.

Flora said, 'I hadn't thought of that. Thank you for telling me.' And she turned away from him, snuggling her bottom against his crotch.

Thirty-nine

It was early, the air fresh; sun, slanting through the plane trees, dappled the pavement, shone on the tablecloths of the café. Hubert had left Flora asleep on her stomach, her face buried in the pillow. What on earth am I up to? he thought. She is only seventeen.

The waiter brought coffee and set it on the table with crusty rolls and glistening butter. Would Monsieur like a newspaper? Yes, please.

Buttering a roll, Hubert watched stout pigeons hurrying to and fro among the café tables, pattering after crumbs snatched by speedier sparrows. The rage which had swept him from his safe and boring job, spurring him across France to catch up with Flora, had subsided; having acquired her he was unsure what to do with her. She will cling, he thought, as he poured his coffee and gulped it down. I may have made her pregnant; she will expect me to marry her. Oh God, I am hoist by my lust. I need my freedom, there is so much I want to do. Morosely he munched his roll. Then, counter to these thoughts, he remembered the night before and his loins pricked with desire. He was filled with immense tenderness.

The waiter, taciturn and observant, brought the newspaper. Let's see what's new in the world; what Hitler, Mussolini, and the terrified-of-Communist British look like through the eyes of the French. Hubert shook the paper open. I do not think Ramsay MacDonald is right when he says war will go out of fashion, he thought; bellicosity is ingrained in human nature. He poured himself more coffee.

From the corner of his eye he saw Flora emerge from the hotel, cross the street and disappear into a chemist shop. Was she ill? What was the matter? Was he responsible? Anxiety wrenched his gut. Flora re-appeared and, re-crossing the street, joined him. 'Hello,' she said. 'Good morning.'

Hubert stood and pulled out a chair for her. 'Would you like breakfast? The coffee and rolls are good.'

'Please.' She sat, she smiled. She looked all right.

Hubert ordered coffee and rolls. 'Are you all right?' he asked. 'I hope you are. I saw you go into the chemist; not ill, I trust?'

'No.' She transferred her smile to the waiter as he set coffee, milk pots and rolls before her. 'Perhaps Madame would prefer croissants?'

'No, thank you.' She was happy with rolls. She bit her tongue, amused at being called Madame. Hubert, still wary, watched her eat. Nothing wrong with her appetite.

Forgetting the crumbs the cock pigeons now chased the females, hurrying after them through the maze of tables and chairs. The females rose in negative flutters to avoid their attentions.

Flora drank her coffee and ate her rolls. 'Was what we did last night exactly what married people do?' She looked away from him down the street, to where an old lady walked slowly so that her Pomeranian dog could stop, sniff and lift its leg without an indecent hurrying jerk to its lead. It was similar in appearance to Irena Tarasova's Prince Igor, though a different colour. 'D'you remember Madame Tarasova's Pom,' she said, 'long ago?'

'That little pest, yes. Well, in answer to your question – ' Hubert felt himself begin to perspire – 'in a manner of speaking, yes. Though from what I gather – ' Flora turned attentively towards him, eyes large and dark – 'there was a don at Oxford who was forever saying "in a manner of speaking", it sounds so pompous. Well, yes, married people do it and – er – um – lovers. People who love one another or—' Hubert hesitated and came to a halt.

'Do you want to marry me?'

'No! Yes, I mean, oh, er—' Sweat prickled his armpits and his groin. 'I—'

'Because I don't,' said Flora.

'Don't what?'

'Don't want to marry you. I can't, actually.' Impossible to tell him that there was Cosmo and had been, still was Felix, although Felix seemed to have attached himself elsewhere, married. 'I can't,' she repeated apologetically. 'I'm sorry.'

Feeling a huge lift of relief, but at the same time outrage, Hubert said huffily, 'Why the hell not?'

'I am too greedy.'

'But last night you—'

'Oh, it was lovely,' said Flora. 'Marvellous.'

'Then why—'

'You said married people do it, and lovers, and people who love one another. Well, they aren't all married, so—'

'So you—'

'Yes.'

'But suppose you have a baby; you might easily have a baby,' he said, anxious now that she should want to marry him, to tie her down, bind her to him with legal cords for ever.

'I am not going to have a baby.' Flora flushed. 'That's why I went to the chemist just now to buy – well, I've got the curse,' Flora said, embarrassed. 'It happens.'

Hubert said, 'Oh, darling,' and took her hand. 'Are you all right?'

Flora said, 'Of course I'm all right.' (A bit sore, but she wouldn't mention that.)

From the doorway of the café the waiter looked back into the dark interior where the *patronne* sat at her desk. The *patronne* jerked her chin upwards in a sardonic gesture. She had seen it all before, heard the whoop.

270

Flora said a little touchily, 'I may know nothing about nightclubs but I have learned a little basic biology.'

Hubert said, 'Oh dear, fate intervening. Giving us time to be sensible.'

Flora, mistrusting the word, asked, 'How do we set about that?'

Forty

Angus Leigh, having had his hair cut at Trumpers, walked briskly through the parks on his way to his club in Pall Mall. He would glance through the papers, drink a glass of sherry and lunch solo. With luck he would not run into a club bore and be compelled into politeness. But, turning into Pall Mall after passing St James's Palace, he sighted Freddy Ward and Ian MacNeice heading in the same direction. He slowed to let them get ahead and diverged into Hardys where, browsing through its delights, he wrestled with his conscience. Dear old Freddy and Ian were not yet bores but on their way to becoming so; they would expect him to be sociable, would— 'I don't really need these, I tie my own,' he said to the shopman as he chose flies. 'And that lure, I haven't seen one of those. No, no, I can't buy another reel, can I? I have so many – well, yes, perhaps as you say. Yes, my son fishes and my son-in-law; it will be interesting to hear what they think of – Yes, if you would post them up for me. Thank you, good day.' Stepping into the frosty street his inner ear heard not the shopman's goodbye but Milly: 'Not more fishing stuff. Really, darling! Never been able to pass that shop, have you? The house is cluttered with tackle,' and so on and so on. 'And so on and so on,' he said out loud, almost bumping into a girl on the pavement.

'General Leigh,' said Flora. 'Hello.'

'Hello, my dear! Well met,' said Angus in delighted recognition. 'You are just what I need. Can you help me? Have you half an hour?'

'Both,' said Flora.

'I have bought a lot of expensive unnecessaries; to balance, I must buy something for Milly. Do you understand?'

'Yes,' said Flora, 'I do.'

'Splendid girl. Where should I go?'

'Floris?'

'Oho!'

'Or Fortnum's?'

'Or Fortnum's? Why not?'

'Chocolates?'

'Indeed yes.' Angus tucked Flora's hand in his arm. 'Off we go.'

'I say, isn't that Angus,' said Ian MacNeice, looking out of the club window, 'with a girl?'

'So it is,' said Freddy Ward. 'His daughter?'

'Doesn't look like his daughter. His daughter is fair.'

'Out of sight now,' said Freddy Ward.

'Are you lunching with anyone?' asked Angus, as they emerged from Fortnum's into Jermyn Street.

'No.'

'Will you lunch with me? Could you bear it?'

Flora said, 'Yes, please.'

'Perhaps we had better visit Floris too,' said Angus. 'Then we could lunch at Quaglinos. Do you know it?'

'No.'

'Come, then, tell me what to buy her at Floris. Then with conscience doubly clear I shall enjoy your company the more.' Flora laughed.

She thinks I am quite a dog, thought Angus, watching Flora choose bath oils for Milly; she's grown up, lost none of that charm. I wonder what she is up to these days. What was it she had that one liked? Reserve? Secrecy? One wondered even then, and so I think did the boys, fools if they didn't. 'Great piece of luck running into you,' he said, as they settled at a table in Quaglinos. 'I had intended lunching alone at my club where the food is rather dreary; I would have taken you there if it had been passable, but it isn't.' (With old Ian and Freddy peering at us, coming up to

273

be introduced? God, no.) 'Now, what shall we eat?'

Flora ordered oysters and sole with wine sauce. Angus also chose oysters but opted for sole plain grilled, studied the wine list and ordered. While they waited Angus chatted, giving her news of Milly; of Mabs and Nigel, living in London now, as no doubt she knew; the dogs, poor little Bootsie still alive but incredibly ancient – 'snaps at everybody'; the horses; Cosmo reading for the bar. The garden had had a good year; a new young gardener seemed keen. Tiresome loss of the butler, Gage, infected, one surmised, by Bolshie ideas encouraged by Hubert. Did she remember Hubert Wyndeatt-Whyte? Flora nodded. Such a loss, such a good butler. Milly insisted it was better now to make do with a parlourmaid since the fellow was irreplaceable, worked somewhere in London to be near Molly. Did she remember Molly, nice girl, under-housemaid? Well, she was with Tashie and Henry now, remember them? Flora said she did.

The oysters arrived. Angus watched her eat and drink her wine. 'So what are you doing with yourself these days?' He gulped an oyster.

'I am being sensible,' said Flora.

'Sensible?' He was stumped.

'Yes.'

'I thought,' said Angus, remembering, 'you were to join your parents in India. They are well, I hope?' What had he heard sieved through via Mabs to Milly? Something about rabies?

Flora said, 'They were well when last heard of.'

'So you are off to India?'

'I decided not. It wasn't sensible.' Flora watched the waiter refill her glass. Beside her Angus whooshed breath through his moustache. 'They don't like me,' she said, 'I have always known that. I am an impediment; they are wrapped up in each other. They left me in a deadly school for seven years. The only time I left it was when your wife invited me to Coppermalt. But now I am grown up. They sent me a list of clothes to have made which they would pay for, and a ticket for

Bombay. Their plan was obvious: I would get married and be off their hands. I had known this, I suppose, but it became clearer on the ship.' Flora reached for her glass and gulped wine. 'I am talking too much, boring you.'

Angus said, 'Go on.'

'To be fair,' said Flora, 'I don't like them.' Angus raised startled eyebrows. 'So I got off the ship.'

Angus said, 'Good God! Where?'

'Marseilles.'

Imagination racing, Angus said, 'When was this? What have you been doing since?'

Flora grinned. 'October. I've been catching up. Growing up,' she said sedately.

She seemed pleased about that. Angus blew out his moustache. 'What did your parents say?'

'I haven't heard. I wrote, but I had no address to give them. They will get the trunk. I only took what I needed, this suit for instance. It's nice, isn't it?'

Was she mocking him, imitating Mabs when talking of clothes? It's nearly Christmas, Angus thought. What the devil has she been up to since October? 'What did you tell them?' he said.

'I thanked them for my education, such as it is. I said that from now on I would earn my living, be off their hands, and not to worry.'

'Good God.' Angus found himself pleasurably outraged. 'You've got a nerve,' he said.

'They won't worry,' said Flora. 'They will be pleased,' she said. 'Pretty delighted.'

Angus repeated, 'You've got a nerve.'

Flora said, 'I hope I have.'

The waiter removed the plates of empty shells and brought Angus' grilled sole and Flora's with wine sauce. He watched her run her knife down the fish's spine, fork a mouthful, smile at him sidelong and wipe her mouth with her napkin. Whatever I say, he thought, 'I must not say, 'If you were my daughter', but what would one have done if Mabs had ever really—? She was watching him. 'It's not as

275

though this was about Mabs,' Flora said. 'You Leighs love each other. There's no love between me and my parents. You may remember them. Dinard? You didn't like them, I noticed. Goodness! When my trunk reaches them, my mother will be thrilled by the new dresses; we are the same size. She told me what to buy. They will think of something plausible to explain my non-arrival.'

Angus said, 'I've never heard anything like it, it's outrageous.'

Flora said, 'Oh, come on—' amused. 'People have run away through history.'

'Boys,' said Angus, munching his sole. 'You are a girl.'

'I admit that.'

'Girls cannot run away without—'

'Getting into trouble?'

'That's it.'

Flora said, 'There are things a girl can do between the extremes of marriage and prostitution.'

'I wasn't thinking—'

'Yes, you were. Marseilles, malodorous place; no place for a young girl. That's what you were thinking.'

Accepting her mockery, Angus said, 'What shall you do? What are you doing at the moment?'

'I am staying with a friend.'

She had not said what friend, Angus thought, watching her fleet departure up Bury Street, and given no indication of an address. It had, as they ate their sole, become curiously impossible to question her; his curiosity had been ably deflected. While he longed to probe where had she been since jumping ship? Who with? Had she any money? Where was she living? Why was she so averse to marriage? In what way could she possibly earn her living? It was she who questioned him. What did he think of unemployment? The collapse of the League of Nations? The National Government? He had swallowed the bait, he thought ruefully, as he watched her retreating back. He had mounted his hobby horses, held forth at length as they finished their sole and worked their way through pudding, cheese and coffee. He enlarged on Ramsay MacDonald, shredded the National Government, lauded Winston Churchill's scaremongering over disarmament, the rise of Hitler, the disgrace of universities stuffed with pacifists and Bolshies. She had let him run on. She read the newspapers and was well informed, a damn sight more interested and interesting than Mabs had been at seventeen or was now for that matter. She had encouraged, flattered, led him on. Clever little bitch, he thought, as she vanished round the corner, she made a monkey out of me.

Could he not have asked her to stay at Coppermalt? he wondered as he cut through King Street into St James's Square. Would Milly make her welcome? Ask a silly question, he thought, remembering the child tarted up in the black evening dress. One had wondered whether she was aware of the facts of life and got one's head bitten off. She had thanked him charmingly for giving her lunch, letting him brush her cheek with his moustache. She called back over her shoulder as she sped off, 'Who knows? I might become a housemaid,' making friendly fun.

Carrying his packets from Floris and Fortnum's, Angus reached his club. In the hall he ran into Ian MacNeice and Freddy Ward on their way out. 'Hello,' they said. 'We saw you earlier with a pretty girl.'

Angus said, 'Yes, a sensible creature, friend of the children's.' He resisted saying she had helped him buy presents for Milly. Men like Ian and Freddy sprang to stupid conclusions.

Forty-one

Hubert left Fleet Street walking on air and cut through
Bouverie Street to the Temple. Early for his appointment with Cousin Thing's solicitor, he assembled his
thoughts as he strolled towards Tweezers Alley. In a
week he would be in Germany, accredited correspond-
ent to a reputable newspaper, commissioned initially
to write three articles on the upsurge of Hitler. After
which, who knows? The editor, who had interviewed
him, had said, 'We'll see'; a different connotation to
'Who knows?' But who cares? thought Hubert, buoyant; it's a start. I can distil onto paper what I have
expounded under the plane trees of Aix, in the Roman
theatre at Orange and on the Pont d'Avignon. Flora,
gallant little listener, had called it a crash course in
international politics, and encouraged the indulgence.
His ideas had clarified and grown more succinct as he
lectured her.

Sighting the names of Macfarlane and Tait on a brass
plate, Hubert straightened his tie and banished Flora.
Yet she returned as he stood in the waiting-room, too
exhilarated to sit. Her mind had wandered when he
grew long-winded on the Fabians. She had pretended
not to know the difference between Socialist and Communist and complained that in *The Times* newspaper
the two seemed to be one, teasing him.

The clerk ushered Hubert into another room. 'Mr
Wyndeatt-Whyte,' said the solicitor.

'Mr Macfarlane,' said Hubert.

'Tait, actually, Macfarlane's dead. Do sit down. Cigarette? Don't smoke? Mind if I—'

Hubert sat and watched the solicitor light a cigarette, prop it on an ashtray, reach for a bundle of documents tied with pink tape, shake it, lay it in front of him and clear his throat. He had the moon face of a clown, with monkey eyes. 'These are the deeds of Pengappah and your cousin Mr Hubert Wyndeatt-Whyte's will,' he said in a depressed voice.

'Do call me Hubert.'

'Oh, well, thanks. Well, there are – um – yes – do you know the place, er – Hubert?'

'No.' Smoke was spiralling up from the ashtray. How much revenue did the government rake in annually from tobacco? How much did this Tait contribute to the bourgeois system? 'My cousin never invited me. I rather gathered he was a recluse.'

'Recluse? My goodness, no, not a recluse. You couldn't call him a recluse,' said Mr Tait. 'No, that would not fit.'

'What would?'

'Does it matter now?'

Hubert was surprised by a note of acrimony. 'Not if he's dead.'

Mr Tait said, 'Well, he is.'

Hubert said, 'Good.'

There was a pause. Mr Tait rested his hands on the documents. Hubert said, 'Let's get on, then,' hoping he sounded polite; he would never get back to Flora at this rate.

Thus urged Mr Tait got on. 'Pengappah, such as it is, is yours for life. I believe you are aware of that? Your cousin left a small income, this.' Here he pushed papers towards Hubert. Hubert read, registering the amount of the income with pleasure. It was not his idea of small. 'That's for the upkeep of the house, such as it is, and the land, such as it is. You say you have never been there?'

'No.'

'Ah.'

'All I know is that there are six baths in the bathroom.'

'No, Mr – er – Hubert, not any more.'

'Why not?'

'You were not informed? Perhaps not. You see, half the house burned down six years ago.'

'So that's why you say, "such as it is".'

'Precisely.'

'It's a ruin?'

'No, no, not a ruin. Just half the size of what you expected.'

'I have not known what to expect.'

'I see.' Mr Tait picked the remnant of his cigarette from the ashtray and stubbed it out. 'I believe,' he said, 'your cousin, old Hubert Wyndeatt-Whyte, reorganized the house and sold some of the land to do so. We were not consulted.'

'What a shame.'

Mr Tait said, 'Yes, a shame. We were his legal advisers.'

Hubert said, 'Of course.'

Mr Tait said, 'Not that we would have advised him to do other than he did.'

Hubert breathed in. 'Not a recluse, no six baths and half a house—'

'Oh, it looks whole.'

'Are there things for me to sign?' (It was amazing that the streets of this part of London were not festooned with solicitors dangling from lamp-posts.)

'There were six baths, that would be in my partner's day, and yes, yes, of course, there is this and this for you to sign – I will ask my clerk to witness – and a map of how to get there.' Being rushed came as a surprise to Mr Tait.

It did not take long; anxious to get away, Hubert thanked Mr Tait and prepared to leave. Mr Tait said, 'You'll need a car, it's rather isolated.'

Hubert said, 'I'll borrow one.' He would take Cosmo's. Cosmo was going up by train for Christmas at Coppermalt; Cosmo wouldn't mind.

'I would like you to lunch with me.' Mr Tait would not take no. Hubert thought that time need

280

not be wasted; he could pump Mr Tait about Cousin
Thing and Pengappah. Mr Tait took him to Simpson's
and, while they ordered their roast beef, admitted that
he had never met Cousin Thing or seen Pengappah.
His recently defunct partner had handled all Cousin
Thing's affairs.

Hubert resolved to remove his affairs from Mr Tait
as soon as feasible, but now the man undermined his
fury by asking, 'Are you married?'

Hubert said, 'No.'

Mr Tait said, 'Do you intend?'

Hubert said, 'I—'

Mr Tait said, 'You should bear in mind that your
property is entailed on a male heir but *don't*, oh,
Hubert, *don't*. My wife left me this morning – the
grief, the desolation, the despair.' The monkey eyes
glistened, then in a choking voice he said, 'The bloody,
bloody bitch. I shall kill her.'

They had reached the cheese stage. Hubert swallowed his mouthful of stilton, crunched a piece of
celery and murmured, 'Each man kills the thing he
loves.'

Mr Tait raised his head and voice. 'But *he* was
a queer.'

Several people looked round, then quickly away.
Hubert said, 'Maybe he *was*, but he screwed out a
couple of sons. I say, Mr Tait, I must go. I hadn't
realized the time. Thank you so much for your help
and lunch,' and began shuffling to his feet.

Mr Tait said, 'It's been a pleasure. Waiter, my bill.'

Shaking Mr Tait's hand, looking into the little monkey eyes in the clown's face, Hubert said, 'You won't
kill her, will you, not really?'

Mr Tait finding his pocket book, looking embarrassed, murmured, 'I shall think of something better—'

Escaped into the Strand, recovering his balance,
Hubert decided that Mr Tait was mad, but what
did it matter? He had the keys of Pengappah in his
pocket, the deeds in his hand, and the prospect of an

interesting job. Cheered by his thoughts, he set off to borrow Cosmo's car.

Cosmo, in shirt-sleeves, was packing a suitcase. 'Borrow the car? Of course, here are the keys. Treat her kindly. Sorry, but I'm in rather a rush. I am catching the train with Father and he will skin me if I miss it.' He folded a coat, laid it in the case. 'Shoes, socks, shirts, pants. Where are you going?'

'Pengappah.'

'So you've *got* it? It really *exists*?' He paused in his task.

Hubert shook the keys in the air. 'Keys! Deeds!'

'After all these years, it's yours. Congratulations. Lord of Pengappah, a landed gentleman. Shall you change your political mores?'

Ignoring the tease, Hubert said, '*And* I've got a job.'

'No!' Cosmo was delighted. 'How splendid.'

'Germany, commissioned to write articles on the Nazis—'

Cosmo, mouth open, listened to details of the job. He said, 'You will be so much happier than working in that bank.'

'Much.'

The friends stood smiling at one another, then Cosmo said, 'I must get on; Father's getting old, he fusses. I wish you were coming to Coppermalt for Christmas, but I quite see you can't wait to see your house. Knowing you, you want to savour it alone.'

'Who is going to be at Copper—'

'Mabs and Nigel, Tash and Henry. Infants too, of course.'

'Joyce?'

'Gone to the Canaries with Ernest.'

'It's over, then?'

Cosmo said, 'Joyce is not a habit, she's an incident. You should know.' He laid a pair of trousers in the suitcase and closed it. 'Now, what have I forgotten?' He looked round the room. 'I was tempted to hare after Flora when we saw her off. If you must know, I realized the thing with Joyce was on the wane. I wonder how she's getting on?'

Hubert said, 'I'm sure she's all right. Well — many thanks for the car. I'll leave it back here in a week,' and left.

Mounting the stairs to his own flat twenty minutes later with jubilant step, filled with pleasurable antici- pation, Hubert called, 'Flora?' The flat was empty, the bed they had lain in the night before cold. His stomach contracted in panic. Confidence evaporated, he was filled with manic rage. 'Where the hell have you been?' he yelled, as Flora appeared in the doorway. 'What have you been up to? Where have you been?'

'Out.'

'Where? Doing what?'

'Spending a sensible day.' She stood on tiptoe to kiss him. 'Why so cross?'

'I thought you had gone. I was bracing myself against disaster.' He held her close.

'Why should I go? How was the meeting with the lawyer?' Disturbed by his fury, she disengaged herself, kicked off her shoes and lay back in an armchair. 'Don't tell me there is no Pengappah? What was the old man like?'

'Not old, rather odd. Gave me the keys and so on, and insisted on giving me lunch. His wife has just left him. He wants to kill her.' Joyce had lain back in that chair in much the same attitude, but Joyce was aware of the effect. 'I thought we could start at once, this afternoon.' He would not tell her yet about the job; he would keep the news as a treat.

She said, 'Wonderful,' smiling. 'Was the man de- ranged?'

'Drive through the night,' ignoring the question.

'Drive?'

'I've borrowed a car.'

'How splendid.'

'Have you had anything to eat? Are you starving?'

The habit of privacy wrapped her too close to tell

283

him of her lunch with Angus. 'I've been sensible.' She smiled up at him.

Joyce had smiled too. 'You look very cocky,' he said, looking down at her.

She had learned why the men she had danced with on the ship grew lumps in their trousers. It had happened too at Coppermalt, but she had not then known the reason. 'Goodness,' she said, as Hubert picked her up out of the chair, 'not on the floor!' They fell onto the bed. 'We seem to be doing rather a lot of this,' she said, as Hubert pulled off her knickers. 'You smell nice,' she said. (Not a bit like my parents, she thought.) Then, while Hubert swooned, she thought of how she had been waiting all her childhood and seven interminable years at school for something to happen and now it had.

Hubert said, 'I love you. I might even marry you some day.'

'If I don't marry someone else.'

'Who, for instance?' He stroked her silky thigh.

'Felix?'

'He's married.'

'His wife might die. Or Cosmo.'

'Can't have that.' He felt a twinge of guilt. Should he not this afternoon have been more open—

'You may have to "have it".'

'Come to think of it, I promised I would share you. We were pretty young at the time.' Hubert got off the bed. 'But as St Augustine said, "Not yet, oh Lord".'

Flora said, 'What cheek! Without asking me? Share?' She was shocked.

'You had gone, swept off by Miss Felicity Green. We had a fight.'

'Who won?'

'Nobody. I blacked his eye, he trod on my foot. Come on, get cracking. We should be on the road.'

Driving past Hammersmith Broadway, Flora said: 'Is this car Cosmo's?'

'Actually, yes.'

'Thought so.'

'How d'you guess?'

Flora said, 'He came to see me off at Tilbury with Joyce. You must remember.'

'And?'

'It smells of Joyce.'

'A lot of things smell of Joyce; she wears scent which hangs around. Jolly girl, though, Joyce.' I should be grateful to Joyce, he thought; catching up with Flora at Marseilles wouldn't have been much fun if Cosmo had made it too.

Flora did not want to think of Joyce, jolly or not. She was sorry she had brought her up; there had been faint unsettling traces in Hubert's flat. She supposed they shared Joyce, as they had agreed to share her. She stared ahead as they drove past the suburbs towards the Great West Road.

They had left London far behind when Hubert said, 'For the sake of propriety I shall tell people at Pengappah you are my cousin.'

'You did not bother about propriety in France.'

'Pengappah is different.'

'I am not your cousin. Why not pretend I am your sister? We are both dark. That would be much more proper.' She was contemptuous of his new respectability.

Ignoring the acidity in her tone, Hubert said serenely, 'I could not marry a sister.'

Flora spaced her reply. 'I – do – not – want – to – marry – you.'

Hubert was indulgent. 'You will change your mind.'

Bearing in mind her phantom trio, Flora said, exasperated, 'How could I?'

Hubert did not answer.

Presently Flora asked, 'How long shall we stay?'

'Not long. You can stay on if you like it. I have to go to Germany.'

Flora turned towards him. 'Germany? What for? What's this about Germany?'

He told her about the job; she listened bleakly as he outlined the project. It was a wonderful chance, just the kind of life he wanted. He viewed his immediate prospects with enthusiasm. So he too could be secretive, she thought. She said, 'How jolly for you,' keeping her tone neutral.

Ignoring her chill, Hubert said, 'Far jollier than banking. I was going to tell you, but you were not there when I got in—' He could not tell her of his terror when he found the flat empty and thought her gone. He was glad that he could reproach her, conscious, too, that he had deceived Cosmo, and pleased when she said: 'You are a selfish beast.' Driving on in silence he began to wonder why the hell he had brought her. Had he not looked forward in his dreams to the moment when he would at last acquire Pengappah, to doing it alone? There had never been anyone else when he put the key in the door and pushed. Was she in the way?

Flora thought, If he plans to leave, would I not do better to stop now, go back to London and get a job, any job? There must be some jobs I can do. Who do I know who could help me? She opened her mouth to say, 'Stop the car, let me out,' but remained silent, afraid her voice would shake and betray her desolation.

She had been sleeping and woke when Hubert stopped the car to pore over a map by the light of a torch. She said, 'Where are we?'

'Nearly there. I am memorizing the way, it's a very secret place. Like some chocolate?' He snapped a bar in half and handed it to her. 'Now don't talk, I must concentrate.'

Realizing that she was painfully hungry, she ate the chocolate as Hubert drove down a lane which dipped into a valley and over a hill. Beside her, Hubert muttered, 'Right, half-right, left, left again, cross over, turn right, left through the splash, right here, that's right, here's the clearing, aha, and there's the gate. Could you hop out and open it?' There was excitement in his voice. She got out of the car, stiff from the journey, opened a gate and closed it when Hubert drove through. 'Go on,' she said, 'I'd like to walk.'

'But it's still dark.'

'There's a moon. Go on, it won't be very far.'

'Really? D'you mean—'

'Yes, go on.' She waved him on and stood watching the car lights twist through trees as the track led downhill. If I had not been asleep, she thought, I would know how far I am from the nearest village. I could go now, turn round and go, but I can't, my suitcase is in the car. She started to walk.

The house squatted black in the moonlight with silver eyes. Standing on the grass of an unkempt lawn, hearing the sea at the foot of the valley and the brush and creak of trees in the wood, she listened, hearing too the click of the car's engine cool where Hubert had left it, its door swinging open in the quiet. The chocolate had made her thirsty but she was loath to disturb Hubert; she felt *de trop*. A stream trickling from a gravelled gully at the side of the house fell from pool to pool stepped down the slope into a wood. She squatted, cupped her hands in the reflection of her face and drank.

'Come with me.' Hubert took her hand, still wet from the pool, and led her in through a door which opened immediately into a stone-flagged room where she breathed in years of woodsmoke. 'Look.' He pointed to a Regency mirror above the mantelshelf. Stuck round the rim was a collection of postcards arranged in order of date. 'Expect me sooner or later,' read the messages in English, German, Italian, French, Dutch, and pasted in the middle one bearing a message in Russian. 'And this,' Hubert whispered, shining the torch close to the glass. 'Can you read it?' Traced in the dust on the glass Flora was able to make out the word 'Welcome'.

'Makes me look a proper Charlie, a perfect fool,' said Hubert. 'I thought I was being so funny; what possessed me to be so crass?'

Flora said, 'The one in Russian says, "May you be happy and blest". Something like that. The spelling is all haywire, of course.'

Hubert shone the torch in her face. 'So you *cheated*?'

287

There was anger and relief in his voice. 'You deceived me?'

Flora pushed the torch aside; it seemed to her then that there had always been an element of deception in their relationship. 'We don't need that,' she said, 'it's getting light.'

Hubert said, 'I don't think the welcome was for me, do you?'

Flora said, 'I think it was for both of you.'

'I certainly hope so.' Hubert shook off remorse. 'I should hate to think I contributed to his demise.'

'You wished him dead,' said Flora matter-of-factly, 'and now he is.'

'Only,' Hubert prevaricated, 'because he would not make friends. If he had, it would have been quite different.'

Flora said, 'Might have been,' sceptically.

Hubert laughed. 'To be honest, what I used to want was to be invited to stay, to bath in a bathroom with six baths. It sounded so exotic. But this morning, oh gosh it must be yesterday, the solicitor told me half the house had been burned down and the baths—'

'Five of them are dug into the slope, transformed into pools, I was looking at them when you came out just now – rather fun.'

For a moment Hubert felt he could throttle her for cheating him of part of his discovery. 'Tait told me something – oh—'

'What? What did he tell you?'

Hubert began to laugh. 'He reminded me that Pengappah is entailed on my male heir. Perhaps,' said Hubert, chuckling, 'we'd better look sharp, get married and beget.'

Flora said, 'You are a swine,' and hit him.

When the quarrel stopped Hubert held Flora in his arms, but she said, 'I must get away. Where's my suitcase? I should never have come, never!'

'Darling, I was joking.' He stroked her hair. 'I'm sorry, so sorry. Don't let's quarrel, please. Look, it's light, it's Christmas. Happy Christmas.'

She said, 'All right, but I can't marry you. I can't explain. I'm sorry about it, but Happy Christmas.'

Hubert said, 'Come and explore the house with me,' and surprised himself wishing Cosmo was with them.

Forty-two

Coming down to breakfast Milly viewed the Christmas tree in the hall. Cosmo and Mabs, Nigel, Henry and Tashie had decorated it the previous day. It was beautiful, silver and gold with white candles, a far cry from the jolly but glaring arrangements that had been the genre of nursery and schooldays, when every colour of the rainbow had jumbled so thickly on the tree it had been almost impossible to see a pine needle. Their parcels under the tree were sophisticated, artful wrappings of pale blues and pinks tied with gold and silver ribbon. She could recognize her own contributions in the glaring reds, greens and yellows she was used to using. Perhaps, thought Milly with nostalgia, we shall revert to bumptious vulgarity as the grandchildren grow?

'Happy Christmas,' she said, opening the dining-room door. 'Happy Christmas.' She kissed her husband. They had kissed already when Molly's successor, Bridgid, brought their morning tea, a kiss rasped against Angus' bristles. Now he was shaved her kiss lingered on his sweet-smelling weather-beaten skin. 'Happy Christmas, my darlings.' She sat down. 'Is this my post? What a heap of last-minute cards; people do cut things fine. I do enjoy Christmas.' She looked round the table at her family, and Tashie and Henry so close they almost counted as family, as did Hubert and Joyce, habitual visitors but absent this year. 'I popped into the nursery on my way, the Nannies are already trying to contain the tinies' excitement.' Round the table Milly's darlings gave her cheerful greetings as they opened their letters, or ate their breakfasts.

Cosmo brought his mother coffee. 'What can I get you, Ma?' He kissed her cheek.

'I think I'll look at my post first.' Milly sorted through letters. 'What is this? And this?' she exclaimed, discovering two parcels tied with ribbon. 'A mystery. No name on them.'

'Presents extra for an extra special wife.' Angus beamed as Milly flushed with pleasure. 'Open them,' he said, pouting out his moustache. She was a fine woman, he thought, watching her untie the parcels, as fine as she had been at eighteen, the darling of his heart. He would have liked to voice this thought but was inhibited by the presence of his children, who were exchanging surreptitious smiles. Come to think of it, he had never actually called her the darling of his heart; would she laugh if he did?

Struggling with tight knots, Milly exclaimed, 'Oh darling, you shouldn't,' and 'Floris, my absolute favourite,' and 'Honestly, Angus, how could you? Fortnum's chocolate truffles. What about my figure?'

Angus was delighted by the success of his parcels. 'Your figure suits me as it is.'

Milly said, 'What a cheat to spring such a surprise. My mingy contributions are under the tree. What a darling you are.' Nigel, catching Mabs' eye, hoped that their union would be as affectionate in twenty years' time; Henry, infected by the atmosphere, kissed Tashie; Cosmo, reaching for the toast rack, experienced a twinge of loss, wishing he had Hubert to keep him company.

Milly began opening her letters. 'Cards, cards, there are always some from people I forget.' She sipped her coffee. 'Ah, Rosa, and her good news! Felix has a son. I'd forgotten he was expecting when we were told last week.'

'Felix?' Mabs raised an eyebrow. 'Felix?'

'His wife, silly. Oh dear, a card from Felicity Green, I never send her one. And look at this, from your dressmaker, Mabs. I don't go to her these days.'

'A hint that you should?' suggested Tashie.

Angus, looking up from bacon and egg, said, 'Touting.'

Milly said, 'Hum, well, perhaps. Who do we know in India? I don't recognize the writing.'

'Try opening it.' Cosmo reached for the marmalade. 'Pass the butter, Nigel.'

Milly slit the envelope. 'Vita Trevelyan. Who is Vita Trevelyan?'

'Flora's mother,' said Tashie.

'You must remember her,' said Mabs. 'You couldn't stand her.'

'What can she want? Difficult writing.' Milly looked at the letter askance.

'Try reading it,' said Henry, who was enjoying his grilled kidneys and deplored conversation at breakfast. Tashie kicked his shin to remind him that he was not in his own house.

Nigel got up to help himself to kedgeree.

'You'll get frightfully fat if you eat so much,' said Mabs with wifely disapproval.

'Fortifying myself against Christmas lunch,' said Nigel amiably. 'The more I eat, the more I can.'

Pursing her lips as she read the letter, Milly said, 'My goodness, how peculiar.'

'Out loud, Ma,' suggested Cosmo.

Milly read: ' "Dear Mrs Leigh, Forgive me for bothering you but I remember you were kind enough to have Flora to stay" ' (but I did not invite her again when I should have, oh dear, oh dear, how can I have been so mean?). ' "She was to have joined us here" – here must be, yes, it's postmarked and addressed Peshawar. Where's that?'

'North-West Frontier,' said Angus. 'No pigsticking. They hunt jackals. Good fun, I'm told.'

'Father,' said Mabs, 'you digress.'

Milly read on, her voice rising on a tide of incredulity. ' "She sailed from Tilbury in early October, seen off by one of the mistresses from her school, but when our bearer met the ship at Bombay there was only her

292

trunk with all the lovely clothes I had had made for her by the little dressmaker we all went to in Dinard that year" – I'd quite forgotten how she monopolized her—'

'Go on, Mother,' urged Mabs.

' "We wrote to the school thinking she might have returned there" – why should she do that? – "but they were as surprised as we are and had received no news." – Why do tiresome people receive not get?'

'Mother—'

' "– a letter arrived here in early December to say she does not want to come to India, she will earn her own living" – from the girl?'

'Bravo,' said Nigel. 'Spunk.'

'Nigel dear, she goes on. "Not unnaturally, since she is only seventeen, we are concerned and would like to get in touch – we wondered whether you or any of your family had been contacted – apologies for troubling you." What a peculiar letter. What a strange way, oh, here she says in a postscript, even more peculiar, she seems to have left the ship in Marseilles. Good heavens, what an extraordinary—'

'White-slavers.' Nigel forked kedgeree into his mouth. 'They drug and kidnap.'

'Don't be stupid,' said Mabs. 'Idiot.'

'She came to see me,' wailed Tashie. 'She seemed – we were just going away for a week's shooting. I told you, Mabs, d'you remember? I telephoned. You were in your bath.'

'She didn't want to go to India and we did absolutely bloody nothing,' said Mabs. 'Oh, God.'

'Don't swear, Mabs, it's ugly,' said Milly.

'Hubert, Joyce and I saw her off,' said Cosmo, 'at Tilbury.'

'How did she seem?' asked Henry.

'All right.' But had she been all right?

'We were all rather jolly, cracked a bottle of champagne to wish her well. Joyce's idea, actually.' I was drunk, thought Cosmo, and Joyce seemed to have charge of me. I was sleeping with her, wasn't I? Why didn't I latch on? Why didn't I help?

'When she stayed here,' said Milly, examining Vita's letter for non-existent clues, 'I thought she was rather – it strikes me that – well, she was quite—' (Quite what? A danger? A girl one couldn't ask to come again in case one's son or husband found her attractive? Which she was. Oh God, I am belittled.) 'Well, my goodness, to step off the ship just like that and disappear seems strange, if not actually disreputable.'

Angus said, 'Is that the telephone? It's all right, I'll answer it. I'm expecting a call. She seemed a sensible girl to me,' he said as he left the room.

'Nothing wrong with Father's hearing,' said Mabs. Or mine, thought Cosmo. Listening to his father in the hall, he heard:

'Yes, my dear fellow, yes, of course. I'll see about it, yes. Happy Chris – Goodbye.' Angus replaced the receiver. His heart was beating uncomfortably; he went to sit in the library. Why, he asked himself, had he not told Milly at the time? Nothing had happened, no need to feel guilty; since when was it wrong to give a pretty girl lunch? Nothing wrong in that. Then the second chance to tell her had come just now when Milly opened her presents. He could have made a joke of it, told her how he had been extravagant in Hardy's – those salmon flies, the lures – told her how Flora had suggested Floris, suggested Fortnum's, been charming at lunch, been in her own words 'sensible'. Oh yes, thought Angus, the girl was sensible, sensible in the French sense. I am sixty-six, old enough to be her grandfather, but not, he thought ruefully, too old to think how beautiful it would be to get her into bed. One wouldn't try, of course, it was only an idea, but try explaining that to Milly. 'Oh bugger,' said Angus out loud. 'Bugger, bugger, bugger.' He walked to the window and stared out at the winter sky.

Coming into the room Cosmo said, 'Father, there's an argument. The girls want to bring their babies to church; Mother wants you to decide.'

Re-focusing his thoughts, Angus said, 'Let infant shrieks drown the Christmas message, slew the carols off course? Bloody good idea, all hell let loose, whyever not?'

His father's tone was so belligerent Cosmo took a step backwards, but in the doorway he said, 'You've seen her, haven't you?'

Angus said, 'Who? Certainly not. No idea.'

Cosmo said, 'Thanks,' and retreated into the hall, convinced that the telephone had not rung.

Forty-three

Finding the door open Cosmo peered in; Hubert knelt with his back to him, puffing with a pair of bellows at a recalcitrant fire. The wood was damp and his measure of success small, for each time a spark crackled and pale flames licked a down draught billowed smoke in his face, making him rock back on his heels cursing. Then, suddenly, flames took hold with a hungry crackle and purred sweetly up.

Cosmo said, 'Eureka. Bravely done.'

Hubert swung round. 'What brings you here? How did you find the way?'

'There are such things as ordnance maps, trains, taxis and so on. I walked from the village.' Cosmo stepped inside. 'Shall you not be hospitable and ask me in? I brought you a bottle of whisky. Nice,' he said, looking round. 'Is Pengappah what you expected? Dreams come true? Will you show me round your estate?'

'I thought you were spending Christmas at Coppermalt,' said Hubert ungraciously.

'I was. I did. Your presence was sadly missed.' Cosmo sauntered round the room and peered out of the window. 'Is that the sea down there through the trees? What an idyllic situation; sheltered, secret and remote.' He turned back into the room. 'I say, nice books. I see your cousin Thing was quite erudite. Furniture not to be sniffed at, either. Some decent pictures, too; do show me round.'

'I had rather intended to be alone, but as you are here, shut the door. It's only open to let the smoke out.'

'And not uninvited guests. Do I gather I am not welcome?'

'I have rather a lot to do – I hoped—'

'A solitary gloat is understandable,' said Cosmo amiably, 'but since I am here, welcome or not, why don't we have a drink?' He unscrewed the bottle of whisky. 'In those nice rummers on the mantelshelf, or are they sacred? A quick tot to drink your health and wish you luck.'

Hubert reached for the rummers. 'I'll get some water,' he said.

Cosmo watched as Hubert went into the kitchen, noted a pile of groceries, fruit, a bottle of wine, another of whisky on a deal table, a loaf, butter and cheese. Hubert brought water. 'Perhaps I need a drink, I've had a surprise.'

'Oh? Nasty?'

'Yes.' Hubert watched Cosmo pour the drinks, took his, gulped, looked at his watch and then at Cosmo. 'Why don't you sit down?'

'Thanks.'

They sat in armchairs by the fire. Cosmo said, 'What was the surprise?'

'My cousin's – my solicitor hanged himself.'

'Why?'

'What a thing to do! I saw him in London. He gave me the keys, read me my cousin's will and gave me lunch. The thing is, he said his wife had left him, and that he'd like to kill her. I didn't expect him to kill himself. It seems all wrong for a solicitor—'

'I suppose they are human.'

'I thought he was a bore. I felt awful. I telephoned from the village when I was doing the shopping to ask him to do various things for me, and his clerk told me.'

'I suppose he has a partner.'

'God, you are callous.'

'He bored you; you didn't like him. You are not really upset. What's upsetting you is that you don't want me here, you want me to leave. You keep looking at your watch.'

'I only looked at it once,' Hubert exclaimed. 'I'm upset, I tell you.'

'So will I please leave? Tell you what,' said Cosmo, 'show me round first, a lightning tour for old time's sake. I did bring you a bottle,' he wheedled. 'Would it be permitted to see the famous bathroom, for instance? The six baths? Come on, be hospitable. Don't let your new status affect your manners. One hopes, too, that now you are a man of property it won't affect your democratic tendencies.' Cosmo sniffed his whisky and drank.

Hubert said, 'All right, but it's got to be quick. These are the stairs—' He led the way.

'So I see,' Cosmo murmured. 'The stairs.'

'The landing,' said Hubert. 'Bedrooms.' He walked past, opening and shutting doors before Cosmo could see in. 'A loft up there full of junk, a lot of it scorched.'

'Scorched?'

'There was a fire; half the house went. Cousin Thing did not rebuild but made a walled garden in the ruined wing. It's rather effective.' Hubert gulped whisky as he walked. 'The bathroom.' He opened a door, gesturing with his glass. '*La salle de bain*.'

'But only one bath.' Cosmo's eyes darted about, taking in a large but solitary bath and, on a wooden bathrack, sponges, soap and flannel.

Hubert closed the door. 'He took out the extra five. Come down, I'll show you the kitchen. He dug the extra five into the slope of the garden so that the stream runs through them, a sort of waterfall. F—, I found them all green with moss. You'd never guess they were porcelain pools.'

'Fascinating,' said Cosmo. 'I must see them. Goldfish?' He followed Hubert down the stairs.

'Trout. This is the kitchen, w—, I – er – eat in here.'

'Most democratic,' said Cosmo gravely.

'And that's the lot,' said Hubert briskly. 'As you see, there is no electricity, candles and oil lamps, no telephone, spring water. Sorry I can't offer you lunch. I'm only camping. I leave tomorrow for Germany. It's

298

been a quick dash, that's all.' He moved towards the door. 'I have these letters – a lot of business—'

Cosmo did not follow him. 'Since you came in my car,' he said, helping himself to whisky, 'I imagined we could go back to London together.' His tone was amiable, his expression obtuse.

Hubert said, 'Oh no! I mean, well, it's not—'

'Where are you hiding her?' asked Cosmo quietly.

'Hiding? Hiding who?'

'Flora.' Cosmo sat in an armchair, stretched his legs towards the fire and set his glass beside him.

'What makes you think she's here?' Hubert blessed the whisky for the amazement in his voice. 'Why should—? What an extraordinary idea.'

Cosmo said, 'Since when have you used a pink bath flannel?'

'Joyce—'

'As we both know, Joyce's bath flannels are always mauve and Joyce has gone to the Canaries with husband Ernest.' Cosmo leaned forward and replenished Hubert's glass. 'Where is Flora?'

'I don't know what—'

' – I am talking about. Sit down,' said Cosmo. 'You are as bad at lying as my father.'

'What has your father got to—' Hubert gulped his drink and sat down.

'I'll tell you. Flora's mother, that pestilential woman, wrote to my mother.'

'What would she do that for?'

'It appears Flora knows no one in England except us Coppermalt lot and her school. Mrs Trevelyan wrote to Mother to ask whether by any chance she had news of Flora. It appears she jumped ship at Marseilles and has not been heard of since. White-slavery is suspected by the gullible, but I remembered that you came with Joyce and me to see her off at Tilbury, and that you, curiously enough, have been in France for a couple of months. Two and two seemed to me to make Flora. Where is she?'

Hubert said, 'This is ridiculous,' and leaned forward to throw logs on the fire.

'I seem to remember,' said Cosmo, 'that we made a pact to go shares.'

'As boys.' Hubert demurred.

'We have not changed gender; we were both in good working order with Joyce.'

'Oh,' said Hubert. 'Joyce.'

Cosmo asked, 'Have you married Flora?'

'Married? Good Lord, no.' (She had refused, had she not?) 'I can't afford to marry.'

'I have a strong suspicion that my father is in touch with her,' said Cosmo slyly.

Hubert burst into spontaneous laughter. 'Your father! How massively comical.'

'Mother does not think it comical,' said Cosmo rather stiffly. 'I say, should we not dilute this a bit before we get squiffed?'

Hubert dribbled water with a careful hand. 'Tell me how your father comes into things.' He sat back, smiling. 'Your honoured Pa, the General.'

Cosmo said, 'There has been one hell of a row over Christmas, a full-blown menopausal eruption, starting at breakfast on Christmas morning, carried on through Boxing Day: low-voiced queries, muttered asides, hints, all behind a bright Christmas-spirity front. Mustn't spoil Christmas. Mabs and I became quite wretched. Oh, do stop grinning. You are as bad as Nigel and Henry.'

'But it is funny,' giggled Hubert. 'Your aged Pa, how could—'

'Would you still laugh if I told you there is something in it?'

'There couldn't be.'

'But there is. Neither Mabs nor I have seen him like it, hangdog, guilty. We've seen so many of Mother's suspicious attacks, but this—'

'But he must be about sixty.'

'Sixty-six.'

'Well—'

'I tell you, when my mother accused him he looked sheepish. It began with Father giving her extra presents, not the sort of thing he would choose himself. Then she got Mrs Trevelyan's letter and began thinking of Flora, remembering her when she came to Coppermalt.'

'She was only fifteen.'

'She remembered that. When she read the letter she began thinking of Flora's last evening, when the girls dressed her up as a *femme fatale*. Mother managed to say, without using the word, that Flora was a tart – disreputable was the word used – and Father left the room pretending he heard the telephone.'

'Oh!'

'During Christmas church – Mabs and Tash brought their infants to counter the carols – Mother was *distrait*; she whispered at Father and Father's neck went red. I was in the pew behind them. He said, "Milly, be quiet," and "For Christ's sake, shut up." Jolly unchristmas spirit. But she wouldn't let well alone. She niggled through Christmas Day and he made a mess of his answers. He did not, as he's always done, laugh at her. She kept coming back to the letter and Flora. "Thrust on us by your girl-friend, Rosa." "I never had any affair with Rosa." "It's not Rosa we are discussing," and then later worrying like Bootsie at a bone. "When I had her to stay that summer I didn't think she was really that sort of girl, and yet when Mabs and Tashie dressed her up she looked very, very tarty." By night she was really needling him. None of us could stop her. Father drank far more than he usually does and punished the whisky decanter after dinner. Then, as we drifted thankfully to bed, we heard her shout: "You met her in London. Stop lying, I know you did." '

'And?' Hubert's mouth hung open.

'Father said, "If you must know, yes I did," in tones of ice.'

'And?'

'Slept in his dressing-room. He never does unless one of them is ill. He adores her. Boxing Day was arctic, they were not on speakers. They both looked

301

wretched. And I remembered what a hurry you were in when you borrowed my car, not a bit like you, and set off to find you and check up.'

Hubert said, 'The silly old man, he made it up,' and helped Cosmo and himself to whisky.

'If he made it up,' said Cosmo, 'you must have got Flora hidden somewhere. Where is she? Up in the loft among the scorched junk?'

'No,' said Hubert. 'No. She's gone out, said she wanted to think.' He lay back and closed his eyes.

'You bastard,' said Cosmo. 'When will she be back?'

'I don't know. She's been gone hours.'

'Why should she want to think? Have you hurt her?'

'Why should I hurt her?' said Hubert violently. 'I love her.'

'I love her,' said Cosmo.

'Not that again. What we should be asking is, Who does she love?'

Forty-four

The sand on the tide line was frozen. Flora's feet
imprinted the crust as she walked across the cove
to the water. The sea was the colour of pewter and
flat.

When Hubert woke he would find her note on the
kitchen table. He would go to the village to buy food,
carry on to the town, exploring his new neighbourhood,
and do his telephoning from there. She had written: 'I
am going for a walk. Flora.' He would expect her back.
She had not said: 'I need to think, to work things out,
to decide.' But finding herself alone on the beach she
had known that that was what she was trying to do.

She watched a flight of herring gulls winging out to
sea in the winter dawn and listened to their lonely cry.
At the water's edge she wrapped her coat tightly round
her, turned up the collar and let her eye follow a pair
of cormorants scurrying close above the water towards
a horizon just catching the pink of dawn. It was cold.
A ship steamed along the line between sea and sky,
heading perhaps to the subcontinent of India. 'Where
shall I decide to go?' she said out loud. 'I cannot stay
here.'

Pacing at the water's edge she reviewed the past
days at Pengappah, very different from the heady
weeks in France when, listening to Hubert, she had
known that their thoughts and emotions blended as at
night her body fused with his. Arrived at Pengappah,
she had stood aside and watched as Hubert discovered
the reality of his inheritance. She had seen him com-
pare the substance with some imaginary dream. Ready

303

for disappointment, he had prowled suspiciously at first, ready to rebuff; grown enthusiastic he had fallen headlong for the place's charm. Excluded by his concentration, and not unwilling to be so, she had watched him with increasing detachment, a detachment of which he was unaware. They had explored Pengappah minutely, walked the boundaries, talked to the old couple, Mr and Mrs Jarvis in the village, who had worked for Cousin Thing. 'Old Mr Wyndeatt-Whyte was a proper gentleman,' they said. 'A proper gentleman was Mr Hubert.' They sized Hubert up, visibly wondering whether the new, the young Mr Wyndeatt-Whyte would do, if not at once, eventually.

Hubert had not been ingratiating and this they appreciated. They agreed to do a bit in the house, light the occasional fire to stave off the damp, keep the garden tidy as they had for Cousin Thing. Cousin Thing, it transpired, had only visited occasionally of late years, preferring to lodge in his club at Bath. 'He didn't like things moved, came in good weather for a change to look at his books, collect the post if there was any, just postcards as a rule and not many of they.'

Hubert, avoiding this conversational lure, had stuck to the point. He told them that he would come when he could. He had to earn his living; his work would take him abroad. The Jarvises had said, 'Ah,' and 'Yes,' and 'That so?' and Hubert had said that he would like his friends to come even when he could not; that they would ask the Jarvises for the key. He did not like to think of the house empty, but giving joy to his friends. His cousin Miss Trevelyan, for instance, would be there a lot. They had nodded, looking Flora over, wondering how much she was part of the package.

Certainly, Flora thought, as she gave an involuntary hop of freedom, Hubert did not wonder. He behaved as though she were the package, taking her for granted as he was beginning to take his property, sure that she would fall in with his plans. He would this morning telephone the solicitor, arrange for money to be paid to the old couple and follow his conversation with a letter of confirmation. He had a strong businesslike streak, Flora thought, as she doubled up with mirth; he was businesslike in the way he made love, when it was the right time, when it suited him. Not that it was not wonderful, of course.

'Wonderful, wonderful,' she shouted up at the sky and broke into a run to reach the rocks at the foot of the cliff. Would Cousin Thing have approved of Hubert? Had Cousin Thing enjoyed the message in Russian? Should Hubert not be ashamed of those silly postcards sent over the years to tease? Above all, should Hubert be so sure she would return from her walk?

Flora clambered round the rocks to the headland and up the cliff, pulling herself up with arms and legs which winced from the strain, flopping down to rest in a sheltered hollow, catching her breath. I am weak from sitting about in cafés, she thought, and love-making. Would love-making with Felix or Cosmo be the same or better?

Able to think freely, for she and Hubert had not explored here – had not ventured so far, the discovery was hers alone, the privacy absolute – she pulled her coat round her, lay back on the short grass and closed her eyes. Listening to the murmur of the sea, she imagined herself in Felix's arms, or Cosmo's, making love out-of-doors instead of in a bed with Hubert, with one's legs getting tangled, as they sometimes did, in the sheets.

When she woke a breeze had sprung up and she was cut off by the tide. She had to climb a long way along the cliff to get back through fields to the woods round Pengappah. Ragingly hungry, she let herself in by the kitchen door. Hubert's shopping was on the table; she helped herself to bread and cheese, found pickles, spread butter, poured a glass of milk.

Reflected through the door into the sitting-room, in the glass of a print of Napoleon pacing the deck of the *Bellerophon* hanging on the kitchen wall, she saw Hubert and Cosmo sprawling in armchairs by the fire, a bottle of whisky on the floor between them.

Munching her bread and cheese, Flora leaned against the wall and listened. Hubert said, 'When I telephoned the clerk told me he was dead, killed himself. It was weird.'

Cosmo said, 'Yes, you told me.'

Hubert said, 'You see when he said he would kill himself, I wasn't really listening. One doesn't expect solicitors to be suicidal.'

'Why not?'

'Well, you don't. All I wanted was to get back to Flora and bring her down here.'

'In my car.'

'In your car. I feel awful now. He must have loved his wife; she'd left him, you see.'

'So you said. Several times.'

'Would I kill myself if Flora left me?'

'Probably not. It would be different if she left me.'

'You haven't got her. I have.'

'So you keep saying.'

'The clerk said somebody would attend to my letter. I've decided to leave Flora here, see that she has enough money and so on, so that she'll be all right.'

'Does she know?'

'I'll tell her. Does what I say, does Flora.'

Flora stopped munching, swallowed, drank some milk.

Hubert said, 'Any whisky left? Lucky I bought a bottle too. Jolly, jolly decent of you to bring a bottle, by the way. Did I thank you? This one is nearly defunct.'

Hubert's reflection poured whisky. Cosmo said, 'At least you got a ghostly welcome from Cousin Thing. He seems to have enjoyed your messages, keeping them stuck up, especially Flora's. You never guessed she cheated, did you? D'you think Thing left it, her message, as a sort of something for you?'

Hubert said, 'You'll have to make yourself clearer than that when you're p – practising at the bar. Less obtuse.'

'Oh, ironic are we now? I wonder where she is?'

306

'Went for a walk. 'nother drink?'

'When I first found her she came walking out of the sea – lovely.'

'Ah me. The Birth of Venus! Ever tell you how I lusted after the Venus?'

'Botticelli?'

'I lusted and lusted. Lovely, lovely seaweedy hair, standing in a cockleshell, her hand modestly sheltering her pussy.'

'Flora was too young – rather skinny, snappy too, I remember – but too young to have a pussy.'

'She has now, dark brown, nearly black, wonderful.'

'Swine,' said Cosmo amiably. 'Is she as good as Joyce? As keen? Extraordinary orange colour Joyce's bush – is she—'

Flora wondered whether to swallow her bread and cheese or throw up. Her cheeks burned. Felix would never discuss her like this.

Hubert's reflection, careful not to spill, poured whisky, added water, said, 'Be careful what you say. You are speaking of my future wife.'

Cosmo laughed. 'Mine, more likely. Don't be so bloody cocksure.'

Hubert exclaimed, 'I am not cocksure. I force myself to be sure. Every day and in every way I try to be surer.' His voice was a lament.

Cosmo consoled. 'When we were young and virgin we wondered what girls would be like. Do you suppose girls wonder?'

'Your sister Mabs did,' said Hubert sharply.

'Mabs?'

'Fiddled with my flies when we were dancing.'

'Our Flora was never like that,' said Cosmo.

'My Flora.'

'Ours. To my mind Flora is still as free as the Venus, free to choose. Tell you what I think, I think she fancies Felix. How does that suppo— supposition strike you?'

'Bosh shot, old friend; it would waste her lovely energies. I have it from Joyce that Felix had a walk out with her brother.'

'The queer as a coot, pretty boy who was at school with us?'

'That's the one.'

'But Felix is married and has a baby. Lucky escape for Mabs if you're right. Makes one think. No, Flora wouldn't − no, hang on, idiotic as it may seem, if you're right about Felix being bisexual, anything can go. There may be something between my Pa and Flora; my mother's nose is rarely off beam.'

Flora stopped masticating, took a step forward and stared in at the young men. They did not see her.

Cosmo carried on. 'Convoluted my thoughts may be, but I get there in the end.' He appeared to think he had scored a point.

Hubert said, 'Rubbish,' and lay back, stretching his legs towards the fire. For a while neither spoke. Hubert's glass rested empty on his chest; Cosmo let his drop to the floor. Presently, rallying thought from far away, he said: 'It wasn't a cockleshell the Venus was standing in, it was a scallop.'

Hubert said, 'Of course, how silly of me. It was a scallop.'

Having worked things out, decided, Flora finished her bread and cheese, drank her milk and ate a banana. She had stopped shaking.

Hubert and Cosmo were asleep when she passed them on her way to the stairs, asleep when she came down carrying her suitcase.

She had not, when she dreamed of lying in their marble arms, known what they would be like live, human and drunk. Hubert had given excitement and passion. The tenderness she had experienced with her imaginary trio was still there, but Hubert no longer fitted. Could she possibly feel it now for Cosmo? They looked very young and innocent as they slept; they did not wake when she stood beside them looking down. They would probably think, if they noticed when they woke, that the spots on the floor were whisky, not tears.

They did not hear the door when she closed it.

Forty-five

'A letter for you.' Denys, sorting through his mail, handed Vita an envelope.

Vita said, 'Oh, thanks. This looks like an answer from the Leigh woman.'

Denys watched her tear the envelope open. 'Well?' he said. 'What does she say?'

Vita glanced up. 'I feel so silly at having written; we don't really know her. I just felt I had to do something.'

'You should cultivate the art of inactivity. Remember the adage about sleeping dogs. Read it out.'

Vita read: ' "Dear Mrs Trevelyan, Thank you for your letter written in December; what a long time letters take from India." – Of course they take a long time! Must she be so discursive? "I fear we have no real news of your girl. She has not been to visit us," – I don't suppose she was invited, they probably found her plain and dull that time – "but my husband remembers that when he was in London before Christmas he ran into her by chance in the street. He says she seemed well and in good spirits." – Oh, so she's got back to London. "She volunteered no address. At that time, of course, we had no idea that she had left the ship en route to Bombay or that you did not know her whereabouts. The encounter was casual. My husband got the impression she was doing a sensible job of some kind. I am sorry that is all I can tell you, I am sure that by now she will have got in touch with you and explained why she did not join you in India. I am sorry to be of so little use. The young can be so thoughtless, can they

309

not? Yours sincerely, Milly Leigh." I wish I had not written to her,' Vita said angrily. 'It makes me look an utter fool.'

'What you do look,' said Denys, 'is radiant. Is that one of the new frocks?'

'Yes.' Vita smothered a laugh. 'I am getting a lot of pleasure from them.'

'Why don't we leave things as they are, then?' Denys leaned forward and stroked her cheek.

'If only we could.' Vita looked away.

'We have no choice to do anything else.' Denys watched her. 'You did not write to any other person apart, of course, from the school?'

'Who would I write to?' Vita was glad she had not written to the Russian dressmaker; those sort of people gossiped. She looked down at the letter in her lap and the large handwriting of a confident woman, black ink on blue linen paper, the discreet but definite letterhead: Coppermalt House, near Hexham, telephone Coppermalt Halt 25. What had been in Mrs Leigh's mind when she wrote it? 'What about missing persons or the police,' she murmured, 'or the Salvation Army?'

'What about them?' Denys slit open an official-looking envelope. Vita wished he would not use the butter knife. 'Aha,' said Denys, pleased. 'Confirmation of my new posting. It is to be Delhi.'

'Delhi?' Vita was delighted. 'Oh good.'

'You will like that?'

'Oh, yes. It's wonderful, and what a step up for you. I am more than ready to move on, but—' her voice drooped, 'what about—'

'She is not my child, is she?' Denys's voice was level, his pale eyes holding hers cold.

Vita felt the blood drain from her face. She felt sick and her mouth went dry.

The bearer came to tell Denys his car was waiting to take him to his office.

'So.' Denys stood up. 'Let's forget it, shall we? Providence appears to have intervened. You can wear those

310

dresses with a clear conscience. They will come in useful in Delhi,' he said cheerfully.

'But—' Vita's hands shook as she gripped Milly's letter.

'This does not make the slightest difference to you and me,' said Denys. 'Now I must go or I shall be late.' He bent to kiss her. 'Don't shrink from me. I did not, as you imagined, arrange a murder in Marseilles.' He kissed her again.

Vita blurted: 'Of course not. She has been seen in London.'

Denys chuckled, then, 'I want no more discussion,' he said, 'ever. Understood?'

Vita said, 'Yes. If that's what you want.'

'See you this evening at the polo. You are coming to watch?'

Vita said, 'Of course I am.'

PART FOUR

Forty-six

Flora moved about her employer's house checking a list. She liked the house; she had spent contented years working in it. She wondered whether she would ever work in it again. Robbed of its pictures, its silver and books, pale patches on the walls startled and empty bookshelves accused. The rooms had a forlorn appearance. The house was gutless, its innards removed to the country to grace other rooms and adorn walls of different proportions. She felt sorry for the house, as though it were sick and grieving for a civilized comfort disrupted by the war.

But the house had escaped the bombs; its windows were intact, its walls unscathed. It was clean. Had she not, as she did periodically, spent several days sweeping, dusting, polishing? It smelt all right; it would, given the chance, revive. Should it survive unscathed, her employers could, if they wished, move back to London and restore it to life.

Standing in the partially furnished drawing-room, watching a barrage balloon hoisting up into the evening sky from Thurloe Square, Flora speculated whether, should her employers return to London, she would come with them. She rather thought she would not. Her horizon had widened; she was no longer content with the view of a street bounded by a square garden.

The list. She must pay attention. She checked, read: *Newspaper cuttings in drawer sofa-table.* Mr Fellowes had been one of a minority who had paid attention to dire warnings in the years leading up to the war. She opened the sofa-table drawer. It was a good table, she

315

thought it deserved evacuation; Mrs Fellowes thought otherwise. She gave the table a consolatory rub. The drawer yielded packets of elastic-banded newsprint which recalled the Reichstag fire, Mussolini's bombast, the plight of the Jews, the Munich Crisis, the growing Nazi threat. Some of the articles were by Hubert; the name Wyndeatt-Whyte looked both strange and familiar. Hubert had foreseen the war reporting from Berlin, Spain and latterly Prague, a war of which Mr and Mrs Fellowes wished no part for they were Quakers and, anyway, even if they had wished, too old to fight.

Hubert's articles read dead sober, Flora thought, recollecting Hubert when last seen with a chuckle.

The Munich Crisis had made up the Fellowes' minds: they had moved to the country, bought a farm. 'War brings starvation,' they said. 'We will grow food.' And Flora, with an innate aversion to violence, had moved with them.

As she packed the newspaper cuttings away she remembered her horror when war was declared; how shocked she had been by the aggression of people who hoped to take part and were anxious to join the fray.

She ticked her list, read *embroidery scissors*. It was possible the scissors, errant for several years, had slipped down the side of the sofa. She removed the dust sheet and went to shake it from the balcony. Hearing the crack of cloth above him a man passing below looked up, startled.

Flora, laughing, called out, 'Sorry.' Then, '*Felix?*'

And Felix, looking up, said, 'Who?' in a guarded voice. Then, 'It's Flora. So you grew up.'

Flora said, 'Yes,' bunching the dust sheet against her chest.

Felix said, 'Shall you come down?'

'Wait a minute, I will come down.' But she delayed, running her hand down the side of the sofa and finding the lost scissors, which pricked and drew blood. Replacing the dust sheet, she ran downstairs to open the door.

Felix came in quickly and said, 'Ah,' as she closed

316

the door. He stood with his back to a patch on the wall where a regency mirror had hung.

She was amazed that she had recognized him. She said, 'I supposed you were in Holland. I imagined you there.'

Felix said, 'Technically, I am.'

Flora said, 'It's lovely to see you, how are you?' as convention decreed.

'Well,' said Felix, leaning against the wall. He was sweating, she noticed. She said awkwardly, 'And I am not technically here. I live in the country. I only come to London occasionally to see to the house; that is what I have been doing.' Idiotically she wondered whether he would notice the smell of furniture polish.

Felix said, 'Your finger is bleeding. You have blood on your skirt.'

She said, 'It doesn't matter.' She sucked the finger. 'Would you like some tea or coffee? I can't offer you a drink; my employers are teetotal.'

Felix said, 'I would like to sit down.' He glanced round the empty hall.

She said, 'Come upstairs. There's a sofa.' Then, backtracking, 'But you say you are in Holland?' She led him towards the stairs.

'As you are in the country.' He followed her to the drawing-room and sat on the sofa. 'I am not officially here. I am a bird of passage.'

Flora said, 'I will get us some tea.'

He said, 'No, just let me sit here while my heart settles.'

'Your heart? Are you ill?'

'Scared. That cloth cracked like a pistol.'

Flora laughed. 'No pistols in Thurloe Square.'

Felix leaned back and closed his eyes. 'No pistols, that's nice. So I'm safe, am I?' He looked tired. His hair was grizzled and he had put on weight. What did he mean safe? Watching him, she thought, It was I who felt safe all those years ago when he held my hand, safe when he waltzed with me. She found herself thinking that she would not feel safe with him now. He had a closed expression which she did not recognize. His face was a funny colour; his hand, when she had taken it, had felt damp, not dry as she remembered it at Dinard. Nor is he cool, she thought, as he was all those years I lay in his arms.

He was watching her.

'Are you really in Holland?' she asked.

He said, 'Of course not, I was joking. I am here, sitting on this sofa in London. Why is the room half-empty?'

She explained that most of the furniture had been moved to the country, that only the basics were here. 'It's half-empty because of the war.'

'As I am half-empty,' he said.

She said, 'I don't understand your joke.'

'What joke?'

'About Holland.'

'Oh, that.'

'Rather mysterious.'

'Oh, all right. It was a slip. I am visiting. I am not supposed to meet anyone I know. You surprised me into telling the truth.'

She said, 'Is that another joke?'

Felix began to laugh. 'I am not very good at this, am I?' His laugh was strained.

'Good at what?' she asked.

Felix said: 'Never mind. Actually I am here secretly to meet some people, Hubert Wyndeatt-Whyte among them. D'you remember him?'

She said, 'Yes.'

'He's something in intelligence; the navy, I believe.'

'I thought he was a newspaper man.'

'The work intertwines in wartime.'

'I did not know that,' she said.

Felix smiled. 'You offered me tea, but what I would really like is a bath. The hot water failed in the place I am staying at.'

Flora said, 'Of course, have a bath. When are you meeting these people?' She would not stress Hubert's name.

'Could I stay the night? It would be wonderful to stay where nobody knows where I am, liberating.' She remembered his slight accent.

Flora said, 'Yes, do stay.'

'Then I could have another bath in the morning,' he said.

She did not remember him as one of the world's great washers, but what exactly did she remember? She would put him in Mr and Mrs Fellowes' bedroom, take the sheets to the laundry afterwards; no need to tell them they had had a visitor. 'I will make up a bed for you,' she said, 'and after your bath, I could give you something to eat. An omelette? Would you like that?'

'Real eggs?' he asked.

'And a salad. I bring them up from the country.'

'Is there a telephone?' He looked about him.

'Disconnected for the duration.'

'I wish I could be.' He smiled; she had forgotten his teeth. 'Now, what about that bath?'

She said, 'I will get you a towel, then we will eat in the kitchen; this house is put away, so to speak, for the war.'

Felix said, 'What a luxury to be put away, how nice,' stressing the word nice.

Was this a joke, too? She felt she should not question him. He followed her to the bathroom. She said, 'When you are ready, I will cook supper.'

In the doorway he said, 'I was persuaded to come because I know Hubert. How is he?'

She said, 'I have not seen him for years.'

Felix said, 'I should not have mentioned his name. I am hopeless at this. Never mind, it is nice to talk to you. Now for my bath. Oh good, bath salts!' He sounded derisive; she had not known him derisive. Had she ever known him?

Presently, eating his supper, Felix said, 'It's a pleasure to talk to you, to be indiscreet. I so long to be indiscreet.' Then he said, 'I suspect you are the soul of discretion. My wife is not discreet; I can't talk to her.

319

I hardly dare share her bed. Does that sound true?'

Flora said, 'Not particularly.'

He said, 'It takes someone like you who has been hurt to be discreet.' (How had he known she had been hurt?) 'I remember your small closed face in France,' he said, 'and Irena Tarasova was another. I used to talk to her. The secrets were there, but different.'

Flora said, 'I see her sometimes.'

'Give her my regards if you do. Does she still dress-make?'

'Yes.'

'I cannot talk to my children, they chatter like their mother.'

'In Holland?' It was difficult, watching Felix eat his omelette, to believe in Holland; she had imagined England separated by the Channel from occupied Europe for the duration. Had he really come from there? 'Your mother and sisters?' she asked.

'I dare not endanger them. We are occupied by the Germans, as you know. This is good.' He ate his salad and Flora's ration of cheese. 'I shall get into trouble for disappearing,' he said. 'It will do them good to fuss. English people in their nice safe offices are too bloody pleased with themselves—' He was contemptuous.

'They will think you spent the night with a tart,' she said.

Munching his last mouthful of cheese he observed her thoughtfully. 'I shall spend the night with you,' he said. 'It's a long time since I held a strange body in my arms.'

It was not the first time she had noticed that the urgency of war inclined men to cut the preliminaries, but Felix surprised her. Belatedly resentful, she said, 'When you took me out to lunch from school, you were afraid of catching my cold.'

'You haven't got a cold now.' Felix laughed. 'And later I heard that your cold was measles. Come on, darling—'

She was glad to hear him laugh. 'You don't laugh much,' she said.

'It's difficult if you are in a permanent state of fear. Come on, Flora.' He took her hand. 'Come to bed?' He smothered a yawn and stood up, stretching his arms.

She said perversely, 'I must wash up the supper things.' Then, distancing herself, 'I can't see what good you can do in Holland if you are stunted by fear.' What was he doing that made him so afraid? Anxiously she adjusted her thoughts, finding it hard to believe what he said. 'Have you really come from Holland?' she said.

'Oh yes, I am not making it up.'

'Then why not stay on now you are here?'

'Come on, Flora. Upstairs.' He watched her. 'You haven't changed much,' he said, 'but you have filled out in the right places. At Dinard you looked like a bundle of sticks, but your eyes glowed.'

'Why can't you stay?' She altered her question.

'There are things I can still do.'

'Such as?'

'Irritate the Germans for one.' He spoke lightly. 'What it amounts to is what's called "standing up to be counted". Oh, come on, Flora, leave the washing up.'

This is a mistake, Flora thought as she undressed. Felix, already in the bed, said, 'Hurry up.'

Sensing that what she was about to do in her employers' bed would not meet with their approval, Flora hesitated.

Felix reached from the bed and pulled her knickers down. 'Come on,' he said, 'get in.'

A love-making, expert but impersonal, slow, slow, quick, quick, slow, ending with a thunderous chord. The marble Felix was never like this. She stifled a laugh.

'Did you enjoy that?' He stroked her flank. 'Nice,' he said, not waiting for an answer. 'You are muscular, like a boy.'

'I work outdoors. I am a farmworker.'

He was not interested in her work. 'Do you remember the picnic?' He stroked her. 'Billy must have been about eleven.'

'Who was Billy?'

321

'The girl with white eyelashes and buck teeth's little brother, Billy Willoughby.'

'She re-arranged her looks, married a rich American.' Flora could not remember Billy.

'Dear Billy. I wonder what he is up to these days?' Felix murmured.

Flora lurched away from Felix. Perhaps it would be better if she turned her back.

'Don't turn away.' He pulled her round.

She tried to remember what he had looked like in Dinard: not grey and middle-aged.

'Mr Fellowes, who I work for, is working on a book which hopes to prove the Nazis could have been defeated by peaceful means,' she said. 'He is a man of peace.' Felix snorted. This bed was Mr Fellowes'; she had felt obliged to mention him. 'He collected Hubert's articles for reference,' she said, 'before the war.'

Felix was fingering her biceps. 'Billy was about your size in adolescence,' he said, pinching her.

'I am not Billy.'

'I wish I had time to look him up.'

Flora debated whether she might retreat to her own bed on the floor above. 'I think I should leave you to sleep,' she suggested.

'Don't leave me alone. I need to talk.' He held her tightly.

'About what?' If I went to my own bed, she thought, I could kick, bite the bedclothes, scream, laugh or whatever. She felt as though she had knitted a gigantic garment which unravelled as she watched.

'Stay with me, listen to me.' Felix held her. 'My family,' he said, 'my children, they are so pretty, so small, so trusting. The boy is clever. One had had hopes – my wife Julia has hopes and much spirit. She battles with the rations and the black market. You cannot understand. We have money. Of course, we are better off than most. My mother and sisters try to help people who are at risk. It is absolutely diabolical existing under an army of occupation, one feels helpless. A lot of people fight this—'

322

'Don't you?'

'Not enough. One's efforts are puny. The Jews—'

'You help them?'

'They disappear, my dear; here one minute, gone the next.' His tone was bitter.

'Oh.'

'And one does not want to follow them. Am I boring you? Elizabeth and I used to wonder whether we bored you, you were so much younger.'

'I was not bored.' She noted the stubble on his chin; she would find him a razor in the morning. Felix began to talk. He talked of the price of vegetables in Holland, the lack of petrol; he seemed obsessed with minutiae. She grew sleepy and struggled to keep awake. His body beside her was taut. 'One has to watch oneself all the time,' he said. 'One slip might mean many lives.'

After a while he was quiet. Then, in a new and desperate voice, he said, almost shouting, 'Actually I take damn good care not to get involved, not to risk my neck. This trip is a stupid one-off risk. I shan't let myself get talked into another, I have to think of my family.' As she remained silent he said more soberly, 'That is the truth and I have really very little need to be afraid.'

She said, 'Then why on earth did you come?'

'Why on earth does one do anything?' he said angrily. 'Perhaps I was showing off. Perhaps I felt I must try just once to do what other people do all the time.' He held her close and pressed his face between her breasts. 'I am not a hero,' he said, his voice muffled.

Presently he propped himself on his elbow and in a formal voice said, 'You must understand that it is not so bad for us; we are fairly well known, respected, rich. The Germans hesitate to interfere with people like us. All we have to do is behave ourselves.'

She said, 'I should have thought that could make things more difficult.'

He said, 'It cuts both ways.'

She remembered Felix's mother and sisters arriving at the Hôtel Marjolaine in 1926; the head waiter bowing and scraping, the English families' sibilant whispers, six baronesses, six.

She said, 'But you helped the Jews.'

'I did *not* help the Jews. If I had, I would have put my family in danger. I feel guilty, can you understand? Doing nothing breeds guilt.'

'I think I understand.'

'I was *afraid* to help the Jews. As I am *afraid* to work for the Resistance, and even worse, more terrible to contemplate, *afraid* to collaborate.'

'Collaborate?'

'With the Germans. People do,' he said.

Flora was shaken. 'I did not know,' she said.

Felix said, 'So I feel helpless. I think I am only out to save my own skin.'

She said, 'Try not to be ridiculous. Do not denigrate your courage, it's absurd.' Lying in Mr and Mrs Fellowes' bed after a colourless love-making, this seemed a pompous thing to say, but she repeated it. 'Do not denigrate your courage.'

Felix said, 'Funny little Flora.' He lay back and presently dozed.

When he woke he was cheerful; he put his arm round her and pulled her head onto his shoulder. 'Do you remember that picnic? How beautiful Cosmo and Hubert were, and those girls, so silly and lovely. It was amazing when they sang.'

Flora said, 'They have families now, like you, to care for.'

He said, 'I do not suppose they are any less silly. It is a form of courage; my wife has it. It is a gift not to take life *au grand sérieux*. Do you think I am too old to learn?'

She said, 'You do not need to learn about courage. It is brave to admit that you are afraid. You shouldn't harp on it.'

'Does it bore you?'

'A little.' She felt out of her depth.

Then Felix said, 'Shall I tell you one of the things which frightens me most?'

'What's that?'

'I am shit-scared of the Gestapo arriving to arrest me when I am in my bath.'

Flora said, 'That I can understand. Was that why you came to England, to have a carefree bath?'

He said, 'One of the reasons.'

She said, 'Do you tell your wife your fears?' She tried to imagine his wife; he had not described her except as silly and brave.

He said, 'She would not understand. I dare not upset her, but I can talk to you.'

As one talks to strangers, she thought.

Towards dawn he fell asleep. She eased herself from the bed and went to her own room. She bathed her face, brushed her teeth and combed her hair. When she was dressed she went quietly about the house, finishing the task Felix had interrupted. When Felix was gone she would have a bath, check that all was well in the house and catch her train back to the country.

There was no time now to question Felix; it was too late. He would wake, have a bath, eat the breakfast she would provide and go, leaving her with the price of cabbage and swedes in occupied Holland. And the knowledge that he loved a brave and silly wife, that he loved or had loved Billy Willoughby, and that he was afraid. Quite a lot, really.

All the same she felt numb and resentful. He had shown no interest in her life; he had asked no questions, used her. 'A convenient receptacle for his fear,' she said out loud, and went in search of Mr Fellowes' spare razor. He will tell the person he should have spent the night with that he has been with a tart, she thought with sour amusement. Then she thought, Come now, play fair, the poor man has no idea of the part he has played in your life. Trying to recapture the Felix she had known for so long she laughed out loud and went to knock on Mr and Mrs Fellowes' bedroom door and wake him. 'Time to get up. I have brought you a razor.'

At breakfast Felix was cheerful; he had had a wonderful bath, he said, and breakfast was delicious. What a treat to have real coffee. She must come and stay after the war, she would love Julia. On the doorstep he kissed her. 'It's done me so much good to talk. You must have thought it a lot of nonsense.'

'Take care of yourself,' she said.

He said, 'Never fear, I will.' And, 'It would be best not to tell anyone I was here.'

Flora said, 'I won't. My employers might not understand.'

But he was not interested in her employers, she thought as she watched him stride jauntily down the street, any more than he would be interested to know that he had used up all the hot water for his bath. At least I was able to supply a carefree bath, she thought, watching him reach the pillar-box at the corner and disappear. In spite of her numbness she felt sadness for Felix and sadness for herself, for the man she had shared Mr and Mrs Fellowes' bed with did not seem to be anyone she had ever known.

As she stripped Mr and Mrs Fellowes' bed she wished she had not seen Felix; he had robbed her of an agreeable, if faded, dream.

Forty-seven

'We must not be too long.' Mabs stood while Irena, on her knees, pinned the hem of her skirt. 'We are meeting Hubert for lunch.'

'How is he?' Irena's mouth was full of pins.

'Well, he sounds well.'

'I have not seen him since he was a boy.'

'You wouldn't know him; he's filled out, going grey. But his eyebrows are bushier than ever.'

'Is he married,' Irena asked, 'yet?'

'Says he'll get married when the war is over, meanwhile lots of girls. He's sort of in the Navy, just as Cosmo is sort of in the RAF,' she said.

'His mother died,' said Tashie from the *chaise longue*. 'He has a bit of money now.'

'And a reputation,' said Irena, pinning, 'as a left-wing journalist. There, how's that?' She sat back to watch Mabs twirl.

'We could have done without Hubert's reputation in our family,' said Mabs, easing herself out of the dress. 'Shall you need another fitting?'

Irena said, 'Yes. Now your dress, Tashie.' She was making them warm evening dresses to wear in the cold wartime winter.

'Tell Irena about the chandelier,' said Tashie, as Irena lowered a half-made dress over her head.

'The chandelier?' Irena looked from Tashie to Mabs.

'It was a chandelier which made Father change his mind about Hitler,' said Mabs.

'Stand still,' said Irena to Tashie, her mouth full of pins.

'Tell her,' said Tashie. 'She's English now; she will get the gist.'

'Father was dining at his club during an air-raid,' said Mabs, 'with Freddy Ward and Ian MacNeice. They were too proud, of course, to go to the shelter. This was early in the Blitz. Now nobody in the Club had thought to remove the chandeliers, so when a bomb dropped in Pall Mall the chandeliers flew. Father was cut and Freddy Ward needed five stitches. Father was *enraged*. Up to then he had still been muttering that Hitler had a point.'

Irena sniffed disapproval.

'If it had not been for Hubert's articles General Leigh would have changed his mind long before,' said Tashie.

'Why?' Irena was fitting a sleeve. 'Stand still, Tashie.'

'Honestly, Irena! You read them! Hubert kept stressing how anti-Communist Hitler is. General Leigh is too. *That* was the point they had in common.'

Irena said, '*Tiens.*'

'Nigel maintains Hubert has a genius for rubbing old gentlemen up the wrong way,' said Mabs. 'But Father's all right now.'

'Didn't he paint *Heil* Hitler on some main road?' teased Tashie.

'That was someone else,' said Mabs. 'How does it feel to have Russia on our side, Irena?'

'Bolsheviks,' said Irena. '*Ça finira mal.*'

'You and father should get together,' said Mabs. 'Careful with that pin.'

'Perhaps we are too set in our opinions,' said Irena. 'Some people disassociate themselves from the war altogether.'

'I wonder who she was talking about,' said Tashie as they drove in a taxi towards Wiltons. 'She didn't get your joke about your pa and the chandelier.'

'Well, she's Russian,' said Mabs. 'Here we are and there's Hubert just going in.'

'Hubert,' she said presently, as they sat eating oysters, 'do you know anyone who is *not* taking part in

328

the war even minimally, like Tashie and me?'

'Yes,' said Hubert.

'Gosh, Hubert, who?'

Hubert thought of Felix, who would rather take no part, but said nothing. He swallowed an oyster. Mabs and Tashie were wonderful, he thought, but one could not talk to them, too silly.

'Who? Tell us,' said Tashie.

'Joyce's young brother, for one.'

'Really? How does he manage? Is he ill?'

'He's a conscientious objector.'

'I call that jolly brave,' said Mabs.

Hubert adjusted his opinion. 'Got himself sent to prison,' he said.

'My word,' said Tashie. 'Wasn't he a queer?'

'Still is, no doubt. He's now been sent down a mine.'

'So he *is* taking part, and much less minimally than Mabs and I bringing up our tots in the safety of Wiltshire, and keeping up our husbands' morale by being silly.'

Hubert laughed. 'You keep up my morale, too, you know. Are you two going to buy hats after lunch? Hats, like oysters, are unrationed. Shall we have some more or would that be greedy?'

'Let's be greedy,' said Tashie.

'I could do with a hat,' said Mabs. 'Clever fellow to remind us.'

'Are you sad about your mother, Hubert?' Tashie enquired. 'Or didn't you like her?'

'Not sad, no, but I got to like her latterly. I used to buy her hats to console her for my boring step-father's demise. It worked. I even took her to Pengappah and she quite liked it.'

'So that's all right,' said Mabs. 'Has she left you a lot of money?'

'What was left after the racing; she was keen on the gees.'

'But you earn a mint.'

'I did up to the war. It wasn't bad.'

'You should get married,' said Mabs.

'Time enough,' said Hubert.

'We could pick you someone suitable,' said Tashie, teasing.

'I'll pick my own, thanks,' said Hubert. 'I'm off to North Africa soon, by the way.'

'Oh, *Hubert*. If you possibly can, send us some cans of olive oil. Will you do that? All the oil I hoarded had to go to help premature babies.'

'What premature babies?'

'The ones I work with in the local hospital. Oh, Hubert, you really believe we sit around doing nothing, don't you?'

Watching the two friends disappear towards Bond Street, Hubert felt great affection for them. Their relentless shopping represented continuity. Wartime shortages only whetted their appetites; when the war ended they would snap back into peacetime quicker than most. Did Mabs ever regret Felix? he wondered. Or had she forgotten him? She seemed content with Nigel. As he headed back to his office, he wondered where Felix had disappeared to that night. It was not like Felix to pick up a tart; his explanation had been unconvincing. He hoped he had not done anything rash, like looking up old friends.

Forty-eight

Back in London a year later, Flora stubbed her toe on the kerb, stumbled onto the pavement and landed on her knees. In the ochre-coloured gloom the driver of the car which had nearly hit her sounded his horn. As she groped across the pavement to the railings its tyres squeaked, slithering against the kerb. She had laddered her stockings and grazed her knees, and the latch of her overnight case had burst open. She swore, 'God damn and blast,' as she straightened her skirt and spat on her handkerchief to wipe the cuts. 'God damn and *blast*.' Her voice was muffled by the fog. She snapped the lock of her case, kept close to the railings and limped on. The monsters in the street crawled invisibly, adding their exhausts to the fog. Her knees hurt, the pain made her gasp, and gasping she inhaled the fog as she bumped into a fog-coloured uniform. The American was stationary. Flora said, 'Sorry, I didn't see you.' She had hit the man's legs with her case.

He said: 'That's okay, lady. I was just wiping my glasses; they get kinda misted in this climatic speciality of yours.'

Flora said: 'Oh, I say, you've got a map.'

The American held the map close to his face. 'How else would I find my way around in this goddam city, where none of the streets run straight?'

'We are in Farm Street,' said Flora helpfully. 'I can tell you that much.'

'Wrong, lady. This is Bruton Street. Don't you know your own city?'

Flora said: 'I thought I knew the way. I am trying to get to Piccadilly. I must be lost.'

'Catch hold of my arm,' said the American, 'and I will get you there. This is Bruton Street, right?' He stabbed at the map. 'We turn right at the end and go down Bruton Lane. See it?'

'Yes.'

'Takes us into Berkeley Street; turn left and Piccadilly's at the bottom. Keep close to the railings or we get run down by a nut.' Flora took hold of his sleeve and they started to walk.

'You are very kind,' she said. 'I have never actually visualized seeing the air I breathe. Are you a navigator?' (It would be good manners to chat.)

'I do a desk job. Back home I deal in real estate. In San Francisco we get fogs, but nothing like this.'

'At least it stops the air-raids.' Flora was grateful for his company.

'Been in many raids?' Her escort stopped to wipe his glasses.

'Not many. I live in the country.'

'They scare the shit out of me, but we have a great shelter in Grosvenor Square.'

'I'm afraid of shelters, of being buried alive.'

'We should turn left here, and Piccadilly's at the end of the street. My name is Roger.'

'I thought all Americans were called Chuck or Wayne or Hank.' Flora could now hear heavier traffic; there would be buses, a taxi perhaps, but it would be quicker to get in the tube.

'Only in the movies,' said Roger. 'If we can get across your Piccadilly we could reach the Ritz. What d'you say to a drink in the bar, or lunch?'

'I have to catch a train,' said Flora. 'I've never been in the Ritz. It's kind of you, though.'

'If we could get out of this fog, I could see your face.' Roger stopped yet again to demist his glasses. 'My mom back home wrote that I would be too shy to proposition an English girl. Come on, help me prove her wrong.'

332

Flora laughed. 'Sorry, I must catch my train. But thanks all the same.'

'There ain't no trains in Piccadilly,' said Roger sarcastically. 'I know that much. You want to get away because I'm homely.'

'No!' said Flora. 'No.' Homely was exactly what he was, kind and homely. 'There are buses and the tube,' she said, 'which will get me to my train.' She felt ashamed. She had taken advantage of his map.

'She said not to bother with English girls. Maybe she was right.' Roger's face had a mulish look. 'Hey!' he exclaimed angrily, as a man coming out of the fog at a run cannoned into them. Flora was swung out into the street. 'Where the hell are you going?'

'Sorry,' said the man, 'I didn't see you. Here, get back where it's safe.' He reached for Flora's arm. 'I don't want to be responsible if you're squashed. My God,' he said, 'it's Flora. *Darling!* Where have you been? I've been looking for you for ten bloody years.'

Flora said, 'Cosmo,' leaning back against the railings and clutching her suitcase with both hands.

'D'you know this guy?' asked Roger.

'Yes, she does,' said Cosmo. 'Where have you been hiding?' He towered above her. 'Look, you'd better come with me, I have to catch a train. We can talk on the way.'

'But does she want—' said Roger.

'Of course she wants.' Cosmo put his arms round Flora, pinning her to stand still. 'We don't want this between us.' He snatched her case from her and bent to kiss her. 'Can't you fuck off?' he said to the American.

'The lady has a train to catch too,' said Roger, speaking to Cosmo's back.

'It will have to wait, won't it, darling?'

'Paddington,' Flora gasped, as he kissed her again.

'Me too,' said Cosmo. 'Come on, there's an empty taxi in the gloom, let's try it.' He picked up Flora's case. 'Come on. Do you think you can get us to Paddington?' he asked, as he opened the taxi's door and pushed Flora in.

'You'd do better in the tube,' said the driver, 'but I'm going that way; might as well be paid for it. But don't blame me if you miss your train.'

Flora pulled the window down. 'I must say thank you. He invited me to the Ritz. Thank you, thank you,' she shouted into the fog. 'You've been very kind, thank you.'

'You're welcome,' said Roger's disembodied voice.

Cosmo pulled her in and shut the window. 'Getting yourself picked up by GIs,' he said.

'He was a captain. I counted his pips.'

'What has he done to your knees? You're bleeding.'

'I fell, tripped on the kerb—'

'That'll teach you to rush off without me.' Cosmo held her close, hugging her. 'Oh God,' he said, 'this is wonderful. Ten long years.'

'Why are you crying?' asked Flora.

'Shock. Don't speak for a moment.' Cosmo gulped, sniffed and blew his nose. 'Could one ask why you are crying too?'

'I hurt my knees. I am so glad to see you and—'

The driver slid the glass partition open. 'What time is your train, sir?'

'Oh, any time. It doesn't matter.'

The driver closed the partition.

'And what's the third reason?' asked Cosmo.

'I can't talk about it. I have not been able to cry, it is *so awful.*'

'One of those? Something really bad?'

'Yes.'

It had been the most terrible thing. She had heard it on the radio and later read it in *The Times*. Infuriated by the Dutch resistance the Germans had taken hostages. Two mayors, a well known banker, some prominent people. One of the hostages had been Felix. The hostages had been shot. She had heard the news on an exquisite autumn morning of clear skies and early frost. The beauty of the day made the news worse. Her grief bunched in her stomach and froze in her brain. She had been stunned.

'Ah,' said Cosmo, 'I can guess. Felix.'

She said, 'Yes,' and the tears came. Felix had seemed so slight, so afraid. Had he not talked of his fear? She had felt doubtful about him, found him dull as a lover, resented his taking all the bath water. How could I have been so petty? she thought. I should have been able to comfort him and give him love. I only thought of myself when I watched him go. I was disappointed. I cannot tell Cosmo that I saw him; I cannot tell him that we spent the night together. 'He didn't expect to be a hero,' she said, weeping.

Watching the tears make points of her eyelashes before they tipped onto her cheeks, Cosmo's mind went back to Madame Tarasova's room above the horse butcher in the Rue de Rance. They had been sitting on the floor; he had plucked an eyelash and measured it. Felix had come in and told them that it had stopped raining. He said, 'He was a very brave man. I bet he made the Germans who shot him feel funny.' Flora choked. Cosmo said, 'D'you remember when he came and told us that the rain had stopped? We had the picnic next day.'

'Yes.' And he had waltzed with her on the sand.

Cosmo said, 'We are fortunate to have known him.'

It was private sitting in the taxi with Cosmo's arm round her, cocooned in the fog, the taxi's engine chugging as it inched along.

'The fog is khaki,' she said, still weeping, 'not pea.'

Cosmo said, 'I could not cry when my father died.'

'Not your father? I did not see it in *The Times*. Oh, Cosmo, when?'

'Six months ago. Heart attack.'

'He was such fun at the picnic, he had a flask – and kind; he gave me lunch at Quaglinos. I'd never been to a restaurant like that. And afterwards we shopped for your mother at Fortnum's and Floris. I ran into him in the street.'

'My mother thought the worst—'

'Not? Oh, no! Oh—' Flora began to laugh. 'Oh, with your father?'

Cosmo noted that she had stopped crying, or rather that she was laughing too. 'Mixed emotions,' he said. 'Are you pleased to see me? D'you observe that I wept for joy?'

She said, 'Yes, very pleased,' and 'Tell me about your father. Was he in a rage?'

'It wasn't rage. There's a girls' school in the house for the duration. Mother and Father moved into the flat above the stables. He was too old to get back into the Army but he was overdoing it: Civil Defence, ARP, Min. of Ag., everything local. Everyone came to him all the time. It was the way he died which upset Mother. She was shattered anyway, of course; funny old things, they were in love. No, it was the way he died,' Cosmo paused.

'What way was that?' The shy little girl would not have asked. Cosmo studied the adult's face; the eyes were the same but the cheeks were slightly hollowed, the mouth grown more sensual. Where had she been these ten years? What doing, *who with*? 'Tell me,' she said.

'He'd had a drink or two, I gather—'

'Go on.'

'The headmistress of the school came to make a complaint. Father was jollying her along, she was a bit of a stick, and he'd got to the stage when he would begin telling stories. You wouldn't remember—'

'Yes, I do.'

'Apparently he got to his favourite—'

'*Ces belles choses?*'

'You remember? Oh Lord! The woman was not amused when Father finished with his *comme ci comme ça etcetera*; he looked at her, Mother says, and said: "She wouldn't understand, would she, Milly? She's as flat as a plank, not like you, darling." And he pouted out his moustache in that way he had, gave a sort of cough, and died.'

'But that's a lovely way to die, making a joke.'

'Mother thought it undignified.'

Cosmo, mirrored in the glass partition, had begun

336

to weep. She hoped the driver would not choose this moment to open the partition, look back and launch some cockney quip.

The noise of the traffic altered; they were moving faster. She thought she could see trees loom out of the fog. They must be in Hyde Park. The last time she had seen Cosmo mirrored, he had been drunk; there had been no runnels for the tears from nose to mouth.

Presently he fumbled for a handkerchief, blew his nose and said, 'That's better. Thank you.'

Flora said, 'What's this uniform you've got on? Where are you going?'

'RAF, as you can see, and I'm going to North Africa.'

'To fight?'

'No. Intelligence is what they call it. I am out of the fighting, too old. I was a rear gunner for a while.'

'Then you are lucky to be alive,' she said crisply. (Thank God I did not know.)

'I gather I am.'

'And Blanco – Hubert?'

'In the Wavy Navy. He's attached now to the Free French, aide to one of the squabbling Admirals.'

'Mabs and Tashie?'

'Sharing a house in Wiltshire with a friend who has children the same age as theirs. They do all sorts of war work and get batches of Italian POWs to work in the garden.'

'Nigel and Henry?'

'Treasury and Ministry of Information.'

'And Joyce?' She looked out at the fog, remembering Joyce.

'Joyce is in London. She actually enjoys air-raids, hasn't missed one. She's very popular with our Yank allies, indeed with all our allies. As you may remember, she's full of bounce. She extracts the maximum of pleasure out of everything she does.'

'I don't know,' Flora snapped.

'Perhaps you wouldn't.' Cosmo was amused. 'Her elder brother was killed in the Dieppe raid.'

'I loathe and detest this war. I want nothing to do with it,' said Flora violently.

'And how do you manage that?' Cosmo teased. 'Were you not called up?'

'I don't manage. I am in the Land Army, it's the least of the evils.'

'So you make hay, commune with cows.' She found his tone mocking.

'And pigs and geese,' Flora shouted. 'Yes.'

'Nearly there,' said the driver, pushing open the partition. 'This is Sussex Gardens.'

'Jolly good.' Cosmo looked at his watch. 'I shall be in time for my train. But don't think,' he said to Flora, 'that this is the last you will see of me. I am taking you with me to where I catch my flight. You have yet to tell me why you ran away from Pengappah and where you have been since. You can tell me on the train.'

'Why should I?' asked Flora disagreeably.

'You owe it to me.'

'I owe you nothing. You are as arrogant and pleased with yourself as ever; you haven't changed in ten years,' Flora exclaimed. She felt a resurgence of the rage which had assailed her, standing over them slumped and drunk in front of the fire at Pengappah. 'I bet you have grown as bossy as Hubert,' she cried. 'As selfish as he is, as—'

The taxi had come to a stop. A porter opened the door and snatched Flora's case. 'Which train, sir?' he said to Cosmo.

'I'll take that.' Flora reached for the case.

'No.' Cosmo caught her wrist. 'Stand still a minute, darling. How much do I owe you?' he asked the driver. 'I have all my gear in the left luggage,' he told the porter as he fumbled for change with one hand. 'We need the Cornish train. Eleven o'clock.'

'Number one platform,' said the porter. 'Very crowded today.'

'Always is,' said Cosmo. 'Stand still,' he said to Flora.

Flora said, 'Let go,' and kicked his shin.

'I won't,' said Cosmo, handing money to the driver. 'Thank you very much. Ouch,' as Flora bit his hand. 'Bitch!'

'What a pair of love-birds,' said the taxi driver. 'You should be ashamed,' he said to Flora, 'him going off to war. He might get killed and be remembering your last words as he died,' he said, using the intimacy engendered by the fog.

'Oh, shut up,' said Flora. 'Please give me my case,' she said to the porter.

Cosmo, still holding her wrist, said: 'Darling, please—'

Flora said: 'All right, but let go of me, you are hurting.' She did not add that she was destined for the same train. She had her return ticket in her bag.

Cosmo looked at his watch. 'We have just time to find a First Aid place and do something about your knees,' he said, 'and my bite. You've drawn blood.'

Flora said, 'I'm sorry,' but did not look it.

Forty-nine

Squashed in the corner of an overcrowded carriage, Flora was disgruntled and annoyed for letting herself be beholden to Cosmo who, travelling first-class as an officer, had insisted on paying the difference on her third-class ticket.

The compartment was full of officers poisoning the atmosphere with tobacco smoke which, making her feel sick, added to her disadvantaged feelings. 'Perhaps we could have a window open,' she suggested to the palpable horror of a Frenchman on the seat opposite.

'*Et le brouillard?*' he protested, with an outraged sniff.

Flora said, 'Please,' in the voice Cosmo's mother used when she would brook no No. A Royal Marine Major in mid-carriage stepped across the Frenchman's legs and pulled the window open. Flora said, 'Thank you very much,' warmly.

The French officer, appraising Flora's ankles, let his eyes rise to and rest at her sticking-plastered knees. Flora pulled her skirt down. The train began to move from the shadowy platform into fog.

'Well, now,' said Cosmo, more briskly than he felt, 'we have a lot of catching up to do.'

'We can't talk here,' said Flora, looking round at their audience.

'Darling, there's nowhere else.'

'Catching up on what?'

'On what you have been up to these ten years.' Cosmo kept his voice low. 'Are you married, for instance?'

'No. Are you?'

340

'No, and nor is Hubert. Not that that— where did you vanish to when you ran away from Pengappah? You were gone when we woke up. We were in despair. We searched the woods and cliffs, yelled ourselves hoarse and imagined you drowned, until we realized your case was gone. Your trail went cold at the station.'

'You looked like rag dolls lolling there,' said Flora. 'You discussed me. Dissected me. I was furious, livid. I heard every word from the kitchen,' she hissed. Then, leaning forward, she said, '*N'écoutez pas, monsieur; c'est une conversation privée.*'

'*Et qui manque d'intérêt,*' said the French officer, closing his eyes, turning aside and hunching his shoulders at the draught.

Flora repeated in Cosmo's ear: 'I heard every word. You discussed me.'

'Most lovingly,' said Cosmo, remembering the conversation. (Oh dear.) 'What did we say?'

'If you've forgotten, I shall not remind you. I am still furious.'

'Darling, we were plastered. I remember the hangover; it was a humdinger.'

'I wish you would not keep calling me darling.'

'You did not object in the taxi.'

'I had forgotten how angry I was – am.'

Cosmo looked out at the fog and glanced round the carriage. Several people besides the Frenchman were trying to sleep, the rest deep in newspapers. 'What's this about reading *The Times*?' he asked.

'At Coppermalt Nigel advised me to read *The Times*. I think he was shocked by my ignorance; he said I could follow what happens to people, deaths, weddings and so on, and get a grasp of what's going on in the world. It was my last evening, the time that Mabs and Tashie, oh and Joyce, dressed me in black and your mother— Well, anyway, I thought about it and took his tip. I've been reading the papers regularly ever since.'

'I see.'

'I've read some of your cases in the law reports.'

'Really?' Cosmo was pleased to hear this.

341

'And Hubert's articles and despatches during the build-up to the war. He made me aware of a lot of things the politicians didn't seem to want us to know. I learnt to distrust politicians and hate war. It's filthy.'

'It's going on, we are all involved—'

'As little as possible, me. I don't want to kill anyone, it doesn't help, or for anyone I love to die.' I don't want you to die, she thought, or Hubert. 'Look what's happened to Felix,' she said, 'a neutral murdered in a neutral country. What's going on over there in Europe? I never really knew Felix and now I never shall.' (I loved but did not know him.)

'And you would have liked to?'

'Of course I should. And you, how well did you know him?' (She felt a fierce nostalgic hunger for the Felix of her childhood.)

'He came to stay once or twice. Mabs was keen on him. What was there to know? He was the kind of person people talk about. That charm and good looks breed gossip, engender jealousy. At various times I heard it suggested that he was (a) a womanizer or (b) a homosexual. It was even hinted that he was illegitimate. My father said that was rubbish, that although he did not look like old Jef, as Pa called him, he was in manner exactly like him. Pa sometimes made his old friend sound rather a bore, I admit. Felix was a good man, that's all, and that's enough, but above all he was bloody brave. Not many people choose to get themselves shot to shield some person or persons they don't know. In theory yes, but in actual cold-blooded practice, that takes guts.'

'Is that what happened?'

'I imagine so.'

So he had stood up to be counted, she thought. But boring? Well, perhaps. He had not, come to think of it, been exactly sparkling company when he took her out from school. Had she been blinded by love when she blamed herself for the flop the day had turned out to be? And more recently in the Fellowes' bed, what had he

342

been like? A most unexciting lover, she thought bleak-ly. It would have been so much better to remember him as the marble persona of her childhood. 'Felix was a charmer,' she said. 'He took me out to lunch when I was at school. It was terrible. I was going down with measles. *He* was bored.'

Cosmo laughed. He would laugh a lot louder if I told him I'd slept with Felix and was unmoved, she thought; if I let him know that in bed with Felix it was *I* who was bored.

Cosmo said, 'Poor devil. What hell.' He turned to look out at the fog. He was grown leaner. His large nose made him look hawkish and arrogant; his hair, once so fair, had grown darker than she remembered. He turned back to look at her. 'You haven't changed much in these last ten years,' he said. 'If anything, you are lovelier.' Then, startling her with parallel thought, he said, 'Cerebral love sticks; it's impossible to get it out of your system. I do so want,' he muttered in her ear, 'to make love to you.'

'Are you suggesting,' she said, 'that I am in your system?'

'Yes.'

'And you want me out of it?'

'I did not say that; cerebral and carnal can link very nicely.'

'Oh look,' said Flora, 'the sun.'

The several occupants who were still awake looked up as the train moved from one moment to the next into sparkling sunshine. 'Let's shut the window; I am cold,' she said.

Cosmo closed the window. Two fellow occupants got up to struggle along the corridor to the lavatory. 'What happened to you? Where did you go,' Cosmo persisted, 'when you disappeared?'

'I moved where nobody would look for me. I changed class.'

'What?'

'I became a servant.'

'What kind of servant?' He was disbelieving.

343

'A housemaid. In Thurloe Square.'

'But that's five minutes from Mabs' house.'

'Yes.'

'I've often walked through that square. I could have—'

'You wouldn't have found the person you were looking for.'

'Are you that person?' Cosmo tried to see Flora's eyes, but she turned away.

'Look,' she said, 'Maidenhead, the Thames,' in a bright voice. 'That is the river Thames.'

'Please, Flora,' he said, 'tell me how you did it.' And, he thought, who you have become.

She said, 'Any fool can sweep floors, make beds, polish furniture.'

Cosmo said: 'How did you set about it?'

It had taken from Truro in Cornwall to Maidenhead for her to make up her mind, on that flight from Pengappah. She had counted her money at least six times to see how much was there, each time forgetting in her pain the exact sum. Between Maidenhead and Paddington she devised a strategy for survival, and the manic panic which had bunched her insides for six and a half hours subsided to a manageable knot. She found a cheap hotel and set off next morning for Knightsbridge to find Irena Tarasova. In Beauchamp Place she ran into Alexis coming away from Irena's establishment, recognized him, and he her. Supposing her to be with Hubert – for had not Hubert stopped in Paris on his way to Marseilles for a game of bridge? – Alexis enquired after Hubert in a sly and jocose manner. 'I was afraid,' she told Cosmo, 'that he would give me away, tell Hubert that he had met me, so I went with him for a cup of coffee and a bun in the Kardomah café in the Brompton Road.'

'Did he make a pass?' asked Cosmo, suspicious.

'Alexis? He was old and fat; at least forty-five.'

Cosmo said: 'Sorry to interrupt. Go on.'

Over coffee, Flora said, she had made it clear she wanted none of Hubert or Cosmo, that she was on her way to ask Irena for help; she thought Irena might find her a job. Alexis advised strongly against this; he was returning next day to Paris. His own visit had been fruitless; Irena had refused not only to lend him money but had also, and this was heinous, refused to remarry him so that he could apply for British citizenship. He was sick, he said, of being stateless. He was brazen and unashamed. Irena, he said, grown selfish with success and security, was not in the business of helping anyone but herself. 'She will make you clothes and take your money and that's the lot,' he had said. 'And what's more,' he said, 'she will betray you, talk.' Flora had realized later, she told Cosmo, that Alexis, having been refused help by his ex-wife, did not wish her to help anyone else. 'You learn about people as you grow older,' she said with amusement.

Cosmo said: 'I suppose so,' wishing to learn the new Flora. 'What happened then?'

'Actually he came in handy.'

'Oh?'

'He agreed to post a letter to my parents from Paris. I wanted them to think I was in France. I wrote on plain paper, with no address. I gave him money for the stamp. I was trying to behave as decently as I could. I did not want to be with them, but equally I did not want them worrying about me.'

'Did they get the letter?'

'I don't know.' She turned to face Cosmo, flinching as she brushed his knees with hers. 'I thought it was my fault that I did not love them. I suppose I hoped for some vestigial bond. I was haunted by the family love I'd seen between the Shovehalfpennies and you Leighs at Coppermalt; you are so lucky.'

'Did they get in touch?' Cosmo strove to understand.

'I had given no address. But four years later, when I was twenty-one and felt safe, I wrote care of my father's bank to tell them that I was all right and to congratulate my father. I'd seen his name in the New Year's Honours.' The train was drawing into Reading. Few people got off, many more squeezed on. There was

345

shuffling and jostling in the corridor; the officers near the door fended off intruders. 'Full up in here, I'm afraid, try further along,' closing the door which had been hopefully opened, stretching their legs across the compartment. 'Bloody hell, travelling these days.' The guard blew his whistle and the train moved on.

'I got an answer that time,' said Flora, speaking quietly, 'via a solicitor.' She stared at the French officer, who was temporarily awake; he closed his eyes.

'What did the solicitor's letter say?' asked Cosmo, puzzled.

'The letter was to the effect that I am not my father's child, that I am no concern of his. My mother was not mentioned.' In spite of herself Flora's voice hit a high note.

Cosmo said: 'I call that absolutely splendid, terrific. Wasn't it a great relief?'

'Yours is a robust view,' said Flora drily. 'I agree with you now, but at the time I felt I did not exist, that I was nobody.'

'I think it's wonderful.'

'I am still my mother's child.'

'Put her out of your mind, forget her. Now, back to Alexis. Did you go to Irena, after all? Who helped you? Alexis?'

'Actually,' said Flora grinning, 'he did make a sort of pass. I – er – fended him off.'

Cosmo felt fury. 'What happened?'

'Nothing. He may not have posted my letter, just pocketed the stamp money.' Flora laughed. 'I went to Molly.'

'Who is Molly?'

'Molly was your parents' under-housemaid at Coppermalt; she left to work in London for Tashie. She was in love with your butler, the one who was a closet Communist.'

'Gosh,' said Cosmo. 'I never knew that! Gage!'

'They are married now,' said Flora, 'and have a tobacconist's business in Wimbledon. He votes Conservative.'

'But why didn't you go to Mabs or Tash?' Cosmo was at sea.

'They would have talked. They would not have been able to resist talking. Molly was my bridge.'

'Bridge?'

'From middle-class to working-class, to where it would not occur to anyone to look for me.'

Cosmo took this in rather slowly. 'Please go on,' he said respectfully.

She had telephoned Molly, Flora said, when she guessed Tashie would be out, visited, and over cups of tea in the kitchen learned the hows and whys of becoming a servant; servants, she had noticed, got free board and lodging, something she badly needed. Much amused, Molly told her where, apart from *The Times*, to look for advertisements. 'In the Thirties,' said Flora, as though talking to an idiot, 'there was fearful unemployment, but a shortage of servants. People did not want to be servants, *The Lady* was simply full of pleas.'

'I remember,' said Cosmo. 'Constant fuss and worry among one's aunts. Go on.' She had answered an advertisement for a housemaid in Thurloe Square, a Mrs Fellowes. 'I told Mrs Fellowes that this would be my first job, which was the truth. I was nervous. I handed her my references; Molly had stressed that I must have references. They said that I was honest, hard-working, clean, tidy and came from a good family, that I had no experience but was willing to learn, and of good character.'

'And?' Cosmo was fascinated.

'Mrs Fellowes read them. She asked whether I liked dogs. I said I did. Then she said, "Did you write these yourself, these, er, excellent references?" I had pinched a sheet of Tashie's headed notepaper and, what I thought was rather brilliant, ventured into the Knightsbridge Hotel for a piece. Actually I wrote the references in the hotel lounge. So I said actually yes, I had written them, I was sorry but I'd thought it worth a try, and again that I was sorry and I would go now and not waste her time. She said, "Wait a minute, just tell me who," and she looked at the references, "is Alexander Butler, Justice of the Peace? And who is Hubert Wyndeatt-Whyte, doctor of divinity?" I said, "I know a butler but he is called Gage, and that Wyndeatt-Whyte was dead, a friend of mine's cousin." I was frozen with shame, sitting on the edge of a chair like a dolt. It was awful. Mrs Fellowes began to laugh. When she stopped, she said, "When can you start?" I've been with them ever since, as housemaid up to 1939, and from then on as a Land Girl at their place in the country.'

Cosmo said, 'Tell me about it. What is it like being a servant?'

She said, 'There isn't much to tell.' How could she explain to him that as a servant she was distanced from people, that she watched them as though they were characters rehearsing a play, and that this distancing made her secure.

'Did you, for instance, wear a cap and apron over your black dress?' He would lead her as he led witnesses in court.

'In the afternoons I wore black, in the mornings pink, like Molly and the other servants at Coppermalt.'

'What did you do on your days off?'

'I walked my employers' dogs in the park.'

'And?'

'Sometimes I went to the cinema.'

'And?'

'Museums, galleries. I explored London, rode on buses.'

'Alone?'

'Mostly.'

If only he had known where to find her. 'I can't get over your being just round the corner from Mabs. What did you do for money?'

'I had my wages. Then there were tips. Visitors leave tips on the dressing table when they leave; some are quite generous,' she said.

'What else?'

'When I had enough money I went to the theatre. Once, from the pit, I saw Tashie and Henry. Tashie was wearing a green dress.'

'Oh, darling.'

'Mrs Fellowes sent me to the Cordon Bleu cookery school. I learned to cook. She is a kind person.' She had been in the company of debutantes sent by their mothers to learn something practical. They had sized her up, tried to place her and failed. 'Why all these questions?' she asked.

'I am trying to fill in the ten years during which I lost you.'

'Nothing much happened to me, Cosmo. I like the Fellowes, I like working for them. I was damn lucky to get that job. I fell on my feet. They made me feel safe.'

'Safe?' He considered safety. It was probable, he thought, remembering her parents, that to feel safe would be a novelty. 'What else besides safe?'

She said: 'I suppose the word would be content.'

'I have not been content; how could I be content without you?'

Flora laughed. 'Oh, come on. You were forging ahead with your career.' She mocked him. 'I bet that's what you were doing. Putting Cosmo first.'

Leave my career out of this, thought Cosmo. 'So now you are a Land Girl,' he said. 'Do you enjoy it? Does it make you content?' He longed to wrest her contentment from her. How dare she be content?

Flora said, 'I like the work. I can ignore the war.' I have found a niche, she thought; how can I explain that? 'I fit into village life,' she said. 'I seem to be accepted.'

'You must be cleverer than I'd imagined,' said Cosmo. 'That's quite a feat.'

'I like the people.'

'And they you?'

'I hope so.'

'And men? Have you lots of boyfriends? Lovers?'

'That's none of your business.' Flora looked out at

349

the countryside. I have the lovers I have always had, she thought. I have had trouble shaking them off and here is one of them in RAF disguise sitting beside me.

'It is my business. Tell me about them.'

'No.' She would not tell him of the men who wanted her. They had nothing to do with Cosmo, and precious little, she thought, to do with me. 'There is nothing,' she said, 'to tell.'

Cosmo felt like slapping her but the Royal Marine Major had opened an eye. 'Are you happy?' he asked.

Ah, thought Flora, happiness. 'I live a very busy sort of life,' she said.

'With cows, geese and pigs?'

'Dogs, too, lots of dogs, and there are of course cats.' She was making fun of him. 'And ferrets.'

'But are you happy? When can you remember heights of happiness?'

'I was happy several times that year in Dinard,' she answered simply.

'And?'

'When I stayed with you at Coppermalt.'

What a meagre ration. 'But in Aix-en-Provence with Hubert you were happy?'

'That was different.'

'I'll say it was. Hubert your lover, your great great love,' said Cosmo bitterly, 'rushing off, stealing a march. Damn him getting in first, I can't bear to think my best friend, the sod.'

Flora said, 'Don't be silly.' She turned away from him. Hubert and Aix-en-Provence were long ago, a lovely period of fun, good food, sunshine and loving, but over, as was Felix. She shivered, thinking of Felix.

'You always loved Hubert best,' Cosmo heard himself say.

Flora got up, struggled through the carriage and battled her way along the crowded corridor to the lavatory. Cosmo thought, I am unwise to bring Hubert up. When she came back he said, 'When do you find time to read *The Times*?' (Try some neutral ground.)

350

'When it's a day old, after Mr Fellowes has finished with it.'

'All those years,' Cosmo heard himself saying nastily, 'you must have longed for love, for Hubert.'

Flora stared at him. 'Don't be so cross,' she said, her voice rising. 'You two were all for sharing me as though I was a *thing*, an *object*, somebody who didn't matter, a sort of plaything, a *tart*,' she shouted. Several people in the carriage looked up and hastily looked away. Flora found herself glaring at the French officer; he had stretched his legs while dozing. The movement of the train jogged them against Flora's. She kicked his shin with her toe.

Waking with a jerk he muttered, *'Je vous dérange, Mademoiselle.'* He drew his legs away. *'Pardon.'*

'Vous écoutiez—' she accused.

'Mais non, Mademoiselle.' He suppressed a smile.

'He was asleep, poor chap. About the only one who wasn't listening,' said Cosmo, choking with mirth.

'I am getting out at Taunton. I think it's the next stop,' said the Major in the Royal Marines, clearing his throat.

'Exeter for me,' said another officer.

'I go as far as Plymouth,' said a third, coughing nervously.

'Look how you've embarrassed them,' said Flora meanly.

Cosmo was reduced to simmering silence.

When the train stopped at Taunton two people got out and their places were taken by a couple who had been standing in the corridor. The carriage rearranged itself yet again at Exeter. Cosmo thought, We are wasting precious time. He caught the Frenchman's eye and looked away.

'How do Mabs and Tash manage for clothes?' asked Flora conversationally. 'They must be hampered by rationing.'

'They foresaw the shortage and bought bolts and bolts of cloth. They stocked up for years. Mother was rather ashamed of them and said it was unpatriotic, but I notice she wheedles a dress length from one or other of them quite often.'

Flora laughed.

Cosmo said, 'I'm sorry I made you angry.'

Flora said, 'I should not have snapped.'

Cosmo said, 'Tell me about your life.'

Flora thought, If I were counting times of happiness, I would rate this train journey pretty high. She said, 'What you tell me about Mabs and Tash explains why Irena Tarasova is kept busy.'

'So you see her?'

'Occasionally. I got in touch with her after some years; she was kind to me when I was a child in France.'

'I remember, the Tsar and Tsarina, the noble officers.' Cosmo smiled. 'The silk clothes.'

'It's all our King and Queen now, she is more British than the British and wears wool.'

'Her husband?'

'Alexis? He appeared among the French who came over with de Gaulle. Irena tried to push him into an English regiment but he was not welcome; last heard of he was with the Free French in Djibouti.'

'Your life – tell me.'

She told him about her work, how she tended Jersey cows, loved the different seasons: haymaking, harvesting, threshing, being out of doors. It was much more enjoyable than being a housemaid, she said. Was she aware that what he wanted to know was: was there a man in her life, someone she was in love with, someone other than Hubert he might lose her to? 'Have you got a lover?' he asked. 'Or many lovers?' Somehow it would be better if she filtered her emotions among the many rather than just one.

Flora countered, 'How many have you?'

He said, 'All right. Sorry. What right have I to ask? you say. I apologize. You are content.'

I *was* content, she thought. I suppose I was content in the fog this morning trying to find my way to Paddington. I had done all the things I had to do in

352

London. I was looking forward to getting back to the farm, to getting away from the war. She said, 'Perhaps, and you?'

'Not at the moment. I am mad with longing. I want to make love to you. I am prevented by this crowd of people. It is abominable that Hubert was able and now I—'

'That was long ago,' she said, turning towards him, 'and you have something else on your mind.' She slipped her hand in his. 'I can smell it.' She held his hand.

'You wouldn't understand,' he said, taking both her hands in his. 'It is not something one should talk about. It is not right to tell you about it, but yes, it is simply that I am afraid.'

'Ah,' she said, 'yes,' and, 'of course you are,' remembering Felix's fear. 'This hateful war,' she said.

'I am afraid of the flight I have to make to North Africa; I am afraid of being a passenger. I am afraid of death,' he said, involved with the war.

'Ah,' she said, 'yes.'

'Stay with me until I go. I haven't long.'

'But—'

'Please.' There might be a few minutes when he could get her alone; there might be a delay. If there was a delay, would it not be possible to spend the night with her in an hotel? He longed to be alone with her to make love. 'I do so want,' he said, 'to break through this barrier of chastity.'

'My knees,' she said, 'would hurt in any position.'

'Oh God,' said Cosmo. 'What a selfish bitch you are.'

'Don't let's start squabbling again,' said Flora. 'Where do you leave the train? I get off at Truro.'

'Come on with me to Redruth.'

'I shouldn't.'

'Give the cows a miss, please.'

'I shall have to telephone,' she said. 'But I don't like getting so close to the war; you are involving me. Normally I shut it out.'

'You will be safe with me,' he said obtusely, 'perfectly safe. No raids there.'

'Don't you see,' she said, 'that I am afraid now I have seen you? I have lost Felix, I am afraid to lose you.' She did not mention Hubert.

'For me?' Cosmo was dubious.

'Of course,' she said. 'Naturally.'

Cosmo said, 'Oh good, that's lovely. If only we could spend the night together.'

'Try and be cerebral,' she said, more lightly than she felt.

'My brain still tells me that you are in love with Hubert,' he said jealously. 'Sorry, I am stupid. I thought you were as glad to see me after ten years as I am to see you. You don't mean it when you say you are afraid for me. Oh God, my head goes round and round. You had better be shot of me and get out at Truro.'

'I shall come on to Redruth,' she said. 'I will telephone from there and tell Mrs Fellowes that I got carried away. I don't think I am doing the right thing, but I will do what you want.'

At Truro the French officer got out. He was going to Falmouth, he said, adjusting his kepi. '*Bonne chance.*' His space was filled by an American Air Force Colonel who was talkative, smoked Lucky Strikes and held forth about his home town in Texas and the war in the Pacific. Cosmo gave up trying to talk and Flora, leaning against his shoulder, surreptitiously eased knees which, bruised and stiffening, hurt. She was content on this last lap of the journey to memorize what she could of Cosmo, his voice, the smell of his hair, his long fingers.

Sitting uncomfortably in an American bomber en route to North Africa, Cosmo reproached himself. He should have let her get out at Truro, he thought, instead of dragging her on with him to the RAF base at St Evel. At St Evel there had been a loud party going on in the officers' mess, a mix of American and British. Flora was the only civilian girl among the few WAAFs.

There had been a lot to drink and he, with pre-flight nerves, had not stinted himself. He had, too, talked loud shop with the RAF to bolster his fear and then, when a man asked Flora to dance and she accepted, seeing her with a stranger's arms round her he had exploded and made a scene. 'Your knees don't stop you dancing, I notice. You could perfectly well have made love,' he had said, as though there had been somewhere to go, a snug bed in a cosy hotel, warmth and privacy, when of course there was no such thing. She had not snapped back at his outburst, not pointed out that he had not asked her to dance, not said she was bored, which she must have been, by the noise and the ballyhoo, mounting decibels, baying voices of fighting youth, all strangers to her. Rather her expression had been as withdrawn as he remembered it when he saw her sitting on a bollard on the quay at Dinard, before he asked her to go with him to buy his father a revolver in St Malo. Their parting had been bewildered and stiff.

Now, high above the Atlantic, mentally composing a letter of love and apology, searching his pockets for the address she had given him, he found he had not lost the piece of paper she had written on but used it to write his own unit, rank and number, his own address in North Africa. He could see her put it in her bag as he swilled his last drink. 'I will write the moment I get there,' he had said.

When meeting Hubert in Algiers a month later Cosmo told him of this catastrophe. Hubert said, 'People only do things like that in books,' and laughed immoderately.

PART FIVE

Fifty

In her late sixties, having come to terms with widowhood, Milly began fussing about Cosmo. She had moved back into Coppermalt, reducing its now unmanageable size by turning the top floors and back premises into flats which she rented to grateful couples. The long battle to get planning permission and builders to do the work kept her occupied for years and also, as her son-in-law Nigel said, out of everyone's hair. But now the contests with bureaucracy were over she had time for other things, as she said to Felicity Green who was on what had become, since the war, an annual visit.

'It is time I did something about Cosmo. Do you realize, Felicity, that Nigel and Mabs' children are practically grown-up and Cosmo is not even married?'

Felicity did not answer this rhetorical question but waited for Milly to go on. The practice of listening had come in useful in her profession of novelist; while her better self hoped Milly was not about to make a fool of herself, her novelist self hoped she would. She had often put bits of Milly into her increasingly successful novels and supposed, since her novels lay on the bed tables in Milly's spare rooms, that the bits she had used were sufficiently camouflaged.

'Cosmo should marry,' said Milly firmly. 'Even his flighty friend Hubert has settled down and has children.'

Surely, thought Felicity, the term 'flighty' is only applicable to girls? 'Has Cosmo ever been engaged?' she tested.

'No.'

How does one ask a woman like Milly Leigh whether her son is homosexual? 'Perhaps he enjoys being a bachelor?' she suggested. 'Does one still use the term "eligible bachelor"?'

'He has had lots of girlfriends,' said Milly.

'Well, then.' (Not homo.)

'But it is time he settled down,' said Milly.

'Does he know?'

'How would I know? Honestly, Felicity.'

'Shall you tell him?'

'Angus would have if he were still alive, the poor darling. Angus would have come straight out with it.' (Felicity raised doubting eyebrows.) 'Angus would have told Cosmo that it was his duty to marry and have children. He will inherit Coppermalt. I don't really want it to go to Mabs' boy, he doesn't wash and that long hair is a bit much. You may doubt it, Felicity, but I know what Angus would have done. By dying he passed the responsibility on to me.'

'Oh.' Felicity the writer was pleased. 'Well,' she said, 'has Cosmo ever been really in love?'

Momentarily baffled, Milly said, 'He's had affairs, I'm sure he has. I've met some of the girls. He's a normal man.'

'Yes, of course – but love?'

'There speaks the novelist in you,' exclaimed Milly. 'I had a long talk once with Rosa, a Dutch friend of ours, such a sensible woman. She married off five plain daughters. She was in favour of arranged marriages; apparently they last. There is far too much divorce these days, it's dreadful.'

'Was yours arranged, your marriage to Angus?'

'Of course not. Ours was a love match, wonderful; no quarrels, no jealousies, no doubts. But our marriage was exceptional, one in a million. I can't expect perfection for my children. You should see Mabs and Nigel. They quarrel as much now as they did before they married, yet they thrive.'

'Um,' said Felicity. 'I seem to remember a row; it

was at dinner. I was shy, I had a stammer in those days, quite useful in a way. Yes, I remember your husband turning them out of the dining-room—'

'What a bark he had!' Milly remembered fondly.

'Wasn't Cosmo interested in that girl you had staying almost the first time I stayed here? You got me to give her a lift down to London.'

'Oh, *that* girl,' said Milly. 'She was only fifteen.'

'Must be more than that now,' said Felicity.

'No,' said Milly, as though pushing something away, 'I *don't* think she—'

'Her father became a top dog in the Indian Civil Service, don't you remember? One read his name in the papers at the time of partition in 1947. You must remember, very distinguished, one of Mountbatten's right-hand men.'

'Oh, really? I had not made the connection. So he's that Sir Denys Trevelyan. Oh, I *see*. Rather an awful wife, I remember *her*.'

'A misfortune which failed to impede his career.'

'How interesting, how very – well – interesting. How silly of me not to have taken that in; Angus would have noticed. I do so miss Angus.'

'Then he was in the papers again. People wrote articles about him and his wife.'

'A scandal?' Milly's mouth remained open.

'No, no, odder than that. They decided to stay in India when everybody left. It was a sensation at the time. They said they could not see themselves settling in Cheltenham or Tunbridge Wells.'

'People did find it hard. It must have been similar to being widowed, wrenched roots. Will they wither and die out there? I suppose the girl looks after them.'

'I did hear,' said Felicity, 'that she refused to join them, went her own way. Actually she—'

'Oh, my dear!' cried Milly. 'I remember now, the mother wrote to me. The girl had become a tart.'

'Actually she works for some friends of mine in the West Country.' Felicity felt weary. She thought, Shall I forget this conversation and in years to come distil something quite else from it which will trickle onto the page like acid?

'She must be quite old by now.' (That too could be stored.) 'What a vast cross-section of people you do know, Felicity.'

'I always think people are interconnected. I am interested in people,' said Felicity blandly.

'To put in your books, you clever thing. But what am I up to, imposing my family worries which are of no earthly use to you? I shall get cracking, as my son-in-law says, and have a Christmas house-party as we did in the old days. I shall get splendid Joyce to help me, she knows lots of young people. It's time I pulled my finger out, as my grandson says, the awful boy.'

'Do you know what it means?'

'He explained it. I said, "Dear boy, I was not born yesterday." Yes, I shall invite Joyce, she will be a great help. And it will be nice for her, she's at a loose end between marriages.'

'I thought you deplored divorce,' said Felicity, laughing.

'I do, but Joyce is different. She's an old friend. We used to stay with her stepfather, such a dear man, for the grouse shooting in Perthshire.'

Fifty-one

When Flora read of Hubert's marriage in 1949 to
somebody called Victoria Raglan she was agreeably surprised to find herself unmoved. Victoria whoever she
was would not experience the ebullient innovative passion she had shared with Hubert in Aix-en-Provence.
The honeymoon would not be a first-time abandoned
fling for Hubert, for he would – whether he remembered it or not – have her, Flora, as a yardstick. Victoria
Raglan might well be prettier, and certainly richer,
but she would not be the same. I was his first love,
thought Flora; his first adventure. She did not then, nor
had she ever, compared herself with Joyce. She knew
about Joyce, had always liked her since the early days
in Dinard. Joyce was fun; there was no lasting malice
in Joyce. She thought of Joyce rather in the terms of a
necessary sexual assault course to be surmounted by
young men such as Hubert and Cosmo, just as, as
boys, they had manoeuvred through the scholarship
or common entrance to their public school. She was
glad for Hubert, hoping he would be as happy in his
marriage as he was successful in his career. She went
out to call in the cows for the evening milking with a
cheerful heart. As she ushered them into the milking
shed she supposed that at some time prior to their
meeting Felix, too, had passed through the hands of
some skilful woman similar to Joyce. As the years passed she thought of Felix with less pain. Quite often in
her thoughts he reverted to the cool recumbent lover of
her early adolescence. When her employers sold their
large farm to a merchant bank (Nigel's bank, she noted

with amusement), she agreed to move with them to the smaller property they were buying; she was promised a cottage of her own and more responsibility, and was content. It was after the move that she realized the new farm was within easy reach of Pengappah. She need not go near it; she need not be bothered. If she had wanted, she could always have reached it; it had never been so far as to be beyond reach. Yet one day, resolving to lay the memory of her painful eavesdropping and anguished flight, she took the bus and, getting off at the village, walked through the woods to snoop.

The house was unoccupied, crouching in its clearing rather sad, its windows closed and blind, as she had first seen it with Hubert. The small garden was choked with weeds, the creepers Cousin Thing had planted in the ruined wing smothering the walls. The five baths were slimy with rotting leaves, the fish gone. The old couple Hubert had left in charge must be dead, she thought. It seemed natural to unchoke the water-course, clean the baths, cut away a few dead branches. She enjoyed herself and came again from time to time on her days off. She got to know the house from an angle which was superimposed over the memory of Cosmo and Hubert's drunken conversation, and her rage and hurt.

Sometimes there would be traces of visitors – empty milk bottles, tyre tracks, tools left out to rust, a diminished log pile. One year, approaching Pengappah along the cliff, she heard voices. She looked down at the cove and recognized Hubert, sturdy and greying, seen from above going bald. He was playing with children who shouted to him, 'Daddy, Daddy, look what I've found. Come and look, Daddy,' splashing by the edge of the water, trailing armfuls of kelp.

'Don't let them get wet, darling, remember they have stinking colds.' Victoria, once Raglan, now Wyndeatt-Whyte wife and goodness me three tots, lithe and maidenly in her wedding photographs on the steps of St Saviour and All Angels, hanging onto Hubert's arm, looking up at him full of trust, now sat on a dry rock watching her family, knitting what looked like a sock.

Flora, with her back to a gorse bush, watched Hubert build a sandcastle, surround it with a moat, deflect the little stream which had higher up run through the five baths to reach the sea, and make a complex of dams and locks. She heard him say, 'No! No! Stand clear,' to his eldest child. 'You'll ruin it if you do that. Victoria,' he shouted, 'could you keep Emma away? She keeps stamping on Julian's dam.' Flora wondered, watching Hubert, whether he was as bossy with Victoria as he had been long ago with her. I could never have lived with him for long, she thought; that period in France was just right. I spoiled it by letting him bring me to Pengappah, just as I spoiled my train journey with Cosmo in the war. I was snappy and nervous. I should have got out at Truro, not given in to him, not stayed with him till he left. It was nice, though, she thought, retracing her steps along the cliff, to think Hubert and Victoria were using Pengappah. She was glad to see Hubert so well arranged in marriage. Making a detour to peep at the house, she was pleased by the substance and size of Hubert's station wagon and by the sight of cases of wine in the back. Going home in the bus she thought of Hubert with pleasure and affection.

It was another matter when she read of Cosmo's marriage in the Chelsea registry office; he was laughing in the photograph. In the background Hubert and Victoria looked serious. It was difficult to read Milly's expression.

Fifty-two

'And how was India? You've got yourself a nice tan.' Cosmo took stock of his nephew, hoping that under a superficial resemblance to Mabs he was right to see a preponderance of Nigel's solidity. 'What will you drink?' he asked. They were lunching at his club; he was amused to see that Charles had put on a suit.

'Water, please,' said Charles.

(Dear me, what virtue!) 'Teetotal?' Cosmo asked.

Charles said, 'Not altogether.'

Cosmo said, 'Your father put it away at your age. When under stress, that is.'

'Not any more,' said Charles. 'Mum makes him mind his liver.'

'What a sensible woman she has become,' said Cosmo drily. 'She used to glory in hepping him up with rows.'

Charles said, laughing, 'She still does. He likes it; it keeps him on his toes.'

They ordered their meal.

Cosmo seemed happy to sit in silence. Charles, rather strained, said, 'Er – my mother tells me you want to talk to me, Uncle Cosmo.'

Cosmo said, 'Did she tell you what I mean to do?'

Charles said, 'Yes. It's incredibly generous. I think you should change your mind.' He flushed under his sunburn.

As well as wearing a suit he had had his hair cut, Cosmo noted with amusement, white skin edging his neck, forehead and ears. He must be trying to make a good impression. He said: 'Shall you feel tied, trapped?'

(Perhaps I am interfering with this boy's life, doing him actual harm?)

Charles said, 'Oh no, no! It's the most wonderful, the most – I can't think how you can bear to give Coppermalt away.'

'I can bear it,' said Cosmo. 'Besides, as your father will tell you, it's the only way to keep Coppermalt in the family. Death duties cripple. But tell me about India. I cannot discuss business while I am eating. Where did you go?'

Charles said, 'All over, it's wonderful. I was there a year. I could talk about it for a week.'

'Please don't do that; condense.'

'That is what I want to do. Hubert has promised to help me place articles, he is very kind—'

'So he should be. He "arrived" long ago.'

'He suggested that I write a book. I'd like to go back and see more; there is so much, and so many different peoples.'

Cosmo said, 'So one hears.'

Charles thought, God! I am boring him. I've never known him well; he's stiff and difficult. 'Oh, by the way, before I forget, Mum said I must tell you about the pockets of old Raj hands who stayed on; you know some of them.'

'I do?'

'A couple called Trevelyan. Mum says Granny and Grandad had their daughter to stay at Coppermalt when you were young. Dad remembers her; he says you and Hubert were in love with her, that if it had not been for getting engaged to Mum he would have had a stab himself.'

(Bloody cheek! Nigel with his short legs.) 'First I've heard of it,' said Cosmo, with chill.

'Anyway,' Charles rushed on, 'there they are, these old things, must be at least as old as Granny, living in rather a super house they built for themselves. In some style, too, up in the foothills, the Himalayas—'

'Not the Nilgheri?' Cosmo teased.

Charles said, 'Sorry, I'm a fool—'

367

'Go on.'

'Well, these old – they look like preserved fruits; they still have servants, boss them about. They grumble that "nothing is what it was, of course," but they are not going to budge. It's a sort of time warp. The Indians are either extremely tolerant or find them amusing. What excited Mum and Tashie, who was at dinner – Henry had gone to Brussels for a couple of nights – was that this old Mrs Trevelyan still writes to the same dressmaker they both went to and Granny too, it seems, to order a dress a year which she then gets copied cheap by the Indians. Some old woman in Beauchamp Place.'

'Rue de Rance,' murmured Cosmo.

'What?'

'She was in the Rue de Rance above the *boucherie chevaline*.'

'Come again?' Charles looked lost.

Cosmo said, 'Nothing. What else?'

'Oh, just that, you know Mum and Tash, they next started a hare about finding the girl you all loved. They have a guilt thing about her. They'd like to see what she is like now. Then Joyce said, "The trail has gone cold." Oh!' said Charles. 'Perhaps I should not have mentioned Joyce. Have I put my foot in it? She was at dinner, too. Sorry.'

'Not at all,' said Cosmo. 'Joyce is an old friend. She was a childhood friend of us all. You should have seen her teeth at fourteen.' He laughed. 'Would you like some stilton? It's excellent.'

'No, thank you.' (Why did I have to mention Joyce? Should Mum still be friends with Joyce? Still friends when Uncle C. has divorced her? What does he mean, see her teeth? I don't understand his generation's morals.) 'No cheese, thanks.'

'Coffee?' suggested Cosmo.

'Yes, please.'

'Cigar?'

'I don't smoke.'

(It would be cruel to ask him whether he fucks.) 'Coffee, please, waiter. Do you smoke pot?'

'Sometimes.'

'Glad you admit to one vice.'

The waiter brought coffee.

'Now then,' said Cosmo. 'You must be dying to get to the point and I must get off to Bodmin, for the Assizes. You do not, I gather, wish to work in the City like your father, or live in London. As well as wishing to travel and write, you are not uninterested in country matters. You could learn to manage an estate. Do you feel able to grapple with Coppermalt? With your consent, I propose to make Coppermalt over to you; you will, I trust, let my mother live on there until she dies. I have no children, but if I live another whatever years are necessary, death duties will be saved. I hope you will be as happy there as we have all been, and find a girl to be happy with. I have made an appointment for you with my solicitors. Did you ever hear how, when Hubert got the keys and deeds of Pengappah, the solicitor hanged himself? It was not funny but it makes some people laugh. It shocked Hubert, he drank a whole bottle of whisky. Anyway, mustn't digress, the whole thing should be wrapped up in no time. That's the lot, I think.' Cosmo pushed back his chair and stood up, anxious to leave.

Charles said, 'I am at a loss for words.'

'Good.'

'May I ask a question?'

'Which is?'

'Why do you not want to retire to Coppermalt when you stop working? I know you have no children, but you love the place. It seems so—'

Cosmo thought, I like this boy, he'll do. 'One should never go back to where one has been happy,' he said. 'The beautiful memory is in danger of getting overlaid. Case in point: I recently went back to a place in France where I remembered being extremely happy. It has been gobbled up by progress; it is unrecognizable. I found a café proprietor I remembered as an ebullient young man in love with his pregnant wife, old, stuck in a wheelchair. The gunsmiths had metamorphosed

369

into a gift shop. My God, I beat it. Any other questions? As I say, the solicitor has it all. It's been nice. Give my love to Mabs.' He was in a hurry to get away.

On the steps of the club Charles, shaken by his need to render thanks in some adequate fashion, blurted out: 'Why did you marry Joyce?'

A smile spread across Cosmo's face. 'To teach my mother not to interfere perhaps, not to try and manage my life?' Charles, watching him go, thought, He seems detached. Can he be lonely? Then, forgetting Cosmo's detachment, he made haste towards the nearest telephone to ring up the girl with whom he was in love, break the good news and ask her to marry him.

Fifty-three

Cosmo locked his briefcase in the boot and got into his car. Although this was the third or fourth car since his divorce, he rolled the window down to let air in and any residue of scent out. He opened the window from habit. On the rare occasions he thought of Joyce, it was to reproach himself for stupidity. There's no surer way to lose a good friend than to marry her. High-spirited, bouncy, generous Joyce had in middle age and close proximity become a bore; and as for sex, so good in experimental and lusty youth, that had switched to something akin to aerobics. But now, after the Bodmin Assizes, he had a free weekend. He would dawdle back to London, bird-watch on the way. Should he head for Slapton Ley and the Exe Estuary for migratory birds, or chance the cliffs of North Devon? He drove as far as Launceston enjoying his indecision. It was agreeable, he thought, to have no ties, not to have to rush back to wife and family as did, for instance, Hubert, always in a hurry to fit in the children's holidays or Venice or Paris because Victoria must go between the children's half-terms, and still constantly travel for his own work. No wonder he was threatened with ulcers. Cosmo rolled up the window.

Heavy rain squalls hit the windscreen. Late September brought equinoctial gales; the north coast might be too rough. He would cut south from Launceston; stay in a pub, perhaps? He could spend the night at Pengappah. He was welcome, as were all Hubert's friends, to collect the key in the village and make himself at home. But I am not at home there, Cosmo thought irritably. I have never felt at home since Flora told me she had heard us discussing her. Then he thought, It is eighteen years since that happened. Hubert is married and has found success; I have married and divorced; I have a good practice. I have no room for sentimentality. I must take a pull and be sensible.

Thinking this, Cosmo remembered his father. Had he not, during that awful row that Christmas at Coppermalt (patched up, of course, but unforgettable), said something about Flora being sensible? One wondered, thought Cosmo, driving through the rain, who under their veneer of ordinariness was sensible. I cannot claim good sense, he thought; it was stupid to marry Joyce, cheaply cruel to my mother. I have often been idiotic. Look at that trip I made to Brittany; nothing could have been stupider. St Malo destroyed in the war is rebuilt. There is a barrage across the water where we crossed in *vedettes*, the beach beyond St Briac is built up with villas and a concrete car park covers the site of our picnic. Even giving Coppermalt to Charles has not erased anything. I remember the silky feel of the water when Hubert and I drifted down the river that hot day. The sight of Flora undressing, and catching her unaware in the water. Sometimes I hear her voice or remember the salt taste of her eyelashes when I kissed her on the last night of her visit. Or finding myself, as I occasionally do, getting out of a taxi at Paddington, I remember the feel of her wrist as I held her. It is ridiculous. I remember it all. I am fifty years old yet I am frequently tempted to seek out Irena Tarasova. Nothing could be simpler but I am afraid. Then he thought, more cheerfully: I make my living from other people's lack of sense; who am I to complain?

In the dusk a policeman flagged him down. There were fallen trees blocking the road; it would be best for Cosmo to take the main road to Plymouth. Cosmo said, 'I will wind my way round by the lanes.' The policeman remarked that the lanes were tricky, it was easy to get lost. Cosmo replied jauntily that he was in the mood to get lost and turned the car.

Quite lost some ten miles on, rounding a bend, he found cars parked by the side of the road and jamming a disused quarry. Groups of people were straggling up a moorland path. Reaching for his binoculars, Cosmo focused them on a bonfire on top of the hill, a frieze of happy and skipping children. On impulse he got out of his car and started walking towards the fire. As he climbed he smelled roasting lamb on the damp wind and heard harsh shouts above the cries of children. He overtook a wheelchair pushed by two boys. The woman in it ordered them to make haste; she had an authoritative voice. Cosmo said, 'Can I lend a hand?' and, pushing, asked, 'What's the picnic in aid of?'

'It's not a picnic, it's a ram roast,' said the woman in the chair. Cosmo felt snubbed.

One of the lads pushing said, 'Some 'ould call it a barbecue. You all right there?' He shot off at a gallop, leaving Cosmo to push.

'You shouldn't have given him the chance, he's a lazy bugger,' said his mate.

Cosmo said, 'I'm sorry.'

'So long as you get me up there,' said the woman. 'I don't want to miss anything.'

'What are you celebrating?' Cosmo ran through a few historical dates in his mind.

'We are not celebrating anything,' said the woman in the chair. 'It's her idea, "A bit of fun at the end of the season," she said. She gave the lamb.'

'Celebrating the end of the grockle season,' said the boy.

'Tourists, trippers,' explained the woman.

'I know what grockles are.' Cosmo was tempted to stop pushing. When they reached the top, he wondered what had possessed him to get involved. He was out of breath. He went and sat on a rock apart. He would not stay long. The woman in the wheelchair had barely said thank you.

As well as the bonfire proper there was a second, more seriously built fire, where men were turning a sheep on a spit. Fat dripped into the fire which flared up, illuminating the men's faces. Young women held babies in their arms and small children by the hand; the larger children and adolescents chased each other, shrieking. A group of older women, taking orders from the woman in the wheelchair, tried in the wind to anchor a tablecloth onto a trestle table under which crates of beer were stacked. The wheelchair woman cried, 'Not like that! Do it the way I tell you.' Dogs ran about, getting in people's way. Some of the men in charge of the roast had started on the beer. Cosmo thought, This might be a scene from Breughel. Then, unhappily, My thoughts are unoriginal. He felt he should leave, but if he was seen leaving it would look ill-mannered; he sat on.

The sheep was presently removed from the spit amid bonhomous shouts. The woman in the wheelchair screamed shrill directions but the men paid scant attention as they began to carve. Soon the men were handing out chunks of meat to the crowd. One detached himself and came towards Cosmo with a helping on a paper plate. He looked hard at Cosmo as he gave him the plate, but did not speak. Cosmo felt he should offer some explanation of his presence, but the man carried a second plate which he was taking to someone behind Cosmo, beyond the firelight.

Cosmo had not known that there was anyone behind him. He had thought himself outside the circle. He felt self-conscious, exposed, afraid to look round. He thought, This is ridiculous. I am fifty years old, what have I to fear?

A considerable amount of drinking was now going on. Round the fire some of the shouts had an anarchic ring and the laughter was raucous. Cosmo thought again that he should leave; he had not been invited. Should he thank somebody? Say goodbye politely? Should he slink off? He could perhaps thank the woman in the wheelchair. Had he not helped push her up the hill? Was she the host? Standing up, he felt cramp in his leg. Stamping to rid himself of it,

374

he turned about and saw the person behind him who had received the plate of lamb.

A woman sat on a rock dressed in anorak and jeans and wellington boots. She had a dog at her feet. The dog was watching its mistress, who was watching him. Cosmo could not see the woman's face but he thought, She will do. I can thank this woman, apologize for gatecrashing, be on my way, make a lame explanation, sound courteous. As he stepped towards the woman the bonfire crackled up and he recognized Flora.

He must have been standing there some little time when three men detached themselves from the festivities and closed in. They carried mugs of beer; he could smell their breath. One of the men, pressing close to Cosmo, said, 'You all right, Flora? Making a nuisance of himself, is he? Shall us sort him out?'

Flora said, 'It's all right, Jim. I know him.' Then she said to Cosmo, 'They think you may be a man from the Ministry; we have not got permission to have the bonfire on this hill. Are you from the Ministry?'

Cosmo thought her voice had not changed at all. He said, 'I am not from the Ministry.'

The man called Jim said, 'Not a snooper, then,' and laughed. He seemed a friendly sort of fellow.

Cosmo said, 'But I gatecrashed your party. I wanted to say goodbye and thank you, to the lady in the wheelchair perhaps? She seems to be in charge.'

Flora smiled and the men burst out laughing. Cosmo saw he had been mistaken. He said, speaking at last to Flora, 'I've forgotten her name.'

Flora said, 'Everybody called her "The Natural Leader". It's a type.'

A little puzzled, the man Jim said, 'Right then, we are going to see about the music.' He drifted away with his friends. Flora called after him, 'Thanks, Jim.'

By the light of the bonfire he could see her hair was still thick and dark, her teeth when she had smiled at Jim white and even. He had not particularly remembered her teeth. He said, 'Portable gramophone, squeezebox?'

Flora said, 'Pop. They run it off one of the land rover's batteries, I think. I don't understand these things.'

Cosmo said, 'Nor do I. May I sit down for a minute? I think my legs are giving way.' Flora made room for him on the rock. The dog sniffed Cosmo's trousers. Cosmo said: 'Is she called Tonton?' He stroked the dog.

Flora said, 'No.'

Presently Cosmo said, 'There's nothing wrong with my legs, I'm as strong as a horse.'

Flora said, 'Good.'

Cosmo said, 'The fact is they were shaking. I thought, too, that I might have a coronary.'

She said, 'Please don't.'

Flora's dog leaned its chin on her knee and groaned. Flora said, 'She's terrified of the bonfire, that's why we are sitting here.'

Some of the party had managed to get a land rover up the hill. A voice said, 'Testing, testing,' and there was a burst of the Everley Brothers.

Cosmo said, 'When those friends of yours closed in on me just now I realized what a stranger I am. I was quite scared.'

She said, 'They'd love that.' She laughed.

The Everleys sang 'Come Right Back', the volume wobbling in the wind. Flora put her mouth close to Cosmo's ear and asked, 'And how is Joyce?' Her breath tickled his neck.

He said, 'We were only married about five minutes. Didn't you see our divorce in *The Times*?'

'I gave up reading *The Times*,' she said.

Cosmo said, 'I have wanted to find you, but I hadn't the nerve. I knew I might be able to trace you through Irena Tarasova. Once I went to backtrack in Brittany, but it was horrible. There wasn't a sniff of you. Then I thought if I did find you, you would give me the brush-off.'

376

'You brushed me off when you went to Algiers.' She was furious.

Shouting above the Beatles, Cosmo yelled, 'That was a bloody stupid mistake, you must have known it was.'

Flora's dog jerked itself up and bared its teeth. Flora said, 'I thought you were going off to get killed and wouldn't want an involvement,' gentling the dog.

'Christ!' Cosmo shouted. 'Any chance of my getting killed was long gone. I was on my way to a desk job.'

Flora thought, We are grown people, adults. We should be managing better than this, and was silent.

Cosmo said, 'I remember you coming up out of the sea with that dog, carrying your clothes in a bundle. You were pretty stroppy then.'

He had shouted, 'Espèce de con, idiote!' She remembered that.

The younger people were dancing round the fire. The men who had managed the ram roast drank and laughed in sharp claps of sound. They could see Flora from the corner of their eyes; she was all right. 'She's away,' said Jim, and his voice was caught by the wind.

Mothers with children began to leave. A group of older women disappeared suddenly over the brow of the hill, pushing the woman in the wheelchair in a flurry of precautionary shrieks. Flora said, 'I hope they don't tip her out.'

Cosmo said, 'D'you like her?'

'She's kind.'

'Rather interfering?' he suggested.

'Qualities which run in tandem,' she said.

Cosmo thought of his mother; he must not talk of her yet. What was safe? 'All those years in London when you say you were working as a maid, what did you do?' He had asked this before when they sat side by side in the train.

'I went to the theatre; the pit cost very little. Museums, galleries.'

Who had gone with her to the galleries, who had

shared her enjoyment, who had had a part in those lost years? 'Alone?' he asked dubiously.

'Usually.' It had been safer, less trouble to be alone. Childhood habits die hard.

'Do you still prefer living and working in the country? Are you content? You told me in the train that you were content.' It rankled that she should be content. He was resentful of such a state.

'You will run out of innocuous questions soon.' Flora stroked her dog's ears, looking straight ahead. Her voice was steady.

'All right. Are you married? Are you living with somebody? Have you had many love affairs?'

Flora said, 'Phew, how brave.'

Cosmo said, 'Well?'

'Are you like this in court?'

'Much better. The wig gives presence, the gown threatens.'

'Ah.'

'So?'

'Not married. Not living with anyone. Yes, I have had affairs.' It would be peculiar, she thought, watching the men stamping out the remains of the fire, if I had not. The affairs, such as they were, had been ephemeral, pleasant; there had been no risk of hurt. 'You did not ask,' she said, 'whether I have children. I haven't.'

Cosmo thought, I don't believe I have ever been alone with her; there have always been people. Oh yes, that time I found her by the river and muffed it in some way. God damn all those people. He remembered the French officer and the Colonel from Texas in the train. But we were alone, he remembered, that first time on the beach.

The bonfire was dying, and people dribbling away. The men had finished stamping out the fire and others loaded the trestle tables onto the land rover. There were shouts of, 'Night, Flora,' 'Night,' and, 'Thanks a lot, see yer.' Somebody started the engine and the land rover tipped out of sight down the hill.

Cosmo, watching it go, said, 'Were you the host?'

378

It was almost dark but the rain was reduced to a drizzle.

'I gave the ram. It was a communal do. A bit of fun for the village.' As they sat she too thought back, remembering the picnic and her terrible despair the following day. 'I went back to the beach,' she said, 'the day after the picnic. There was a circle of black where the fire had been; that was all.'

She had written their names in the sand: Cosmo, Felix, Hubert. The sea had washed them away.

Cosmo said rather crossly, 'Well, I'm here now.'

The wind which had dropped now gustily renewed its energy, bringing with it rain. Flora's dog whined and shook herself. Flora said, 'If we go on sitting here, we shall get the most awful rheumatism.'

'I am afraid,' said Cosmo, turning up his coat collar, 'that if I ask you to marry me, you will refuse.'

'You could always ask me again,' said Flora, getting to her feet, 'when we have got into the warm and dry.'

Getting to his feet, Cosmo was annoyed to find he was stiff.

Flora's dog sneezed and started off down the hill at a joyful canter. Flora followed at a half-trot.

At the foot of the hill the last of the ram-roasters were piling into their cars, switching on headlights, revving their engines, shouting goodbyes before driving off. Flora, cantering sideways down the steep slope, thought, If I put on a spurt I could join them, get away, leave him behind, go back to my cottage, light the fire, have a hot bath, put the cat out, and go to bed with my book. Then she thought, He is not someone to be remembered with amused affection like Hubert, or with regretful pity like Felix who, for all his heroism, failed me. Cosmo is here, behind me, trying to keep up, he is *real*. Then she thought, He doesn't know this path as I do, he may trip in the dark and fall, and she slowed her pace. She heard Cosmo slip and curse. He yelled angrily, 'Don't run away from me, damn you. Wait.' And, catching up with her, he said, 'I nearly went to Pengappah to spend the night, but there are unfortunate

379

memories.' Flora's laugh was snatched by the wind. 'And as I began my drive from Bodmin to London I resolved to take a pull on myself and be sensible.'

Flora said, 'Wouldn't that be rather risky?'

The last of the cars had gone as they reached the road. Cosmo said, 'Where's your car?'

She said, 'I walked.'

He said, 'Get into mine,' and unlocked his car door.

Flora said, 'My dog is muddy.'

Cosmo said, 'Stop quibbling.'

The dog leapt into the car and sat on the back seat. Cosmo said, 'That animal has a lot more sense than we have,' and put his arms round Flora and, holding her close, hugged her. Then he said, 'Let me kiss your eyes,' and, 'Don't tell me you are crying.'

Flora said, 'It's the rain.'

Cosmo said, 'First time I've come across salt rain.'

Flora said, 'Why don't we get in the car, which is dry?'

Cosmo said, 'I'd better warn you, I've given Coppermalt to my nephew, Mabs' boy.'

Flora said, 'I'm not marrying you for Coppermalt.'

Cosmo said, 'Oh, darling, what a lot of time we have wasted. How shall we ever catch up?'

Flora said, 'There will be less time for squabbling.'

THE END

Jumping the Queue
by Mary Wesley

'A virtuoso performance of guileful plotting, deft
characterization and malicious wit'
THE TIMES

Matilda Poliport, recently widowed, has decided to End It
All. But her meticulously planned bid for graceful oblivion
is foiled, and when later she foils the suicide attempt of
another lost soul – Hugh Warner, on the run from the
police – life begins again for both.

But life also begins to throw up nasty secrets and awkward
questions: just what was Matilda's husband Tom doing in
Paris? How is the soon-to-be-knighted John (or Piers as he
liked to be called) involved? Was Louise more than just a
lovely daughter? And why did Hugh choose Matilda as his
saviour?

Jumping the Queue is a brilliantly written first novel
brimming over with confidence and black humour,
reminiscent of Muriel Spark at her magnificent best.

'Great verve and inventiveness . . . (Matilda is) a
convincing original'
TIMES LITERARY SUPPLEMENT

0 552 99082 5

BLACK SWAN

Second Fiddle
by Mary Wesley

'She writes like an avenging angel, with a freshness, vigour
and zest for sex (but never for sleaze) that belie her years.
The lovely Miss Wesley has a steel-tipped talent. Long
may she hone it'
SUNDAY TELEGRAPH

Laura Thornby, independent, individual, and slightly
exotic manages her life with exquisite control. Her affairs
are brief but delightful, her career fulfilling, and she copes
with her two rather peculiar elderly relatives with wryness
and humour.
But when she meets twenty-three-year-old Claude
Bannister, struggling to be a writer, she is swept by an
irresistible desire to interfere, manipulate, experiment
with him – for his own good of course.
What she does not foresee, however, are the possibilities
that he, one day, may write well, and that she might fall in
love.

'SECOND FIDDLE' will delight the healthily growing
number of Mary Wesley enthusiasts and offer a delicious
treat to those who have yet to discover this unique author'
PUNCH

0 552 99355 7

BLACK SWAN

The Camomile Lawn
by Mary Wesley

'A very good book indeed . . . has the texture and smell of real life, rich in detail, careful and subtle in observation, mature in judgement'
SUSAN HILL

Behind the large house, the fragrant camomile lawn stretches down to the Cornish cliffs. Here, in the dizzying heat of August 1939, five cousins have gathered at their aunt's house for their annual ritual of a holiday. For most of them, it is the last summer of their youth, with the heady exilarations and freedoms of lost innocence, as well as the fears of the coming war around the corner.

The Camomile Lawn moves from Cornwall to London and back again, over the years, telling the stories of the cousins, their family and their friends, united by shared losses and lovers, by family ties and the absurd conditions imposed by war as their paths cross and recross over the years. Mary Wesley presents an extraordinarily vivid and lively picture of wartime London: the rationing, imaginatively circumvented; the fallen houses; the parties, the new-found comforts of sex, the desperate humour of survival – all of it evoked with warmth, clarity and stunning wit. And through it all, the cousins and their friends try to hold on to the part of themselves that laughed and played dangerous games on that camomile lawn.

'Extraordinarily accomplished and fast-moving . . . plotted with great deftness and intelligence'
MARTIN SEYMOUR-SMITH, FINANCIAL TIMES

'Nothing old-fashioned or even ladylike about it. With the verve and jollity of youth . . . a book as scatty and chatty as a gossip column'
MAIL ON SUNDAY

'Delightful . . . wholly believable and exact. I like the mixture of warmth and wit . . . More, please'
DAILY TELEGRAPH

0 552 99126 0

BLACK SWAN

A SELECTED LIST OF FINE TITLES
AVAILABLE FROM BLACK SWAN

THE PRICES SHOWN BELOW WERE CORRECT AT THE TIME OF
GOING TO PRESS. HOWEVER TRANSWORLD PUBLISHERS
RESERVE THE RIGHT TO SHOW NEW RETAIL PRICES ON
COVERS WHICH MAY DIFFER FROM THOSE PREVIOUSLY
ADVERTISED IN THE TEXT OR ELSEWHERE.

☐	99248 8	**The Done Thing**	Patricia Angadi	£4.95
☐	99201 1	**The Governess**	Patricia Angadi	£3.95
☐	99385 9	**Sins of the Mothers**	Patricia Angadi	£3.95
☐	99322 0	**The Highly Flavoured Ladies**	Patricia Angadi	£3.95
☐	99351 4	**Blue Heaven**	Joe Keenan	£4.99
☐	99243 7	**Confessions of a Failed Southern Lady**	Florence King	£3.99
☐	99376 X	**Reflections in a Jaundiced Eye**	Florence King	£3.99
☐	99377 8	**Wasp Where is thy Sting?**	Florence King	£4.99
☐	99375 1	**When Sisterhood was in Flower**	Florence King	£3.99
☐	99337 9	**Southern Ladies and Gentlemen**	Florence King	£3.99
☐	99239 9	**Babycakes**	Armistead Maupin	£4.99
☐	99106 6	**Further Tales of the City**	Armistead Maupin	£4.99
☐	99383 2	**Significant Others**	Armistead Maupin	£4.99
☐	99384 0	**Tales of the City**	Armistead Maupin	£4.99
☐	99086 8	**More Tales of the City**	Armistead Maupin	£4.99
☐	99302 6	**The Love of Good Women**	Isabel Miller	£3.95
☐	99126 0	**The Camomile Lawn**	Mary Wesley	£4.99
☐	99210 0	**Harnessing Peacocks**	Mary Wesley	£4.99
☐	99082 5	**Jumping the Queue**	Mary Wesley	£4.99
☐	99304 2	**Not That Sort Of Girl**	Mary Wesley	£4.99
☐	99258 5	**The Vacillations of Poppy Carew**	Mary Wesley	£4.99
☐	99258 5	**Second Fiddle**	Mary Wesley	£4.99

All Black Swan Books are available at your bookshop or newsagent, or can be
ordered from the following address:

Corgi/Bantam Books,
Cash Sales Department,
P.O. Box 11, Falmouth, Cornwall TR10 9EN

Please send a cheque or postal order (no currency) and allow 80p for postage
and packing for the first book plus 20p for each additional book ordered up to
a maximum charge of £2.00 in UK.

B.F.P.O. consumers please allow 80p for the first book and 20p for each
additional book.

Overseas customers, including Eire, please allow £1.50 for postage and
packing for the first book, £1.00 for the second book, and 30p for each
subsequent title ordered.

NAME (Block Letters) ....

ADDRESS ....

....